REALM OF LIES AND SHADOWS

REDEMPTION OF REALMS BOOK 1

E.J. WIGHTMAN

Paperback ISBN: 978-1-7396023-1-4
Hardcover ISBN: 978-1-7396023-3-8
Publisher E. J. Wightman
2022
United Kingdom

Realm of Lies and Shadows is an adult fantasy not meant for readers under 18. This is book one in a series filled with redemption and hope. Unfortunately, our characters will go through some dark times along the way. The following content is present in the book which some readers may find distressing. Though none of these items are glorified, I understand some readers might rather not read about them.

Sensitive Content:
   Violence
   Sexual Assault
   Systemic intolerance of LGBTQ+ individuals
   Racial slurs (based on fictional races, not skin tone)
   Intrusive Thoughts
   Panic Attacks
   Brief mention of attempted suicide in the past
   Death of a loved one
   Narcissitic abuse
   Controlling abuse
   Single chapter from villain POV

Other Content readers may wish to avoid:
   Adult Language
   Acts of sexual intimacy
   Drugs and Alcohol
   Blood
   Vomit
   Brief discussion of diet/exercise routine

THE THR
VORRA
The Veil
FYLIOS
Dakyto
Sea
Lithari Mountains
Iris Meadow
N
W E
S
ROLIOS
Tormund
Braktyn
Gela Forrest

REALMS

The Veil
MESTERRA
ERIMOS
Prifma
Oasis
Baom
The Ravine
Zoi River
DENDRON
Avato
Sea
Paralon
Coruscis
Swamp
THALLOS
The Veil
Brumalis
Castle
NOTOS
aphyr

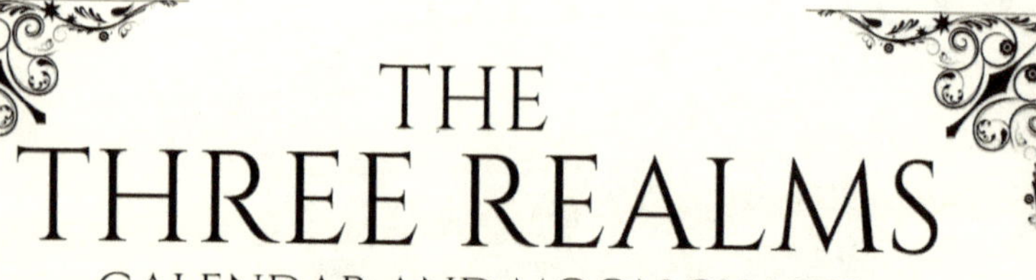

THE
THREE REALMS
CALENDAR AND MOON PHASES

Jairos   Full moon

Fevaros

Maros   Quarter moon (Spring Solstice)

Allos

Majos

Jonios   Half moon (Summer Solstice)

Yojos

Avgos

Sevtos   Three-quarter moon (Autumn Equinox)

Okvos

Novios

Dekemos   New Moon (Winter Solstice)

PRONUNCIATION

Characters

Ashton	Ash-tuhn
Wren	Rehn
Samael	Sam-I-ell
Kenna	KEH-nuh
Sera	SAIR-uh
Aryn	Air-inn
Zola	ZOH-luh
Ilan	EE-lahn
Varis	VAIR-iss
Lailah	LAY-luh
Echelous	Eh-kuul-uhs

The Ancients

Soldivus	SOHL-di-vuhs
Luniva	Loo-NEE-vuh

Places

Mesterra	Mehs-tAIr-uh
Notos	Nah-tOHs
Sapphyr	SAff-ir
Braktyn	BrAk-tin
Vorra	VOr-uh
Brumalis	Broo-mAh-lis
Castle	

Magical Items

Fostone	FAH-stohn
Eriksomb	Er-ik-somb
Geolift	Gee-OH-lift
Surgati	Ser-GAH-tee

CHAPTER 1

King Ashton Moonbriar had been locked in this battle for almost an hour, and his muscled, fair-skinned torso was slick with sweat. The winter sun shone through the open shaft overhead, and dust particles floated through the rays of morning light.

Relentlessly, Ash forced Wren to shuffle backward along the stone flags of the sparring arena in Brumalis Castle. Then Wren landed a blow to Ash's ribs. The king grunted.

"What's the matter, old man? Can't keep up?" Wren taunted with a smile that only fed Ash's growing need to draw blood.

He growled and launched himself at the winged fae, sword drawn. Ash was an angel, so of course, he could have attacked with magic, but today he needed to feel the punishing impact of each clash of their blades. Ash lost himself to the rhythym of the fight, allowing his thoughts to stray.

Despite the perpetual winter in this part of Notos, Summer Solstice was tomorrow. That meant there would be an influx of elves from Mesterra. They arrived in the realm of Notos with their heads filled with nonsensical ideas of hope and freedom from the angels on the High Council.

If only the elves knew the truth.

Tomorrow, Ash would select a female elf from among them. It didn't really matter who.

He'd charm her and earn her trust. Eventually, she'd come with him willingly.

And she'd fall for him. She'd give herself to him until she loved him heart, body and soul.

When the time came, he would betray her in the worst possible way, just as he did every year.

And Ash would have to live with what he'd done.

Again.

That was his curse.

With every clang of metal against metal, the chanted truth rang in his mind.

I. Am. A. Monster. I. Will. Never. Change. Wren met each strike of the sword with skilled defense. After all, the king was the one who'd trained him.

Then, with a final burst of energy, Ash brought Wren to his knees and held the blade to his throat.

"Enough." Ash said, slinging his weapon across the floor and sitting with his back against the solid limestone wall of the sparring ring.

Wren flopped onto his back, his dark brown chest heaving. "Thank fuck. I don't think I could've gone another minute."

He gave Ash a sidelong glance. Wren understood Ash's rage. Understood his tortured thoughts.

"Are you alright?" Wren asked.

Ash ran both hands through his perpetually messy black hair. "I don't have a choice. Do I?"

"But this year, I thought—"

"There hasn't been a single whisper of the treaty's terms being fulfilled. No one knows anything. My father should have ended Mother's life and cast her out of this world to stop the war instead of making his ridiculous treaty."

All the angels referred to the Ancients, Luniva and Soldivus, as their mother and father. Though angels weren't born. They were created by Ancient magic.

Ash stood and extended a hand to Wren, helping him up. They crossed the dusty stone flags and headed out of the sparring arena.

"Perhaps I deserve my curse," Ash confessed. "I was the one who betrayed Elenya."

He'd betrayed his mate in the worst way imaginable. Every year since then he'd been stuck in this cursed cycle of reliving the greatest mistake of his life, betraying every elvish woman who fell in love with him.

Year after year after year for three hundred and twenty nine years with no way out.

Wren shook his head. "You can't speak that way. You can't give up. I can feel it in my bones. The treaty will be fulfilled, Ash. You'll be able to make amends for everything."

Ash gave a non-committal grunt as they reached the bottom of the stairs.

Wren asked, "Do you want me to come with you to Braktyn?"

"No. I'll take Varis." Ash's answer never changed.

Wren gave a curt nod, though his distaste for Varis, the hateful dungeon master, was clear. Both of their boots scuffed along the polished stone steps as they climbed in silence.

Wren had offered to accompany Ash every year for the twenty years of their friendship. But Ash didn't want Wren to taint his soul by helping Ash trick an elvish woman into trusting him.

Wren was a good man, and he'd never judged Ash. The king had found Wren in Gela forest on the side of the road twenty years ago. Wings clipped and body beaten beyond recognition, Wren's only crime had been being born a winged fae.

Hoping for some shred of redemption, Ash had helped him. He'd taken him in and given him a home, training, and a position on the royal guard. But Wren would never fly again.

When they reached the main hall, two female servants took their time cleaning the large mirrors, their eyes lingering on the bare torsos of the two men as they passed. Wren winked at a woman with a round figure and said, "Morning, princess."

She smiled and blushed, looking away as though suddenly very interested in attacking a tiny speck of dust.

"She and I had a lovely evening together yesterday. Quite the handful between the sheets, in all the best ways." Wren wiggled his eyebrows. "Honestly, I wish all women were as plump as her. It's my life goal to let every servant here know how beautiful she is."

"Well, you know I won't stop you from pampering the servants. Our esteemed prince might have something to say about it though." Ash clenched his jaw. Though he was king, he could do nothing about how the servants or prisoners were treated in his own castle. When Luniva had crowned Ash king after the Void War, she'd also granted Samael the title of Prince. The prince had a penchant for cruelty, but he was vital to fulfilling the treaty, and therefore under Luniva's protection.

A group of courtiers passed in the hall and one paused to sneer at Wren. "Fae mut."

That, Ash could do something about. He clenched his fists and whirled on the angel. Rather than giving into the instinct to punch him in the jaw, he forced the angel to his knees with his wind magic. The group of courtiers who'd accompanied the kneeling angel stopped and turned towards the king. They kept their eyes lowered to avoid attracting the king's wrath.

Ash laced his words with a tone of merciless authority. "You may think yourself above fae and elves, but you are a newcomer to my court. In fact, I do not even know your name."

Ash paused, waiting for the courtier's introduction.

"Lord Franick. At your service, Your Grace," the courtier simpered.

Using his magic, Ash probed the angel's mind briefly and confirmed he'd given his true identity.

"Well, Lord Franick, if you cannot treat my Captain of the Guard with the respect due to his station, then you will be removed from this court. Or perhaps I'll allow Prince Samael to oversee your punishment. Are we clear?"

"Yes, Majesty." The lord bowed his head, his face pale. "My sincere apologies."

"I am not the one to whom you should apologize." Ash jerked his head towards Wren.

"Apologies, Captain," the angel said, looking like it caused him physical pain to apologize to a winged fae.

"You are dismissed." Ash released the force of his magic.

Wren pointedly scratched his jaw with his pinky, a subtle use of the obscene gesture eluding to the size of the angel's manhood. Then he smiled, winked and blew the courtier a kiss. With a barely veiled look of disgust, the angel stood and rejoined the others. Every courtier in the group bowed or curtseyed before turning to continue on their way.

After a few minutes of smug silence, Wren cleared his throat. "So... blonde or brunette this year? Or a red head? Not that it matters. I'm sure she'll run like Hel when she realizes you've got a tiny, shriveled, old man di—"

"There's something wrong with you." Ash reached out with his boot, tripping Wren. The fae stumbled but caught himself. They both laughed.

He appreciated Wren's lightheartedness, but Ash's smile soon faded.

He'd tried to fight the curse in the past. Not only had he endured the physical agony caused by his resistance, but three of his brothers had been tortured and imprisoned for Ash's insolence. The Winter Solstice ritual had still taken place that year, and he'd still betrayed the innocent woman who'd fallen in love with him.

The only way to live with himself was to abandon himself to the urges of the curse. Urges that made him into a predator.

So, he brushed off his pain and self-loathing, and replaced them with swagger and charm. He armed himself—ready to strike with dazzling blue eyes, crooked smiles, and whispered flirtations. He would use every weapon in his arsenal at exactly the right moments. In the end, she wouldn't resist.

They never did.

CHAPTER 2

Nothing truly violent ever happened in Tormund, but Kenna and all the elves in the city carried the heavy threat of punishment with them every day. Even minor crimes were severely punished.

As for the more serious crimes like rebelling against the angels on the High Council, she'd witnessed what happened to elves who were accused of that. Kenna blinked away the memory of the female elf in the fiery cage, and the woman's screams as the rebel was carelessly thrown from the treetop capital city of Dendron to the forest floor.

There were no humans left, so Kenna and the other elves were at the bottom of the hierarchy of intelligent beings in the Three Realms. And females were the lowest of the low.

It was the day before Summer Solstice, and the late morning sun beat down on her olive skin, chestnut hair, and midnight blue tunic. She strolled along the cobbled Main Street, flanked by whitewashed shops and thatched-roofed taverns. She valued her tentative safety enough to try to pretend that nothing happened in Tormund, even though everyone knew that elves failed the trial every year.

She should have picked up her pace, but she was in no hurry to face the task ahead. If she arrived early, she would have to sit and wait. And waiting was the worst kind of torture.

The combination of stifling heat and rising anxiety made sweat pool unpleasantly underneath her full breasts and in every crevice of her voluptuous figure.

There's nothing to worry about, she told herself. Like a large, dry chunk of stale bread, the lie lodged in her throat, reminding her of everything she had to lose.

Her churning insides were at odds with the excited chatter and bustling preparations that seemed to be on the agenda of everyone else in the city. Did other citizens feign happiness in their oppressed existence or were they actually happy?

How could any elf in the realm of Mesterra ever feel safe enough to be truly content?

She'd never know, since city guards hovered everywhere, waiting for someone to make a mistake.

The Three Realms had been at peace since the war ended. Only five angels remained, the High Council. They assured all of the elves in Mesterra that the Ancients had allowed the few angels to stay in Mesterra to rule—to maintain peace and order. The Veil kept the rest of the angels in the realms of Notos or Vorra, so that elves and angels might live their respective lives in peace.

Obviously, the Council's version of peace was extremely subjective. Elves weren't allowed to discuss the fact that they lived under the constant threat of banishment, enslavement, or execution if they stepped out of line.

If the Ancients had known the noble angels would use their superior magic to become totalitarian rulers, would they still have appointed them to rule Mesterra?

It didn't matter. Luniva and Soldivus were dead, and there were no gods left.

Shaking her head, Kenna attempted to clear away the existential questions plaguing her mind. She tried to join in with the positive energy of the chatter around her, but feeling anything other than dread was impossible.

She was one of the twenty-five-year-old elves on the way to her trial.

The conversation in the air was secondary to the insistent whisper that she imagined drifting on the breeze. Thinking the wind could speak to her was ridiculous; elf magic came from the Aqua, Terrane, and Flame elements of the land.

Lucky me. A Spectrum elf who can wield all three elements, but with absolutely no control over my own path in life.

With a final gust, the wind seemed to hiss a warning into her delicately pointed ear. *Eyes open.* As the current died, she was surrounded by the stillness of the summer heat.

Kenna fixed her eyes on the remarkable view at the end of the street, where a stony track continued out of town and around the meandering shore of Lake Audral. From her vantage point, she couldn't see Iris meadow, but the towering, snow-capped obelisks on the far side of the aquamarine lake looked like they shot straight out of the water. She could almost smell the colorful meadow grass that stretched between the lake and the Lithari Mountain pass.

Taking a deep breath, she attempted to relax into memories of simple days laying in that rainbow-carpeted meadow and escaping into the imaginary worlds on the pages of her books. The colorful meadow was a vivid reminder of where the Ancients' blood had been spilled in the war.

Kenna dreamed of visiting the other sacred locations throughout Mesterra, but memories and dreams were not enough to chase away her trepidation about the trial. Every year, at least a few elves failed the trial and were never seen again. Instead, she opted for an active distraction—some last-minute Flame practice while she walked.

She reached out with one hand as she passed the smithy, using her power to summon a tiny spark from the blacksmith's forge. She directed some magic from her internal Vessel into the spark until a flame danced over her open palm. When she stumbled over a stone, her brief lapse in concentration made the fire flicker. Her stomach clenched, and the flame winked out entirely.

Thankfully, she saw Sera turn onto the street ahead. Mindless chatter with her housemate was exactly what she needed to take her mind off the looming disappearances at the trial.

"Sera! Wait for me!"

"Well, well, well, if it isn't Kenna Duras, my favourite contributor to the continuation of our patriarchal society," Sera said, the only member of their graduating class more worried about misogyny than safety.

"Here we go again." Kenna rolled her eyes, though she welcomed the conversation—would have welcomed anything—to take away her sense of impending failure.

"Your father is the Dean," Sera stated. "Surely you could try again to convince him to change things." Sera's emerald eyes flashed with rage, and she flicked her glossy black waves over her shoulder. "It's so archaic. Why should males get to have all the fun learning to make shields?"

"You know I'm on your side, Sera. I've already mentioned it to Father. I usually have him bent to my will, but it seems that's not the case with the trivial matter of societal change and potential banishment. Unlike you, I'll stick with the tasks deemed worthy of our fairer sex and not cause problems, thank you very much," Kenna said with finality.

Kenna had approached her father about the prospect of changing the curriculum during her first year at the academy, but his response had been clear: *Young women shouldn't ask questions about such things.* She'd been annoyed, but accepted her father's answer as just another thing she'd have to tolerate.

Sera, on the other hand, had been furious. Undeterred, she'd found her own means of learning. Holt had been happy to have any excuse to spend time in Sera's presence.

Until the Shadow snatched him away after his Emergence.

Sera's tiny waist and the perfect curve of her hips, combined with her tragic past and emotional defences, gave her an undeniable sense of allure. But she hadn't opened her heart to anyone since Holt.

"I'm sure you must be feeling incredibly nervous about filling glasses of water and lighting candles at the trial today, oh all-powerful Spectrum elf." Sera bowed to Kenna.

"I'll have you know, I'm going to pour the best damn glass of water you've ever seen. And you'll be able to eat off the ground after I've vanquished the dust with my mighty power." She nudged Sera playfully with her shoulder.

Neither of them knew exactly what to expect from the trial, since the events were supposed to be confidential. However, all the students at Tormund Elemental Academy had solid assumptions about the tasks based on whispered rumors, as well as the gender and element specific training they'd received.

At the Academy, there was very little emphasis on defensive magic, even for males. Tormund was nestled safely in the southwest corner of Rolios in the Realm of Mesterra. The Elders, the High Council's elvish lackeys, were extremely adept at keeping the peace by quickly diffusing any person or situation that upset Tormund's peace.

The only reason anyone would need to be able to defend themselves was if they planned to purposely cause trouble. The males learned just enough defensive magic to lure elves into thinking they didn't live under constant oppression, but not enough that any of them would dare rise up against the town's Elders.

Discontent as Kenna was, her only forms of rebellion were a sarcastic attitude and forward-thinking friends. But Sera was definitely a troublemaker; Kenna would never forget the afternoon in Iris meadow when Sera had demonstrated her defensive skills. She had looked like a fiery goddess clothed in glowing flame. It was almost enough to make Kenna want to follow her trailblazing ways – until Sera collapsed from overusing her magic.

Those flaming shields might come in handy someday, but thankfully, Sera wasn't planning a revolution. Kenna just hoped that was enough to keep her friend safe.

"You know, as much as you complain about the plight of females, you don't seem to mind it so much when you have males panting after you everywhere you go." Kenna raised her brows.

"I have absolutely no idea what you mean." Sera batted her long dark lashes.

"Yes. I can see that you're completely unaware," Kenna said dryly, but she couldn't help smiling.

Sera would never become some pretty prize with a broken spirit. She knew exactly how powerful a weapon her beauty was. Whether with Flame shields or a vivacious personality, she'd learned to protect herself from pain.

Their chatter had carried them to the end of Main Street, where the road ended in front of the City Hall, and they turned left toward the Trial Amphitheater

"Try not to be jealous of my superior fire-lighting skills!" Sera called.

"Good luck, Sera."

"Oh, I don't need luck." A smirk wrinkled Sera's light brown cheek, and she sauntered ahead, pushing open the large, wooden gates that led directly into the ground level of the trial amphitheater. When Sera turned back to Kenna, her expression was earnest. "Be careful, Kenna. Don't do anything stupid."

Kenna took a deep breath and hoped that they would both walk back out of the gates again when the trial was over.

CHAPTER 3

Kenna padded onto the earthen floor of the open-air stadium where the atmosphere fluttered with contagious, nervous chatter. Opposite the gated entrance, the four Elders sat in their ornately-carved, wooden chairs waiting to exact their judgement.

The amphitheater was arranged in circular stone tiers, with wooden benches providing onlookers an unobstructed view of the pit in the middle where the trial would be performed.

Sera flounced up the steps and was instantly surrounded by an eager gaggle of male Flame elves, while Kenna squared her shoulders and took her seat with the other Spectrum elves.

The tasks ahead should align with her simplistic education. Surely, the Elders would have no reason to trick the students into failure. Only students and the city's Elders were permitted to be present for the trial, so at least if Kenna failed, her shame would be limited. Though, there was the small matter of potential banishment, but she refused to dwell on that.

None of Kenna's closest friends could access the entire Spectrum of elements like she could, so she contributed to the low buzz of conversation by making polite small talk with a fellow Spectrum elf, Paisley, who sat in front of her.

The bell tower announced midday, and her mind whirred with expectation. The amphitheater fell silent as the last reverberation died, and the still air gave birth to another imagined, cautionary whisper. *Be alert.*

Was Kenna the only one who heard that phantom voice?

Ilan, the head Elder, stood to address them. Ilan's long silver hair and soft eyes made him look deceptively kind and caring. His appearance was one of the few things that aided her futile efforts to believe what her parents had taught her: the Council had no choice but to use formidable means of maintaining peace, order, and morality for the good of the people.

Kenna would never quite understand why the only forms of punishment for anything were banishment, enslavement, or execution.

Ilan interrupted her thoughts. "Welcome, esteemed students of Tormund Elemental Academy. Congratulations on having completed the first phase of your Emergence by passing your theoretical examinations. Today, you will demonstrate your control over your elemental magic. I will call each of you forward in turn, and your elemental Elder will give you the tasks that will make up your trial. Should you be successful today, you will proceed to the Emergence Ceremony tomorrow to take the vow."

Thanks very much for that reminder.

If the sacred Chalice found her unworthy of taking the Emergence Vow in front of everyone...

She was thankful that her shapeless tunic was navy blue, so the pools of sweat in her armpits weren't too noticeable.

"I'm sure our Elders need no introductions, but I would be remiss if I did not give them the honour of thanking them for their participation today.

"I am Ilan, your Spectrum Elder." Ilan inclined his head in acknowledgement of the requisite applause.

"Please welcome Cai, your Aqua Elder." Ilan paused for more clapping.

"Peder, your Terrane Elder." Increasingly bored clapping.

"Last but not least, Xavier, your Flame Elder." Clapping that seemed to beg Ilan to put the students out of their misery and just begin the trial already.

"Without further ado, we shall begin." There seemed to be a collective, thankful sigh that there would be no more mind-numbing formalities.

"Drake Shaver," Ilan's booming voice ricocheted around the amphitheater, signalling that her friend, Drake, would be the first of the Aqua elves to demonstrate his capabilities.

She sat up, anticipating a magnificent display. Drake had a flare for performance. They'd been practically inseparable since they'd met at the age of twenty-one on their first day at Tormund Elemental Academy. Her relationship with Drake was the source of much jealousy and chagrin for Kenna's oldest friends Sera, Zola, and Aryn. What her other friends didn't know is that she'd been Drake's primary confidante since he'd told her about his attraction to males. He was also attracted to females, but he and his boyfriend, Ezra, had been in a secret relationship for over three years.

Drake was from Dendron, the capital city of Mesterra. When Drake had tried to discuss his inclination with his parents at the age of eighteen, they'd sent him off to complete his education at the Academy in Tormund "for his own good." Or so they had said.

The lack of equal education for females wasn't the only societal issue in Mesterra steeped in traditional views. Those with any sexual preferences beyond the opposite sex were suppressed into silence or cast out into the unknown. Even so, Drake swaggered through life, refusing to let the raised eyebrows and furtive whispers on Main Street deter him from being confident and adventurous.

On his first Spring Equinox in Tormund, he'd even dared to cross the Veil, where all types of proclivities were accepted. If the Elders found out that Drake had crossed the Veil, he'd be sent back to Dendron and punished by the angels.

She'd never see him again.

Thankfully, Drake made it back with stories that whispered of the promise of intrigue across the Veil in Notos.

If Sera wasn't so jealous of Kenna's friendship with him, he and Sera would find they had a lot in common. Though, whenever Kenna managed to get them to speak to each other, there was barely enough space for both of their egos in one room.

Aqua Elder Cai, stood and gave Drake an encouraging smile. A large trough filled to the brim with water stood between them—the trial tasks would require three elemental sources. Not even the most powerful among the elemental elves could conjure water, earth, or fire from thin air.

"Welcome, Drake." Cai's voice was just loud enough for the other students to hear if they strained their ears. "Let us begin. I will give you a series tasks so that you may demonstrate your aptitude with your elemental power. First, please create a cloud of mist from the pool of water and swirl the water that remains in the trough."

Studying the fingernails on his left hand and not bothering to look at the water, Drake reached forward with the upturned palm of his right hand. As he raised his arm slightly, a dense cloud of fog settled over the trough. Then, Drake used one finger of his left hand to draw a small circle in the air near his blond, wavy hair, creating a small whirlpool in the trough as directed, while doing a cheeky little tapdance. All the students laughed at his performance, and even the Elders barely stifled their smirks.

"Now, please return the water to the trough," the Elder said.

Drake brought his palms together deliberately at his chest, and the water in the trough immediately looked as though it had never been disturbed. He bowed and beamed at Kenna, his blue eyes gleaming, while everyone whooped and cheered.

His nonchalance and self-assured attitude were byproducts of his magnetic personality and magical prowess. He made it look so effortless. If this was what the trial would be like, surely Kenna didn't need to fret. Drake's easy confidence made her feel like she was capable of anything, and she was sure some of his eccentric performance was for her benefit. He knew how anxious she was feeling.

The Elder gave Drake a nod of approval. "Excellent work. Though I need not remind you to behave, Drake."

The celebration died, and Drake's smile faltered. The Aqua Elder continued, "Now, you will complete one task of a defensive nature. For this task, you must shield yourself from view in whatever manner you see fit using the resources available to you. Proceed."

Turning his entire body in a measured circle with one palm upturned, Drake coaxed a thick coil of mist to himself. The tendril of mist slithered over the side of the trough and along the ground toward Drake's heels. As the serpentine fog contacted his fair-skinned hand, he sped up. He twirled in a quick, graceful motion and was swallowed into a thick white cloud. If not for the oddity of seeing a cloud in the middle of the arena, his presence was entirely undetectable.

"Well done, Drake," Drake reappeared, surrounded by an aura of pale mist.

Drake flashed one of his most charming smiles as he twirled again, sending the water back into the trough.

As his loyal companion, Kenna enjoyed the privilege of basking in his ambient charm and talent. She just wished it was contagious. Unfortunately for her, she didn't thrive under pressure like Drake or Sera. Knowing she'd soon be standing in front of everyone made her gulp, and she rubbed her clammy hands down her tunic.

Both Cai and Ilan nodded at Drake. "Excellent work, Drake You have proved your competency and will proceed to the final phase of your Emergence at the Ceremony tomorrow."

With a slight bow to the Elders, Drake sauntered back to his seat, taking his place amongst the Aqua elves next to Ezra.

Over the next three hours, the rest of the Aqua, Terrane, and Flame trials passed in a haze of both impressive and simple magical tasks.

Finally, it was time for the Spectrum elves, including Kenna, to complete the Trial. Overhead, a cloud drifted across the sun. No one had failed the trial yet that day, but the darkness that crept through the arena was oppressive. Like it wanted her to fail.

Images of the black Shadow stealing Holt away flashed in her mind, and her heart hammered in her chest as she waited.

The first Spectrum elf beckoned forward to complete the trial was Paisley. She completed all of her menial tasks with ease, and she gave Kenna a friendly smile as she returned to her seat.

Next, Ilan called forward a shy, withdrawn male named Trevan. Whenever she'd spoken with Trevan, he'd been cordial enough. He was from Thallos, the southeastern territory, and Kenna knew little about him beyond their limited interactions in class.

Trevan seemed agitated by the time he reached his position in front of the Elders, and the air vibrated with expectancy. Ilan spoke to Trevan so quietly that the rest of the students couldn't hear, probably soothing his nerves.

After his quiet words, Ilan indicated that Trevan should stand in front of the trough of water. When Ilan spoke again, his voice was loud enough for all the graduates to hear, and he gave Trevan his first task.

"First, Trevan, we will test your competency with Aqua magic. Your task is simple, please create mist with the water in the trough."

It was the same, easy task that Drake had completed before, but everything felt different.

Trevan stomped around the back of the trough with stiff, unnatural movements. When Trevan looked up, Kenna saw a wild look in his eyes that sent a feeling of unease skittering down her spine.

Something was very, very wrong.

CHAPTER 4

$\mathcal{A}$s thunder rumbled through the trial arena, a single Shadow rose from the dusty ground. Dark clouds hung overhead and the balmy, humid air rested heavily around her. Kenna's fear of failure was suddenly oppressive. Her inadequacy felt like a physical weight, anchoring her to the wooden bench as the sentient presence of the dark Shadow washed over her.

The black Shadow resembled the mysterious, omniscient presence that had snatched Holt away three years ago.

But something about this Shadow was different. It radiated undiluted evil—malice that smothered every one of her senses.

The darkness slinked past the Elders and around the center of the ring. The Elders exchanged a glance but made no move to stop the Shadow on its serpentine path around the edge of the arena.

Why aren't they doing anything?

Kenna's eyes returned to Trevan, poised to complete his trial. As he reached out his hands, his movements were jerky and his eyes looked panicked. The water rose quickly into mist as dark as the legendary Void, gulping down any hints of light in its vicinity. Then, he directed the fog into slender, spiked peaks of black ice, and angled the chilled knives toward the Elders.

He was ready to strike.

Paisley turned to Kenna, whispering, "He's actually going to fight them. We should help." Paisley stood, determined.

But Kenna stayed seated, frozen with fear. She noticed other students standing with courage written on their faces. They were all going to join Trevan's fight against the Elders. Had these students planned this attack?

Suddenly, Trevan spun wildly on one foot. Though the Elders seemed to be his target, the obsidian daggers hurtled randomly in all directions. It was as though he hadn't quite mastered control of his magical weapons.

As he spun, Kenna ducked and threw her hands over her head just in time to dodge the frigid projectiles.

However, her hands didn't shield her from the crimson shower as an icy arrow struck Paisley.

She crashed into Kenna's hiding place, lying in front of her with a gushing, crimson gash across her throat. On instinct, Kenna pressed her hands to the woman's neck in a futile attempt to stop the bleeding, but the blood flowed effortlessly through her fingers. Within moments, Paisley's eyes were wide and vacant—dead.

Kenna's hair was wet, and some warm liquid dripped down the side of her face. She stared at her blood-soaked hands. She might as well have struck the killing blow herself when she'd ducked and hidden. She gripped Paisley's hand tightly, saying a silent prayer to the long-dead Ancients, Soldivus and Luniva, as if that could somehow make up for her cowardice.

The frantic commotion gave way to whispers and crying throughout the stadium. She dared to peek over the ledge in front of the benches toward the center of the arena. All four Elders had their hands raised, and Trevan was shackled to the spot. His feet were buried under piles of dirt, his hands were bound with liquid manacles, and his path was blocked by a wall of flame. With wide, panicked eyes, he struggled against and shouted at his captor.

"You can't do this! You can't control us forever!" he yelled at the Elders.

Why had Trevan attacked? He had to be insane.

Ilan, the town's chief Elder, held his captive in place with as little effort as a spider holding a fly in its web. Then, he spoke in a tone forged with steely authority, "Trevan Balthilon, for your crimes of unprovoked violence, you are banished from Tormund. May your actions today follow you, and our esteemed brethren on the High

Council punish you as they see fit."

The High Council would surely execute Trevan for this.

Trevan sneered but didn't respond. The liquid chains twisted his arms and he winced. Finally, he gave Ilan a curt nod, acknowledging his defeat.

"Is anyone hurt?" Ilan silenced the crowd with his words. Meanwhile, the three other Elders milled about, giving quiet instructions as they assessed the situation.

"Here..." Kenna spoke as loudly as she could, but she couldn't form any more words. She hadn't realized she was still clutching Paisley's cold, limp hand until some male elves lifted the woman's body to carry her down the stairs to where the Elders gathered the dead and injured.

The attack had all happened so fast, and Kenna's thoughts and emotions hadn't caught up with what she'd witnessed. She counted seven dead elves once they'd assembled all the victims in the center of the amphitheater. All the students who'd stood to join in the attack were dead.

How was it that Trevan attempted to kill the Elders but only ended up harming those who were willing to fight alongside him?

The Elders looked at each other, coming to some silent agreement.

In unison, the four members of the City Council brought their hands over their heads. After a blinding flash of lightning, wings materialized on their backs. Each of the Elder's feathers were different colors, but the beautiful feathers were the least of Kenna's concerns.

Wings. The Elders had wings. They were angels.

Seconds later, a thunderous clap rumbled through the arena as Trevan vanished. Simultaneously, all the dead elves disappeared, and the entire crowd fell into stunned silence.

That was when Kenna started trembling, as the truth echoed through her mind.

The Elders are angels.

But if the five angels on the High Council weren't the only angels in Mesterra...

What else had the angels erased from history since the Void War?

Until recently, Kenna hadn't understood how the humans had been foolish enough to attempt a revolution against the angels. She'd been taught the Void War was a foolish, impossible endeavor that destroyed the entire human race.

But if the Elders were angels, the history the elves had learned in the three hundred years since the war was a lie. Kenna now understood what had driven the humans to the madness of rebellion.

Her existence as a female elf in Mesterra was increasingly oppressive. It could barely be called living anymore. And after what she'd witnessed today…

The High Council and the Elders were keeping more than order in the realm of Mesterra. They were keeping secrets.

Kenna looked around at the other jaded faces. Everyone floundered to understand not only what had just occurred but also the angels standing before them. The stillness gave way to uneasy whispers while the guards and Elders made sure all the students were accounted for.

Then, the guards barred the gates.

Before she had time to consider why the guards locked them in the arena, Ilan raised his hands to signal he was about to speak.

"Your attention, if I may. I understand that the events you have just witnessed are incredibly distressing. My fellow Elders and I are here to protect this city at the behest of the High Council. This includes ridding our city of those who are a threat to the safety, peace, and order of Mesterra."

It sounded like Ilan saying that this attack was staged. Like this year's trial was not about the elves proving their magical capabilities at all, but instead was a cover— a way to weed out emerging students who might attempt to rebel against the angels.

She breathed a sigh of relief. At least Sera hadn't been among them, though she also wondered what had held her fiery friend back from taking action today.

Kenna's hands were still shaking and covered in blood, and Ilan had the audacity to claim that the Elders were keeping Tormund safe and peaceful. Did the Elders seriously expect the city to go back to normal after everything that had just happened?

In spite of Ilan's attempt to calm the crowd, the hum of conversation grew louder. Kenna wasn't the only one with questions. She wasn't the only one who seemed angry.

As soon as the Elders dismissed them, she'd speak to her parents and brother. For years, she'd suspected they were keeping something important from her. She needed to find out exactly what they knew.

In the center of the arena, Ilan raised his arms overhead, then slowly lowered them like autumn leaves lazily floating to the ground. As he moved his arms, all the Elders' wings vanished.

A gasp next to Kenna drew her attention, but it had nothing to do with the Elders.

She followed the other student's gaze and looked down. Tiny streams of purple mist rose between the cracks in the wooden benches, forming a dense cloud filled with swirling white lights. The rising cloud surrounded her with a distinct sweet and spicy scent—licorice.

It was soothing as it settled over Kenna, and she inhaled the fog's licorice scent, feeling a deep sense of relaxation trickle through her body. She watched as the blood on her hands vanished.

For a moment, she felt a deep sense of gratitude toward the Elders. She was thankful they were so kind. But then, she realized the Elders were using some sort of magic to wash away or change any recollection of what had just happened.

She wanted to remember what happened. She needed to remember the truth.

She refused to take another breath, clinging to the memory of the attack. She looked toward the exit. City guards still stood sentry at the locked gates. There was nowhere to run. She couldn't do anything to stop it.

Her lungs burned, and her vision blurred at the edges.

When she finally gasped for breath, the purple mist flooded her lungs. A cage door in her mind clanged shut, locking the memories away. In an instant, every hint of shocking truth was replaced with euphoric ignorance.

CHAPTER 5

The next thing Kenna knew, Trevan was gone. She blinked away a slight sense of confusion. She honestly didn't care where he'd gone or why. It was nearly her turn, and she was positively euphoric. Though, she felt sure there was something important she needed to remember…

Oh yes, she had two more dress deliveries after the trial. Excitement for the Emergence Ball had washed away her nerves about the trial and the ceremony.

Everyone looked as dreamy eyed and content as she felt when her name was called. Wasn't it lovely to live somewhere so peaceful? She was so thankful that the city's Elders and the angels on the High Council kept them all safe.

"Kenella Duras, please step forward and take your position in the center of the elemental sources," Ilan, the Spectrum Elder, announced from somewhere that felt very far away. She remembered watching the other females sail through their domestic tasks, and she was sure that nothing could go wrong. Unless…

That feeling of forgotten memories and the weight of potential failure slowly settled over her, like some anxiety-numbing agent was wearing off. She wished she could have more of whatever had made her feel so blissfully calm moments earlier.

I'm safe. I'll pass the trial. I can relax.

She stood before Ilan and the three elemental sources—the trough, the lantern, and the rock pile.

"Good afternoon, Kenella. Since—"

"Kenna," she blurted on impulse, slapping a hand over her mouth. She removed the hand to apologize. "Sorry. Only my mother calls me Kenella, and that's only when I'm in trouble." She hoped she wouldn't be punished for interrupting.

Ilan gave her a warm smile, and something within her eased slightly. "Very well, Kenna. Since you are a Spectrum elf, I will ask you to prove your competency within the full spectrum of your elemental powers. You will perform one task each with your Aqua, Flame, and Terrane magic. To complete the trial, you will perform a task which showcases your ability to wield all three elements in unison. Understood?" Ilan asked her.

When she nodded, the Spectrum Elder instructed,

"First, without touching the glass, please fill it with water."

Sera would never let her forget that she had been right about this trial task. If Kenna had any chance of avoiding her merciless teasing, she needed to make her efforts count. There were no rules saying she couldn't employ a strong measure of creative flare.

Channelling Drake's stage presence and clinging to her last bit of false, euphoric confidence, she pointed to the trough with her index finger. She coaxed a stream of water into three parallel, spiralling arcs through the air that converged into the glass. She filled it to the brim without spilling a single drop.

Ilan looked amused by her flagrant exhibitionism. "Most impressive, Miss Duras. Next, I would like you to use your Flame magic to light the logs."

Ilan gestured to a makeshift campfire. The logs had been lit and extinguished repeatedly throughout the trial. However, at that moment, they sat charred and lifeless, waiting to be born anew with her Flame.

Upon being asked to light a fire, something Kenna could have easily done with a flint, she felt the acute sting of truth in Sera's outlook on female education. The life paths for females in Tormund were limited—cook, baker, seamstress, waitress, mother. But were any of those things what Kenna wanted? She could do those things without a single drop of magic in her veins, so what was the point of her education and Emergence?

Suddenly, she felt doomed to live out her days without purpose—filling glasses, lighting fires and doing exactly what was expected of her. Too dejected to waste any more effort on theatrics, she threw a spark from the lantern to the firewood with a flick of two fingers. She swirled her hands around each other, until orange flames licked steadily at the logs.

"Exemplary Flame magic, Miss Duras. Next, please use your Terrane power to move this small pile of dust and rocks from here to there. You must not leave any debris behind."

Chores? This is a sham of a trial.

Using her magic, Kenna deposited the stones and dirt to the point Ilan had indicated. She was ready for the trial to be over.

"Very good. Now you will need to prove your ability to use all three elements on the magical spectrum simultaneously. Using the sources in whatever way you see fit, please create a heated pool of water. The pool must be large enough to hold all of the water in the trough. Begin."

She took a moment to think, but the magic was simple and a plan materialized quickly.

First, she scooped and swirled one hand, using her power to dig a circular hole in the soil. At the same time, she used power flowing from her other hand to arrange stones in a circular border around the makeshift pool. She also deposited a few stones into the base of her creation.

Having formed a suitable container, she reached out toward the trough, forming a floating sphere of water. As she directed the liquid globe to its destination, she channelled the heat of the Flame into the stones at the base of the pool. She released the clear liquid into the hole, and the cool water hissed and sizzled upon contacting the heated stones. Twirling wisps of steam rose from the surface.

"That water looks rather inviting, Miss Duras." Ilan raised his voice to address all of the students, "I dare say that if this pool was any larger, you would have all had to avert your eyes as I submerged myself to ease my aching bones."

The assembled students laughed politely at the joke, trying to ease the awkwardness of imagining their Elder stripping into his undergarments to soak in the steaming water.

How old was Ilan anyway? It didn't matter. He was at least two hundred which was far too old to be stripping in front of a crowd full of twenty-five-year olds.

"Well done. I will see you tomorrow at the Emergence Ceremony."

She bowed her head in thanks and returned to her seat. Her Vessel's capability for holding magic was limited, since she'd not yet taken the Emergence Vow which would allow her to access her full measure of power. Even so, she hadn't neared her stilted power's boundaries with the domestic duties of the trial.

Her head was still a little fuzzy as the rest of the Spectrum elves completed their tasks, and the Elders congratulated everyone. No one else failed. Seven students had failed earlier, including Paisley. The details were fuzzy.

Before she could examine the memory too closely, Ilan spoke again,"Go now in peace as you prepare for the Emergence Ceremony tomorrow. May the magic of the land within the Emergence Chalice find you worthy to celebrate with us at the ball in your fine ensembles."

Her trial was over. Now, she just had to be found worthy at the ceremony. She slung her satchel over her shoulder, and joined the flow of the crowd toward the gates. She had two more deliveries to make today, and then she'd treat herself to a victory cinnamon bun.

CHAPTER 6

*A*fter exchanging congratulations with Drake, Ezra, and a few other fellow students, Kenna continued back to town with Aryn and Sera. Aryn, a Terrane elf, was another one of Kenna's oldest friends. Aryn's blonde curls and blue eyes gave an impression of innocence befitting her strict morals. The fact that she could move elements of earth and stone was entirely fitting, too. Sometimes, Aryn's stubbornness was a nuisance. More often than not, her views were infuriatingly correct.

Only seven people had failed the trial, though none of the students seemed to remember exactly why. Since they weren't supposed to discuss the trial, they moved on to the safer topic of clothes.

"Won't you tell us anything about your dress for tomorrow?" Aryn asked Sera.

"It's red," Sera replied.

"Oh really? I had no idea," Kenna quipped. "This is not new information. *All* of the Flame elves wear red."

"Let's just say, my magic isn't the only thing capable of heating up this city."

Sera gave nothing away. Kenna already knew that her spunky friend would wear a dress that pushed the boundaries of modesty and convention.

Aryn crossed her arms. "Do I need to blindfold my fiancé or not?"

"Don't get your knickers in a twist, your holiness. All of my fun bits will be covered. Mostly." Sera winked.

"Well, I don't want to get a peek at your nipples, so if you can keep them contained, my eyeballs and unsullied memories will thank you," Kenna said.

They all laughed and then carried on walking in an uncomfortable quiet. Kenna wondered if she was the only one trying to piece together memories from the trial, but the listening ears of the guards patrolling the road kept her from asking.

Trying to worry about something other than the ceremony, Kenna daydreamed about her beautiful dress for the ball the following day. It was red like Sera's. Like blood.

She felt a niggling memory just beyond her reach. Then, they arrived at the butcher's shop.

"I need to stop here. I have a delivery for Finch's wife. See you tomorrow, Aryn. Remember, Sera, breasts covered." Kenna gave her a mockingly stern look.

"I'll do my best, but I can't promise anything." Sera shrugged as she and Aryn carried on walking.

Kenna shook her head, smiling to herself, before entering the shop. As she stepped inside, she resisted the urge to pinch her nose closed against the scent of blood and death. She wanted to be in and out as quickly as possible.

"Hello, Finch," she said to the butcher. "Would you mind terribly giving this to your wife for me? I can drop it off at your home if that would be more convenient." She did her best impression of the polite and respectful young female everyone expected her to be.

"No problem at all, Kenna. Say, did you hear about our parakeet? It's disappeared. Poof!" The butcher walked around the counter to close the door to the shop. Still, he lowered his voice, leaning in to give her a hushed warning. "You didn't hear this from me, but some folk reckon they saw a Shadow prowling around the temple earlier today. Keep your head up, Kenna."

As she listened to the butcher's cautionary words, she couldn't stop staring at the red liquid leaking from the cuts of meat behind the glass window. Was there always so much blood? She could have sworn she saw blood dripping from her hands and felt it in her hair. She ran clean hands over her dry hair, tucking a couple of loose strands behind her pointed ears. No blood.

Still, she needed to get out of there. Thankfully, the door of the shop swung open.

"That's terrible news about your bird. I'd better go or I'll be late!" She said it more loudly than was necessary, just for the prying ears of the new customer, before she escaped the butcher's shop. After a few breaths of fresh air, she fixed on her normal mask of confidence and wit and headed to see Zola.

The entire town was buzzing with preparation for the Emergence Ball. The Summer Solstice was a strange juxtaposition of anxiety and pretending to enjoy the revelry.

Panic began to rise in her chest. If she didn't ignore it, she would crack under the weight of it. The trial was over, so why did thinking about it make her feel so uneasy?

Ancients. I think I'm losing my mind.

The hot sun and her spiralling anxiety were making her sweat more than ever, so she quickened her pace toward the promise of a cool shop interior and the smell of freshly baked bread at the destination of her final delivery.

A moment later, her worries were washed away by the comforting scent of baked goods. Through the window of the bakery, she spotted her oldest friend, Zola Barsden.

Zo's slender, dark brown hands meticulously kneaded bread dough on the counter, and her rosy lips were set in concentration. She'd tamed her tight curls into a high ponytail, but a few dark tendrils peaked out of her yellow headband to frame her face.

Kenna opened the door of Barsden's Bakery, welcoming the comforting aroma of sweet icing and yeasty bread. Zo lifted her dark brown eyes before Kenna dropped a carefully wrapped parcel on the flour-dusted, wooden counter in front of her.

Though Zo was twenty-five years old like Kenna and the others, she didn't need to take part in the trial. She had no elemental magic, only the special gift of Sight. Because she was an anomaly, her magical education was non-existent and her life's path was already decided for her. As long as Zo was found worthy when she took the Emergence Vow and drank from the Chalice, she would live out her days in

Tormund helping her mother in the bakery, under orders to report any visions to the Elders.

"Done," Kenna said, plopping a parcel down on the counter. She punctuated her week's work and let Zo know she'd completed the trial with the single syllable.

The unassuming brown paper package on the counter belied the beautiful cream garment inside—Zo's gown for the Emergence Ceremony. Kenna's mother was the most talented seamstress in town, and every female wanted to wear a Heidi Duras gown to her Emergence.

"How was it?" Zo asked.

"It was fine." Kenna helped herself to a warm cinnamon swirl from the basket on the counter.

"Aren't you going to tell me what happened?" Zo pressed, continuing to work the dough.

"You know I can't talk about it." Kenna shrugged, stuffing her mouth.

"Hmm." Zo looked like she knew something.

"What?"

"I just…I Saw something this morning, and— "

"You *Saw* something? Are you okay? What happened?" Kenna interrupted, nearly dropping the cinnamon bun.

The first and only other time she knew of Zo having a vision had been three years ago at Aryn's birthday. Zo had gone into a trance before spouting some nonsense about the moon and sun and feathers. Then, she'd fainted and hit her head on a table, unable to remember anything she'd said.

"Calm down. I'm fine. I didn't fall ill this time. I saw a few flashes of the trial amphitheater that seemed…I don't know…dark. But it was blurry. If the trial went okay, then I must have misunderstood it. I still don't quite understand how my Sight works."

Zo was still speaking, but Kenna's thoughts were elsewhere. Something in her head was pounding, desperate to be let out. She just needed to give it words and set it free. She choked on the need to tell Zo…something.

Damn it! What is it? Think, Kenna. Remember.

Zo suddenly seemed to realize Kenna wasn't listening.

"Nevermind. How did Sera do?" Zo asked, snapping Kenna's focus away from that angry thing in her head.

"Oh. She was amazing. You didn't hear this from me, but even lighting a campfire she looked like a goddess. It's not fair."

They both chuckled.

"What about Aryn?" Zo enquired after the other member of their "Pixie Pack", the nickname Kenna's mother had bestowed upon Kenna, Zo, Aryn and Sera.

"She was perfect," Kenna said.

They stood in silence for a moment, while Kenna chewed her cinnamon bun, wishing the delicious treat would soothe her worries, but both she and Zo seemed to realize there was something they should be worried about.

Even though Kenna passed the trial, something wasn't right. And there was still a chance Kenna could be banished if drinking from the Chalice revealed her unworthiness.

"I should go. I'm sure dinner will be filled with Mother going over every detail for the ceremony tomorrow."

Another customer arrived, so Kenna headed out, pausing on her way out the door of the bakery and turning back to her friend. "I'll see you tomorrow, Zo. You're going to be stunning."

Zo smiled awkwardly, darting a glance at the customer. "Yes. I guess. If you say so. Thanks." She was terrible at accepting any sort of compliment.

Kenna stepped back out into the blazing afternoon, and let out an appreciative sigh as she savored the last bite of decadent cinnamon bun.

She'd only made it two steps when she heard Zo shouting behind her. "Kenna! Wait!"

She paused a beat, allowing Zo to catch up. With her own favorite sweet treat in hand, Zo said, "You're trying to brush it off, but I know you're worried about tomorrow."

Clearly, Zo knew her too well.

They walked for a moment in silence, until Zo said, "I can't believe it's really time. What if..." she stumbled over the question and lowered her voice slightly. "What if something goes wrong at the ceremony?"

Kenna stopped, turning to face her friend and looking right into her dark eyes. "Zo, there is no way in the Three Realms you won't be found worthy."

Kenna's gaze implored Zo to understand that she was one of the most beautiful individuals she'd ever met. Zo was loyal, creative, kind and humble. Her gentle strength and ability to know when to stay quiet and when to speak her mind were both traits that Kenna admired and envied. She was certain she wouldn't have made it through the last fifteen years without Zo, and she didn't think there was anyone in the world more worthy of magic.

Zo looked away. Even as a grown female, she seemed uncomfortable with Kenna's—with anyone's—belief in her.

Kenna didn't waste precious words trying to convince Zo how wonderful she was. Throughout their lives, they'd often discussed their search for worth and purpose in a world that told women they weren't valuable.

Still, Kenna often found herself lost in her own struggles and forgot to try to understand what it might be like to be in Zo's position. To have an unheard-of magical gift must make Zo feel very different. Lonely.

Zo fiddled with the chocolate chip cookie in her hand, breaking into smaller and smaller pieces but not taking a single bite. Her eyes glistened with emotion. "Whatever happens tomorrow, I want you to know how much this friendship means to me. Sorry. I know you don't like to talk about this stuff."

"You've known me since I was six, Zo," Kenna replied. "I think we both know I'm perfectly capable of ignoring your emotions if they make me uncomfortable."

Zo laughed. "I love you, even if you are emotionally stunted." Her smile faded. "Really, Kenna. I love you. Remember that."

"Right. Okay."

Kenna licked the sticky icing from her fingers, and watched Zo jog back toward the bakery. Zo turned to look at Kenna.

Something about the expression on her face made the panicky feeling Kenna had been fighting ever since the trial pinch her chest. Though she was glad she could reassure Zo, she felt like she was fighting a losing battle with her own worry.

CHAPTER 7

Kenna's parents both had successful careers, and their two-story, stone cottage was cozy but large enough to host small gatherings. Though the décor was not overly extravagant, the tiled foyer always had fresh flowers to welcome guests. It was a true home and the backdrop of many memories from a time before Kenna realized that her life and freedom were under constant threat.

She'd promised her mother she could help her get ready for the Emergence Ceremony, so Kenna had slept in her old bedroom last night. Her room hadn't changed much since she'd moved into Sera's house three years ago, strewn with supplies for numerous failed or abandoned hobbies.

Though she fought the butterflies in her stomach, she was thrilled to finally wear her Emergence gown. She bounced on the balls of her feet, and thrummed with the need to turn and look at herself in the full-length mirror behind her.

Her mother was lacing up Kenna's corset when she said, "Eventually you need to clean up this mess. Just because you decided to move out doesn't mean that I'm going to tidy everything you've left behind. I'm not a servant, you know."

Servitude was forbidden everywhere in Mesterra except in the capitol district of Dendron where the upper-class families kept slaves. The slaves were unfortunate folks serving time as punishment for supposed crimes or in exchange for keeping their families fed or educated. Drake's boyfriend, Ezra, was from Erimos. His parents had offered themselves as slaves in exchange for his education.

"I just wanted to be sure you didn't forget me." Her response was muffled as her mother slipped the dress over her head and began lacing up the bodice. Kenna shifted her weight restlessly.

"Kenella Duras, hold still before I turn you into a pin cushion." Her mother gripped her shoulders, forcing her to stop her impatient wiggling. The use of her full name reminded Kenna of the trial, when Ilan had called her Kenella and…and…

It was there. On the edge of her memory. Roaring to be let out, but just beyond reach.

She closed her eyes. Instead of trying to remember, she pictured herself in the most beautiful garment to ever exist. Of course, she'd worn lovely dresses on previous Summer Solstices, but they were nothing like this dress. It was a masterpiece.

She looked down at her ample cleavage. *Well, girls. Tonight, we flaunt your rotund beauty and all will swoon.*

As long as she could remember, she'd imagined her Emergence. After all, it was one of the few aspirations females were allowed to have. She used to have girlish fantasies about the perfect dress and dancing with a handsome man at the ball, until she realized the Emergence Ceremony could just as easily turn into a nightmare.

If her Emergence Vow was successful, then her ceremonial robe would disappear and the beautiful gown would be revealed for all to see. But if drinking from the Chalice revealed her unworthiness…

Her breathing was shallow both from the rising panic in her mind and the tight-fitting bodice of the dress. She was suddenly sure there was something physically wrong and that she was about to die. Her breath came in short, panting gasps and her heart galloped in her chest.

What is wrong with me? I'm losing my mind.

Mercifully, her mother released the back of the dress, and Kenna gulped down a breath in the sudden reprieve. Her mother stepped around to face her.

"Are you okay?" her mother asked, concern shining in her eyes.

A few seconds passed, and Kenna's breathing slowed slightly.

At her very core, she was afraid she wasn't good enough, that she wasn't meant for much, and that she'd be cast out because of it. She'd always tried so hard to present an image that conformed to other's expectations of her. When she took the vow, she couldn't hide from scrutiny behind the shield of her carefully crafted wit or sarcasm. The thought of being so thoroughly examined—so thoroughly seen—terrified her.

"What if I'm not worthy?"

"Don't be silly. Of course, you're worthy. You love this dress, and you look stunning in it. Just focus on that. Breathe."

Kenna closed her eyes and took three deep breaths as she regained her composure.

"Shall we try again?" her mother asked gently.

Kenna opened her eyes and nodded.

A few minutes later, she was dressed, and her mother looked like she might cry as she asked, "Are you ready?"

Kenna felt like the question held weight beyond whether or not she was ready to look at her reflection. Was she ready for the Emergence Ceremony? For the possibility of being separated from her family forever?

It didn't matter, because she didn't have a choice. She nodded.

Her mother held her hands and spun her around to face the full-length mirror.

Kenna grinned at the sight of the dress, her worry vanishing. It was everything she'd imagined. The glittering, feminine piece was vibrant crimson, complimenting her olive skin, shiny brown hair, and dark brown eyes. The neckline of the bodice perfectly accentuated her breasts, and loose, sheer sleeves brushed her arms. The skirt flared out from her waist, with a light smattering of silver, gold, and bronze crystals. The carefully arranged whorls of sparkles looked like dancing flames.

She'd struggled to accept her figure before her magic manifested on her twenty-first birthday. Now, her curves filled her with confidence. She only wished she could find the same confidence in who she was and what her life meant.

As usual, her mother seemed to sense Kenna's thoughts. "Kenella Duras. You are wholehearted, generous, and kind. When I look at you, I see a woman who is beautiful inside and out. If you see anything other than those things when you look within yourself, remember how I see you. How your friends see you. Your father and I are so proud of you."

Kenna couldn't help the tears that welled in her eyes, and she looked away. She'd never felt like she was anything other than ordinary and found it difficult to believe her mother's words, but was thankful for them nonetheless. She swiped the tears away and attempted a shaky smile.

After her mother had arranged her hair into sweeping twists that joined in a low, relaxed bun, she gave Kenna a final hug. "I love you, my girl. I'll see you after the ceremony."

Her mother hesitated on her way out the door, as though she wanted to say something else. But then she left Kenna alone.

Kenna closed her eyes.

Suddenly, she was overcome by a pounding headache accompanied by confusing flashes of inky darkness and blood-stained hands. Her hands tingled with the sensation of phantom gore. The sight of her scarlet gown, the color of blood, made her stomach roil. That thing in her head seemed to writhe and scream, trying to get out. She sat on her bed before she could crumple to the floor in pain. The images were getting more and more vivid and disturbing—more insistent. Like memories, but they couldn't be. She'd never witnessed anything so gruesome.

A knock on the door brought her back to reality. She was sharing a carriage to the ceremony with the Pixie Pack girls. They must have arrived.

She used a few extra spritzes of her lavender perfume and inhaled deep breaths of the calming oil. She finished applying her cosmetics, and was pleased with the result of the shimmering powder dusted lightly over her cheeks and eyelids and the pink sheen of her lips. She donned the navy blue, ceremonial robe over her dress.

There was another knock on the door, and her brother's muffled voice filled her room. "Surely there isn't anything left to paint, curl, or pluck at this point, little sister."

She jerked the door open, sniping, "Not everyone is a magical genius who can get away with a face as ugly as yours."

In spite of her handsome, older brother's success, he'd never made her feel like she was any less important than him. She admired Jona, even though he was a flagrant overachiever, and they'd always had an easy relationship.

Jona whistled. "You're in a mood this evening, aren't you? One might think you were facing potential banishment."

"Ancients, Jona. Please don't joke about it. I'm already trying not to vomit."

"I'm sorry. I remember the feeling. You know I'm not good at this." He looked sheepish and maybe a little worried on her behalf. "You look lovely, Kenna. Everything will be fine. Really."

She couldn't stay too mad at him, since the propensity for ill-timed humour was a genetic trait just like their Spectrum magic. Unfortunately, whatever genetic trait the made Spectrum elves some of the most gifted elves in Mesterra seemed to have forgotten about Kenna. Perhaps only the males were worthy of exceptional magic.

"The carriage is here!" her mother called from downstairs.

"Good luck, Kenna. I...love you." He stumbled over his words, looking at the floor. She loved her brother and knew he loved her, but they were both excellent at skirting around the discussion of any real feelings. The fact that he was telling her he loved her felt like some sort of omen.

"You too, Jona," she said, heading downstairs to meet her friends.

Her parent's house was only a ten-minute walk from the temple, so the carriage the Pixie Pack had hired was purely a luxury. Navigating the town center in a carriage would take nearly as long as walking to the temple, but none of them wanted to worry about messing up their hair or cosmetics in the summer heat. Plus, they wanted to have a few minutes to speak privately.

Just in case.

"I know he lives on the opposite side of town, but are you sure you wouldn't have rather ridden with *Drake*?" Sera chided, turning to Kenna with her joking emerald eyes.

Kenna rolled her eyes dramatically. "Sera, I've told you. Just because Drake and I are friends doesn't mean you three aren't my favorite people in the entire realm."

"Well, just as long as we're clear that we are your favorite friends, I guess I can live with you spending some time with Drake and Ezra." Sera gave her an appeased wink.

They sat quietly for a moment until Aryn cleared her throat. "If everyone's done fighting, I need to tell you all something."

There was an extended pause as the three others waited for the big revelation.

"Last night was the night." A blush crept into Aryn's cheeks.

"What?!"

"Really?!"

"Seriously?!"

They declared, all speaking at once.

As far as romance, Aryn was the most conservative of them. She was mercilessly teased by the others for her inexperience with males.

Kenna saluted Aryn with a conspiratorial smile. "Lo and behold, virginal Aryn has submitted to her fleshly desires at last. I guess it's official. We'll have to share your heart with Daniel forever."

The new development was long overdue, since Aryn and Daniel were engaged to be married.

Aryn endured their frenzied inquiries with grace, but stalwartly refused to give too many details. Having exhausted their questions and collapsing into a fit of giggles, they fell into uneasy silence as they approached the temple.

Sera's eyes took on a haunted look. Sera had been happily unattached since losing Holt, though she had plenty of flings. Zo had just broken up with a long-term boyfriend a few months earlier. Kenna had been in a few relationships, but she hadn't found a man she felt truly connected to.

The carriage slowed to a stop, and they all clasped hands without a word, forming a circle. Looking at her beautiful friends, Kenna was crushed by the reality that the Emergence Ceremony could irrevocably change their lives.

After tonight, she might never see her friends or family again.

Affection for the three sisters of her soul poured through her. "Whatever happens and wherever life takes us, we'll always find our way back to each other. To this friendship. True North."

She meant the words with every fiber of her being, though she didn't know how she would achieve such a feat. She only knew that even if she was banished, she'd find a way back to her friends.

The carriage door opened, and Kenna didn't have time to wonder at the pained glance that Zo and Sera shared.

CHAPTER 8

$\mathcal{T}$he ceremonial robe—a glorified blue sheet—ballooned around Kenna as she climbed the steps into the temple. The lofty, vaulted ceilings and cracked tile floors housed wooden pews divided into three sections with wide aisles flanking the center. Even the balcony of the temple was packed, since attendance was mandatory for everyone in the city. But the heady mixture of all the different perfumes couldn't mask the distinct smell of decaying parchment and mildew.

They reached a pinch point at the aisle on the way to their seats, and the anticipation in the room was palpable. Kenna couldn't be bothered with small talk. She was too busy fighting an aggressive swarm of bees in her stomach and begging her armpits to stop sweating. The crowd shuffled forward, and she finally reached her seat among the other Spectrum elves.

She drank in the sight of the evening sun casting myriad colors through the three stained glass windows over the raised altar at the front of the cavernous hall. The historic tapestry depicting the creation of the Three Realms was divided into four sections. On the far left, a towering, onyx tile mosaic was encrusted with a glittering star and sun —the symbols of the Ancients, Luniva and Soldivus, in the Void that had been their home.

Next, came a vast, bloody, battle scene—the Void War. Her eyes skipped over the carnage to her favorite window. It was an opaque patchwork of every imaginable color that represented the Ancients sacrificing themselves, creating the Veil, and bringing peace to the realms. The final pane depicted Mesterra with its four current districts.

Kenna's father stood at the front of the temple in the center of the altar. The sacred basin filled with the Emergence serum and the silver Chalice were behind him. Zo was also seated on the platform, in a place of honor. She was as motionless as a slim statue, and her normally pleasant expression looked stricken, like she might vomit at any moment. Kenna tried to catch Zo's eye to send her what she hoped was a bolstering smile.

A few minutes passed before the humming in the air was swallowed by the sixth echoing chime of the bell tower, and anticipatory silence settled over the crowd.

"Good evening," her father addressed the crowd. "I am Dean Quinn Duras of Tormund Elemental Academy, and I would like to thank you all for joining us to celebrate the Emergence Ceremony of our fine, young elves."

Turning his attention to the elves gathered in the middle of the temple, her father addressed the students, "We are honored to celebrate with each of you as you take the Emergence Vow today. The Summer Solstice has marked the entry point from early adulthood into true adulthood for elemental elves throughout Mesterra for three hundred and twenty-nine years. Since the Void War, Mesterra has known peace, but that peace was bought with the price of bloodshed to conquer the corruption of the rebellious and greedy human race."

He gestured toward the stained-glass window behind him which depicted the Void War. The look on his face, and the familiar timbre of his voice were telltale signs he was about to go off on a tangent with one of his famous history rants. Ilan, the head Elder, nodded in approval and agreement with her father's droning.

Soldivus save me. There's no stopping the deluge of information he's about to let loose. Might as well settle in.

"All of the angels apart from five of the most noble and pious—dead. All because of humanity's insane desire to steal angel magic. Mercifully, the Ancients were willing to destroy themselves and the humans, a steep price to rid this realm of human corruption. Luniva and Soldivus poured out their lives to create the Veil so that we elves could live in peace and safety in Mesterra, allowing the angels to live in their own realms.

In light of the Ancient's sacrifice, it is our responsibility to train each generation in the laws of magic…"

Kenna didn't need to listen to the spiel she'd heard so many times before. Notos and Vorra, the other two realms across the Veil, were supposedly full of angels. The High Council insisted it was best for elves and angels to remain separate.

People like Drake had snuck across the Veil, and from her friend's reports, he'd not seen any angels in Notos. Perhaps it was just another one of the Council's lies in their continued oppression of the elves in Mesterra.

Kenna scanned the crowd for her mother and brother and spotted them seated a few rows back on the right-hand side of the temple. When she caught her brother's attention, she jerked her head in their father's direction and rolled her eyes. Jona stuck out his tongue and made a rude gesture at Kenna while Mother wasn't looking just like he used to do when they were younger. Kenna snorted, but quickly tried to cover it up with a fake cough. The noise still attracted the attention of those around her.

I should at least try to pay attention.

"…worthy of the Emergence Vow. When you drink from the ceremonial Chalice it will become clear. In the rare event that you are found unworthy, the guards outside the temple will escort you home for a short time to gather your things. Then, you will be escorted to the shore of Lake Audral to begin your journey to Dendron."

She shuddered at her father's words.

"My fellow professors and I are exceedingly grateful to have had the privilege to be part of your lives, and we wish you well in all of your endeavors as you venture forth into the next chapter. Without further ado, I believe it is now time for you all…" he paused dramatically, "to take the Vow." He indicated the waist high basin of liquid to his left which began to glow with a faint purple-hued light. Ilan, the lead Elder, took up the center position on the altar.

Jona was a celebrated genius, her father was the Dean of the Academy, and her mother was the most renowned clothing designer in town. Kenna would either Emerge or be cast out forever into some unknown fate. She shifted on her sweaty rear end.

Why would I possibly feel any pressure?

All of the Academy students stood in unison as the applause faded away to the mellow quiet of the hall. The only sound was a tinkling melody floating lightly from the fingers of the harpist in the back corner of the cavernous room.

Although the Aqua elves were standing in the back row, they would be the first to speak their vows. They all wore the same navy robes, but the robes would reveal dazzling ensembles in a splendid array of watery-blue underneath.

Without further instruction, the Aqua elves filed out of the rear pew and up the left-hand aisle. They'd all rehearsed their positions and cere-monial movements ad nauseam earlier in the week, so she didn't have to turn around to know Ezra and Drake were the first two in the procession of Aqua elves.

Ezra passed first, squeezing her hand. Drake followed, impishly pinching her robed ass on his way, eliciting a tiny yelp. The little noise earned cross glances from other students and a confused look from Ezra. Drake gave her a sly smile even as she stared back at him, stunned.

Sera is right. Drake is the worst being in the Realms. Why am I friends with him?

Seconds later, Kenna was already smiling about the incident and thankful to be distracted from her anxiety, which was probably Drake's intention. Only he could get away with pulling that stunt in the middle of a sacred ceremony in a temple.

Ezra reached the altar and the harpist stopped playing. Looking stoic as ever, he ascended the steps of the raised platform and walked to the center to kneel before Ilan.

Kenna's heart quickened. Ezra's face was visible in profile as he spoke the words of the Aqua Emergence Vow. All of his brethren would repeat the same phrases before they returned to their seats.

Ilan placed a hand on Ezra's head, prompting him to recite practiced words:

"As still as the morning mist and as fierce as the rushing river, I accept the flowing whisper of the water within my soul. With this vow and the blessing of the land, may the Aqua magic within my Vessel Emerge."

After his vow, Ilan motioned for Ezra to rise and he passed him the jewelled Chalice. Kenna held her breath as her friend sipped the consecrated liquid.

The moment the solution touched his lips, he was transformed.

His oversized, blue robes evaporated into azure mist that blended into the rainbow of light from the stained glass windows. Ezra's golden skin glowed faintly, and he beamed as he continued across the dais and down the stairs on the right-hand side. He took his place to wait for the rest of his fellows.

Meanwhile, Drake climbed the stairs, as self-assured as ever, and approached Ilan from the left. Kenna could tell by his grin that he wasn't worried.

Drake repeated the ritual, and, as his robes disappeared to reveal an impeccable ensemble. The Emergence glow made him even more handsome than usual. He was resplendent in a deep teal waistcoat marbled with gold filigree. The gold embroidery coordinated with matching stitching on black breeches. His loose white shirt sleeves and gleaming black boots completed the outfit perfectly. His blue eyes sparkled as he followed Ezra's trajectory down to the other side of the steps.

One by one, the rest of the Aqua elves completed the Emergence. Dozens of ceremonial robes trickled away into nothing, the thing caged in her mind grew more and more insistent, scratching at her thoughts like a reminder of a forgotten truth. No matter how hard she tried, all she could think of was the vision of blood on her hands. Like a memory from an awful nightmare, and yet...

Eventually, the last of the Aqua elves finished the Emergence. After a final round of applause from the crowd, they filed back to their seats in a kaleidoscope of blue. The Chalice hadn't found any of them unworthy, which was wonderful news for the Aqua elves, but it meant that the odds were not in Kenna's favor. The vice in Kenna's chest tightened a little. At least a few elves from each university in Mesterra were found unworthy and banished every year.

Next came the Flame elves. Sera was, of course, stunning. Her robes gave way to a perfect, crimson gown which showed entirely too much cleavage. *Just the right amount*, Sera would say.

By the time the final Flame elf, Aubrey, took her place in front of the gathered townsfolk, the atmosphere had grown more relaxed to the point of feeling almost boring, as though they'd all forgotten what was at stake. Aubrey spoke the sacred vow of the Flame elves.

"As insignificant as a single spark and as immense as the fiercest fire, I accept the wild will of the Flame within my soul. With this vow and the blessing of the land, may the Flame magic within my Vessel Emerge."

Aubrey stood and sipped from the silver goblet, and as they waited for her robes to disappear and reveal her Emergence glow…

Nothing happened.

CHAPTER 9

The silence in the temple was all-consuming, and Kenna's heart dropped like a stone into her gut. Aubrey's cheeks flushed and tears streaked her face as she stood, shamed and rejected in her ceremonial garb. The crowd didn't move as she hurried across the platform, down the steps, and along the aisle to exit the temple with her head bowed against the harsh quiet.

Her friends and her family wouldn't even be allowed to say goodbye. Kenna thought she heard someone sniffling quietly in the crowd.

The shift in the mood was jarring as everyone snapped out of the brief sense of false security. Aubrey's exit was a reminder that the magic in the Chalice could find any of them unworthy. No one was safe.

Reality pressed down on Kenna, and she couldn't draw enough air into her lungs. She was sure these were her last moments of freedom. She'd be cast out. Just like Aubrey. As the Flame elves journeyed back to their seats, the Terrane elves proceeded to accept their gifts or be doomed to the same fate as Aubrey.

Kenna barely registered any of the Terrane elves taking their vows. She scarcely noticed Aryn's stunning bronze dress overlaid with cream lace. She refused to feel anything at all as three more elves were banished, and she pondered the complete helplessness and lack of control over her entire life.

A pointed cough to Kenna's left shook her back to reality, and she wrestled the onslaught of helplessness into submission. It was time for her to lead the row of Spectrum elves to the altar.

It was time to discover her fate.

In the span of the ceremony, she'd flitted from bored to despondent to numb to whatever emotion now settled like lead in her legs, making it nearly impossible to place one foot in front of the other.

Don't trip. This is it.

The silent refrain dragged her toward the altar step by step. Her earlier excitement over the beautiful gown felt comically inconsequential.

By some miracle, her feet carried her to the stairs. Her father smiled at her, which gave her the jolt of determination she needed to climb the steps.

Everything hinged on what happened after she took the vow.

Standing silently in front of everyone in the city, she couldn't mask her trembling uncertainty. There was nowhere to hide.

She knelt, and her kneecaps jolted with pain on impact with the stone altar. She wasn't sure why, but she closed her eyes to take the oath. She repeated the oaths for Aqua, Flame, and Terrane magic before moving on to the Spectrum oath:

"As varied as colors in the rainbow, I accept the diversity of the spectrum of elements within my soul. With this vow and the blessing of the Chalice, may the Spectrum of magic within my Vessel Emerge."

She stood on quaking limbs and eyed the hand that offered the bejewelled, silver Chalice.

Feeling like she was moving under water, she raised the goblet and glimpsed the swirling liquid in detail for the first time. It was deep violet, so dark it was nearly black. Tiny white lights with shimmering tails danced through the solution, a tangle of shooting stars. The way it glittered reminded her of something she'd seen before. A dream.

The temple doors crashed open. Everyone turned toward the noise, but there was nothing there; it was only a gust of wind. Then they all looked at Kenna again. Waiting.

That thing in her head pounded in time with her racing heart. It was roaring at her to think. To know. To *remember*.

The Chalice was cool in her hand and the gentle breeze that now meandered through the temple seemed to purposefully tickle her nose with the scent of the liquid as she raised the Chalice to her lips. It was the stringent smell of metal and the cloying scent of liquorice that finally freed the caged animal in her memory.

Her vision blurred, but the memories were clear as they rushed through her mind.

Trevan in the icy, swirling darkness. Paisley's vacant eyes. Paisley's warm blood dripping down Kenna's face. The mysterious Shadow. And the Elders.... They were angels.

No one would believe her if she told them. For over three hundred years, elves had believed that only five angels lived in Mesterra, but now...

She stared and stared into the goblet, watching the dancing lights. There were only seconds to make a choice. The liquid smelled just like the mist the Elders had used to control their memories. If she drank it, would the truth of what had happened be locked away forever? The Elders discovered and killed rebel students at the trial every year. It seemed like the angels had controlled Trevan somehow...but how? And did anyone else in Tormund know what really happened at the trial?

"Miss Duras? Are you quite alright?" Ilan's prompting voice sounded so far away as Kenna remembered where she was.

No. She couldn't drink this poison, even if it kept her safe. She had nothing but her instincts to guide her as she lowered the Chalice and extended it back to Ilan. There were a few audible gasps.

"Miss Duras." Her name wasn't a question. It was a warning.

"I... I'm not ready," she stammered.

"Miss Duras. If you do not drink, you will not Emerge." He pushed the Chalice back toward her like moving a chess piece.

Sera would be proud of the way the Flame within Kenna bristled at the presumption.

"So be it." She forced the goblet back in his direction and waited for him to clasp it before she let go. She wouldn't be a mindless pawn. She needed to remember the truth, even if it meant putting herself in danger.

There was a flicker of something in Ilan's eyes—Anger? Surprise? Confusion? It was difficult to tell what he thought as he formulated his response. "Very well. This is most unprecedented. The other Elders and I will—"

An almighty *BANG* rattled through the night and seemed to rock the foundation of the world. Screams filled the temple.

Ilan's head snapped towards Kenna, and his lip curled over his teeth in a snarl as though it was somehow her fault. He must have seen the shock and confusion written on her face.

He turned away from her to face the murmuring crowd.

"Silence!" Ilan's shout elicited immediate obedience, and the temple fell quiet. "The other Elders and I will investigate the disturbance. Everyone stay where you are until we have returned," he said. Then he swept down the stairs. All four elders swept down the aisle towards the doors, their robes trailing behind them in the wind.

The newly emerged elves with their glowing skin and dreamy-eyed expressions seemed unphased by the explosion. Kenna's eyes searched for her friends and family. Jona was no longer seated next to her mother. Thankfully, Ilan didn't seem to notice her brother's absence.

She looked behind her. Her father's jaw was tight, and Zo still seemed frozen in place, though tears were streaming down her face now.

"I'm so sorry," Zo mouthed silently.

The fearful quiet still blanketed the room as Ilan addressed the two guards stationed at the temple doors. "You two. No one leaves the temple until the other Elders and I have investigated what is happening outside. Bar the door and open it for no one but us. Understood?"

The two guards each placed a fist over their hearts. "Yes, Elder Ilan."

Once the Elders exited the temple, the guards shut the doors. After a few seconds, one of them peeked through the door and then turned back to Kenna's father, nodding.

"They're gone," the guard said.

Immediately, conversation filled the silence, along with quick footsteps and a sudden flurry of movement from many people in the temple. Her father was at her side in an instant. "Kenna. You must come with me. Now."

"What? What's happening?" she said, shaking her head as he guided her down the steps toward the temple's exit.

Her father rushed Kenna down the aisle towards the door, Zo following at their heels. "There's no time to explain. I'm so sorry. Everything will become clear in time, but you must leave Mesterra before midnight tonight. It's not safe for you here anymore. Drake and Ezra have volunteered to make the crossing with you. They will meet you there."

Zo hugged her close, before she released her quickly. "I'm sorry. I should have told you. I wanted to come with you, but the Elders watch me more closely than the others. Please. Please be careful. I love you."

"Zola," her father said, handing Zo a bag. "You know what to do."

Zo opened the bag and peaked inside. It was a tiny vial filled with a liquid that looked like pure light.

Her best friend didn't wait for Kenna's response before she jogged back towards the altar. A few other citizens ran to her father, and he gave them orders.

Kenna barely registered as she watched Zo run away and urge the emerged elves to drink the shining liquid. As they drank, their emergence glow faded, and they looked around in confusion. Many of the gathered citizens were hastily removing doublets and ladies were ripping away the skirts of their dresses to reveal trousers beneath. Some of them were already clad in armor and carrying weapons. Two additional city guards were handing out armor which must have been stashed somewhere within the temple.

Still, just as many citizens bore perplexed expressions as the armor clad elves seemed to explain what was happening.

Kenna's body moved as though she were in a dream. Turning to her father, Kenna asked, "What is happening?"

Someone knocked in a sequence that sounded like a code, and the guard opened the temple door. Jona was back, and his face was streaked with soot.

Her brother said, "It's chaos. City Hall is a pile of rubble, and the guards and the Elders are distracted for now trying to find the cause of the explosion. But we need to move quickly. Before they come back."

"Wait!" her mother shouted. As Kenna turned, her mother careened into her and smothered her in a hug. Kenna's mother fixed her father with an imploring look. "Are you absolutely sure she has to go? Can't she hide in the camp?"

"Heidi, for the thousandth time, we have to let her go. It's time," her father said.

"I just… it's so dangerous, Quinn."

"We can't protect her from this. She's not a child."

Her mother's voice cracked and tears spilled down her cheeks. She placed a hand on her chest. "She's *my* child! She will always be my child."

"We've always known she was destined for something greater. Despite her destiny, she sealed her fate the minute she refused to drink from the Chalice.."

Kenna finally found her voice. "What are you talking about?"

Her parents looked at her like they'd forgotten she was there.

Her mother was crying. "Kenna, I'm so sorry. We just wanted to keep you safe, we just…"

Kenna looked at her brother. "Jona, do you know what they're talking about?" Her brother looked at the floor. He knew.

Her nerves were already frayed, but seeing her family like this…her mind whirled with hundreds of possibilities, and rage burned in her chest. "Tell me what you're talking about. What is going on?"

Kenna's father placed a hand on her cheek, and the callouses she'd never noticed before rasped against her soft skin. "For years, I've taught you safety was the most important thing. Please forgive me, and allow me to tell you the truth now. If you remember anything I've ever told you, let it be this: Freedom is worth fighting for. No matter how feeble it seems."

"So…what? This is a revolution? Why would you hide this from me? Why wouldn't you prepare me for this?" Kenna's hands trembled and her cheeks were wet.

"We couldn't risk the Elders watching you. Suspecting anything of you. I'm sorry," he said. "You have to make the crossing."

Kenna's eyes widened. "The crossing? Why? But I might be trapped in Notos. I might not ever see you again."

Her mother cut in and pulled Kenna into a tight embrace. "Don't you dare say that. I love you, my girl."

The moment her mother released her, her father hugged her and said, "We have a plan to bring you home. For now, all you can do is take the next right step. That means you must leave. I love you, Kenna. Everything I've done… it's because I love you. I've written you a letter that explains everything."

Next, Jona gave her a short hug. "Get out of here, little sister. I'll see you soon."

"How? There are guards everywhere. Or are they all rebels?"

Jona answered, "Not all of them, but there are enough. Plus, the smoke from the explosion obscures the view of the lake. They're all distracted for now." Her brother took off his leather rucksack and thrust it into Kenna's hands. "Meet Ezra and Drake at your bench by the lake. Stay hidden until they arrive. This should have everything you need."

Kenna looked around for any sign of Aryn, Sera or Zo, but couldn't see them in the crowded temple.

Finally, she took a deep breath and looked at her parents, tears blurring her vision. Both of them were crying too, and she knew they loved her. She trusted them, and if this is what she needed to do. "I love you. I... I'll miss you."

Before she could change her mind, she opened the temple doors.

It was like watching a glass falling in slow motion as she spared one final glance at her family. Finally, Kenna slipped out the door and ran.

And the falling glass shattered into thousands of pieces along with everything she'd ever known.

CHAPTER 10

She ran through the shadows towards the lakeside path, sobbing as the air burned in her lungs.

Clouds of smoke surrounded the ruins of city hall and hid Kenna as she picked her way down the banking towards the lake. The only stairs down the hillside were behind city hall, and she didn't want to get any closer to where the Elders were investigating the explosion.

She didn't question the air current keeping the smoke from invading her lungs or the wind keeping the air clear enough for her to see the next step. She whispered a curse as her feet tangled in the skirt of her dress, and she tumbled down the grassy bank towards the lake.

Standing up quickly, she settled into a steady jogging rhythm. Kenna focused on placing one foot in front of the other, and her thoughts began to flow with the cadence of her feet. She'd always been impulsive, but refusing to drink from the sacred Chalice was the first time it had ever put her in any real danger.

She emerged from the smoke and looked over her shoulder towards Tormund. Towards her family.

It didn't matter what secrets her family was keeping, she still had to leave. She'd never doubted they loved her, but they'd hidden something from her. Leaving without knowing why they'd lied to her seemed wrong. Her heart ached, and she wished they'd had more time to explain everything.

And what about her friends? Zo...

She and Zo had always understood each other. They both saw the world a little differently, and she never felt like she had to be anything other than herself with her very best friend. But Zo had hidden this rebellion from her.

Had Aryn and Sera known, too? Kenna's eyes filled with tears as she remembered the promise she'd made to her friends before the ceremony.

They didn't warn her, even as they'd held hands and vowed to always find their way back to each other. She'd meant every word, but she hadn't known she'd be fleeing for her life tonight.

With only the sound of her ragged breaths and her footsteps crunching along the stony path, Kenna allowed the tears to fall. She allowed herself to feel all of it. The fear, the betrayal, the loss.

She'd tried to be good for so long. To play a role and stay safe. She wouldn't hide who she was. Not anymore. What would her life look like if she finally took off the mask and found out why she could hear the wind whispering to her when no one else could hear that phantom voice?

She could have sworn she heard that voice urging her on.

Faster. Run.

After the longest twenty minutes of her life, Kenna reached the bench where she used to meet Drake and Ezra to practice their magic.

She shimmied into a hiding place between some shrubs, trying to quiet her breath and listen for footsteps.

If Drake didn't arrive before midnight, Kenna wouldn't be able to make the crossing. All she knew about crossing the Veil was that the nearest port was invisible, somewhere on Lake Audral, and only open on the equinox and solstices. Drake was the only person she knew of who'd made the crossing before.

She checked the time on her Fostone—eleven thirty. The small sapphire on her bracelet was a feat of her brother's genius. He'd invented the fostone three years ago to light or extinguish candles with a single drop of elemental magic transferred by touching the stone. He'd made improvements to the fostones since then, adding glowing hands that showed the time.

Time that was now slipping away.

Five minutes passed. Then ten. Then twenty.

Then, it was eleven fifty. Only ten minutes until the crossing would close and she'd be stuck in this realm. Would she be hunted by the Elders? Everyone she loved seemed to be involved in this plan to help her leave Mesterra. But why?

And where were Ezra and Drake?

As if in answer to her silent question, she heard quick footfalls crunching along the stony path.

She held her breath as a male silhouette drew closer. Then, the moonlight illuminated a familiar face—Ezra.

Sighing with relief, she scooted out from her hiding place in the bushes and threw herself at him, hugging him tight.

"What was that explosion? Where's Drake?" she asked.

He squeezed her back, breathless from his run. "The explosion was something your brother calls an eriksomb. Drake's just behind me."

She heard the next people arrive before she saw them, since they were shrouded in a natural-looking mist in the valley next to the lake. From the sound of their footsteps, they were running. But they weren't too winded to argue with each other.

"Ancients save us," Kenna muttered.

"All I'm saying is that Flame is much more exciting to work with than Aqua magic," Sera said.

"Oh really?" Drake countered as he appeared through the mist, reaching out his hand.

A shimmering, liquid lion rose out of the water in response to his magic. The lion bounded over the lake's surface next to him in the bright moonlight, before it crouched, prepared to pounce. It fixed translucent, predatory on Sera. "And how much experience do you have wielding Aqua magic?"

Sera snorted. "Obviously, I don't *have* Aqua magic. But if I had a Flame source, I could prove why it's better."

"Obviously," Drake said, smirking and allowing the lion to disappear, just as he and Sera reached Ezra and Kenna.

"I'm just on the run for my life in the middle of a revolution I knew nothing about, but we'd all love to know whose head is bigger. Please, make more of a scene. Don't let me interrupt." Kenna folded her arms.

"We all know Drake's head is bigger," Sera muttered.

Drake scoffed. "Oh, please."

Ezra cut him off. "Can you two shut up for two seconds? We need to hurry, and you need to be discreet."

Drake led the way, setting a quick pace, and the other three followed behind him.

Sera said, "You worry too much, Ezra. I'm always discreet. Just ask the man I spent a happy few minutes with in the bathroom at the Tranquil Tavern last night."

"I agree with Drake," Kenna said, a smile creeping onto her face. "You really are insufferably arrogant."

"Ha!" Drake said in triumph.

Given the severity of the situation, their lighthearted argument was entirely inappropriate. Still, Kenna found the familiar banter comforting, momentarily forgetting her burning legs and the grave situation.

Kenna glanced at her Fostone—ten minutes until midnight. She spared a look over her shoulder towards the city. Between the smoke from Jona blowing up city hall and whatever the rebels were doing, it seemed the guards and the Elders were still too busy to search for a lone female elf.

"I hate that I'm putting anyone else in danger," Kenna panted as they veered off the path towards the lake's shore.

For once, Sera was serious. "Too bad, Kenna. This isn't just about you. I spoke to Aryn. She loves you but she doesn't approve of the rebellion. She can't understand why anyone would do something 'so utterly stupid and reckless.' Her words, not mine. I tried to convince her it was safe enough to come say goodbye, but you know how she is once she makes up her mind."

Drake was a little breathless as he asked, "Care to explain what was important enough to risk the Elder's wrath? Why did you refuse to drink from the Chalice?

"The Elders have been lying to us," Kenna told them.

"I am shocked. And appalled." Sera feigned melodramatic surprise.

"Sera, can you be serious for one minute? It's worse than ingrained tradition and misogyny," Kenna said. "What do you think happened at the trial? To Trevan and Paisley and the others that disappeared?"

They'd not yet had a chance to discuss yesterday's events.

Sera shrugged. "Before tonight, I thought they'd just failed and been banished to our angelic rulers on the High Council to be slaves or some other wonderful future. But did you see the vial Zo took from your father?"

Kenna nodded.

"It was an antidote of sorts. To counteract the effects of the Emergence Serum. It restored my memories of the trial. There's not enough antidote for all the rebels, but enough of us know the truth to spread the word. And now that the revolution has started, I'm planning to cause as much trouble as I can." Sera winked.

Kenna shook her head. "But I remembered. Before I drank the serum, I remembered everything. The mist the elders used to wipe our memories. If they're angels, it must be angel magic. After the trial, I was having flashbacks and panic attacks. I didn't say anything. I genuinely thought I was losing my mind. When I smelled the Emergence serum in the Chalice, it smelled just like the mist and my memories came flooding back. I was certain I'd forget again if I drank it. Honestly, I almost wish I could go back. Part of me wants to forget."

She wasn't sure if she imagined the angry flames dancing in Sera's eyes, or if it was something the Emergence serum had unlocked in her friend. "Don't you dare say that. It's time to take those bastards down. It's one thing for them to be controlling, totalitarian assholes. But how dare they control our memories? Our history? You were right to defy them."

"I never thought I'd agree with someone so insufferably arrogant, but Sera's right. You did the right thing, Kenna," Drake said.

Sera raised a brow. "Insufferably arrogant? Really? That's rich coming from you, you tap dancing son of a—"

"Stop. Both of you. We're on the same side, remember?" Ezra cut them off.

Thanking Drake and Ezra for coming with her tonight wouldn't even come close to conveying Kenna's gratitude. She knew it was selfish, but she really didn't want to cross the Veil alone.

Ezra must have seen the relief on her face. He squeezed her shoulder and said, "The last time Drake crossed the Veil, he went without me. I thought I might never see him again."

Kenna raised her brows, surprised to hear Ezra speaking so openly about his relationship with Drake in front of Sera.

Sera looked between the two men. "Wait. So, you two…?"

Drake shrugged with a sheepish smile and put an arm around Ezra's shoulders.

Sera let out a low whistle and an approving grin spread across her face. "Well, I'll be damned. Good for you."

"What about your parents?" Kenna asked Ezra. He was from Erimos, the poorest part of Mesterra, and only had a place at Tormund Elemental Academy because his parents had offered themselves for twenty years of voluntary enslavement. They'd given up twenty years of their lives for the chance to offer him a better future.

"For years, I've tried to make them proud. I've let the fear of what might happen to them guide my actions. The more time Drake and I have together, the more certain I am my parents would want us to act. They wouldn't want us to have to hide. That's why I joined the rebellion."

Drake's eyes softened as Ezra spoke, and he reached for his partner's hand. "I really hope I get to meet them one day. They sound about ten million times better than my parents."

"Well, for what it's worth, I don't think you should have to hide," Kenna said. She looked at Sera, expecting her to declare that she would make the crossing too, but she seemed to be having some sort of internal debate.

"I want to come with you more than anything. But I have somewhere else I need to be," Sera said, exchanging a knowing look with Drake and Ezra.

"No. No more secrets. Damn it. Someone just tell me *something*!" she demanded.

"Your dad and your brother have been growing the rebel force for years," Sera informed her. "Holt was an integral part of it, too. We think that may be why the Shadow targeted him after his Emergence. It's why your father has been working so hard to bring in so many students to the university while he's been dean. Growing the rebel force is part of why Tormund's population has grown so much.

Theres's a camp in the mountains where thousands of rebels are living in hiding. There's a rendezvous point near the bottom of the mountain pass. They're waiting to lead small groups of women and children to safety as soon as we can sneak them out of the city. There are others waiting for my signal to come to Tormund and fight alongside us."

Kenna always knew her fiery friend was a revolutionary at heart, but she'd never dreamed that almost all of her friends and her family had been part of something like this right under her nose. And they'd kept it from her. Did they not trust her? How had she not figured it out? She was a fool.

"My family knew. You all knew."

"Aryn didn't t know anything until tonight, either," Sera said. "She wouldn't have approved. Ancients, can you imagine what would have happened if her father found out about the rebellion? He would've run and told the Elders faster than you could say, 'You're a misogynist prick.'"

Her three friends laughed, but Kenna didn't find anything about the situation funny. Her lips were numb and her body was too hot. She felt like she might burst, like all the anger welling up inside of her was begging to be released. Instead, she pushed it down. She would deal with it later.

"Come here," Sera squeezed her into a hug. Her words were hurried. "I'm sorry I didn't tell you. Your father was very clear. He told us that if the Elders discovered your involvement in the rebellion, it would be detrimental to the Three Realms."

Kenna's voice was a hoarse whisper. "Why me? What's so special about me? And why wouldn't he tell me any of this? Does he not trust me?"

"I don't know, Kenna. He said it wasn't safe, and he also threatened to find a reason to have us banished if we told you about the rebellion before tonight. Whatever his reasons, your father was willing for people to die in order to protect you. Try not to worry. We have to believe it will all work out. We'll see each other again. True North, right?"

Kenna just nodded, trying to numb the emotions and swallow the lump in her throat. "Goodbye Sera," she whispered. "I love you. Tell Aryn and Zo I said goodbye. And that I love them, too."

"All being well, Ezra and I will be back tomorrow night. Try not to burn anything down before we get back," said Drake.

"If he gets lost on your way across the Veil, I probably won't cry about it," Sera told Kenna.

With that, the Flame elf disappeared beyond Drake's mist towards the mountains.

CHAPTER 11

"So, now what? How do we make the crossing?" Kenna asked from where she stood with Drake and Ezra on the lake's shore.

"Think about why you want to cross. Then, just walk out onto the lake."

She leaned around him to look out over the water.

"Then, we swim? Or …?"

Drake rolled his eyes. "Just think about why you want to cross and follow me."

He turned and walked toward the water, until he was walking *on* the water. Was he using Aqua magic?

He turned and beckoned her and Ezra closer. She went first, thinking as hard as she could about why she wanted to cross.

I want to be safe.

She looked at Drake and stepped forward.

Her foot got soaked, and the water pooled in her shoes.

"It doesn't seem to be working. Care to give me any more help?" she said.

"I already told you. You need to think about why you want to cross," Drake replied.

I want to be free. I want to know the truth.

A wooden jetty appeared under Drake's feet. Kenna took a tentative step nearer. Straining to see the end of the pier shrouded in mist, she was reminded just how little she knew about Mesterra. She knew even less about the realm of Notos where they were headed.

Drake led the way over slick, wooden planks toward an old sailor who was seated near the end of the pier.

"Hello, Drake." The old man must have recognized him from his previous trip across the Veil.

"Good evening, Raziel." Drake's response was unusually curt.

The ferry master stood to face them with his back to the tiny, wooden raft behind him— a ferry of sorts. He looked at Ezra as he joined them on the pier. "And who's this?" Sweet smoke hovered around Raziel's wiry gray hair and weathered face. He looked as though he'd had a hard life.

"This is my partner, Ezra," Drake answered.

"So, you found love after all. How wonderful." The ferry master's weathered face twisted into a satisfied grin. Something about his smile hinted at darkness lurking beneath the surface.

Drake addressed the captain. "My friends and I would like to make the crossing, please. But Ezra and I need to return as soon as possible."

"That can be arranged. You'll need to be at the ferry port before nightfall on your first day in Notos. And it will cost you, of course."

"What is the cost?" Drake asked.

The ferry master gripped Drake's forearm, pulling him close and whispering in his ear.

Drake's mouth formed a pinched line, and he hesitated. "Fine. I'll pay it."

As soon as he agreed, a coil of light swirled around their linked arms before disappearing with a flash. Drake rubbed his arm and stepped onto the ferry

"And you? Will you pay?" Raziel asked Kenna.

She began removing her leather rucksack to procure payment. "I've been saving my wages, so—"

The captain held out a hand to stop her. "Oh. You didn't think that *money* would be sufficient payment, did you?" He laughed, a grating, unnatural sound. "Oh no. That is not how things are done across the Veil. Your elvish money may buy you insignificant things in Notos— food, drinks, lodging—but when it comes to things you truly need or desire, a bargain is required."

"Um. Okay. What kind of bargain?" she asked.

"Well, that depends. What is your name?"

"Kenna Duras."

"What is it that you are seeking, Kenna Duras?" the ferrymaster's eyes bored into hers.

"I…" She looked to Drake, unsure of how much she should tell the captain. Drake gave her a nod of encouragement. "I need somewhere to hide."

"And is that all?"

"Yes," She lied to him. She lied to herself.

Raziel scoffed. "I think you should be on your way home. If you have a home, that is."

The wooden pier beneath her feet shimmered, and the water rose. She was sinking. She scrambled back to the shore, panting. The hem of her Emergence gown was soaked.

Ezra, Drake and Raziel disappeared into the mist. The pier was gone.

"Drake! Ezra! Wait! Come back!"

Despite her shouting, the pier didn't appear again.

She'd always been inconsistent. Impulsive. Her recklessness at the ceremony had upended her entire life. At least she'd tried to be brave. But who did she think she was? Perhaps she could catch up with Sera. Hide in that rebel camp in the mountains.

Go. The wind seemed to roar in her ears.

"Go where, exactly? I can't go back to Tormund. To Notos? Into the mountains?" She said aloud to no one.

Trying to go to Notos was insane, but going back to Tormund would mean death. Looking north across Iris meadow, she made her choice. She'd flee into the Lithari Mountains.

But as soon as she took her first step toward the path that would lead her into the mountains, she saw the Shadow swirling in the moonlight.

The dragon-shaped Shadow slowly lumbered back and forth at the fork of the path. It looked angry. Or hungry.

The shadowy beast swished its tail and wings intently, daring her to move.

Keeping her eyes on the Shadow, she squatted and picked up a large rock. She had no idea what she'd do with it if the Shadow attacked. She stood and backed away from it, slowly.

The Shadow creature prowled toward her. Kenna was too afraid to draw breath.

She jumped, darting a glance over her shoulder when she heard the crunching footsteps behind her.

"Kenna? What are you doing? What's with the stick?" Ezra asked.

Her eyes shot back to where the Shadow dragon had been a moment before. It was gone.

She blinked and rubbed her eyes. "Didn't you see...? Shit. I'm actually losing my mind." She shook her head, throwing down her icy weapon and turning to face Ezra. "I thought you'd left."

"Without you?" he asked.

He stood in front of her, the wind tousling his dark waves. His gaze was solemn.

"I spoke to Raziel. He says you can try again, but you have to be honest about why you want to make the crossing.

She looked toward the mountains. Toward a place where she might be able to run away from answers she was both desperate and terrified to find.

"What did you tell him? About why you want to cross?" Kenna asked.

Ezra ran a hand through his hair, seeming to consider his words. "Do you know how it feels? To have to hide who you love?"

Kenna had always felt different—like she had to wear a mask— but she didn't know how it felt to face the threat of death because of who she loved. She shook her head.

"Drake is so confident. It's one of the things I love about him. But every damn day, I worry that someone will discover our relationship. I worry that someone will finally prove the rumors about him are true, that we'll both be executed or enslaved and separated forever. Maybe my parents will be punished, too. I don't know. But loving him...it makes the risk worth it. It makes fighting for a better world worth it. The love I feel for him makes it worth..."

He took a deep breath, like he wanted to say something else. Whatever he was going to say never materialized. Finally, he said, "I would give anything to be able to love him without fear."

His pleading gaze and unspoken question hung between them. Was Kenna willing to look deeper within herself? Could she admit why it was so important to uncover whatever secrets the angels and her parents were keeping?

Kenna threw her hands up in defeat. "I already told the captain the truth. What else am I supposed to say? I can't get across if he won't let me."

"Did you give him the real reason? You have the choice of whether or not to lie to him," Ezra said.

"I didn't lie. I need to cross the Veil to hide."

"If you wanted to hide, why didn't you just drink from the Chalice and forget everything? You could have pretended you didn't remember anything. But you didn't pretend. So, why do you want to cross?"

She whispered. "Why does all of this have anything to do with me? It feels…. The weight of it makes me feel like I can't move."

"You don't have to move alone, Kenna. But do you really want to hide?"

"No!" She took a shuddering breath, exhaling all of the truth she'd kept pent up for so long. "I don't want to fucking hide. My whole life, I've had to hide. I don't even know who I really am, because it's never mattered. I'm a woman, so why does it matter what my purpose is? What I want?" Tears blurred her vision. "I'm so tired of pretending. Of doing whatever it takes to be safe. I want my life to mean something."

A smile bloomed on Ezra's face, and he extended a hand to her. "Well, that makes two of us. Now, come tell Raziel what you told me. The weight of it might feel heavy, but you don't have to carry it alone."

The wind picked up around them, giving rise to purpose. With a surge of determination she'd never felt before, Kenna resolved to find out why the angels were hiding things. She needed to find out why her parents had hidden the rebellion from her.

As she acknowledged her deeper need, the pier shimmered into existence again. She looked toward the ferry and took one last look back at Tormund.

Then, she walked hand in hand with Ezra out over the lake.

CHAPTER 12

*R*aziel stood on the end of the pier with his arms crossed. Drake stood behind him on the ferry, the wooden raft bobbing gently on the water.

"Well?" the ferry master prompted.

"I need answers. I need to find out what's happening outside of the lies I've been fed my entire life. And I need to find out who I really am. I'm willing to pay to learn the truth," she said.

"Now, *that* is an answer worthy of a bargain." Raziel's eyes gleamed.

"What is the price?" She asked, hesitating slightly.

"A wise question. Here is what I require from you in return for safe passage." As he'd done with Drake, he grabbed her forearm and pulled her close. His whispered demands tickled her ears, and the longer he held her close, the more she felt a primal need to pull away from him. To run.

"First, during your time in Notos, you must participate in a new life experience with an angel." A thread of ice extended out of his pointer finger, wrapping around her arm.

"Second, you must discover a previously unknown truth about the Ancients from an angel." A string of fire flowed out of his middle finger.

"Third, you must accept two offers of help from an angel." A line of dust shimmered next to the other two elements.

The thought of interacting with an angel in these ways after a lifetime of oppression under their rule was nearly enough to make her jerk her arm away.

"You will not be permitted to cross the Veil back into the Mesterra until you have completed all of these requirements. Do we have a bargain?" The elemental rope held their clasped forearms together.

"Finally, there is one element of this bargain that will remain hidden until an opportune time. A risk in order to find what you seek." The three strands wound together into a cord of all three elements.

"What type of bargain is this? I've never seen anything like it before," she asked.

"It is an elemental bargain. You will be bound by it until the terms are satisfied. Or until you die." Raziel shrugged like her death was as inconsequential as that of a squashed insect. Then, he asked, "Kenna Duras, do you hereby swear by the Ancients to pay the price for crossing the Veil in pursuit of the answers you seek?"

She couldn't see any other way.

"I swear," she answered.

"I accept your word. By the Ancient Luniva, I grant you safe passage to Notos. You will arrive in the morning." With the briefest prick of searing pain, their bargain was sealed. A silver cuff appeared on her wrist, and she stepped onto the ferry.

Once she was aboard, the ferry began to move further out into the mist, as though set in motion by some invisible pulley system.

"Doesn't he come with us? How do we steer this thing?"

"Some sort of magic," Drake replied. "I asked him that last time, and he got terribly angry and said that he'd made a bargain for safe passage. As though his word was enough."

Calling the glorified slab of wood a "ferry" was a stretch. They stood aboard a large, floating pallet with a mast. She wasn't sure how it was going to get three adult elves anywhere, much less through the Veil. She just hoped it would keep them afloat.

The fact that Drake had made the crossing before made her feel a little better.

On the other hand, she wasn't sure if she could trust the ferry master's word. She had the distinct impression she'd been tricked. She'd definitely felt the magic of the bargain, and she had the bracelet as proof. The silver cuff had no clasp, no way to take it off. It was engraved with three scrolling words and a tally mark coinciding with the bargain:

Life I

Truth I

Help II

"What were your bargains?" She asked Ezra and Drake.

Drake's lips moved as he tried to answer, but no sound came out. Drake shrugged, as if to say he knew they wouldn't be allowed to tell each other the terms of their crossing.

"Drake, don't be ridiculous. Just tell us," Ezra said.

Drake wiggled his eyebrows at his boyfriend. "I'll show you mine if you show me yours."

Ezra rolled his eyes before glancing in Kenna's direction. When he tried to speak, she heard nothing. She tried to read his lips, but they were a blur of indistinguishable motion.

Kenna shook her head, and Ezra let out a deep sigh. She couldn't decide if he looked frustrated or relieved.

She held out her wrist for them to examine the bracelet. Ezra's brows furrowed. "There's nothing there."

Drake smirked.

"Oh, don't look so smug," Ezra said.

"How long does the journey take?" Kenna fiddled with the bracelet.

"Impossible to say. Time doesn't seem to move the same in the Veil." Drake showed them his Fostone, a dark ruby at the end of a chain that he kept in his pocket. On Drake's Fostone, the glowing hour and second hands flickered and jumped randomly. "If I had to guess, I'd say it's a few hours. Last time, I left Tormund in the afternoon, but it was morning when I arrived in Braktyn. But, it was nearly midnight when we left, and Raziel said we'd arrive tomorrow morning, so who knows?" He shrugged. "I think we should try to get some sleep though."

"Can one of you unlace this?" Kenna asked, desperate to get out of her fine gown. The dress was ruined now anyway.

As Kenna changed into a simple, linen dress, Ezra and Drake settled down for the night. They used their rucksacks as pillows and laid down on the ferry's deck. It wasn't long before both of them were fast asleep.

Kenna pulled her cloak tight against the misty chill. After the night's whirlwind of events, she finally felt some sense of safety on the dark, quiet water with her friends.

She sat down and leaned against the mast, fighting the heaviness in her eyelids. Her eyes had barely closed before she sat up suddenly, remembering her father's letter.

Rifling through her pack, she found the carefully folded piece of parchment with her name written in her father's handwriting.

With shaking hands, she unfolded the letter. Her father had promised it would explain everything.

But the parchment was blank.

Why would her father promise her answers and then give her a blank letter? It made no sense. After staring at the parchment for what felt like an hour, she eventually folded it up and shoved it back into her pack. She leaned against the mast again and closed her eyes. Worrying about the ongoing battle in Tormund and swirling questions kept her awake even as the ferry tried to rock her to sleep under the moon't watchful light.

WHEN THEY EMERGED from the Veil, the air was crisp, cool, and sunny. She looked behind them, but there was no sign of Lake Audral or the Lithari Mountains. No sign of the realm she'd left behind. No sign of her friends or family.

"I can tell you exactly what kind of things occur in Braktyn." Drake informed Ezra happily.

"Here we go again," Kenna said, yawning.

"There are some benefits of fleeing our oppressive city. I know the circumstances were less than ideal, but you've been positively robbed of all of life's greatest pleasures. Soon, very soon, you will see."

"Alright, alright. I'm not totally innocent, you know," she said.

"Sure," Drake prompted, "but have you ever had someone kiss you while they're —"

Before he could finish his explicit interrogation, Ezra interrupted him with a slight chuckle. "Give it a rest, Drake."

"Well, I just feel obligated to deliver my knowledge to my friends." Drake's earnest expression could have won an award in the actor's guild.

Ezra huffed in response just as their ferry docked.

"We're here," Kenna said, dumbstruck as the bustling arrival port came into view. She'd actually crossed the Veil.

Drake looked at her with a sense of pride shining in his eyes. "We are, indeed."

CHAPTER 13

When they'd departed Tormund, it had been a tepid summer night on a quiet lake. Here, they were greeted by a chill, autumn morning and the cacophony of a crowd. Drake had warned Kenna that it was perpetually autumn in Braktyn, but it was still odd to have been transported into a different season within the span of a few hours.

As the ferry drew closer to the port, she saw dozens of boats moored there—ferries, sailboats, and ships of various sizes.

Most of all, she noticed the many people with wings among the crowd. Their feathers were as varied in color as the types of boats. Were they winged fae or angels? Whatever they were, people seemed to keep their distance from the winged folks.

She looked at Drake and Ezra. Ezra's shoulders stiffened, and he seemed as jarred as Kenna to see winged individuals moving amongst the crowd as though it was ordinary.

She noticed Ezra step away from Drake, as though he was suddenly afraid of punishment like he had been in Mesterra.

Ezra dropped his voice low and said, "Why didn't you tell us this place was crawling with angels?"

Kenna answered on Drake's behalf. "I don't think he remembers. When he came back from Notos three years ago, he told me he hadn't seen any winged fae or angels."

Drake shook his head, finding his voice. "I knew I'd made a bargain to forget something important, but I could never remember what it was. I guess I know now. But I remember that we don't have to hide our relationship here."

Surrounded by so many angels, Kenna couldn't quite believe Ezra and Drake would be safe.

But then, A woman ran down the gangplank of one of the ships. She launched herself into the arms of another woman, kissing her fiercely in a happy, romantic reunion. None of the winged people looked twice at the women.

Kenna's tension dissipated, and Ezra released a loud sigh. Drake put an arm around Ezra's shoulder and kissed him on the cheek. "See? Nothing to worry about."

Still, there was plenty about Notos they didn't know. Plenty of things to fear.

Drake turned to Kenna. "Ezra and I will see you safely to the Red Lantern, but then we'll need to go directly back to the port."

With a bump, their ferry docked, and they disembarked. The new surroundings teased all of Kenna's senses as she followed Drake along the dock toward the road that would lead them to the city. She squinted her eyes against the bright sun and wrinkled her nose against the pungent, fishy breeze.

Not watching where she walked, she bumped into the solid chest of a burly, tattooed male who smelled like fish guts and brine.

"Watch it," he snarled.

"Sorry," she said. She might have made a huge mistake coming here. Then, Drake took her hand, leading her onward and bolstering her courage and need to find the truth.

Traveling the length of the pier and squeezing their way through the crowd took almost fifteen minutes.

The dockworkers, including Kenna's new friend whom she mentally referred to as "Fish Guts", were clad in drab brown or grey work tunics and breeches. They loaded and unloaded barrels, boxes, and pallets from trade ships. In contrast, a number of people seemed to be travelling for pleasure, dressed in a dazzling array of red, orange, yellow, and gold. The vacationers flitted toward their destination like swirling autumn leaves carried by the wind. Where had they come from?

Kenna looked down at her own simple lilac dress, suddenly feeling even more out of place.

They followed the sign toward Braktyn, and the journey was uneventful. Kenna learned two new curse words—rutting and sarding. She was already busy thinking of an opportunity to use them. She'd also overheard a tale centered around bedroom escapades she'd not realized were possible. She was still trying to puzzle out the mechanics of the positions she was sure could only be accomplished by extremely flexible acrobats when her thoughts were cut short.

"How long is the walk to Braktyn?" Ezra asked Drake.

"I think it took about four hours last time."

"Four sarding hours?" Kenna stopped abruptly, employing her new vocabulary.

"We'll be there before you know it. I'm hoping to find a friendly merchant who'll let us ride in their cart. I may be able to persuade the right driver with my irresistible charms. Trust me." Drake winked.

"Just because I trust you doesn't mean I want to walk for four rutting hours." She deserved top marks for using both of her new words so soon. She looked enviously at two males riding atop horses walking in front of them. But she'd never ridden a horse, and her envy was stifled when the horse plopped a trail of stinking excrement right in her path.

Kenna dodged the steaming blobs, muttering. Trudging on, Kenna examined their surroundings. She looked down, making sure she didn't run afoul of any more horse shit, and noticed that the dirt road was flecked with what looked like specks of gold.

Trees lined the road, dressed in the colors of autumn like the more fashionable arrivals she'd seen at the docks. It wasn't as crowded here, and groups of winged folk and elves mixed together, engaging in pleasant conversations with their travelling companions. It seemed the angels weren't feared here, after all.

After they'd been walking for nearly two hours, there were more trees. Eventually, they entered a stunning, autumn forest.

Kenna said, "If we don't have something to eat soon, I might turn into a dragon. I could eat both of you and still be hungry."

Ezra placed a hand on her arm. "Please don't eat anyone, Kenna. I've got some cheese and bread in my pack."

"Thank the Ancients. You'll both be spared from my inner dragon's wrath. For now." She smiled, but her smile faded as she remembered the Shadow dragon and wondered who or what it was and where it had come from.

They found a mossy stone on a bed of crunchy leaves, a makeshift bench where they could sit to rest their feet and munch on some bread and cheese.

When they returned to the road, Kenna spotted a merchant with a head full of curly auburn hair and a jolly smile approaching with a cart full of barrels.

Drake jumped up and offered Kenna a hand.

"Okay, Kenna. One of us is about to have to woo this merchant, unless you'd prefer to walk the last two hours. Put on your most charming smile, and follow my lead. Best assets forward." Drake gave her breasts an approving nod.

She tried to channel her inner Sera, and sauntered seductively nearer to the road. At least, that was the effect she was aiming for.

"Hello there, good fellow!" Drake donned his most charming smile and called to the merchant, beckoning him to stop.

"My companions and I were wondering whether we might trouble you for a lift the rest of the way to Braktyn? We're headed for the Red Lantern. Do you know it?"

"Oh, I've spent many a night in the Lantern. In fact, I happen te know the landlord. I'll give ye a lift," the driver answered in a lilting accent Kenna hadn't heard before. His jade eyes crinkled at the corners as he smiled. He looked like the sort of person you could trust immediately—honest and kind.

She slouched back into her normal posture, and Ezra shifted next to her, probably relieved that Drake didn't have to flirt with the merchant.

"Thank you," Kenna said to the man on the cart.

"Nae bother, lass. Happy te help. Might even say I'm yer guardian angel." He winked.

The idea of a kind angel who'd go out of his way to take care of her felt utterly foreign. Without thinking, Kenna blurted, "You're an angel? Where are your wings?"

"Don't need em at the minute, do I? They're glamoured."

"They're what?" she asked.

The merchant smiled, and two enormous wings the color of pine needles trickled into view.

Her mouth formed a silent "Oh."

"Most of the folk struttin' about with their wings out are winged fae. And good on em,'" he explained as his wings vanished again. In Mesterra, schools taught children that winged fae were evil abominations, mixed offspring of elves and angels. But none of the winged people she'd seen seemed evil.

"Hop on in. All of ye. Make yerselves comfortable." After the three of them clambered aboard, he tutted to the horses, and then they were moving again as the merchant whistled a jolly tune.

CHAPTER 14

*A*s they drew closer to the city's center, the road became busier. The merchant, who seemed to have a perpetual twinkle in his green eyes, turned to smile at them.

"I think ye'll be better walkin' the last few minutes. Ye'll get there quicker. I need to go te the stables, but the Red Lantern's just across the city square. If ye find the Sacred Tree, ye can't miss it."

"Thank you again for your most generous help, good sir," Drake said with a bow to the merchant.

"No need te thank me," he said, looking like a child bursting with a secret.

"Thanks again," Kenna said.

He tipped his chin to her. As the three friends walked away from the merchant, she could hear him chuckling behind them and wondered what he found so funny.

The gold-flecked road beneath their feet carried them past white limestone shops, taverns, and inns. Kenna read the names on all the signs: Sun Inn, Smoking Leaf, Crimson Chalice, Flaming Arrow.

"Oh look! Isn't that the Flaming Arr...ohhh." Her mouth dropped open as her brain registered the illustration on the sign: a handsome, winged male with a flaming "arrow" protruding from his hips.

Ezra's eyes were wide, and Drake howled with laughter.

"The Flaming Arrow is the local hub for the most sought-after male courtesans in the city," Drake informed them.

"That sign is a bit much. Don't you think?" Ezra asked.

"Oh, I think it's just the right amount. What's the matter, Ez? Feeling jealous?" Drake winked. He'd told Kenna how he spent most of his time in Braktyn three years ago joined at the lips with a male courtesan whose name he'd never learned.

Kenna giggled, still looking at the brothel and wondering if she'd get a chance to have a look inside. "Don't wind him up, Drake."

"We should keep moving. I'm afraid the nature of experiences within The Flaming Arrow will be rather unhelpful in uncovering any truth that may help Kenna or the rebels back in Tor—"

Drake was suddenly rendered speechless as a gorgeous man stepped out the front door of the Flaming Arrow. The man turned inside, smiling and speaking to someone she couldn't see. He had a chiseled jaw and a dazzling grin. He was carrying a crate, his loose white sleeves rolled up to the elbows to reveal dark-skinned forearms.

When the male turned toward the road where the friends were standing, his smile disappeared and the stranger dropped the box he was carrying, its contents clanking together.

"Drake," he said, his voice quiet. "You're back."

This must be the courtesan he'd spent so much time with.

But Drake seemed confused and gave Ezra an apologetic look. Drake walked over to the man and picked up the box. "I'm terribly sorry. I can't seem to remember your name. It was so long ago."

"Nik. And it was three years and eighty-seven days." His words were strained with emotion.

"If you say so. I haven't counted." Drake seemed flustered.

"Well, I have." Nik clenched his jaw, and his beautiful eyes pinned Drake with a smoldering stare. "How long are you planning to stay in Braktyn?"

"We are just escorting our friend to the Red Lantern. We plan to return to Mesterra sometime before midnight tonight."

Kenna could practically feel the pulsing waves of jealous heat rippling off of Ezra. She looked at anything other than her friends or the courtesan, wishing she could extract herself from this awkward encounter. Finally, Drake seemed to remember he wasn't alone. He turned and beckoned Ezra and Kenna forward.

"This is my partner, Ezra, and my best friend, Kenna."

"Nice to meet you." She gave the courtesan a polite smile.

Ezra said nothing, but offered a short nod of acknowledgement.

"Your partner. I see." Nik cleared his throat. "Well, it was nice to see you again, Drake."

Nik leaned down to pick up the crate he'd dropped. It was full of gleaming candlesticks. He turned and started to walk away, but stopped for a moment to look back at Drake.

"Are you happy?"

Drake looked at Ezra, affection softening his features. Addressing Ezra rather than the courtesan, he said, "Yes. I'm happy."

Ezra's stiff shoulders seemed to relax as the man he loved reached out and took his hand. Kenna looked at Nik, but Drake was still looking at Ezra.

Drake didn't see the courtesan's face crumple before he turned and disappeared down the alley.

"What was *that* about?" Kenna asked.

"Yes, please enlighten us." Ezra pulled his hand away and folded his arms across his chest.

Drake shook his head and rubbed the back of his neck. "It seems even courtesans can't resist my charms. My time with him meant nothing, Ez. It was purely physical. Trust me. I love you."

"Bleck. Can you two do this later, please?" Kenna asked. "I can't handle all these emotions."

"We can definitely do this later," Drake said, giving Ezra a pat on his behind. Ezra rolled his eyes, but smiled as they continued on.

If Tormund was a drab collection of ordinary elves, Braktyn was a brilliant mixture of extraordinary folks. The sheer number of feathers proudly displayed, protruding out of specially designed slits in clothing, was shocking.

A cart was crossing the road ahead, and they were stuck in the crowd behind a winged man cloaked with shining, blue feathers so dark they were almost black. Kenna didn't know if he was an angel or winged fae, but she was mesmerised by the way the glossy feathers reflected the sunlight. She didn't even mind that she couldn't see anything past his towering plumes.

She reached out a tentative finger.

She just needed to feel—

"You would dare touch my wings?" The man spun, growling at her, his teeth inches from her face.

Her finger had barely brushed a single feather. Yet he acted as though she'd committed some great crime with his large hand clenched around her wrist.

His features were staggering in their cruelty. He towered over her, immense power thrumming in the air around him. The wind swirled around them in a cyclone filled with debris. She couldn't see anyone beyond the swirling grey cloud that encased them.

She cowered before him. "I didn't—"

The male leaned in close to whisper in her face, his reeking breath seeming to carry a chorus of thousands of voices speaking along with him in the swirling wind. "You stupid fools are all the same. You come to our realm with your heads filled with nonsense. Do yourself a favor, and learn the truth before you make a fool of yourself with an angel who is less forgiving than me."

Kenna shuddered at the thought that there were more wrathful people in the city than the one who stood before her.

The wind died down, revealing a wide circle of people watching them in awestruck silence.

"There is one grain of truth in your worthless education. The winged fae are useless muts," the angel said. Kenna noticed a few sets of wings on different colored faces among the crowd bristling at the slur. "No self-respecting angel would ever debase themselves by rutting an elvish piece of rubbish." The angel spat at her feet. "*Never* touch an angel's wings unless you have a death wish."

Then, he turned and stalked away. Those shining, feathery appendages that she couldn't resist touching belonged to one of the oldest and most powerful beings in the Three Realms. Before he could shove his way through the crowd, his wings shimmered out of existence like the angel merchant's had.

"Are you alright?" Drake asked, checking her over as the crowd dispersed.

"I'm fine. He didn't hurt me."

He may not have hurt her, but that was the closest she'd ever been to an angel. She could still feel the power pulsing against her. She felt the lingering echo of the ancient rage cascading over her.

Kenna raised a shaky hand to tuck her hair behind her ear, taking deep breaths to slow her racing heart and ease the pit in her stomach.

The way angels could hide their wings reminded her of the ceremonial robes vanishing at the Emergence Ceremony. She'd never witnessed any other magic that could make things disappear like that. The sight only fed into her suspicion that the mind-altering mist from the trial and the Emergence Serum were made with angel magic.

The Council and the Elders may have lied about many things, but they'd been honest about one thing. Notos was home to some angels who would prefer for the elves to stay in their own realm.

∼

ASH LEANED CASUALLY against the white exterior of the tavern in civilian clothes with his hood pulled low to avoid recognition. He was not as well-known in Braktyn as he was in Saphyr, but the last thing he needed was to draw attention to himself. He'd been watching people arrive into the citiy from the docks for the last hour, waiting for the perfect target.

She needed to be naïve, but confident enough to take risks. Every year there was at least one. A female stupid enough to touch an angel's wings. All he needed to do was wait.

And there she was.

Varis snarled in her face, and Ash lost sight of them in the cyclone. Ash tugged at his shirt sleeve, waiting patiently for the storm to pass.

When the air stilled, Varis spoke loud enough for everyone in the crowd to hear.

"There is one grain of truth in your worthless education. The winged fae are an abomination. No self-respecting angel would ever debase themselves by rutting an elvish piece of rubbish."

Ash's hands shook with rage. The fact that he still needed Varis was the only reason he didn't make a spectacle and show the angel exactly who was a piece of rubbish in this scenario.

"*Never* touch an angel's wings unless you have a death wish."

As the hulking brute pushed through the crowd and glamoured his wings, the female's wide brown eyes blinked rapidly. Her two companions rushed to her side, speaking to her in hushed tones. Shortly after, the crowd continued flowing toward the town center.

Ash pushed off the side of the building, sauntering along with the rest of the crowd and keeping a respectable distance from the friends.

"We'll get you settled at the Red Lantern, but then Ezra and I need to get back to the ferry before midnight," said one of them.

That was all Ash needed to know

CHAPTER 15

Kenna had finally stopped shaking from her encounter with the angel when she was stunned by the sight in the center of the city.

She gaped as she studied an enormous oak tree standing proudly in the main square. The sun trickled through light saffron, vibrant orange, and deep burgundy leaves that fluttered in a gentle breeze. Shards of Autumn light danced like fireflies between the shifting landscape of color, but some otherworldly magic seemed to stop the leaves from tumbling to the earth below. The veins in the enormous trunk shimmered like burnished bronze.

On the northern side of the square, to the left of the tree, stood a monumental temple. Wrought in pale stone with arched crimson doors and spires pointing like swords at the sun above, the ivory temple looked as though it could accommodate thousands of worshippers at any one time.

Directly opposite the temple, on the southern side of the square, lay the Red Lantern. When they entered, Kenna found the inn to be a rather cheerful looking place. The bottom floor of the inn was a tavern covered in dark wood panelling and filled with patrons enjoying lunch. A welcoming fire danced in the hearth.

Kenna inhaled the yeasty smell of ale and eyed the shelves behind the bar, which were lined with glass bottles of all shapes and colors. As she leaned on the counter, the bare skin of her forearm stuck to a residual spill.

Gross. When was the last time anyone cleaned this? She promptly peeled her arm off the mahogany surface. There wasn't even anyone to meet them.

"Hello?" Drake shouted. No one appeared right away. He called out again. "Excuse me?"

Moments later, a wooden door behind the bar swung open.

"Fancy meetin' ye here." It was the red-headed angel with kind eyes who'd given them a lift from the docks.

Drake smiled. "I'm afraid we need your assistance again. Do you have a room available for the lady?"

"Sure thing. Let me just ask the landlord…" The male behind the bar did not make a move to ask anyone. For a moment, Kenna thought he was going to refuse her lodging.

"He says there's room." The man, who it seemed was the landlord, chuckled at his own joke. The endearing exchange reminded Kenna of her father's sense of humor. "How long will ye be staying?" he asked.

"I…I'm not sure how long," Kenna said. "Will that be a problem?"

"Nae bother, lass. I'm sure we can work something out." He offered a warm smile and turned to fetch two keys hanging from hooks on the wall behind him. He was probably just shy of six feet tall, and Kenna marvelled at his burly form. She imagined only the strongest of opponents could beat him in a physical altercation.

He handed her the keys to her room. "Ye're in room two, lass. First door on yer right, second floor. Sorry I can't show ye to yer room, but I'm on me own and absolutely rushed off me feet. If ye want a pint or a bite to eat after ye settle in, ye know where to find me."

Looking around the inn, Kenna saw no other servers helping the barman. Unlike some taverns, the Red Lantern seemed family friendly. Parents with winged children occupied many of the tables. Whoever had taken care of breakfast for the inn's patrons must have finished their shift as soon as the landlord returned from the docks. In light of his kindness, she couldn't judge him too harshly for the sticky counter. She only hoped her bed wouldn't have lice

For lunch, Kenna and her friends ate their fill of succulent roast chicken, potatoes, and vegetables.

The cool autumn evening air drifted in every time the door opened, leaving the air in the room chilly. The fire near their table had been roaring with warmth when they'd arrived, but it was only a small pile of embers now. Remembering how busy the barman had seemed, Kenna stacked a few logs on the fire and used her Flame magic to stoke it back to life.

"Okay." She sat back down. "Now what?"

She and Ezra looked expectantly at Drake. Now that she was in Notos, she had no idea what to do next.

Drake shrugged sheepishly.

"Don't you remember *anything* important from your last visit?" Ezra asked.

"I did hear that the king is a sight to behold. Rather large…wings." Drake wiggled his eyebrows.

Kenna laughed. "Honestly, Drake. Do you ever think with anything other than your—"

He chuckled. "Alright, alright. My trip last time was not a particularly educational one. At least, not in the way that will help. However, I can highly recommend the Golden Flagon. They have the most stunning mixture of notelixirs."

At the mention of the infamous elixirs, Kenna remembered her parents' warnings against them and why they were banned from Mesterra. Despite her reasons for being here, something about Braktyn beckoned her to new experiences.

Kenna said, "Honestly, now that we're here, that sounds amazing…I need a distraction."

"Pleasurable distraction is my forte. Isn't it, Ez?" Drake put a hand on his boyfriend's leg, and Ezra's cheeks flushed. Kenna grinned at them.

Ezra suggested, "Given everything that's happening, Kenna should learn to do some defensive magic. Surely that would be a better use of her time than drinking."

"Would have been nice of you to suggest that while you were training with the rebel forces behind my back," Kenna spat. Ezra and Drake both flinched.

Ezra answered, "We would have, but your father—"

"I know. He told you I was a delicate flower who shouldn't take part in such things," Kenna said, her voice laced with bitterness. "I'll find a way to learn. I just don't know where to start."

Ezra looked at his Fostone. "We need to be back to the docks at midnight which gives us three hours before we leave. Maybe Drake and I could teach you a few basic things."

"Fine, but will you walk me to the Golden Flagon on your way back to the docks?"

"Of course. I'll even tell you what to order," Drake offered.

As she climbed the stairs to her room, thoughts swirled in a dizzying mixture of everything she needed to learn, everyone she'd left in Mesterra, and the knowledge that Drake and Ezra were leaving after lunch and she'd be alone. Her mind was a jumble of all of it. Getting drunk just long enough to quiet all of the noise in her head sounded like bliss.

Of course, Ezra was right that she should start to learn defensive magic, but she was stuck in Notos. There wasn't anything she could do to help everyone back in Mesterra tonight. Exhaustion and emotion threatened to swallow her whole. Would it be so bad to find an escape from her feelings tonight?

She wadded up her undergarments and stuffed them into the small chest of drawers. One by one, she hung her dresses on the small closet rail. They'd all end up slung over the back of a chair eventually, but it was nice to be organized for the time being. As she pulled the last dress out, the blank piece of parchment from her father fluttered to the floor, falling open.

But it wasn't blank anymore.

She stopped unpacking and sat down on the floor to read her father's words.

KENNA,

First, I must beg your forgiveness. If you're reading this letter, you're gone. I purchased magic ink which would only appear if you made it safely to Notos.

Your mother and I have long suspected the Emergence serum wouldn't work on you.

I know it will be hard to understand why we kept this from you, but it was our sacred duty to protect you. We received instructions written in the hand of Soldivus himself. Despite our duty, we have loved you with our whole hearts from the moment we found you in Iris meadow.

For the first six months of your life, we hid you. Your mother feigned her pregnancy, and then an early birth. We kept you hidden for a while longer under the pretense of illness. Jona was young enough that he didn't understand or remember any of it.

Found. They'd found her.

Why had her birth parents abandoned her? And why didn't her parents openly adopt her or tell her the truth sooner?

Kenna wanted to stop reading. Her face was hot and she could hear her heart beating in her ears.

While you were hidden as a babe, I traveled to Notos in search of some way to keep your true identity secret. I met a kind merchant who sold us a glamor potion at a fair price. With a single drop of my blood, my intention to keep you hidden and safe activated the magic in the potion. For as long as I live, no creature in the Three Realms will be able to guess who you truly are.

You are the human princess, thought to be killed with the rest of the human race three centuries ago in the Void War.

Time seemed to stop. That was impossible. The humans were all dead. If she was a human, she'd have to be over three hundred years old. Three hundred and twenty-nine.

At the end of the War, Soldivus forged a treaty with Luniva, which saved the human race by placing them into a sleep state. Each year that passes is a second of sleep to the humans.

We do not know the full terms of the treaty, but we know Soldivus gave you angel magic. Because of this, you were to awake during the three hundred and fifth year after the Void War. You are humanity's only hope.

Kenna was sure the air was sucked from the room. Still, she couldn't look away from the life altering words on the page.

I'm afraid this was everything in the letter we found with you in the meadow. The only other instructions we were given were to destroy the letter after memorizing its contents. You must do the same with this letter, Kenna. For your safety, you must not reveal this information to anyone. Even those who are closest to you.

I'm sorry we kept the truth about the resistance from you. But we are optimistic about the outcome of our first stand against the angels. You'll know by now about the explosion during the Emergence Ceremony. Rebel forces in all the towns and cities in Rolios launched coordinated attacks. If we are successful, the elves will control everything in the southwest.

We have been fortifying our numbers near the borders to keep angels out. The rebels are continually growing in strength and numbers throughout Mesterra.

And Kenna was stuck here while her friends and family risked their lives.

Though you may not believe it, I'm sorry for keeping all of this from you. I hated lying to you, but if you'd been involved in the resistance and the Elders caught you, if they discovered who you really were, it would have been more dangerous than you know.

I love you, Kenna. You are a piece of our family that we didn't know was missing until we found you. From the first moment you wrapped your tiny little fingers around mine, my heart has belonged to you.

I'm so proud of the woman you've become. I hope that one day you can forgive me for keeping all of this from you.

WITH ALL THE love in my heart,
Father

Kenna's eyes burned. She read the letter over and over and over, absorbing it all. Remembering the attack and then fleeing Mesterra had been hard enough.

So had finding out her family and friends had been hiding the rebellion from her, but she'd never expected this.

Found in a meadow. Human princess. Angel magic. Hope of humanity.

She hurried down the stairs as fast as her legs would carry her, the letter balled in her fist. She went straight to the fire and threw it in, watching it burn for a few seconds until it was nothing but ashes.

"Are ye alright, lass?" the landlord asked.

"Fine. Just going for a walk."

Kenna needed to breathe. To fill her too-small, too-tight lungs. Her heart skittered like it would stop. She would die, and then the entire human race would…

What would happen? How was she supposed to restore the human race? If she failed, would the humans be trapped in their perpetual sleep? How could any one person carry such a burden alone?

Leaving the inn, she collapsed onto a bench under the sacred tree in the city square, sheltered beneath the ancient branches. Unsure what to do next, Kenna put her elbows on her knees, leaned her head into her hands, and cried. She reminded herself to take deep breaths while she sorted through the barrage of thoughts and emotions.

Her whole life she'd never felt like she could truly be herself. Like there was some part of her she needed to hide, though she'd never been sure what. But she'd always believed she had a greater purpose than becoming a subservient wife and mother.

Now, she understood the part of herself which had been aching to become known. But how was she supposed to truly be herself when she needed to keep her human identity a secret? And how was she supposed to embrace the purpose of saving the human race when she had no idea where to start?

She didn't want to go back to her ignorance, but she felt paralyzed in the face of the overwhelming reality.

Plus, the sting of being lied to by her parents hurt like Hel.

Before her Emergence, she'd told her mother how alone she felt. It would have been the perfect time for her mother to share the truth, but she'd still lied to Kenna.

Perhaps her mother knew Kenna would never be able to keep the secret from Zo, Sera, and Aryn—her closest friends. The friends Kenna had left behind and might never see again. What would happen to her family and friends? Surely, it was folly for the rebels to fight the Elders. How could they hope to defeat them?

Pressing her fists against her eyes, she willed the tears to stop. She was in a very public city square, after all.

How was she supposed to keep this from Drake and Ezra?

"Can I sit?" Drake asked warily a moment later.

She gestured to the bench next to her without even looking in the direction of his voice. She couldn't look at her beloved friend without telling him everything. But if her secret was discovered, then it could doom humanity forever. She couldn't be responsible for that.

Drake and Ezra needed to leave before she told them everything. They'd omitted the truth about the impending rebel attack in Tormund. Perhaps she could make them believe she was too angry about discovering the rebellion to accept their help. And so, with a lifetime's worth of practice, Kenna slipped on a mask.

Emotions she rarely allowed to surface boiled over, and unfortunately for Drake, he was the undeserving target. Kenna allowed the culmination of every ounce of suppressed pain, confusion, and indignation to put force behind her words.

"Why didn't you tell me about the rebellion?"

"We already told you. Your father said—"

She lowered her voice. "When have you ever heeded authority. If I'd known what was happening, we could have stayed and fought with them. Now I'm stuck here while my friends and family risk their lives."

"I…Kenna, I'm sorry. I thought it was the right thing to do."

She extended her right arm, palm facing the earth. Beneath the bench, the dust swirled around her feet and the stones trembled at her silent, emotional command. She turned her palm toward the sky, simultaneously raising her arm and beckoning the heavier stones to rise in a violent rain, falling in reverse. The rocks shuddered in their vibrating, static position near her shoulder.

The stones remained suspended, waiting, as she continued her verbal attack: "And what gave my father the right to decide what was best for me? What gave you the right to keep his lies from me? Because you're *men* and I'm just a lowly female who can't possibly make decisions for myself? You're no better than the Elders and the High Council."

If her outburst got any more dramatic, she would probably draw a crowd. Kenna took a breath, calming herself and suddenly wondering how she'd performed the feat of Terrane magic. The dust settled and the stones innocently pitter-pattered to the ground around them.

She stared at the temple beyond. She couldn't look at Drake across the chasm of her secret stretching between them. She'd fled Tormund hoping to find the truth, but she hadn't expected to be the one who'd have to lie to the people she loved.

The realization of how truly alone she was rolled over her. She was fatigued from her magical outburst and profusely aware of her soul's deep weariness. She was battered from drifting through her entire life, tossed around mercilessly by the waves of other people's lies and agendas. If she was ever going to fulfill her purpose and make her own waves, she had to take control of her choices.

A solitary red leaf floated down from the tree, landing on the bench beside her. There wasn't a single leaf on the ground under the sacred tree, so she accepted the gentle offering, picking it up by the stem and twirling it idly in her fingers.

The leaf would serve as a reminder of the reason she was here. She knew at least part of the truth. Now, she needed to discover how she could possibly help an entire race of people. *Her* people. Perhaps she'd meet her birth parents, if they were still alive.

She stood, finally facing her friend.

The expression on his face nearly broke her. "Kenna, I don't know what to say. Did something happen? You seemed fine when you went upstairs."

"I read a letter from my father. And it just reminded me of all the men who've ever expected my obedience. I am done. I am serious, Drake. No man—friend, family, or lover—will *ever* control me or make decisions for me again. If that means I have to be alone, then so be it." Her heart cracked, but her tone was full of ice. "I think you and Ezra should leave now. I wouldn't want you to miss your chance to die along with everyone else I love. You have to leave later today anyway. You might as well get a head start."

"Kenna, you can't be serious." He seemed stunned by her coldness, but from the hurt in his eyes, she knew he believed her.

"You can walk me to the Golden Flagon if that makes you feel any better, but I need to do something first."

"I…Fine. Okay. I'll go get Ezra. The landlord let him go to one of the guest rooms to rest a while," Drake said.

Kenna had meant everything she'd said. She wouldn't let herself be swayed by another man's will anytime soon.

But, damn…

She was going to miss Drake. She turned away and left him there, determined to look ahead, even as silent tears cascaded down her cheeks. And the pain…she shoved it down, down, down. She could deal with the pain another day.

In the aftermath of everything she'd learned, at least she had some sense of clarity. Kenna knew what she needed to do next, so she dashed away her tears and marched into the Red Lantern and straight up to the landlord.

"I need somewhere to live, I need answers, and I need a job." She gestured to the glasses lined up on the bar waiting to be dried and polished. "Clearly, you need help. Can we make a bargain? I'll work for free if you let me live here and provide my meals. And the occasional free drink."

"Ye don't ask for much, do ye?" His eyes twinkled.

"Do we have a deal or not?" She offered her hand, inviting him to make a magically binding agreement like the one she'd made with the ferry master.

He took one look at her puffy eyes and nodded. "Deal. I offer ye a home, meals, and an occasional free drink in exchange for yer employment." The shimmering elemental magic strands extended from the landlord's fingers, forming a rope that wrapped around their forearms. With a sharp sting, their deal was sealed.

Kenna released his arm and stepped away from the bar. Next to the silver cuff on her wrist, she now had a delicate gold bracelet with a small charm that looked like a flame. In the middle of the flame, there was a single word.

Home.

"Great. I'll start tomorrow."

He just raised his eyebrows. "Breakfast preparations start at dawn. Don't be late."

She'd already had quite enough of the bitter taste of her feelings, and she believed the Golden Flagon had just the solution to wash them away.

CHAPTER 16

Kenna, Drake, and Ezra walked to the Golden Flagon in silence. Every moment she spent with Drake and Ezra, her burden felt heavier. With each step she grew closer and closer to telling them the truth. To apologizing for the way she'd treated Drake.

When they reached the tavern, Ezra said, "We're staying for one drink. You might be angry with us, but I refuse to leave things like this."

"Fine," Kenna said, forcing false bitterness into the word.

"I'll get us drinks. What do you want?" Drake asked.

"I'll drink anything that isn't poisonous, won't steal my memories, and will get me drunk enough to forget that everyone I love has been lying to me," Kenna said. Notelixirs were forbidden in Tormund, so she had no idea what to order.

"Ancients, Kenna. Will you give it a rest? We were trying to protect you, and you are acting like a damned *child*." Ezra said. He turned to Drake. "We'll have whatever you're having."

While Drake was at the bar, Ezra whirled on her. "You can treat me however you want, Kenna. But whatever you said to Drake earlier crushed him. You need to make things right before we leave." Ezra was right, of course. But Kenna couldn't tell him that. He continued, "If your father's predictions are correct, the battle could last for days. We'll join the fight when we return. We might… we don't know what might happen."

The heavy silence settled over them again.

She used her magic to swirl the water in her glass and fiddled with her silver cuff. Drake returned with their drinks and placed the glasses on the table in front of them before sitting.

The cylindrical glasses were filled to the rim with crushed ice and shimmering blue liquid. Trails of curling steam flowed down the sides and settled around the bottoms of the glasses like dense morning fog over a field. When Kenna picked up the tumbler to sniff the liquid, the glass was frigid in her hand.

Across from her, Drake took a long drag through the glass straw and hummed his appreciation.

Ezra eyed the beverage warily. "This is glowing. Are you sure it's safe to drink?"

"No." Drake had a twinkle in his eye. "But isn't that part of the fun?"

"Well…I'm not drinking it." Ezra pushed the drink away.

The last time Kenna had been confronted with shimmering liquid, it threatened to steal her memories and lock her into a brainwashed existence. But Drake wasn't convulsing or foaming at the mouth, so that was a good sign. Especially considering how little Drake remembered of his previous trip to Notos. But there was always a chance…

"Do you remember why we're here?" she asked, testing Drake's memory before she was willing to drink.

Drake's smile faded and his jaw tightened. "Because the Elders are angels and we're part of a revolution. We brought you here to keep you safe."

Satisfied that the liquid wouldn't erase her memories, Kenna raised her glass and took a sip. The liquid burned pleasantly on the way down and pooled like molten caramel in her core.

The heady sensation made her moan, and for a moment she forgot the mask she was supposed to be wearing. "If this is poison, I know how I want to die."

Drake gave her a conspiratorial smile.

After about half an hour, Drake had finished his drink. Kenna had helped herself to Ezra's untouched cocktail, and still had about a quarter of a glass left. Her friends stood and collected their rucksacks. The notelixir must have loosened her ability to pretend, because her tears fell freely as she hugged them both.

"I love you. I'm sorry. About earlier," she said.

"Do you want us to stay a little longer?" Drake asked, his brows furrowed in confusion.

"No. You should still go, but please, *please* be careful," she said.

Drake and Ezra looked at her curiously, probably wondering about her inexplicable mood swings.

"We will. You be careful too, and take it easy with that stuff. Maybe head back to the Red Lantern when you finish that one," said Ezra.

She nodded and pursed her lips, trying to keep the truth from spilling out. Her friends hugged her one more time, and she sank onto the cushion as she watched them walk out of the door. She prayed to the dead Ancients that she'd see them both again one day.

CHAPTER 17

The notelixir had done a marvelous job quieting Kenna's thoughts, but her hormones were raging. Drake and Ezra were gone, and Kenna had no desire to lie in her room alone with her worries. Instead, she stayed at the Golden Flagon with plans to drink herself into oblivion.

Her plan was going well so far.

She used her Aqua magic to fill a glass with water from the jug. The water sloshed over the side of the glass as she giggled to herself.

Even my magic is drunk.

Determined not to pass out and wake up on the floor of the Golden Flagon, she gulped down the glass of water. Then, she slammed down the glass in triumph.

Just as she was wiping her mouth with the back of her hand, a striking sable-haired stranger folded himself gracefully onto the floor across from her. His sapphire eyes sparkled as though he was wildly amused by her obvious intoxication.

Her mouth gaped as she ogled the broad-shouldered man in front of her. His dark hair was perfectly disheveled, as though it had been teased by the hands of the wind…or like he'd just rolled out of a bed where he'd been doing everything but sleeping. His strong jawline was peppered with just the right amount of stubble, and she could imagine the feel of it on her skin. His black shirt clung to his shoulders, the open buttons at the top revealing a tantalising hint of a tattoo on the lean muscles of his chest. More than anything, she wanted to take off his shirt and see what was underneath. She shook her head and snapped her mouth shut. Then, she cleared her throat.

"Can I help you?" Kenna asked.

The stranger smirked at her and used his magic to refill her glass. The water spiraled gracefully out of the jug and into the tumbler before her, the artful display of his power a far cry from the drunken mess of hers. He slid the glass across the table on the puddle her magic had left behind. Then, her drink floated right off the edge of the table toward her, carried by a current of air—he was an angel. He had to be. Elves couldn't control air currents.

"Drink." He folded his fair-skinned forearms on the table. She plucked the glass out of the air before taking a sip.

"Thank you," she said, trying not to tremble. His presence wasn't angry like the angel whose wings she'd touched earlier that day, but neither did he seem jovial and friendly like the owner of the Red Lantern.

There was something dangerous about the raven-haired man in front of her.

Suddenly, despite the chill of the autumn air drifting in, the room was too hot. Was her head spinning with intoxication or something much more sinister?

She'd been blissfully drunk and thoughtless moments before, but now her thoughts swirled with suspicions of mind control and false histories. The secret of her humanity. Desperate to get away from the cloying smoke, Kenna stood on wobbly legs and stumbled.

Before she could register his movement, the fascinating stranger was at her side with a steadying hand around her waist. Her body hummed in response to the feeling of his strong arm around her. She could drown in that feeling. She met his depthless eyes, feeling like she might drown in his gaze.

An angel. The enemy. She pushed away from him, and he released her.

"I..." She started. "I think I should get back to my room."

"Can I escort you—"

"No!" She practically shouted before he finished his offer to escort her anywhere. His mouth lifted in one corner, and she hated that crooked smile. "It's not far. I'll be fine."

"I feel as though I should insist. Not everyone in this city is as helpful as I am," he said.

"Helpful? Does bossing drunk females around help you feel more masculine?" She sniped, before she hiccupped loudly and clamped a hand over her mouth.

"I assure you, my masculinity is not in question."

Her smart mouth seemed to have a death wish. "Does that line really work for you?"

He winked. "What do you think?"

"I think it's not working tonight," she said. "I'd like to leave now."

He ran a hand through his hair and shrugged one shoulder.

"I would not dream of denying you anything you desire," he said, though he was still standing between her and her path to the exit. Underneath his words, she sensed a promise.

"Thank you for the water," she managed before skirting around him and out into the night.

Outside, she turned immediately down the narrow alley beside the Golden Flagon. She leaned back against the cool, stone wall and took deep gulps of the chilly air.

The encounter with the stranger had a sobering effect, and after a few moments in the fresh air, she could think clearly again. She turned to walk back to the Red Lantern, but a hulking, hooded silhouette appeared in the alley's mouth.

From where Kenna stood, she couldn't see his face beneath his cloak. But the figure stalking her was huge—obviously male—and his visible wings were ominous. Winged fae or an angel. Terrified, she hoped for the former.

Her heart hammered a warning beat against her ribcage. *Run. Run. Run.* But the alley was a dead end and he was blocking her only escape. Had she fled from the angels in Mesterra to something much worse?

The winged behemoth prowled toward her. "So, we meet again. How delightful."

She recognized the low growl of his voice. It was the angel who she'd riled earlier when she touched his wings. Bile rose in her throat and threatened to choke her. Maybe if she vomited on his boots, he would leave her alone. What was he going to do to her? Her chest constricted.

"My friends are waiting for me," she informed him shakily.

His answering smile was sinister. "Oh, I don't think they are. But perhaps you and I can become friends. You can make amends for your insolence earlier. Personally, I don't like those skinny little things. I like my females juicy."

Puddles swirled up from the ground into coils, stretching her arms wide and binding them to the wall with frigid ropes. She thrashed against the bonds, unable to move her hands to summon any of her elemental power. Not that she'd know how to fight him.

Tears streaked down her face. Why hadn't she let the stranger from inside walk her home? Surely whatever intentions he had for her couldn't have been worse than this.

Like a lightning strake, the male was suddenly in front of her with his hands braced against the stone wall on either side of her head. His long blonde hair brushed her cheek as he leaned forward and spoke: "Poor, helpless, elf. How you must wish that Mesterra's Elders had bothered to teach you how to defend yourself against us."

"Please, let me go." She was ashamed of how feeble she sounded. Sera would fight, but Kenna had no defenses.

"Only way I'm letting you go is if you kill me, little elf." He grabbed a fistful of her hair and yanked her head to one side. She shuddered as his foul breath smothered her senses, and his hot breath made her knees quake.

She felt a trickle of blood where he pressed an icy blade to her throat. "You only need to cut off my wings." He released the pressure of his blade but swiped it across her throat just hard enough for a shallow cut. "Or my head."

He sliced vertically through the laces of her dress from chest to navel and pressed the tip of his blade into the dip between the exposed swell of her breasts. "Or you could stab me through the heart. Though your feeble magic would never allow you to get close enough. Your ability pales in comparison to mine. You and your kind are nothing."

"Then again..." He inhaled deeply along the column of her throat. "You smell interesting. I can smell exactly what you've been thinking. You've had some *very* naughty thoughts tonight, haven't you, little elf?" She realized with horror that the angel could smell the evidence of her body's desire for the stranger she'd just met inside.

"Please," she said, hating the whimpering sound of her voice.

"Oh, I will. But first, I think I need to show you what power really feels like." The angel spun her around, slamming her cheekbone against the freezing masonry. Stars swirled in her vision on impact. It would likely leave a black eye, though a bruise was the least of her concern as he pressed her chest against the cold wall. He leaned in close, his breath nearly making her gag.

"Please. Please, please," she whispered over and over again, squeezing her eyes closed and trying to turn her face away from her attacker's putrid stench. The tears flowed freely now, and there was no one to hear her but the night air.

"Oh, I do love it when they beg," the angel said, pulling on the back of her skirt.

Suddenly, a different voice cut through the night and her attacker went still: "Well, this party looks diverting. Tell me. What game are we playing?"

She instantly recognised the stranger's voice—the haunting union of power and seduction. His tone no longer held any hint of the swaggering protector who'd offered to walk her home. With the precision of the sharpest blade, the authority in his voice sliced through the night. "Go. Now."

The stranger's command left no room for argument and Kenna's reeking captor snarled in response. The brute released her, and she collapsed to her knees, vaguely aware as he pushed off the ground and shot into the sky on his massive, dark wings.

Ash had seen enough. The elvish woman, Kenna, was crying and obviously terrified. Varis found such vile pleasure in her terror. If Ash didn't step in and stop him, Varis would violate and kill the woman. The brute would enjoy every second of her pain.

As Varis flew off into the night to fulfill his sick desires elsewhere, Ash crouched down next to the crying elf.

"Are you hurt?" He reached for her cheek, but she flinched and he dropped his hand.

Her teeth chattered, though from the chill of the night air or shock he did not know. She crossed her trembling arms over her chest. She hadn't seemed to notice that her dress was still gaping, exposing her breasts. Suddenly, she clamped a hand over her mouth and turned away. Her back was to him as silent sobs wracked her body.

The part of the role Ash had taken disgusted him. This woman's tears were because of a situation he'd orchestrated so he could come to her aid. So he could trick her into trusting him.

For a while, he sat quietly beside her, letting her cry. When her breathing returned to normal, she turned to look at him. Even in the darkness, he could see that her eyes were red and swollen. Ash took a deep breath.

I am a fucking monster.

Ash removed his cloak. "May I?"

She looked down and nodded, pulling the ruined front of her dress over her breasts. As he wrapped his cloak around her, he noticed her stiffen. He was careful not to touch her, but he provided a warm cocoon of air around her. Her trembling eased slightly.

"Can you walk?"

She nodded again. When Ash offered her a hand, she took it and allowed him to help her to his feet. His well-rehearsed plan was working perfectly, just as it did every year; it made him sick.

As they walked to the Red Lantern, Kenna felt like she was moving through the thick haze of a dream. The nervous energy pumping through her veins was at odds with the elixir still clouding her mind.

When they arrived at the inn, they stopped outside the front door. She forced herself to turn and face her savior. His cloak was a mercy, covering her indecency and providing much needed warmth. "Thank you. For before."

"No one in this realm will lay a hand on you again. Or they'll answer to me. You have my word." His words rumbled through her.

"Here." She started to take the cloak off. In a surprisingly intimate gesture, he adjusted the cloak to fit more securely around her shoulders.

"Keep it. I'm sure you'll have an opportunity to repay me one day."

That simple instruction reminded her of how readily the huge, powerful attacker had yielded to this handsome angel's command.

Ancients, he was an *angel.* He was the enemy. The oppressor. Angels were the reason she'd had to leave her family and friends behind.

The stranger may be the most handsome male she'd ever laid eyes on, but he was dangerous. She nodded to him and returned to the safety of the inn without saying goodbye. Shutting the door, she paused and leaned back against the wood for a few moments, trying to calm her still-thundering heart.

It was late, and in the empty tavern, the only light came from the faint glow of the fire. She put another couple of logs on the fire, as though the flames might protect her from the monsters of the night. As warmth returned to her body, she realized she didn't even know her rescuer's name.

That was probably for the best.

CHAPTER 18

When Kenna woke, her mouth was as dry as old parchment. Her head pounded and her heart raced. Early morning light streamed through the window of her room. It must have been a few hours past dawn. Her stomach roiled in protest at the amount of elixir she'd consumed the night before. Jumping out of bed, she stumbled to the bathing chamber and slammed the door behind her, before heaving up her stomach's contents into the toilet.

She leaned against the door with her knees to her chest and her head in her hands. All the notelixir combined with the aftermath of the harrowing events of the previous night had left her staring at the ceiling for hours. meant her sleep had been fitful verging on non-existent.

Her mind raced, trying to piece together the details. The memories were fuzzy around the edges. Unfortunately, she remembered the stench of hot, putrid breath swirling up her nostrils. Flashes of other memories waged a sudden assault on her mind—frigid, biting bonds; unyielding stone wall.

She took a deep, shuddering breath, sitting up and leaning over the toilet again, retching. Body exhausted and throat raw, she curled up on the wooden floor and sobbed. She squeezed her eyes shut.

Were her friends and family still fighting in Tormund? She'd thought she'd known fear in Tormund, but she'd been so sheltered her entire life.

Had it been brave to refuse to drink from the Chalice? To follow her father's instruction and come to Notos? If so, why did she feel foolish and more terrified than ever?

She wasn't sure how long she laid there, but eventually she summoned the will to stand. She crawled back into her bed wishing it would swallow her so she wouldn't have to face the day.

Kenna laid there for a good hour, sorting through her feelings about the attack. About her humanity and the way she'd left things with Drake. The trauma of being assaulted faded little by little as she reminded herself over and over that it could have been so much worse.

Her friends and family had started a war, and given the fact that she was a lost human princess…

Well, she supposed the situation from last night was just the beginning of the trials she would face.

When she pulled the covers up over her head, a sharp sensation prickled through her arm from the bracelet representing her employment agreement with the landlord.

"Shit!" she yelped.

Apparently, her elemental bargain with the angel landlord wouldn't allow her the luxury of wallowing in bitterness and self pity. She huffed and threw back the covers. When she sat up, nausea overcame her again. She took some deep breaths until it passed.

She'd been drunk before; she'd need breakfast to settle her stomach.

She looked in the mirror over the small dressing table.

I look rutting awful.

Her eyes were puffy, red, and crusted with the remnants of tears. Her skin was pale, apart from the red splotch on her cheekbone which was sure to turn into a nasty black eye. Her hair was greasy and sticking up in odd places. She scrubbed her face hard with a cloth and cold water.

After splashing more water from the basin on her face and tidying her hair, she put on the same linen dress she'd worn yesterday.

She felt too wretched to care how wrinkled it was or that it smelled faintly of horses from the journey into the city yesterday. She used cosmetics to cover up the red mark under her eye as well as she could. Even in her dishevelled state, she was pretty. She'd realized she was beautiful the moment she turned twenty-one and her magic Manifested. Since then, she'd never felt the need to wait for a man to make her feel good about herself.

Still, she wondered what it might be like to have a true partner. She didn't need a man to complete her, but it would be nice to find someone who didn't hide things from her and who valued her. Someone who wanted to see her strengths grow and shine.

Her father and brother loved her, and they weren't purposefully dismissive of women. Still, they'd kept her human heritage from her for so long without giving her a chance to choose what to do with the truth. Her mother had lied, too. It was belittling. She was twenty-five, and she wasn't some helpless child anymore. She deserved to be the one to choose how to move forward with the knowledge of where she came from.

There would be no answers until she saw her family again. *If* she saw them again.

She pulled on her leather boots, trying to shake off the worry about the revolution in Tormund. What time was it in Mesterra? It was impossible to say. Worrying was fruitless, and there was nothing she could do. Still, she couldn't just sit around all day while everyone she loved fought.

Downstairs, the tables were mostly empty. There were a couple of families with winged children coloring on parchment with some broken colored pencils. Kenna supposed the activities in the city were not exactly conducive to rising early. She made her way to the bar where the tavern owner was busy restocking the shelves. The barman's friendly smile faltered when he saw the state of her.

"Rough night?" he asked.

Kenna sat on a stool and laid her head directly on the varnished wood, not caring when it stuck to her cheek. She didn't bother lifting her head. "You have no idea."

He didn't pry for more details, but instead chuckled. "I've seen a fair share of hangovers in my day."

He was right. She was *very* hungover, and he was laughing at her. So, she decided she hated him. Sadly, it was too early and she was too miserable to form any sort of words to verbalize her bitterness.

"Drink this." He slid her a thimble of bright pink sludge. "Then this." The second beverage was a squat tankard of steaming dark liquid.

She lifted her head. "If you're trying to poison me, you can forget it. I took care of that myself last night."

"Bottoms up." He pointed to the tiny cup.

"Fine. It can't possibly make me feel worse." She shot the tiny cup of syrupy pink liquid down her throat with practised ease—she'd gotten very good at that particular trick while taking shots of notelixir last night. The pink liquid was vile and she put a hand over her mouth, trying to keep it down.

When she thought she could speak without vomiting on the bar, she said, "You're a sadist."

"Am I?" His green eyes glinted with knowledge.

She hated to admit it, but she did feel better. Her insides weren't churning as much and the pounding in her head had dulled to a slight knocking. Slowly, she picked up the tankard. The man behind the bar picked up his own cup of steaming liquid and held it up to her, inviting her to a silent toast.

They clinked their mugs together, and she took a sip of the warm drink. The steaming liquid was bitter, yet soothing. She couldn't decide if she liked the taste, but after a few more sips, she began to feel a pleasant, invigorating zing. It was a little like a liquid hug, and suddenly everything didn't feel quite as terrible.

Last night had been awful, but it could have been so much worse. She shoved the trauma down deep. If she didn't acknowledge it, then maybe she could pretend it didn't exist. Instead, she focused on the drink in her hand.

"What is this?"

"Koffee." Her new best friend resumed his tasks behind the bar. "It's a really, really watered-down version of a very special elixir."

Though she probably should have been more cautious, she didn't care what koffee was or how he had gotten hold of it. She just knew that hot koffee in the morning was one of her new favorite things.

"Well, I love it. And I think I love you. Thanks..." She paused, prompting him to offer his name.

"Pax." He smiled and extended his hand to shake hers.

"I'm Kenna. Would it be terribly cheeky to ask for some buttered bread? I know I'm early. I don't mind helping myself if you're busy."

"The kitchen's through there and there's bread and butter on the counter." He nodded to the door behind the bar. Kenna stood and carried her mug with her to the kitchen, unwilling to part with the koffee.

At first glance the kitchen was immaculate and well-appointed. There was no cook and she still hadn't seen any other staff during her limited time at the Red Lantern.

"Curious," she muttered. Everything in the inn had been perfectly clean and comfortable except for the sticky bar and the occasionally neglected fire.

There was a wooden island in the center of the kitchen where loaves of fresh bread, pots of creamy butter, and jars of strawberry jam waited. It was official. She definitely loved Pax.

He was obviously caring and kind. Despite her trauma, having someone like him on her side made her believe this realm couldn't all be terrible. Surely, things could only improve after what had happened.

She cut a slice of warm bread, covered it in butter, and slathered it in a healthy amount of jam. She drew a spark from the hot brazier and used her Flame magic to reheat her koffee.

Trying to stop the thoughts from buzzing through her mind again, she finished her toast in record time, downed the rest of her koffee and left the kitchen.

"I wasn't sure for a while there, Pax, but I think I'm going to live," she told him as she entered the tavern once more.

CHAPTER 19

Thanks to Pax's miracle cure, Kenna's hangover had disappeared.

She helped prepare and serve breakfast, and then cleaned two guest rooms while Pax did the dishes.

They sat down together for a mid-morning break, while a few patrons enjoyed koffee and cake.

Drinking koffee with him every morning was a ritual she could get used to. Pax immediately began sharing a tale from his childhood featuring one of his brothers.

"And then…" Pax said, trying to catch his breath while he shook with laughter, "I pushed him right off the edge into the lake. He screeched like a little girl the whole way down." Pax was laughing so hard tears streamed down his ruddy cheeks.

Kenna chuckled politely, even though it seemed the story was much funnier to Pax than it did to her. "Do you miss him? Your brother?"

"Aye. I've not seen him in…it's been years. But I reckon I might see him later this year. Perhaps ye'll meet him." There was a twinkle in Pax's eye.

Kenna heard the tavern door swing open and stood up, ready to serve the newly arrived customer. When Pax began to stand too, she scolded, "No, you sit. Finish your koffee."

Pax's cheeks dimpled in an appreciative smile. "I'll come help ye shortly."

She weaved her way through the tables to take her plate to the kitchen. But when Kenna caught sight of the broad-shouldered, dark-haired male standing at the bar, she stumbled and dropped her empty metal plate.

It clattered to the floor, and a few people stared in her direction. The tall stranger turned to face her, his amusement evident. He was dressed in black leather trousers with knee high boots. His navy shirt was so dark it was almost black, and it hugged the lean muscles of his chest and shoulders. His sapphire eyes were on hers, and just as full of mystery as they'd been when she'd first met him last night. His presence commanded everyone's attention.

She crouched down to collect her plate, avoiding his eyes.

Why is he here?

She stood back up, bustling to the kitchen as though she hadn't recognized him. "Be with you in a minute."

Kenna took a deep breath and wiped her hands down the front of her apron before returning to her post behind the bar.

"What can I get you?" she chirped, feigning a casual smile, though her heart skittered when she beheld the playful glint in his eyes.

"Come now, don't pretend you don't remember me."

Of course, she remembered. In order to drown out the memories of her attacker, she'd been focusing on her monotonous duties and memories of this handsome stranger. The way his muscular frame moved with such unexpected grace. The seductive tendrils of his liquid magic. The unyielding authority in his voice when he'd come to her rescue.

She remembered all of it, but now that he stood before her again, she could scarcely remember her own name.

"Oh. Yes! It's you," she recovered. "Nice to see you again. What can I get for you?"

"I'm not here for a drink."

"Okay. So..." She gulped and waited, enduring a stretch of awkward silence before he spoke again.

"Are you well?" He glanced at her face. Then, his eyes scanned her dress, his brief appraisal sending warmth rushing through her.

"Well, you know what they say about a little bit of mild trauma..." Her attempt at dark humor fell flat.

His smile faltered, and his jaw flexed as though remembering the incident. "I believe I owe you a proper introduction. My name is Ash." He extended his hand.

"Kenna." She picked up an already sparkling clean glass to polish and Ash dropped his hand.

"So…Ash, any relation to the big, ugly tree outside?" She nodded toward the door, indicating the sacred tree in the square.

"That's an oak. Distant cousin. Surely you must see the family resemblance," Ash quipped, holding his hands out to the side like branches, before dropping them.

"Well, now that you mention it…" She smiled, returning his sarcasm.

"The rumor around the city this morning is that there is a mysterious new barmaid at the Red Lantern. They say she's a dark-haired, doe-eyed beauty."

Kenna's eyes widened at the statement. It sounded suspiciously like a compliment. She probably looked exactly like the scared deer he'd compared her to. She blinked rapidly, shaking off his words.

"Oh. Yes. I decided to stay in the city for a while. It seemed like Pax could use some help. So, here I am." She gestured to the bar.

"Interesting you should mention helping someone in need," said Ash. "It just so happens that's why I'm here this morning."

"You…want a job?" She asked.

His answer was a low, rumbling chuckle. "No. I assure you, I have plenty of work to occupy my time. Be that as it may, it seems I cannot deny myself any opportunity to offer you my assistance."

"I wasn't aware that I needed any man's assistance today."

"Forgive me. When we met last night, my assistance seemed rather advantageous."

Why did he bring that up? Until Ash showed up, she'd been fine, keeping busy. Besides, nothing had really happened in the alley. It could have been worse. She was fine.

"Well, the last time I checked the Red Lantern doesn't exactly attract the type of clientele that waits to trap unsuspecting females in alleys." She forced a blaze into her eyes which would have made Sera proud. Then, realizing she was behaving like a petulant child, she forced a pleasant smile. "Thank you for your generous offer, and for your help last night. Truly. But I'm fine."

Maybe if she said she was fine enough times, it would become true.

"Well, I just so happen to have certain…skills which could help should you find yourself under threat again. After all, I might not always be around to rescue you."

"Oh?" She scoffed. "And what skills do you have that I can't develop myself? I'm planning to start training by myself tomorrow."

"By all means, train on your own. I only came here to offer my humble tuition to a female in need." Ash bowed gallantly. "Though, I should also tell you training without a partner is entirely useless should you find yourself alone and bound by magic in an alley. If you change your mind, I would be more than happy to teach you how to spar—with more than words."

There was a slight edge of annoyance in his voice. This conversation was a dangerous dance, and she suddenly felt like she was losing.

"The only thing I need is to get back to work. Now, can I get you anything or are you leaving?"

Ash held his hands up in mock defeat, backing away from the bar. "Very well. Though before you make up your mind, perhaps consider a visit to the temple today. The High Priestess is rather inspiring. I think you might decide to accept my help after all." A whisper of wind traced its way over the silver cuff on her wrist.

Ash couldn't possibly know about her bargain with the ferry master. He couldn't know Kenna still needed to accept an offer of help from an angel in Notos if she was ever to cross the Veil back into Mesterra. Back to her family.

She had no idea how to fight with magic. And weapons? She'd never held a sword or a dagger before. Surely, those were the types of skills he'd been referring to. And wouldn't it be beneficial to learn from an angel? Even the thought of accepting his offer was reckless, but that didn't stop her from agreeing.

"Fine. I'll go to the temple this afternoon."

"Excellent. I'll be sure to check in with you later." A rakish grin spread over his handsome features, and Kenna wondered if she was making a mistake.

After her conversation with Ash, the rest of her morning was filled with all manner of tasks. She settled into the rhythm of it easily, finding comfort in the numbing distraction of productivity. She needed all the distraction available to her to keep her from worrying about the rebellion in Tormund.

Now it was her afternoon break, and Kenna was across the square. She was caught in a line of folks waiting to enter the towering ivory limestone temple. With nothing to keep her hands and her mind busy, the anxiety crept in. Was the rebellion still going on in Tormund, and how would she know if the rebels succeeded? Sending letters across the Veil was impossible. Would someone come to bring her home when it was safe again?

Her mind grew quiet as she encountered the most infuriatingly beautiful female she'd ever seen. Her voice was a musical sound welcoming visitors into the temple. From her countenance, it was obvious she was a priestess. Her eyelids were perfectly smoked with dark powder, illuminating her kohl-lined icy-blue eyes. Her wings fluttered behind her as she shared pleasant conversation with those entering the temple.

The priestess's thick, flowing hair was swept to one side where it cascaded over the front of her tanned shoulder in undulating tresses which gleamed like molten chocolate. Her burnished orange organza dress draped effortlessly over her perfect curves. No one should look that good in orange. Honestly, Kenna wasn't sure if she was jealous of her or attracted to her.

But all of her other outward beauty paled in comparison to her wings. They framed her flawless face with graceful midnight black arcs, swooping above her shoulders. The silver tips of her onyx feathers shone like moonlight. Even Sera would look plain next to this woman.

Why hadn't Kenna put on something nicer than her burgundy, linen dress?

Before her sudden insecurity could overwhelm her, she found herself face to face with the priestess. She curtseyed.

Why did I just curtsey? How embarrassing.

"Welcome," the melodious voice greeted her. "It's so lovely to see you this afternoon. Is it your first time visiting the temple?"

"Yes, your…holiness?" Kenna suddenly realized she didn't know the appropriate way to greet a priestess.

The priestess laughed. "I am Lailah, the High Priestess of Luniva. I do not believe in the pretence of titles, so you may call me Lailah. And what is it you seek in the temple on this day?"

"I'd like to look around and then attend the service. Is that allowed?"

"Of course. The service begins in ten minutes. I would be thrilled to have you join us." Lailah swept an arm out, welcoming Kenna to the temple's interior.

As she entered the building, Kenna beheld a blank canvas of white limestone masonry that gave way to staggering stained-glass windows. The colored glass covered the entire wall behind the altar.

The windows were divided into two halves. On the left stood the proud visage of the sacred tree in Braktyn's square. Translucent, painted leaves tinted in shades of crimson, amber, and honey adorned the tree's branches.

The right-hand window transported her imagination into a realm of shining moonlight. The moon was a diamond-encrusted ivory back-drop for the dark silhouettes of bare trees frosted with white and silver and the visage of an alabaster palace nestled on a dark mountaintop.

She walked slowly along the edge of the temple, admiring the stained glass and the pristine interior. She found a shadowed alcove with a few toys and coloring pencils arranged around an illustrated book on a small table—a children's area. Other than the few children at the Red Lantern, she hadn't seen many children in the city, or at least not as many children as there were in Tormund. All of the children she'd seen here had wings, and she wondered if they were all winged fae or if angel children were unable to hide their wings like adults.

Kenna sat on a too-small stool next to the table and thumbed through a children's book, reading from the top of a page.

As punishment for her noble rebellion, Luniva and her angelic host were forced into a treaty with Soldivus and cast into another realm. Luniva watches over us from the sky at night. To this day, it is the purpose of her followers to enlighten the people of the Three Realms.

"The Ancients are still alive?" she whispered aloud.

The smell of cedar and smoke, a bonfire in a winter forest, caressed her senses. She knew that scent. It still clung to the cloak he'd given her last night.

"Indeed, the Ancients still live." Kenna jumped up from her tiny chair at the sound of Ash's voice.

She felt a prick through the silver cuff as the engraved words changed in response to his statement. The word truth vanished.

The word hadn't changed when she read the truth in the history book. Had the history in Notos been tampered with like the history in Mesterra? Or would her bargain only be fulfilled by spoken truth?

"If you wanted a history lesson, I would have been happy to enlighten you," Ash arched a brow at her.

She mindlessly twisted the cuff on her wrist. "I've always enjoyed reading and learning things for myself."

"Well, I understand the angels on the High Council have painted a rather limited picture of Mesterra's history. What is it that you wish to know?"

"What was in the treaty? What happened to Luniva and the angels who rebelled with her?"

Ash looked somber and there was a note of bitterness in his voice as he replied, "The treaty is complicated. Only the royal family know the full details. In summary, Soldivus made Luniva agree to stay in another realm during the duration of the treaty. Apparently, Ancient magic bound her to eternal shores of the moon every night, along with all the evil and tormented souls. Soldivus was bound to the eternal shores of the sun in the same way during the daytime, so that they need not meet in the interim. Apparently, there's a lost human princess who will restore the human race. Winter Solstice this year marks the end of the treaty. But I've not seen any human princesses around, have you?"

"That's impossible," she answered. "All of the humans are dead."

Warning bells peeled through her mind. Thankfully, the bell in the clock tower began to chime as well, giving Kenna an excuse to turn away and hide her reaction.

Ash placed a gentle hand on Kenna's arm, leading her toward the pews. He sat down on the end of the pew where there were two seats, but rather than sitting next to him, Kenna sat on the row in front.

A few minutes later, the priestess began the service. Everyone stood, so Kenna followed suit.

"Blessed be Luniva and her power which watches over us with moonlight." The rest of the congregation chanted back to the priestess.

"This afternoon, we will look at the limitations that hinder us from fulfilling our true potential. Self doubt and lack of purpose."

The priestess locked eyes with Kenna momentarily, and she felt certain the holy woman had seen into her heart's most closely guarded insecurities.

Her musical speech continued, "You have everything you need to go forth and accomplish your purpose and change the world around you. You do not need help. You must simply step into your destiny, go forth, and claim your desires. You deserve to grasp everything you want."

The words were empowering, even if Kenna struggled to believe them. She stopped hearing the priestess when Ash's breath brushed the back of her neck, and the world seemed to tilt beneath her. "Fascinating. Isn't it, love?"

She tried to summon some opposition to the angel addressing her, but it was impossible when his soft accent seemed to carry such subtle promises. "I'm trying to listen," Kenna said.

There was shuffling and disgruntled throat clearing around them. Before she knew it, he'd squeezed himself between her and the worshiper to her left, making the pew uncomfortably tight. She kept her eyes fixed forward, even though people in the row in front of her looked over their shoulders for the source of the disturbance.

Ash placed a casual arm over the back of the pew behind her, his hand dangling dangerously close to her shoulder. It wasn't menacing or intrusive. Instead, she felt an innate sense of protection and comfort from the act. Perhaps it was a lingering sense of trust since he'd saved her last night, but she stiffened nonetheless.

He was an angel, and she was a human. She'd left everything behind to flee from his kind. They could never be anything other than enemies.

"She's quite compelling, isn't she?" Obviously, he didn't care to allow Kenna the privilege of hearing the supposedly compelling words.

"What she's saying is…I've never felt like I was allowed to want anything before."

Why did I admit that?

Ash examined his fingernails.

"Oh, I'm sure there are many things you want." He looked at her again. "But will you let yourself have them?"

She didn't answer, even as she wondered what it would feel like to feel his fingers on her skin.

The male sitting on the other side of Ash coughed pointedly. Then, the High Priestess looked in their direction with narrowed eyes, a silent cue for them to cease their hushed exchange. Did Kenna sense a flash of annoyance from the woman?

She ignored him for the rest of the service, though she didn't hear another word the Priestess said. Instead, her pulse pounded in her ears, and she found herself acutely aware of the disconcerting heat of Ash's body next to hers.

When the service concluded, she jumped up, eager for some fresh air.

Ash chatted pleasantly with other worshipers as everyone filed out the doors once more. Lailah had taken up her earlier post to exchange pleasant goodbyes with people as they left the building. In front of Kenna, Ash approached the priestess. Lailah's beam of pure delight upon seeing him was evident.

Ash brushed a kiss to her cheek, and whispered something in her ear, making her laughter burst into beautiful song as her raven wings fluttered. The priestess seemed to appraise Kenna with more scrutiny now that she'd seen Kenna with Ash.

Not a threat, Lailah's eyes seemed to conclude after examining her.

Ash turned and placed a hand on Kenna's lower back, pushing her forward. "Kenna, allow me to introduce you to High Priestess Lailah Moonbriar."

"Such formalities, brother." The priestess rolled her eyes and turned to face Kenna. "My brother is apparently unaware that we have met."

"Everything you said was illuminating. Truly. Thank you for your words today, Your—Lailah." Kenna curtseyed awkwardly. She rushed down the steps toward the Red Lantern.

"Kenna! Kenna, wait!" Ash called out behind her.

She chose to pretend she didn't hear him at all.

CHAPTER 21

"*K*enna, wait!"

Ash hurried across the square after her and she ignored his shout, surprising him.

He thought she'd be eager to train in the aftermath of the attack. Usually, the desire to learn self-defense combined with Ash's charm was enough to convince elvish women to accept his help.

But this woman…Kenna. She was holding back.

He knew about her crossing bargain with Raziel. And he'd already fulfilled two of the four requirements. That should have been enough to earn her trust.

She slammed the door open and rushed into the Red Lantern before Ash burst through the door behind her. Standing at the bar with his thick arms crossed over his chest was his brother. Pax.

"Can I help ye, yer majesty?"

Kenna whirled to face Ash, shock written all over her features.

"You're…who are you?" she asked.

Ash could practically see the pieces clicking together in her mind. If the redheaded prick could have just kept his damned mouth shut.

He smiled at Kenna. "To my friends, I'm Ash." He turned to Pax, replacing the smile with a withering glare. "To everyone else, I'm King Ashton Moonbriar."

Before his encounter with Kenna this morning, Ash couldn't remember the last time he'd come into the Red Lantern. He only visited

Braktyn once a year, and usually he found his targets in the drug addled interior of the Golden Flagon. Ever since Pax had purchased the tavern last year, Ash had steered clear of the Red Lantern.

"I heard you were the landlord here, Pax. What brings you to Notos? In trouble with Father? Or did you follow some elf here last Summer Solstice to do your duties as their guardian angel?"

Guardian angels were the only angels who could travel freely between realms after all.

"Somethin' like that," Pax said and his posture relaxed.

"Come now, brother. Let's start again. I didn't mean te cause any offence. I just wanna look after Kenna is all." The challenge in Pax's tone was clear.

"Yes, well. I think you'll find the only reason she arrived here safely last night is thanks to me. Where were *you* while she was wandering home from the Golden Flagon drunk and alone?"

Pax looked like Ash had punched him, and he turned to Kenna. "What's he talking about?"

"Can we go to the kitchen for a minute?" Kenna looked around. The patrons were pretending not to listen to the conversation, but all chatter in the tavern seemed to have stopped.

The barman jerked his head to a door behind the bar and led the way. Ash promptly followed. He took his time walking around the bar, aware of the gazes of every female patron tracking his movements. These particular trousers were always a favorite. He looked over his shoulder, smiling as he caught Kenna's eyes rising from his leather-clad ass while following him into the kitchen.

"You're welcome to take a closer look, love."

"Not bad, but did you know your trousers have a hole? I can see your royal undergarments." Kenna raised an eyebrow.

"What?" Ash asked, twisting awkwardly to try and inspect his own ass, before he realized she was teasing. She'd rattled him. Pax guffawed, and Kenna joined him.

"Perhaps I've met my match." Ash chuckled and shrugged.

Kenna's smile faded as she turned to Pax. "Last night, I walked to the Golden Flagon with my friends, but I stayed behind by myself while they went back to the docks."

"Ye shoudn''t have—"

She held up a hand. "I know. It was a mistake. I've already paid for it." She pointed to the now visible bruise under her eye. "Thankfully, he…His Majesty came to my aid before the attacker could cause any real harm. I'm fine, and I learned my lesson."

Her attempted smile was more like a wince. Ash felt the familiar talons of guilt clenching his gut.

"See? She's safe. I'm harmless." Ash turned to Kenna, giving her his best crooked smile. "And you can still call me Ash."

He saw the tension in her shoulders ease.

"Well, *Yer Majesty*. Seems te me that those sorts of folk shouldn't be allowed te wander round yer realm."

"You'll do well to remember your place." Ash tugged on the cuff of his sleeve, doing his best to ooze nonchalant authority. "We're not in Vorra anymore, *Pax*." He spat the nickname at the angel, Pahalaiah, who'd fought against him in the war.

"Oh, I don't need any help rememberin' what my opinion of ye should be," Pax answered.

Kenna looked between them. "Well you certainly fight like brothers, though I can't see any resemblance."

"All angels are brothers and sisters. Doesn't mean we have te be friends."

"Come now," Ash sneered. "We used to be friends."

"That was a long, *long* time ago. Things change."

"If you two are going to have a pissing match, I need a drink. I'm going to get a bottle of wine from the cellar," Kenna said.

Ash sent a flirty look in her direction. "And here I was thinking I'd have to be the one to ask *you* out for a drink."

She rolled her eyes, opened the trap door, and disappeared down the ladder into the cellar. Pax eyed him, and plucked up a large knife to chop some carrots waiting on the counter. His knife came down on the vegetables vigorously again and again.

Neither of the brothers spoke for a while.

Ash wandered around the modest kitchen, enjoying the annoyed huffs from Pax every time he touched something. He felt a twinge of frustration with his progress. Kenna was more standoffish than he'd expected, and he wasn't sure why. Most women were panting after him within hours of meeting him.

Pax had been an unexpected player, but Ash wouldn't let him get in the way. He was a lot of things, but Ashton Moonbriar was *not* a loser.

What did it say about him? That he was more worried about whether or not he'd win this game than what it meant for Kenna's fate.

It only confirmed what Ash already knew about himself. He was beyond redemption.

Pax pointed his knife at the cellar door before continuing chopping the carrots. "What exactly is it ye're after with her?"

"Just a bit of fun."

"Is that so?" Pax stabbed the knife into the wooden chopping board and folded his thick arms across his chest.

"Yes, it is. What is it that *you* want with Kenna?"

"My intention is only te keep her safe."

"And why exactly is that so important to you?"

"Ye may have forgotten the old ways, but some of us still believe that all life is sacred. *Some of us* believe that if someone needs help, ye should help them without expecting anything in return. Just because it's the right thing te do."

"You're just as saintly as I remember." Ash rolled his eyes, and helped himself to an apple out of the fruit bowl. He took a bite, and then returned it to the bowl. "But no. I think you're Kenna's guardian angel."

"And if I am?"

"Then, I'd say you're doing a poor job of it."

"And I'd say ye're just as much of a bastard as when I last met ye on the battlefield."

Their conversation was interrupted when both of them heard Kenna's scream from the cellar. "What the Hel?!"

en, Kenna thought as she rifled through bottles in the cellar. *Apparently, they're the same in every realm and every race.*

After her conversation with Pax and Ash, she needed a moment away from both of them. Pax had oozed trustworthiness, but he'd never hinted that he knew the king. And not just knew him. They were brothers.

And Ash was the rutting *king* of Notos.

She tapped the Fostone in her bracelet to light the candles in the cellar, but when she touched the gem, it sent a vibrating tremor through her finger all the way up her arm.

"What the Hel?!" she yelped in surprise. It hadn't hurt, but the sensation had been unexpected.

"Sorry, little sister." It was Jona's voice

"What in the Three Realms?" She spun around wildly, looking for the source of the voice in the cool cellar. "Jona? Where are you?"

"I'm communicating through your Fostone. Sorry if I scared you," her brother's disembodied voice explained. "Since I knew we couldn't send letters across the Veil, I've been making some improvements to the Fostones. We can use them to contact you, but communicating with them uses a lot of energy. We'll only be able to talk with them about four times a year if my calculations are right, and the connection will drain your Vessel pretty quickly. I'm still working out some of the kinks. So far, I only have it working on mine, yours, and Zo's. This is the first time I've managed to try to reach you in Notos."

Her brother was an actual genius. "I've never been so thankful that you're an overachiever." She heard his garbled laugh and Kenna continued, "Listen, I read Father's letter. I know I'm—"

He cut her off before she could speak her secret aloud. "There's someone else here who wants to talk to you."

"Kenna?!" Zo's voice shouted into the quiet cellar making her jump.

Kenna heard Sera grumble, "You don't have to shout, Zo."

"Oh. Right. Kenna?" Zo's voice returned to a more normal volume.

Happy tears sprung to Kenna's eyes even if she was jealous that they could all be together. They were safe. "Zo! Sera! I miss you already. Is the battle over? Are the Elders gone?"

As if in answer, Kenna heard muffled shouts followed by rattling glass.

"Not yet," Jona said. "We're hiding in the bakery right now. We're using it as one of our safe houses. People come here in shifts when they need food and rest."

"I'm here, too," Aryn said. "And I'm going to fight with them. I'm… I'm sorry I didn't come say goodbye."

"Someone make a note. Aryn just *apologized*," Sera teased.

"Don't be an ass, Sera," Zo said.

Kenna laughed. "It's okay, Aryn. Jona, I need to tell you something. I met the king here in Braktyn. He told me the Ancients are still alive."

"It makes sense," Jona answered. "The High Council wouldn't want us to know the Ancients are alive. The angels can more easily control Mesterra if everyone believes they're the most powerful beings that exist."

Kenna nodded, forgetting that they couldn't see her. It was strange, communicating like this. "How are things going with the battle?" she asked, ignoring the ache in her chest.

As if in answer, Kenna heard someone banging on the door through the Fostone.

"Zola Barsden!" Someone shouted, followed by more banging.

"That way! Quickly! I'll distract them long enough for you to get away," Zo whispered. Kenna heard scuffling and held her breath as she helplessly listened to the events unfold. She felt the strain of exhaustion creeping in from keeping the connection open. She held on, needing to know that Zo and the others were okay.

Then, it sounded like someone broke down the door.

Elder Ilan spoke, "Guards. Hold her. Search the premises."

"Elder Ilan. What is this about? Have I done something wrong? I've been hiding here during the battle. I've been so afraid. I can give you food if you or your men need anything at all," Zo said.

The Elder spoke next, his voice dripping with honeyed condescension, "Oh, my dear. You know exactly why I've come. Delicious as your baked treats are, I'm not here for sweets. It's very quaint that your little elvish rebellion thought you'd have a chance of defeating us. How does it make you feel to know all of you will be dead by tomorrow evening? That it only took four angels to defeat your efforts?"

"I'm not sure I know what you mean."

"Your lies are noble. What a waste. To think that if you had just behaved, you could have used your Sight to help us. Females are too unpredictable." Ilan's voice was laced with obvious disgust. "No matter. At least your blood will be useful, even if you are a rebel fool."

"My...my blood?" Zo stammered, and Kenna's breath hitched.

"You'll understand soon enough." Kenna imagined him waving a dismissive hand. There was a pause. His voice was low and lethal, but it was louder, as though he was right in Zo's face. "You didn't think your part in this rebellion would go undiscovered, did you? Your *friend*"— Ilan's tone was full of amused disdain—"Ezra came to me as soon as he returned. It seems he's been to Notos, and he had some very interesting news."

No. Kenna had no capacity to process what she was hearing. What did Ezra tell them? And why?

"It would seem Ezra made a bargain in order to cross the Veil, just as you foolish creatures always do. Though, I can't complain on this occasion, considering his bargain revealed the location of the crossing." Kenna could practically hear Ilan's sneer. "Of course, that crossing is now closed. Don't want any more rebels sneaking through the Veil."

The crossing is closed...how will I get back?

"Not only that, he also revealed two names who are part of the rebel group. And exactly where to find them."

"I don't know what you're talking about," Zo said, but Kenna heard the tremor in her voice.

What other name did Ezra give the Elders?

It was as though Ilan heard her thoughts.

"You and Quinn Duras. I never would have suspected him. The Dean played his part very well."

Kenna leaned back against the cellar's stone wall and slid to the floor, covering her mouth to stifle the sob that threatened to escape. She was trembling now from the effort of keeping the connection open, along with the uncertainty of her loved ones' fates.

Had Jona, Aryn, and Sera gotten away? Maybe they could warn her father.

"Of course, his bargain must have only stipulated he give us two names. He's been in custody ever since he came to me. We are trying to get more answers and more names, but it seems he has some sense of loyalty after all."

"No," Zo whispered, and Kenna heard her friend sniffling.

"The other Elders and I prefer not to debase ourselves with the distasteful practice of procuring information under duress. However, we have a special facility for people like you, I'm sure the guards at the Hill will get answers from Ezra. And from you.

Ezra had betrayed them. That was the bargain he'd made with the ferry master.

Did Drake know what Ezra had done? Did he know where his partner was? Were they going to torture her father as well?

Kenna's capacity to understand information was dwindling. She could hardly keep her eyes open as her Vessel continued to drain. How long could she keep the connection open? Kenna's tongue felt like it had turned to lead. Her mouth wouldn't move, even if she wanted to speak. She slumped to the side.

"What...where is the Hill?" Zo slurred. She sounded as exhausted as Kenna felt.

"Oh, I could tell you, but it would be much more expedient to let you see for yourself."

There was a thunderous clap, and a whoosh that swallowed all sound. Suddenly, the noises were entirely different. Chains clanked in what sounded like a cavernous space. A prison?

No. No. No! She wanted to shout, but if she made a single sound, Ilan would know about Zo's Fostone. At least if Zo kept it, she might have some hope of contacting Kenna or the others.

"How did you do that? Where are we?" Zo stammered.

"Elves aren't the only one who sometimes have special abilities. I have the ability to terialize. A jump across a vast distance if you will."

Kenna heard the unmistakable sound of metal dragging across stone, getting louder as it got closer to Zo. Chains rattled, followed by the loud clank of a lock. She imagined manacles being fastened to her friend's wrists and ankles as a bitter voice said, "Welcome to the Hill, though most of our residents prefer to call it Hel."

Ilan's voice chimed in, "Isn't Hel the place where monsters live in your elvish children's tales? Zola, you shall have to decide if the nickname is appropriate. I'll ask you when I come back to visit. I need to get back to Tormund. My brothers and I plan to have won the battle by nightfall."

Zo had wished Ilan a good morning, which meant the Elders hoped to win the battle in the next twelve hours. Maybe less. Kenna heard the same thunderous clap as before. Ilan must have terialized back to Tormund.

"Holt? How are you here? *Why* are you here?" Zo asked.

"Because I've seen the light." Holt's voice was vicious, unrecognizable from the man who'd been Sera's lover a few years ago. "Speaking of light. I'll take your that. There are no candles in your cell anyway."

Something clattered and rustled, and then...

Silence. Holt must have destroyed Zo's Fostone.

Whatever happened after the Shadow had snatched Holt away three years ago, it seemed he was working with the angels now. Tears streaked Kenna's face as she finally succumbed to her exhaustion and fell into darkness.

"Kenna," Ash said gently.

The king was crouched down next to her. Why was she asleep in the cellar? How long had she been asleep? Her head pounded like she'd had an entire bottle of notelixir, and she looked at her Fostone. It didn't show the hour. Perhaps it needed time to replenish after the conversation with her brother.

She bolted upright. Where was the Hill? Was there any way to get

Zo out? To get Ezra out? And what would the Elders do to her father? How long until the Elders killed all of the rebels?

"Are you okay?" Ash asked.

She shook her head, and closed her eyes, turning away from Ash to hide her emotion. The sound of Zo being shackled still seemed to ring in Kenna's ears. What did the Elders want with her friend's blood?

And Ezra....

He'd betrayed them the moment he'd accepted the ferry master's bargain. He'd been so desperate to stay by Drake's side that he'd agreed to hand Zo and Kenna's father over to the Elders. It sounded like he was being tortured for information, and she never would have wished that fate on anyone.

Would he break eventually? Everyone was in more danger now that the Elders knew Ezra and Zo could give them information. Any plans the rebels had for the battle. Any of the guards who were secretly rebels who might give the elves an upper hand.

The Elders knew her father and two of her friends were involved in the revolution. City Hall had exploded just as Kenna defied the order to drink from the Emergence Chalice. They wouldn't need to torture Ezra and Zo to connect the rest of Kenna's loved ones to the rebel forces.

Everyone she loved was going to die. And she'd be alone. Truly and completely alone with the secret of her humanity and the responsibility to restore an entire race of people pressing down on her. She couldn't do this. She could hardly even draw breath into her lungs.

Then, there was a warm, steadying hand on her upper back.

Ash. He moved his thumb back and forth in slow, soothing strokes. Surprisingly, it helped.

"Breathe," he said. "Whatever it is. Don't think about it. Imagine something that brings you comfort. Focus on that. For me, it's spring. I haven't seen spring in years, but I remember it. As a boy, I loved the feel of the mud between my toes. The vibrant color of spring blossoms. The steady rhythm of and rainfall. The smell of an afternoon thunderstorm."

She did her best to obey, filling her slowly expanding lungs with long, slow breaths as she listened to the smooth baritone of his voice. In through her nose, out through her mouth, until her breathing returned to normal.

She had to get back. She couldn't stay here while her friends and family fought.

"I have to get back to Mesterra."

At the mention of crossing the Veil, she felt a stinging sensation from the silver cuff on her wrist, reminding her of her bargain with the ferry master. She still had to accept one offer of help before she could cross the Veil back into Mesterra.

"No. *No. No. No,*" she grumbled. Maybe she could beg the ferry master to let her cross anyway. Perhaps his shriveled old heart held some shred of mercy, but she doubted it. Even if he allowed her to pass, Ilan and the Elders had discovered the crossing in Tormund. It was gone. She had no idea where the nearest arrival port was in Mesterra. How long would it take her to get to Tormund?

Ash still had a steadying hand on her back. "Is there anything I can do to help?"

Help.

With that one word, the barrage of thoughts went silent. Kenna turned to Ash, meeting his concerned gaze. She had an idea.

A stupid, reckless idea.

CHAPTER 23

What did Kenna know about Ash's character other than the fact that he'd rescued her in the alley last night? Not much, really.

Any decent person would have stopped the brute from attacking her, but was he *actually* a decent person? And he was the king. Why had he bothered to find her here? Why had he offered to help her? Surely, he must have some ulterior motive.

Ash had some sort of history with Pax, but whatever had happened between the brothers couldn't be too terrible. Otherwise, Pax would have kicked him out of the tavern the moment he'd seen him.

In spite of any logical misgivings she might have, something inside of her soul whispered that she could trust Ash. Something deep in his eyes enticed her to trust him. But she'd been lied to and kept in the dark often enough that her trust was a commodity she wouldn't give freely.

"I will accept your offer of help. I want you to train me," Kenna said.

Ash raised his eyebrows before he removed his hand from her back, and she missed the comfort his warm touch had provided. He casually rolled up his sleeves. "Oh? And what if my offer has expired?"

"Has it?"

He finished rolling up his sleeves, and lifted his dazzling eyes to hers. His mouth quirked up in one corner. "That depends on the terms. You're a clever woman, and a clever woman wouldn't blindly accept help from a stranger. Even if he is a dashing king."

Ash was right. She had terms, and she only hoped he'd agree.

Before she could start bargaining with Ash, Pax stomped down the wooden ladder into the cellar in a huff. "What're ye thinking, lass? If ye wanted training, ye shoulda just asked me."

"I have my reasons, Pax."

From Kenna's limited interactions with Pax, she'd learned he had no love for the High Council in Mesterra. But if she trained with the king in his castle, she might secure Ash as an ally. It would be far too dangerous for him to know she was the human princess, but she could reveal that she was part of the rebellion. Maybe he'd even use his forces to help them.

Pax held her by the shoulders and looked at her. It was a silent invitation to stay there. To stay comfortable. "Are ye sure ye want to do this?" Pax asked.

No. I'm not sure of anything anymore.

As warm and kind as Pax was, he was only the landlord of a pub. And even though he was an angel who could train her to use her magic, staying with Pax would be shortsighted. She sensed that Pax would do anything to protect her. She'd felt an instant sense of camaraderie with him that reminded her of her brother, and it would be too easy to slip into a quiet, safe existence under his care.

But what about her loved ones? She would give up anything, even her own soul, if it would help to keep them safe. Not to mention, she was also the one who was supposed to save the humans. She had no idea how *that* would happen, but Pax had no political power that she might leverage to help anyone.

The silence was tangible as Kenna looked back and forth between Ash and Pax. For all of his charm and arrogance, Ash's eyes held a promise. He could teach her to be ice and steel. A warrior.

"I'm sure." Her conscience wouldn't allow her to hide anymore.

"Let's get you back to Mesterra then, love." Ash smiled.

"What about our agreement? My job?" she asked Pax.

"If yer sure. It's yer decision, Kenna. I only want what's best for ye."

Pax extended his hand, and she clasped his forearm the way they had when they'd made their contract for her to work at the Red Lantern. "I hereby release ye from yer bargain of employment in exchange for food and lodging. And the occasional drink." Pax grinned.

The binding coil of earth, flame, and water appeared around their arms, immediately followed by a feeling like cool water trickling along the trajectory of the shimmering path of the delicate bracelet. The clasp unfastened, and Pax deftly caught the bracelet and stuffed it into the pocket of his vest.

The silver cuff still remained, the bargain with the ferry master and a reminder of what was at stake. Pax fixed Ash with a withering stare. "It's my job to protect her. And if ye hurt her, it'll be me ye answer to."

Kenna wasn't sure, but she wondered whether she saw a brief flicker of fear pass over Ash's features before it was replaced with a lazy smile.

"Don't worry, Pax. You have my word. I won't harm her." His sensuous lips tilted up in a smile. "So, Kenna. What is it that you want?"

Ash leaned casually against the wall by the door, his easy demeanour so at odds with his royal position. As she looked at Ash, she wondered what his word was worth. The questions roiled around inside her like water boiling in a pot.

What would her training look like? How long until she'd be ready to fight? Would he train her himself? Would she live in the castle? Where was the castle located? A wise person would insist on having the answers before agreeing to a magical bargain with a veritable stranger, but she only had instinct to guide her.

She had to get home, and she needed Ash's help to get across the Veil. She couldn't bombard him with questions before he agreed to give her what she required. If he agreed to make an elemental bargain, she could make demands that would ensure her own safety. So, she planned out her words carefully hoping they would guard her against deceit or harm.

She'd had enough of men lying to her, whether their motives were for her protection or not.

~

FOR A MOMENT, he'd worried she'd remain with Pax. He hadn't bought the dragon shit about the *old ways* and taking care of Kenna being *the right thing to do.* Ash had known Pax was Kenna's guardian angel within minutes.

Fortune smiled on him tonight though because Kenna was desperate. And desperation made people foolish.

She'd already made up her mind to accept his help, and he admired her tenacity. His eyes followed the determined set of her jaw up to the hope shining in her dark brown eyes. Or perhaps it was the remnants of her tears.

Ash hadn't planned for her to find out he was the king yet, but it seemed to work in his favor. As she explained the situation with her brother and her friends, as well as some other details about the rebellion, he could practically hear her thinking his position might do something to help win the revolution in Mesterra. He didn't need to divulge that his forces wouldn't be able to help the elves.

Pax closed the tavern for the afternoon, and they returned up the cellar's ladder to the kitchen. The other angel had his thick arms crossed over his chest, and Pax's steady observation revealed a hint of the warrior that anyone would be a fool to cross—someone *Ash* would be a fool to cross.

"Can you give us a minute?" Kenna asked Pax.

He nodded, moving away from the table where Kenna and Ash sat. He stood behind the bar where he kept a keen eye on their exchange, polishing glasses. His measured, deliberate motions sent a clear message: he'd be by Kenna's side at the first hint of trouble.

"You asked for my help. Shall I whisk you away, Kenna?" Ash purred.

She pushed her long brown hair behind her ear. "You're right. I need your help. I want to train, but there's something else I need from you first."

"Very well," Ash leaned back in his chair. He mindlessly adjusted the cuff of his shirt sleeve, unphased by her demand.

"I need to return to my hometown in Mesterra, but I can't until I fulfill the bargain I made with the ferry master for safe passage across the Veil. There were a number of things he required of me before I would ever be allowed to—"

"Yes, I'm familiar with his bargains," Ash interrupted, waving a dismissive hand. "Back at the castle, there's a document listing every payment and debt owed for crossing the Veil."

She pursed her lips with obvious annoyance. "Right. So, one part of the bargain was that I needed to accept two offers of help from an angel in Notos. Pax has been so helpful during my time here, but his help never altered this." She held up the silver cuff on her wrist. "But one of the tallies vanished last night after you helped me in the alley."

"Generally, when Raziel says 'an angel', he has a particular angel in mind. In this case, that angel must be me." Kenna's gaze was wary, and Ash made a mental note to thank Raziel for making his job easier.

"If I accept your help tonight, will it remove the last tally?"

"That would stand to reason. I'm at your service, love." Ash extended his long legs and crossed them at the ankles, reclining in his chair. He folded his hands over his abdomen, smiling when he noticed Kenna's gaze dropping to follow the movement.

"I was also supposed to have a new experience with an angel."

"Oh?" Ash raised his eyebrows and leaned forward, placing his forearms on the table across from her. His eyes twinkled with salacious mischief. "Tell me, Kenna. What type of experience did you have in mind?"

He heard her pulse quicken.

"You'll take me for a flight. That will fulfill the experience."

Pax, who was listening to every word, had a smug smile on his face. Ash leaned back in his chair again, hiding his annoyance. "So, how would you like to proceed?"

"I'd like to make a bargain with you," she answered.

"Pray tell, Kenna. What would you have of me?"

"The truth. I've been lied to my entire life by the Elders. I've also been lied to by people I thought I could trust. I need to know that if I go with you, you won't lie to me. That you don't intend to harm me, and that you'll do whatever is in your power to help me learn to fight and return home."

"Wise demands, indeed. I promise I will not harm you. I will give you a way to test the truth of my words with the magic of our agreement. Though, I feel it's only fair if I counter with some requests of my own."

Again, she didn't seem surprised. This woman was beautiful and cunning, and Ash was enjoying their game more than he wanted to admit.

"First, if you agree to come with me, you must understand that training will be grueling. Second, no matter how unpleasant you find your situation, you will be required to stay to complete your agreement with me. You will be released from your oath at dawn on Winter Solstice. Third, I will fly you across the Veil, and help your friends and family in whatever way I can."

She eyed him with suspicion, seeming to sort through his words to find any subtle tricks he'd woven into his statement. Clever as she was, Kenna missed the loopholes that would be her downfall.

"Very well," she said, extending her arm, clearly expecting an elemental bargain like the ones she'd made before with Raziel and Pax.

Her eyes lit with surprise as Ash silently placed two fingers on her wrist directly over her pulse. She couldn't hide the sharp intake of breath or the way her heart fluttered under his touch. After a moment, his hand glimmered with silvery light. She squeezed the table bracing herself for pain that would not come.

Ash fixed his eyes on her knowingly. He knew *exactly* how good it felt to make an unbreakable oath. He watched her eyes flutter shut with rapturous, undiluted pleasure as a soft moan escaped her lips. It lasted mere seconds, before he removed his hand, leaving behind only the ghost of his touch. Kenna blinked away the remnants of the euphoria, her cheeks tinged with pink in the echo of pleasure and her obvious embarrassment.

Cursed as he was, Ash knew he'd enjoy every moment with her, every chance to make her cheeks flush before the curse forced him to betray her in the end. He imagined her smiling at him, hair tousled and wrapped in nothing but a sheet, and he shifted in his seat as his body began to react to the thought.

For a moment, he'd forgotten Pax was watching them.

Behind the bar, Pax's mouth was set in a tight line, and his eyes burned with anger and disapproval. He didn't know about Ash's curse, but Pax knew exactly what kind of oath Ash had just tricked Kenna into.

Ash looked away, unable to face Pax's scrutiny, even though he deserved it. He deserved so much worse than his brother's judgemental glare.

"What kind of bargain was that?" Kenna asked, her cheeks still pink.

She looked down at her wrist. The silver cuff had disappeared. In its absence, there was a faint scar. A thin white circle around two shining stars—his royal sigil, with an extra star to represent Kenna's binding oath to him.

Ash leaned back again, crossing his arms. "You never specified that you wanted to make an elemental bargain. I assure you, an unbreakable oath is much more powerful. It will be impossible for either of us to go back on our word."

Yet he began this relationship by misleading her. Technically, he hadn't lied, but Kenna had no idea what the true cost of her oath would be now that she was the target of his curse.

CHAPTER 24

"I'll always be here fer ye." Pax grabbed her hand, fastening the delicate gold bracelet which had marked Kenna's employment around her wrist, and she looked at the word engraved there. *Home.*

She couldn't feel any magic from it anymore. "Don't worry. I'll not force ye te work for me. Though if ye want to scrub the chamber pots before ye go, yer welcome te. Ye can take the bracelet off anytime ye like. Thought ye might like te keep it te remember me by. If ye ever need me, I'll find ye, lass."

"Thank you. For everything." Kenna nestled herself against Pax's brawny chest as he hugged her and kissed the top of her head.

Kenna followed Ash out the tavern into the city square, and he extended a gallant hand to her. She stared at his suspended hand. Remembering the effect his touch had a few minutes earlier, she hesitated. But if Ash was going to fly her across the Veil, she couldn't avoid touching him. She took his hand, and Ash's smile widened as his rough fingers closed around hers. The effect of his dazzling smile on his already handsome face was transcendent.

With her hand wrapped securely in his, he asked, "Ready?"

"No."

"Usually, the best adventures begin with an experience that frightens you."

"Well, then I guess I'm about to have an adventure. Because I'm terrified of heights." She looked to the sky above and gulped.

"Are you sure you trust me?"

"My whole life I've believed that all angels were villains. So, no, I'm not entirely sure I trust you," she answered.

Ash leaned down and whispered in her ear, "Good."

In one smooth motion, Ash's wings appeared and he swooped her up into his arms. Before she had time to admire the intricacies of his magnificent white, silver, and blue feathers, they were shooting up into the clear autumn sky. She was sure all of her insides had been left behind on the ground. She clenched her eyes shut, not daring to look, and clung to Ash with all her might.

His voice vibrated against her body. "You're missing the view."

"Unless you want to see what I had for breakfast, I'll keep my eyes shut."

His answer was a deep, rumbling chuckle.

After the harrowing takeoff, Kenna was sure she must be as white as the puffy clouds in the sky. She'd known angels were strong, but holding her sturdy frame seemed to require no effort at all. With each beat of his wings, she started to feel more secure.

She let her thoughts drift to Zo. To Ezra. To her father.

Worrying about losing them suddenly made her tingly all over. It was a burning sort of numbness flowing through her veins, like the feeling when she'd sat in one position too long and her foot was asleep. Except it was flowing through her, from her heart to her fingers and toes, right to the the tips of her ears.

And then Ash looked at her, his eyes wide. "Kenna…your ears. They're not…you're not."

Shit. She clamped her hands over her ears.

Ash stopped sputtering and his jaw clenched, his gaze unreadable. Kenna got the feeling Ash wasn't used to being the one who didn't have all the information. What kinds of secrets might lurk beneath his easy arrogance?

He blew out a breath, and shook his head in disbelief. "Start talking, *princess.*"

When he called her princess, the words from her father's letter rolled into her mind.

For as long as I live, no creature in the Three Realms will be able to guess who you truly are.

But Ash knew who she was. The glamor her father had purchased for her was gone, which meant...

No.

She moved her hands from her ears. She didn't care that Ash knew who she was. If her father's magic had broken, then he was dead. He was dead, and it was all her fault. If she hadn't fled from Tormund, none of this would have happened. Was the battle still going on? Maybe there was still time to help the others. She didn't know how, but she had to do *something*.

"Hurry." Kenna said.

"Not until you tell me what's going—"

"There will be time for answers later. Now, hurry the Hel up and get me to my family before anyone else dies."

"What do you mean?"

"My father is dead. Now fucking *hurry!*" She yelled it. Screamed it over and over again, pounding on his chest with her fist until her screams turned to sobs. She thought she might drown in the pain that consumed her. Like it might actually kill her.

Ash didn't ask any more questions, and he didn't seem to mind the snot and tears that left streaks on his black shirt.

Kenna barely noticed how much faster he flew or the way he held her a little tighter than he had before.

SHE'D FINALLY STOPPED SCREAMING and pounding on his chest, though he hadn't minded any of it. He'd felt the anguish of loss enough times in his life to recognize it in another. Usually Wren sat with him in silence or sparred with him until his breathing was ragged. Perhaps his presence provided Kenna some comfort.

She'd been glamoured. It was angel magic but could be turned into a potion and sold to elves. A drop of the elf's blood who purchased it was the final ingredient of the potion, but the magic only lasted as long as the elf lived. Someone she loved must have purchased the glamor to hide her true identity. It was the only explanation for the sudden change in her physical appearance and emotional state.

But who could have given her a glamor powerful enough to hide her identity from Luniva's high priestess? It must have come straight from the source of all magic.

The woman sobbing quietly in Ash's arms was the lost human princess. And as her guardian angel, Pax had to know who Kenna was.

Wren had been right a few days ago when he'd reminded Ash of the treaty. This was the year the treaty was supposed to be fulfilled, because the human princess would marry a prince of Notos or Vorra. If the treaty was fulfilled, surely Ash's curse would be lifted, too.

This changed *everything*.

For the first time in the last three hundred and twenty-nine years of his miserable existence, Ash felt a flicker of hope.

But as quickly as it had appeared, the hope was gone.

Ash might have ruined it. She was bound to him and his curse in an unbreakable oath. It was highly likely she wouldn't be able to take the Ancient marriage vows with someone else while she was tied to him.

For a moment, there was a wicked part of Ash that was glad. He hated the thought of watching her marry someone else. And not just anyone. Both princes were his enemies.

But if she married neither of them, all humanity might be doomed forever. And he would still be cursed.

There would be no winners in this twisted game they were playing.

He'd known her less than a day, and she'd already proved to be shrewd and resilient. She'd kept an earth-shattering secret from him, just as he'd hidden his true motives from her.

She was a worthy match if he'd ever met one, and the feel of her soft body nestled against his…

Damn.

If he allowed himself, he could easily get used to holding her.

How long had it been since he'd let himself provide another with care and comfort? What would it be like to be with a woman without the gnawing guilt of dawning betrayal? The last time he'd been in a relationship with someone he truly cherished, even above himself, was three hundred and twenty-nine years ago with Elenya.

But he couldn't think of Kenna that way. He had to find a way to help her marry a prince. If he could, he might finally find a way to redeem himself. Maybe he could let go of his hopeless bitterness. Maybe he wouldn't have to play this cursed game any more.

He'd had enough of the lies and the betrayal. How would it feel to earn her friendship and trust without the curse lurking beneath the surface, waiting to leave him riddled with shame?

Ash pumped his wings as fast as he could. Whatever waited for them in Mesterra, it was time to prove he was an honorable, trustworthy man. He could prove it by teaching her to be strong, to take care of herself and the people she cared about.

Though she still sobbed in his arms, Ash nearly laughed with the sheer hope of it all. If he could be rid of his curse, he might be able to feel something *real*. He might be able to set Kenna free so she could have the life she deserved.

And in the process, he'd help her learn to fight. He could make amends for his part in destroying humanity in the war all those years ago. But first, he needed to speak to the prince.

CHAPTER 25

Kenna's eyes were swollen, but her tears had stopped. Thankfully, Ash and Kenna were cocooned in mist, and she hadn't seen the horror that awaited them in her home city.

But Ash could hear everything. Straining his ears, he heard the groans and rattling breaths of people near death. He recognized Kenna's brother's voice from the Fostone. He was shouting orders at people who were crying softly.

The rebels knew they were defeated.

Ash steeled himself, slipping into part of himself he hadn't needed for centuries. With a general's authority, he gave his order: "We are nearly in Tormund. I can hear the battle, and you need to be ready,"

Her eyes widened. "The battle isn't lost?"

"Not yet. Do you have any training? Anything you might use to fight?"

She shook her head.

"Then, you hide. You can't help anyone if you are dead. Do you understand?"

"I understand."

"Kenna, don't tell anyone else who you are. Is it okay if I replace your glamor?" When she nodded, Ash tucked a strand of hair behind her ear, replacing the glamor she'd lost. "Not even the Ancients can see through this magic." At least he hoped they couldn't.

She nodded again, and he could have sworn she leaned into his touch. Just a little.

"Are you ready?"

"Do I have a choice?"

He didn't answer.

They emerged from the mist into a beautiful sunset over Lake Audral and the Lithari Mountains. As the glowing sun descended behind the mountain peaks, the speed of the advancing darkness was unnatural—wrong. Ash circled above the lake, assessing.

The Elders stood on the far side of the lake, wings unfurled. They were four of the angels sent across the Veil to infiltrate Mesterra's leadership. But now, they'd dropped all pretence of being elves. As they cast the lake into shadows, dark tendrils of mist rose from the deep water in spiraling columns; like smoke from the wicks of malevolent candles hidden beneath the lake's surface. The long shadowy coils crisscrossed and billowed into a wall of darkness which stalked toward Tormund as the sunlight faded.

Multiple bodies littered the lake's shore, but there were still a few brave, foolish souls standing with their feeble weapons and elemental shields.

"They said the battle would be won by nightfall. They're going to kill them all," Kenna said, her voice a whisper of the truth.

"Not if I can help it." Ash increased his flight speed, and they plummeted downward before he slowed and set Kenna on the shore. A man and two women dashed toward them.

"Sera, Aryn, Jona!" Kenna half-sobbed, running toward them. She recognized the names of her brother and the friends she'd spoken to on her Fostone.

"There will be time for a happy reunion later." At least, Ash hoped there would be. He looked at Kenna's loved ones. "She stays hidden. Do you understand? They must not take her."

Kenna's brother gave Ash a look full of both knowledge and suspicion before turning to Kenna and placing a hand on her back. "Come with me, little sister."

Kenna looked back at Ash.

"Hide. Now."

Rolling in with swift determination from the far side of the lake, the sinister fog gathered icy arrow heads, preparing to attack. The wind howled and white peaked waves crashed, stirred to life by the predatory darkness.

With a simple thought, Ash set fire to a line of bushes nearby. "Use the flame!" He shouted over the roaring wind to the gathered elvish forces.

One of the females who'd been with Kenna's brother was already in motion, summoning spheres of flame to hover over her palms as she challenged the darkness.

Ash pushed off the lake's shore, leaving a shower of stones in his wake and flew into the heart of the approaching night.

~

FROM HER HIDING place in a thicket of bushes by the lake, Kenna tried to draw on her useless training. Tried to summon a shield. A weapon. Anything.

The nightmare advanced, and her terror transported her back to last night in the alley. Helpless. Trapped.

Her breath came in panting gasps, and her heart pounded against her ribcage. Her ears filled with the howling wind; her vision swirled with blinding spots. Sera, Jona and all the rebel elves were a flurry of activity.

Hide. She just needed to hide. That was good, because Kenna's arms and legs refused to move. She stared while Sera and the others fought, watching everything. Nothing she'd learned helped whatever evil fate seemed bent on destroying everyone she loved.

They're all going to die.

A shower of stones erupted as Ash landed on the shore, summoning her back to reality. He was helping them. Fighting alongside them.

"Flame elves, move to the front of the line. Create a shield for yourself if you are able. Everyone else, weapons raised behind them." Ash's voice sounded far away as he shouted orders over the din of angry wind.

"Kenna," her brother whispered from just outside her hiding place. When she didn't respond, his voice was firm but quiet. "Kenna!"

"I—what should I do?" She stammered.

"Be ready to use Flame magic. As much as you can. Try to cover yourself. If we lose...you must get out of here. I almost told you the truth so many times. I'm sorry I lied. I thought it was the right thing to do."

She nodded, but there was no time to respond as he ran back into the fray. Kenna tried to remember any part of her magical education that might help. The best she might manage was a thin flaming rope.

By the edge of the lake, Sera had her hands raised, stoking the flames into an inferno. Aryn was further back, holding a small dome-shaped shield of vibrating stones out in front of her. She must have better instincts for this than Kenna.

Sera spun, her arms outstretched, reminding Kenna of the way they used to spin around in the rainbow grass of Iris Meadow when they were children. They'd spin and spin and spin until they made themselves so dizzy they'd fall down in heaps of laughter.

The raging Sera looked nothing like the child she used to be. Her vicious twirling goaded the fire into a flaming tidal wave, and Sera was the master of a fiery lake. Seeing Sera like that...

Did Kenna really know her at all?

With one hand, Jona used his Aqua magic to form a shield of water to contain the fire, stopping it from burning everything on the shore, and with his other hand he poured more fire into Sera's weapon. The spiraling orange heat pushed the darkness back.

Sera and Jona seemed unified by their need to fight. To protect.

The black mist was closer, only feet from everyone she loved. But before it could reach the shore, Jona and Sera shared a look.

The flames vanished with a *whoosh*, and the air around them was suddenly at rest. For a single moment, the lake was still—glassy and dark, before...

"Everyone, down! Cover your ears!" Jona yelled.

BOOM!

The entire lake erupted into flame. The lake's water was now a billowing cloud of white steam smothering the dark mist.

Everything fell quiet as Kenna stared at the now empty lake, but by the time the smoke cleared, and the angels were gone.

When the wind died, Kenna's courageous, fiery friend smirked and said, "Good riddance!" Then, Sera collapsed, spurring Kenna to action.

"Sera!" She scrambled to stand up from her position on the ground. Her legs burned as she sprinted to Sera. Aryn was right behind her, and both of them skidded to their knees on the pebbled shore next to Sera's fallen body.

"Sera! Wake up!" Kenna demanded. She refused to lose anyone else.

Aryn placed an ear over Sera's mouth, listening. "She's breathing." Then, Aryn took Sera's limp wrist in her hand and worry creased her brows. "Her pulse is weak, and her hand is freezing."

Kenna closed her eyes, accepting the fleeting relief. At least Sera was alive. Ash approached the women before he lowered himself down next to them. Silently, he closed his eyes and held his palm out, hovering it over Sera's heart.

After a moment, he said, "Her Vessel is severely damaged. She used far too much power. You must find a magical healer. And soon. If not, she may never wake."

This was like the time in the meadow three years ago. Sera had been showing off and lost control of her magic, but Holt had arrived in time to help her. This was so much worse.

"How can you feel her Vessel? Are *you* a Healer?" Aryn asked suspiciously.

"I do have healing powers, but they are limited. If I heal her now, I will not be able to heal anyone else until after Winter Solstice."

"Do it," Kenna said.

Jona interrupted, "Kenna, are you sure? What if anyone else is—"

"Heal her," Kenna demanded. "Now."

Ash nodded. He closed his eyes and hovered his hands over Sera's heart. Light like pure silver moonlight flowed into her chest. For a few seconds, everything was still, and then Sera sat up suddenly with a gasp, and Kenna slumped in relief.

Sera seemed perfectly healthy and calm after a few initial seconds of confusion, and Kenna finally made introductions.

"Sera, Aryn, Jona, meet Ash."

"It's a pleasure to meet you." Ash gave them all a smile. Somehow, he was even more handsome streaked black with grime in the aftermath of the battle.

"Oh, I assure you. The pleasure is mine," Sera's hungry eyes took in every inch of Ash, and something in Kenna ground her teeth.

An uncharacteristic blush crept into Sera's cheeks when Ash turned away. Aryn had just finished vomiting in the grass nearby and he asked, "Are you quite well, Aryn?"

"Do I look *quite well?*" Aryn glared.

"What ails you?" Ash probed.

"What *ails* me is that we all almost died. Meanwhile, if I want my fiancé to be able to touch me without any risk of bringing a baby into this Ancients forsaken world, I have to take a tonic that makes me constantly hurl up my guts."

"Ah, yes. I have known a few females in my time who have been similarly affected by the tonic."

Aryn's eyes narrowed in Ash's direction. "I'm sure you've affected plenty of females."

Ash reached into his pocket and procured a tiny vial of what looked like the same pink sludge Pax had given Kenna for her hangover.

"That stuff tastes terrible," Kenna groaned. " But it is a miracle cure for nausea."

Aryn, obviously desperate, snatched the vial out of Ash's hand and gulped it down. She immediately clapped a hand over her mouth, looking as though she was going to vomit again. Her stubbornness came in handy, helping her to keep the solution in her stomach.

Jona was at her side. Her brother folded his arms and thrust his chest out as he faced Ash. "Thank you for your help. Now, who are you and why do you have my sister?"

"Jona, meet King Ashton Moonbriar. He brought me home to see you all before he takes me to train with him until Winter Solstice."

"Like Hel you are," Jona said. "Your Majesty," he added, seeming to realize it might be unwise to address an angel king with such disrespect. Jona turned to Kenna. "The Elders are gone now; there's no reason for you to leave. We need to go and find father and the others."

He doesn't know.

In the whirlwind of action, she'd almost forgotten about their father. "Jona...Father's...he's gone."

"What? No, He was leading the forces outside the temple."

"He didn't make it, Jona," Kenna said, tears welling up in her eyes.

"But how would you—" Kenna saw Jona's expression change as he pieced it together. He knew who she was and how her father had hidden her identity. Jona knew that Kenna's glamor would fade in the event of their father's death since it was linked to his magic.

"Shit," he whispered, sitting on the ground. He looked down and everyone looked away, giving him a minute alone with the truth. No one else questioned how she knew about her father's death. Kenna didn't feel like she had any more energy to sort through her emotions. They all sat in silence, exhausted from the fight.

Kenna pointed to the white cloud overhead, which was now yielding droplets of water, refilling the lake bit by bit.

"Impressive," she said to her brother.

"I've been developing the eriksomb since I left Dendron three years ago. I got the idea from my work with the geolift and the fostone. I figured if I could blend the elements with inanimate objects for convenience, why not use that same principal to develop weapons to use against the angels?"

Though Ash's wings were invisible again, Kenna was suddenly very aware of his presence among them. Jona seemed to remember who Ash was as well, because he turned to him and said, "I swear to you, if anything happens to her I…"

"I have no love for the High Council or what they've done to your people. You have my word that I will do everything in my power to keep her safe," Ash replied.

"If we had more time, I'd insist on a full inquiry into your motives. Thankfully, I trust my sister's judgement. But don't think for a second that I trust you."

A muscle in Ash's cheek twitched, like he was fighting back the urge to laugh in her brother's face. "Your concern is admirable."

Jona was a reckless fool for posturing himself against an angel—a *king*—in her defense, and Kenna loved him for it.

Sera hadn't said a word or stopped drooling since she'd woken up and introduced herself to Ash after the battle. Kenna hadn't ever seen her fiery friend speechless in the presence of a man before. The novelty of seeing Sera stunned to silence made Kenna smirk. Aryn had observed the exchange, watchful and judging. Her cheeks were a much healthier shade of pink, but she kept her mouth shut.

The wind seemed to pick up, nudging her toward her family's home. *Hurry, Hurry, Hurry.*

Kenna rubbed her ears with sudden clarity. "Jona. Where is Mother?"

CHAPTER 26

When they climbed the steps into Tormund, everything was destroyed. Smoking ash and debris littered Main Street, and large piles of rubble rested where there had been welcoming shops before.

A group of exhausted-looking elves were assembled on the grass behind the ruins of the City Hall. Many of the folk were covered in soot and bloody cuts. By the light of lanterns, some of them set up tents, presumably to provide medical care or to shelter those who remained.

It was so much worse than Kenna could have imagined. Her eyes stung both from the lingering smoke in the air and the reminder that her father would not be there with open arms when she reached her childhood home. Was her mother okay?

When Kenna had left Tormund, the potential to be reunited with her family had felt distant. However, some part of her had held onto the hope she'd see them again. As far as her father was concerned, that hope was gone.

Eventually, they reached her parents' home. Half of the house was reduced to a pile of rubble, the other half only somewhat recognizable.

"I'll make a pass overhead, assess the damage."

"Won't people feel threatened if they see an angel flying above the city? Won't they try to attack you?"

"It's adorable that you're worried about me, love." He winked at

Kenna and she folded her arms. "I'll stay as high as possible, and I'll shield myself. I'll be back soon."

As quickly as they could, Kenna and her other companions picked their way through the ruins to what was once the foyer. A gaping hole existed where there used to be walls with no sign of the front door.

A glistening carpet of glass crunched underfoot as they made their way across the ruined foyer toward the sitting room, and Kenna barely registered the pain as a glass shard pierced the sole of her leather boot, pricking her foot. The door leading to the sitting room hung askew, and puddles of ashen water and discarded stones scattered over the floor.

"We'll wait here," Sera said.

Kenna stopped, squeezing Jona's hand.

"Can you go first? I don't think...what if she's in there. What if she's—"

Before either of them could move, Drake emerged through the wonky door. His gaze darted to Kenna before quickly looking away again. He motioned behind him. "Your mother's injured. Aryn's father is tending to her wounds. It's not good, but he said she's stable. She's sleeping."

Ordinarily, Drake looked impeccable, but Kenna mourned his disheveled state. His eyes were puffy with dark purple crescents underneath, and his usually smooth jaw was covered in stubble and a purple bruise was blooming there. Something in him had cracked.

His heart, Kenna thought.

Drake kept his eyes downcast as he tried to walk past her, but she grabbed his arm to stop him. She wrapped her arms around his neck, and he returned her hug as he released a shuddering sigh. There would be time for words later, but she poured everything she couldn't say into their embrace. The apology for pushing him away in Notos. The shared anguish over Ezra's betrayal. The unbearable knowledge that he and Zo were imprisoned...or worse.

There was no time for grudges. Kenna needed Drake to know that she held none against him. Or Ezra.

"I'm sorry," she whispered.

His eyes were shining when they drew apart. "Kenna, I didn't know—"

She held up a hand to stop him, but gave his shoulder a knowing squeeze. "Later."

"Right." He rubbed the back of his neck. "I'll see you later."

Kenna nodded and refocused her attention on reaching her mother. When she opened the sitting room door, her breath caught. Her mother lay on the sofa, completely still apart from her rapidly rising and falling chest.

Jona had taken the emergency in stride and was speaking in hushed tones with Aryn's father. Formulating a plan.

Kenna rushed to her mother's side, kneeling beside the sofa. The tears in her eyes spilled down her cheeks in a torrent. She couldn't bear another ounce of tragedy. Mother opened her eyes, turning to look at her.

"Kenna." Her mother placed a cold hand on Kenna's cheek and struggled to form words between labored breaths. "It's so good to see you. How are you?"

Laughter barked out of Kenna in spite of her freely flowing tears. "Mother, only you would ask how I am doing while in your current predicament."

One of her mother's eyes was swollen shut, and she was covered in bloody cuts. A binding made from a pink floral bed sheet was wrapped tightly around her abdomen. The makeshift bandage was soaked with crimson.

Kenna wiped her face, scrambling for some sarcastic remark to cut through the pain. All she could manage was a shaky grin and a question: "So did you miss your favorite daughter?"

"I wish you wouldn't do that."

"Do what?"

"Make light of your feelings. Try to push them away. Unless you truly feel both joy and sorrow, life is meaningless." Her mother's breathing was too shallow. "If I hadn't loved your father so deeply, I wouldn't feel the loss of my mate so profoundly now. But our love was worth is. You must not hold your feelings captive."

Her mother was right, but she couldn't loosen the chains on her emotions; the chains were barely holding her together in the aftermath of learning about her father's death.

"Do you know how proud I am of you?" her mother asked.

"Why?" she asked quietly.

Her parents had always been generous with their praise, but Kenna had never had the courage to ask them what they saw in her. Perhaps she was afraid their words were empty and they wouldn't be able to give her an answer. Perhaps there was nothing to be proud of at all.

Now that Kenna knew the secret of her past, she wondered if their pride was for some idealistic version of her who would fulfill her impossible purpose and restore the human race.

"I don't need a reason to love my daughter," her mother answered, as though it was the simplest thing in the world. "How could anyone not love you when you have this?" She placed a hand directly over Kenna's heart.

"But I'm not…I haven't done anything other than run and hide. There's so much happening, and I don't know how to help. I'm trying to learn, but how can one person make a difference against all of this?"

"You are more special than you know. And not just because of where you came from."

"I'm not—"

"For once in your life can you not argue with me?" Her mother started to laugh, but winced in pain.

Kenna's face twisted into a half-flinch half-smile as she remembered all of the ridiculous, raging fights she'd instigated with her mother in her teenage years. "Sorry."

"No matter where you come from or where you find yourself, there is always, *always* a way out of the darkness."

Her mother withdrew her limp arm and folded it across her chest, her eyes fluttering shut. Even their short conversation had been too much.

"You should rest." Kenna kissed her forehead. Though her mother's hands were like ice, her forehead was burning hot. She rested her head on the sofa, listening to her mother's strained breathing.

Her father was already gone. Silently, she begged the Ancients not to take her mother, too. As if they'd heard her prayer, Ash and the others walked in. The king must have finished his flight over the city, and Kenna's heart lifted for a moment as she remembered Ash's healing power. Half a second later, her heart plummeted.

Ash had told her he wouldn't be able to use that power again until after Winter Solstice. He couldn't heal Kenna's mother.

CHAPTER 27

"She needs a healer," Ash stated as he crouched down beside Kenna, looking at her mother.

"There's a rebel camp hidden in a forest valley in the Lithari Mountains," Jona replied. "It's a refuge for those who've managed to escape throughout Mesterra. Some people haven't been able to cross the Veil or were unwilling to accept the ferry master's terms. It's also where the rebellion is based. There's a healer who often visits—Thorne. Do you think he might be able to help?"

The king's nostrils flared. "I know him. If we can get your mother to him, he'll be able to save her."

As soon as Kenna wondered if he was telling the truth, there was a pleasant, warmth on the scar on her wrist. She closed her eyes and focused. She was able to visualize a silvery strand of truth connecting her to Ash. When she opened her eyes, she could still feel it. True to their oath, Ash had given her a way to test his honesty.

Well, that will probably be useful.

"I've heard nothing of a healer in the mountains. Though, there are whispers of other...creatures," Aryn said. Tormund had apothecaries for medicinal herbs, midwives for births, and physicians for other ailments, but the gift of magical healing was unheard of. "Why haven't I heard of this camp in the mountains?"

"You only joined the rebellion after Kenna left and the first battle had already started," Sera responded. " Forgive us if we've not had time to fill you in on every detail. You're the one who chose to spend the last three years with your head in the sand."

Aryn's expression was a mix of anger and shame, but Kenna had no patience for her friends' arguing and she looked to her brother. "You must take Mother to the healer. Now."

"The journey is treacherous, and the climb takes almost two days. That's without carrying an injured person." Jona didn't say what they were all thinking. Her mother would never survive the journey.

"If you tell me where the camp is, I will take her," Ash said.

"Of course!" Kenna stood. She began pacing, each stride full of hope. "You can fly her to the camp. How long will it take?"

"If it's two days on foot, it will probably take a few hours there and a few hours back."

Jona looked uneasy with the idea. "Ash, can I please have a minute with my sister and our friends in private?" Ash dipped his chin in acquiescence and left Kenna, Jona, Aryn, and Sera to discuss their plans.

Jona's voice was low but firm when he said, "We can't just let him fly off with her alone, Kenna."

Aryn agreed with him. "For once in your life would you just control your impulses long enough to stop and think? We know nothing about Ash."

Kenna threw up her hands. "What choice do we have? He helped us in the battle. Plus, we made an unbreakable oath. I don't know how to explain it, but I can feel that he's telling the truth. Look."

Kenna held up her wrist, allowing her brother, Sera, and Aryn to examine her intricate scar.

"You really think just because you have some magic scar that we should believe him? How do you know that he can't make you feel anything he wants through that so-called oath you made with him?" Aryn demanded.

Kenna hated to admit that she hadn't considered that. Making a life altering oath with Ash had been incredibly rash, but it had the desired outcome. He'd brought her safely to Tormund. Had helped turn the tide of the battle against the Elders.

Before that, he'd also rescued her in Braktyn. He hadn't given her a reason not to trust him, other than being an angel. Of course, he also had an insufferably arrogant swagger which told her he was used to getting exactly what he wanted. Still, feeling the thread of truth between them reassured her in a way she couldn't fully explain or understand.

"What else can we do?" Kenna asked her brother. After all, his was the only opinion that really mattered.

Jona stood silent, his thick brows furrowed over his light brown eyes as he thought. "Kenna's impulses aside, none of us are safe anymore. We've started a war, and we're going to have to take some risks. We're sending Mother with Ash."

"What?! You can't actually—" Aryn protested.

"This has nothing to do with us, Aryn," Sera warned. "She's *their* mother."

Aryn's face was so red, Kenna thought the opinions might explode out of her. Just then, Aryn's fiancé, Daniel, burs through the door. He checked her over for injuries and covered her with kisses. The way he cared for her so tenderly was both nauseating and beautiful.

Aryn quickly filled her fiancé in on the entire situation, using lots of angry hand gestures and Daniel whispered to her quietly, placing a steadying hand on her back.

Aryn took a deep breath, turning to them. "I'm sorry. You and Jona have to do what you think is right."

"*Another* apology?" Kenna raised a brow at her friend. "Who are you and what have you done with Aryn."

Aryn's lips twitched into a small smile. "Don't get used to it."

"I agree with Aryn on one account," Jona admitted. "Ash isn't flying Mother into the mountains alone." He raised his voice then and called for the angel king.

"You summoned me, sir?" When Ash entered the room, his presence commanded their attention, even without a crown or visible wings. His playful bow and easy smile did nothing to hide the fact that he was the angel ruler of Notos.

Jona cleared his throat, seeming to remember that he was addressing royalty. "How many of us can you carry at once?"

Kenna's brother had the look that told her his brilliant mind had been concocting a clever solution to a problem.

"Logistically? One."

"What about in terms of strength? I could make a vest for you to wear with multiple harnesses attached to it, so that you could carry more than one."

"I could carry all of you for a short distance, if the situation demanded it. In this instance, I could carry two of you easily enough. How long do you need to fashion the device?"

"I could have it ready in an hour, but I don't want to leave before…" Jona's voice broke with emotion. "We need to make arrangements for the fallen."

"When will you have the funeral?" Ash asked.

Jona looked around at the others. "Tomorrow at sunrise?"

The others nodded their agreement. That would give them enough time to spread the word and assess who else had been lost in the fray.

"I'll go with Ash and your mother tonight," Sera offered. "We have to get her there as soon as possible. I don't need to be here for the funeral, but Kenna needs to be able to say goodbye to her father."

Sera knew the pain of losing loved ones too well, considering her parents had died in a shipwreck nearly four years ago.

Ash spoke, his voice smooth and soothing as he placed a gentle hand on Kenna's lower back. "I can take them to the mountains tonight. Jona, I'll come back for you in the morning before Kenna and I return to Notos."

"Couldn't we just bring them all across the Veil with us?" Kenna asked. "Surely you have gifted healers working for you. You're the king."

Ash shook his head, looking apologetic. " The normal laws of nature and magic don't apply within the Veil. Time and space move differently, and any magical or physical exertion requires exponentially more effort than it does within the Three Realms. Bringing you here was costly. I'll need time to rest."

"What about the crossing? You said you knew all the details of the bargains. Couldn't you just take everyone to a port. They could come with us if you are the one who controls the crossing."

Again, Ash shook his head. "I only know what bargains Raziel makes to allow people safe passage. The Veil belongs to him. No other angels know the locations. Plus, elves can usually only make the crossings on Solstice and Equinox days. As King, I can leverage my position, but there are limits to the favors Raziel will grant me."

Jona placed a hand on her shoulder. "I need to stay here anyway. The rebels need me to show them how to make more weapons if we have any hope of defeating the Council and winning this war."

"Have you forgotten about Zo?" Sera put in. "We have to find her and Ezra. We can't just abandon them if they're still alive. We need to find a way to get them home."

Shame washed over Kenna. In the grief of losing her father and the possibility of losing her mother, she'd completely forgotten about their captured friends. She told Sera and Aryn what she'd heard over the Fostone when Ilan took Zo the night before, hating to be the one to deliver the news.

Her fiery friend had been in love with Holt, and Kenna had watched Sera's heart fracture when the Shadow had taken him three years ago. She watched Sera's heart break again when she shared the short exchange she'd heard on the Fostone.

Jona shook his head in disbelief. Holt had once been one of Jona's best friends and an ally to the resistance. To know of his betrayal, his bitterness now…

"It doesn't make any sense," Jona said.

Kenna nodded. "I don't understand either, but I know what I heard. He said he'd 'seen the light.' I'm sorry."

"I'll find the bastard and kill him," Sera snarled. "Kill him for disappearing and kill him for hurting Zo. *No one* hurts my friends and gets away with it."

"Maybe there's more to the story," Jona suggested.

There was a moment of silence. It was a different type of grief, the loss of finding out their old friend might no longer be a friend at all.

Aryn broke the silence after a few minutes. "What about the rest of the injured? Surely, Heidi Duras isn't the only one in this position after the battle."

Kenna had *almost* forgotten Ezra and Zo in light of her mother's injury, but she'd definitely forgotten the other injured people in Tormund.

"There isn't enough time to take everyone," Ash said. "Spread word throughout the city about funeral arrangements. Meanwhile, you can find out how many more injured require aid. I will make two trips to the camp, but I can't do any more than that. I have duties in my own realm. I can't be away from Notos for more than one night."

Aryn, Sera, and Daniel all nodded. It was a good plan, but Kenna refused to leave her mother's side. Jona looked like he was having similar thoughts. Ash seemed to sway slightly on his feet. "Now, if you'll excuse me. I need to sleep. Wake me in an hour or two."

CHAPTER 28

While Ash rested and the rest of their friends went out to spread the word about the funeral, Jona made three harnesses, despite the current agreement that Ash only take two into the mountains. After that, her brother came to sit beside her on the floor, leaning back on the couch.

"So, you're a human princess. How are you feeling about that?" Jona asked.

Kenna's laugh was dark. "I'll tell you once I've had time to process it."

"Father only told me when I returned to Tormund after my time in Dendron. I was already working with the rebellion, but he didn't trust me with the information when I was so close to the High Council. You saw how they deal with rebels."

Kenna shuddered at the memory, exhausted, and Jona reached out and took her hand.

"Right now, I'm still angry more than anything. You all decided what was best for me, and you lied. I don't know how to feel about it. But now father is… How can I be angry with him when he sacrificed his life fighting our oppressors? Does that make me a terrible person?"

Her brother's eyes softened. "I think everyone will understand if you need some time to sort through your feelings. When I was in Dendron, I had friends who were slaves there. If I learned anything from them, it's that recovering from trauma isn't a linear process."

"But that's just it. I'm not a slave. I had an entire group of people fighting for my freedom, hoping to protect me. Do I deserve to be angry about that? It feels incredibly selfish. Plus, you lost father too. Our mother is barely clinging to life."

"Everyone has their own struggles, but that doesn't minimize what you're dealing with. Kenna, think about everything you've been through. After the Emergence, you left everyone and everything you'd ever known. You had no time to prepare. Then, you discovered you were adopted. And human. You didn't even think humans still existed. One of your friends betrayed us, and your best friend was captured. All of that happened within thirty six hours. It's going to take time to deal with it, and you need to give yourself grace to do that."

"I feel like such a fool. I knew something was going on, but I was too much of a coward to confront any of you. I just let that distance between us grow, hoping whatever was happening would just disappear if I ignored it."

Neither Kenna nor her brother spoke for long minutes, and when she looked at Jona again, his eyes were closed and his breathing was slow and steady as he slept.

Sometime in the night, Kenna woke up to her mother placing a limp hand on her head. "I love you, my girl. No matter what. Remember that."

"I love you, too."

Jona blinked and rubbed his eyes, turning to look at their mother. "I love you, Jona," their mother whispered. "Take care of her."

Hope sparked in Kenna at the sound of her mother's voice but deserted her a moment later. Their mother was saying goodbye. Their mother's eyes fluttered closed, her breath harsh and rasping.

"Go get Ash and Sera," she told her brother. "They need to take her to the mountains. Now."

He nodded his agreement and stood. She turned then, placing a hand on her mother's fevered brow. She was the only mother Kenna had ever known, and she couldn't lose her. It didn't matter that she wasn't her biological mother. This woman on the brink of death had loved her. She'd held her and comforted her. She'd fought for her and kept her safe.

Kenna stroked her mother's hair, the gentle caress reminding her of how Mother used to soothe her when she'd had nightmares. Her mother's words given during those nights danced through her memory. Kenna hadn't understood the truth of the words at the time. She hadn't known the Ancients were alive or how she'd ended up in her mother's arms.

Kenna cried, whispering the words from her childhood over her mother like a prayer: "The Ancients gave you to me, and the Ancients will keep you safe. Nightmares are not real; you need not be afraid. Sleep, now, dear one."

~

"I'LL RETURN in about six hours," Ash said as he gently lifted Kenna's mother's broken body from the sofa.

As Jona fastened the vest to Ash's chest, his wings were visible so Jona could see where to secure the straps of the contraption. Thankfully, Ash had agreed to carrying three people at once, just as Jona had hoped.

Ash's wings were marvelous. They swooped up from his back into a curved peak above his shoulders, and layers of feathers were arranged in a symmetric pattern—short quills near his shoulder with plumage growing longer and thicker near the outer edges. The feathers at the top of his wings were deep navy fading into rounded tips of bright white where at the bottom of his wings near his ankles. A hint of silver sparkled on the underside of the feathers with every shift of his body.

Kenna could practically see the thoughts churning behind Jona's eyes, begging Ash for answers. Before Jona could ask any of his burning questions, he accidentally brushed one of Ash's wings. In an instant, the king's easy demeanour shifted into preternatural stillness. After that, Jona seemed to be very careful not to touch Ash's feathers.

Aryn and Daniel arrived back at her parents' house with their packs.

"All done," Jona said, hands shaking slightly. Kenna couldn't blame him for being wary, having witnessed how much strength and power Ash wielded in the battle.

"Is anyone else coming?" Kenna asked.

"No one else will send their injured friends or family," Aryn said. She darted a glance toward Ash. "They all said they'd rather take their chances than trust an angel."

Of course, no one would trust an angel they'd never met.

"Daniel and I are going first," Aryn continued. "We'll take your mother. Sera's leading some others through the mountains on foot. They've already left."

Sera didn't come to say goodbye, avoiding the emotional exchange. Kenna couldn't blame her. She'd had quite enough of her own emotions, though it would have been nice to hug her friend. Just in case.

"Ash can come back for Jona and take him to the camp after the funeral."

Kenna nodded and helped her brother secure their unconscious mother to one of the harnesses. Aryn and Daniel strapped themselves in on either side of her.

With everyone strapped in, Jona double checked their harnesses and nodded to Ash. "Should be secure."

"Should be?" Aryn raised her eyebrows.

"It is secure," Jona said. Then, behind Aryn's back, "I think."

Kenna noticed Ash mouth twitch as he fought a smile. He'd heard Jona's near-silent whisper from nearly four feet away, which made Kenna wonder how much better his hearing was than hers.

"Please…" the words caught in her throat as she approached Ash.

"I won't let them fall."

Kenna looked down, trying to hide the tears that threatened. Ash placed a gentle finger under her chin, lifting her face to meet his gaze. "I will get them to the camp safely," he said, and Kenna felt that warm thread of truth between them.

There was also a hint of warmth blooming in her chest, gratitude for the man who would carry her loved ones to the rebel camp.

She squeezed Aryn's hand. "Don't let Sera get in too much trouble. Take care of yourself."

"Be careful, Kenna," her friend whispered. "Stay safe."

Kenna turned to Aryn's fiancé. "If anything happens to her, I'll never forgive you."

"I'll do anything and everything to protect Aryn," Daniel promised. "Plus, she's far too stubborn to be killed."

"Go," Kenna ordered, before she could change her mind. And, just like that, Ash flew into the night.

CHAPTER 29

They'd been flying for just over three hours when the glowing firelight of the rebel camp came into view. And not a moment too soon.

Ash was powerful but his energy was still depleted from crossing the Veil into this realm, and his strength had dwindled with each beat of his wings as he'd carried the three elves here from Tormund.

The camp was surrounded by some makeshift walls and watchtowers, and with Ash's keen eyesight, he saw two patrols in the glowing light of a torch nocking arrows and pointing them in his direction.

Ash manipulated the air around himself and the elves he carried, forming a shield as he continued flying toward the camp. The arrows were nothing more than an annoyance, like flies buzzing around his head, as they bounced off his shield and fell into the tall evergreen trees of the forest below.

"Don't shoot! We're friends! Stop!" Aryn shouted.

When they were directly above the camp, Ash circled overhead looking for a place to land. Hundreds of small canvas tents were arranged in rows forming a large square. Camp fires were dotted throughout, but most were only glowing embers since it was the middle of the night.

In the center of the makeshift village, there were a few larger tents, presumably for the rebel leaders. There were multiple cookfires with large cauldrons hanging from wooden frames and barrels full of apples and other produce nearby them. From the looks of things, they'd been building up supplies for years in preparation for the war they'd just started.

There was a grassy clearing surrounded by a fence where wooden swords and shields leaned haphazardly—some sort of training ring. It was as good a place to land as any, and Ash lowered Aryn, Daniel, and Kenna's mother gently until they were on the ground before landing behind them.

A few rebels were running toward them brandishing elemental weapons, swords, and shields.

"Put your weapons down," Ash said. He kept the domed shield in place, fighting to keep his tone pleasant despite his fatigue and exasperation. They had no idea who he was or just how useless their weapons would be. "We've just come from Tormund. The battle was a success, but this woman was wounded. She needs help, and we heard there is a healer who often visits your camp."

As Ash spoke, Aryn and Daniel unhooked their harnesses and Kenna's mother's, laying her on the grass. The rebels exchanged looks and finally one of them, presumably their commander, nodded. They lowered their weapons and their magical defenses.

"Unfortunately," the commander said. "Thorne isn't here."

The commander was wrong. As if he'd been anticipating their arrival, the healer stepped out of the shadows and said, "Hello, Ash."

"Thorne." Ash recognized the angel instantly.

The healer addressed the commander, "I've just returned from the battle on the eastern border of Rolios. We won. Since the rebels took Tormund, Rolios is officially a rebel territory."

A cheer went up from the small group of soldiers while Hawthorne and Ash eyed each other warily.

Both angels were over six feet tall and covered in grime from their recent battles, but the similarities in their appearance ended there. If Ash's appearance reflected snow and ice, Hawthorne's bronze skin, dark brown hair, and mossy green eyes reflected the warmth of the fires and the evergreen of the forest trees. His wavy hair was longer than Ash remembered and tied back by a leather cord. His beard was thicker, and his muscles seemed more solid.

Hawthorne stalked forward, suspicious and observant. Once upon a time, they'd loved each other. They were brothers, after all. But the last time they'd seen each other, they'd been enemies on a battlefield over three centuries ago.

Before they could address their long and painful history, they needed to tend to Kenna's mother.

"This is…"

"I know who this is. Jona, Quinn, and Heidi Duras have been working with us for years." Hawthorne bent to lift the woman and cradled Kenna's mother in his arms. He marched off with her toward one of the tents.

Ash, Aryn, and Daniel followed, observing in silence as the healer laid Heidi on a table. He unbound the wicked slice across her abdomen. Holding his hands over the wound, he spoke quiet words over her in the ancient language. The wound stitched together until only unmarred skin remained.

Hawthorne continued muttering for long minutes, until he finally went silent. "She needs to rest. In a day or two, she will wake and her health will be restored."

Aryn and her fiancé looked at each other. Aryn seemed to sense the rising tension between Ash and Hawthorne and said, "I think we'll leave you two to catch up."

"Of course," the healer said. "Go to the largest tent. One of the commanders will give you supplies and show you where to make camp."

"Thank you," Aryn said, before she and Daniel ducked out of the tent.

Once Kenna's friends were gone, Ash asked, "How long have you been working with the rebels?"

"Three years," Hawthorne said. "I've been gathering forces and allies since then. Slowly, I've gained some of their trust."

"To what end? What is it you hope to achieve?"

"Freedom for the people of Mesterra. If Luniva's priestess hadn't created the Emergence serum…if the angels hadn't infiltrated this land and corrupted the elve's memories of what truly happened in the war, then we wouldn't be in this mess."

The treaty stipulated that only one angel enter Mesterra from Notos each year, but the Emergence serum masked their blood enough for five of them to enter Mesterra every year. With each passing year since the end of the war, Luniva's sway in Mesterra had grown. More and more angels had arrived to distribute the serum throughout towns and cities, taking control of the elves' memories and warping their version of history.

Ash clenched his teeth. "Trust me, when I say that the serum was a mistake. It's a mistake I've paid for the last three hundred and twenty-nine years. She's cursed me to relive my most shameful behavior over and over again, so don't you *dare* assume I have any loyalty left to her."

Hawthorne's expression showed his surprise. A moment later, the surprise in his eyes burned away leaving something else behind. He was angry. And why wouldn't he be? Ash had chosen the wrong side. He'd played a horrific part in this whole mess, but when Hawthorne spoke, it was Ash's turn to be shocked.

"All this time, I thought you were still working for Luniva. I didn't know."

"You're not the only one." Ash's tone was laced with self-loathing. "All the noble elves who attend the ritual year after year believe their beloved king is a willing and eager participant. After the first ritual, when I realized what had happened….In my grief, my mental defenses were lowered. Samael practically danced with glee as he pushed memories of the ritual into my mind until I was sick. Our brother's twisted perspective gave me nightmares about the ritual for months."

After that, Ash had solidified his mind like a fortress. No one would drag any truth from his memories or push any thoughts into his mind ever again. Not unless he allowed it.

"Do you want to tell me what happened?" Hawthorne asked.

The story of Ash's curse was full of pain and shame. "I'm not sure I can tell you, even if I want to. My actions leading to the creation of the Emergence Serum are my life's biggest regret."

Wren was the only one who knew the truth of his curse. He'd witnessed the ritual every Winter Solstice and helped Ash put his life back together by the time he had to repeat the cursed cycle.

Hawthorne had the ability to read and invade minds the same way Ash and Samael could. Ash hesitated, half expecting a probing against his skull, the invasive feeling of another person attempting to breech his thoughts. He would have allowed Hawthorne in; he was ready to try anything to be rid of his curse.

But the pressure of a mental investigation never came.

"You believe me? Just like that? We've been enemies for over three centuries, and you choose to take me at my word?"

"I could comb through your mind if it would make you feel better, but something tells me you'd rather I didn't."

Ash choked on the regret as he remembered what it was like to have Hawthorne on his side before the war. He remembered what it had been like growing up looking up to his older brothers. He'd thrown away any sense of brotherhood he'd felt with Pax and Hawthorne by fighting on the wrong side of the Void War. He already knew he'd made a poor choice following Luniva, but he'd accepted that there was nothing he could do to redeem himself. Sitting in front of Hawthorne, he had nothing left to lose.

The hope that had flickered in his chest when he realized Kenna was the human princess flared brightly now in Hawthorne's presence. Suddenly, he felt sure there was a way to redeem and restore everything he'd lost. So, he laid himself bare.

Whatever history lay between them, Ash was reminded just how much he loved his brother.

He opened his mouth to speak, expecting the curse to prevent the words from passing his lips. He'd only ever been able to tell anyone the truth other than Elenya. She was his mate, the only woman he'd ever truly loved. Once his heart belonged to her, the curse had lost its ability to silence him. It didn't free her from the curse, but at least she'd understood.

Perhaps it was the true, brotherly love between Ash and Hawthorne which allowed Ash to speak freely. Ash didn't pause to question his ability to share the facts as he told his brother everything.

AFTER ASH FINISHED his tale and his tears had dried, he'd rested on a pallet in Hawthorne's tent for a few hours. At dawn, Hawthorne shook Ash awake and beckoned him to follow. Neither of them spoke as he followed his brother out of the camp, through the trees, and up the mountain. Ash still fought down the lingering memories of the previous night's story, along with the shame he'd never be rid of.

Hawthorne led him to a cliff, the whole of the Lithari Mountains spread before them. They sat on a rock ledge with their backs against the sheer face of the mountain behind them. Their feet dangled over the edge of the abyss, watching the sunrise in silence. Ash felt its warmth spread through him. The sun didn't feel this close in Notos.

As the grey dawn turned vibrant orange and pink, Hawthorne broke the silence. "Tell me what you've done to try to break the curse."

Ash huffed a laugh. "How do you know I've tried? Maybe this living Hel is what I deserve."

"If everyone got what they deserved, there would not be a shred of hope in the world. I know you. You've tried. Now, tell me how."

Ash picked up some stones, idly tossing them off the cliff. "Our mother's Ancient magic binds me to this curse. In my deepest despair, I tried to take my own life, but the curse stopped me. My best friend has tried to take my life for me at my request, but when the time came for him to strike, the curse would not allow the blow to fall. The curse has trapped me into this life. There is no escaping it." The truth sliced through the peace of the sunrise like a knife.

Hawthorne was quiet, as though looking for all the answers Ash might not have discovered. So, Ash continued speaking, "Perhaps it's for the best. Originally, I only agreed because I thought it would be better for me to rule than Samael. If Samael was the one chosen to complete the ritual, he would have relished it. My hesitation is the reason the serum only works to warp the elve's memories. If I'd agreed wholeheartedly, I think the serum would have worked to control the minds and actions of any elves who consumed it."

"You might wish to punish yourself for your part in this, Ash," Hawthorne said quietly. "But I think your conscience and your heart are what saved Mesterra. If Samael had been the one in your position... I think you're right. He and Lailah would have been able to fully control the elves. Are there any angels in Notos who are loyal to their king? Or do they all belong to Luniva?"

"My royal guard would follow me if I called upon them. They are loyal angels and fae. Some elves as well. They're under my captain's command and would trust any instructions we give them, but I don't know how I would gather forces without Luniva finding out. She and Samael have eyes everywhere. I don't think we can help in this war if she needs to believe I am still loyal to her. The force is small, but they are good men and women."

"Do you think we'd have a chance of killing her or casting her out of this world? Have you discovered where she'd hidden the source of her power?"

"No. Wren and I have tried. We will continue trying, but after all this time...I doubt we'll ever find it. Sometimes I wonder if Echelous knows." Ash avoided the Guardian of the Wards as much as possible, but Echelous always looked like he was full of secrets.

Hawthorne was going through the same thought process Ash had exhausted in the initial years of his curse. If he could find and destroy the source of his mother's power and then cast her out of the Three Realms, then her Ancient magic would be gone from the world and the curse would be lifted. But Ash's search had been fruitless.

"Can I ask you something?" Ash said.

Hawthorne nodded.

"Do the rebels know you're the prince of Vorra? Does Heidi Duras know?"

"No. Really, it was foolish of me to even give them the name Thorne. I didn't want to risk Samael finding out I was here and trying to prevent me from finding the human princess."

"I'm afraid there's one more thing I haven't told you," Ash said.

"And what's that?"

Ash blew out a breath, knowing Hawthorne wouldn't like the truth he was about to share. "I've made an unbreakable oath with the human princess."

Hawthorne's eyes snapped to Ash, flashing. "But the treaty says—"

"She must be betrothed to a prince. She must choose between you and Samael."

There wasn't a cloud in the sky, but thunder rumbled through the mountains.

"But if you've made an unbreakable oath with her..."

"Her oath is binding until her death. It is very likely she will be unable to speak the ancient marriage vows. Then again, would you really insist on her marrying a man she doesn't love and has not met?"

"I did not hope to force her into anything. I only wish for her to see the truth and hoped that she might choose me. I hoped our marriage would fulfill the treaty and save the humans. If the treaty isn't fulfilled, then the humans will likely never wake. If Samael finds a way to force her into marriage with him, then all of the lives lost in the Void War will mean nothing." Hawthorne's nostrils flared. "You have to keep her away from the castle. She can't take part in the ritual. Samael can't find out who she is."

Ash shook his head. "I have to take her back to the castle. Varis knows I've chosen her, and he's Samael's lapdog these days. The last thing we want is for Samael to look at her too closely. I'll treat her like all the other women who've come before her so he doesn't become suspicious."

"Fine. For now. But we will find a way to break your curse and to nullify the unbreakable oath. We must help her see the logical choice is to marry me. We'll find a way to fulfill the treaty and free the humans in spite of the oath she's made with you."

"You clearly haven't met Kenna. I've known her for less than two days, and I can tell you now, she will not marry a man she does not love. She won't be coerced into a marriage with someone she's never met based on logic. She's confident, clever, beautiful, and far too good for any prince I know." He couldn't help but smile.

"You're making jokes?" Hawthorne's eyes narrowed and Ash's smile fell away.

"I'm not joking, Hawthorne. The man who gets to spend his life with her will be a lucky man."

"We'd better find a way to free her from this mess and offer her a choice. And for the sake of the human race, we'd better pray she chooses me."

Ash looked out over the mountains. Though it was selfish, he wondered if there was any future in which Kenna might choose to marry a king instead.

CHAPTER 30

It was dawn when Jona woke Kenna.

"Morning, little sister." His smile was sad. "You ready?"

Stiff and aching from sleeping on the sofa with the lingering notes of her mother's jasmine perfume, she nodded. But she wasn't ready at all.

She wasn't ready for any of it.

Regardless of her mother's instructions to embrace her feelings, the only thing Kenna wanted to feel was numb. Her thoughts had spun through the night despite her physical exhaustion. The obstacles seemed to build themselves up brick by brick until there was an insurmountable wall before her.

She didn't even know if she could face the small task of getting dressed for her father's funeral. He'd lied to her, but he was still her father. He'd loved her, and in the end, he'd died for her.

She covered her mouth, her shoulders shaking with tears she couldn't hold back. She'd never get to ask him all the questions. Perhaps her mother had some answers, but would she ever see her mother again?

The minutes dragged on as she waited for Ash to return and tell her whether her mother had survived the journey to the village. Would the healer be there?

Her emotions felt raw, leaving her incapable of anything other than laying on the sofa, catatonic and staring.

Jona seemed to sense her paralysis. "Together," he said. And when he held his hand out to her, she took it and stood.

Half an hour later, she'd washed, changed, and dressed in a simple charcoal frock before cleaning her teeth and splashing some water on her face—the bare minimum to look vaguely presentable. She twisted her hair into a simple knot and stood staring at herself in the mirror.

Before she'd fled, her entire life had marched along to a simple, monotonous beat. The only worry was staying in line. Staying safe. In the grand scheme of things, her life had been so easy. Why hadn't she been more grateful?

Before the Emergence, her biggest worry was being found unworthy and sent to Dendron. The old worry seemed almost comical, but she had no dry laughter to spare today. Not when it was the morning of the funeral for everyone who'd died in the attack. On the shores of Lake Audral, she would say goodbye to her father forever.

Mercifully, the bottom of her pack contained a flask of notelixir to help wash away the pain that threatened to drown her. She dug around in her rucksack, finding sweet salvation, and emptied half of the flask in one gulp.

Then, walking next to her brother, she left the ruins of her childhood behind. The elixir had worked, and all she could feel was the blissful tingle dulling her pain. She plodded through town with glassy eyes, ignoring her surroundings.

When she arrived, it looked like everyone in the city was already gathered on the grassy clearing near the pebbled edge of the lake. There was a low hum of subdued conversation from the assembled mourners.

Unfortunately, the fifteen-minute walk through town cleared the anaesthetic of the elixir, and she cursed herself for not drinking more or bringing the flask to chase away the feelings trying to choke her heart.

Dead. Her father was dead. And she'd never see him again.

A tear slipped down her cheek as Jona moved toward the edge of the lake, signaling the beginning of the service. She looked down, kicking the stones. She was alone.

Then, she felt a hand in hers. Drake was standing with her, even after her petulant behavior towards him in Notos. Shame coursed through her. There would be time for apologies and explanations later, though she still couldn't tell him her true identity.

Everyone turned to face the lake in silence, and they waited for Jona to speak. The Elders had always used funerals as another chance to spout their lies, but there was no script this morning. No propaganda.

There was only a yawning chasm of pain and the terrible knowledge that she'd lost her father. Might lose her mother. Might lose Zo and Ezra. She wouldn't find any comfort here because they were at war now. Everything would likely get much, much worse before things got any better.

A rock of grief slid down her throat, lodging in her chest. Her vision blurred as she tried to deny her tears freedom. Drake squeezed her hand, and his small act of physical comfort opened the floodgates. Her knees buckled as her pain threatened to pull her under, but Drake caught her around the waist and didn't let her fall.

Lined up along the shore, dozens of bodies awaited their final rest. They were laid on wooden pyres and covered with white sheets. One of the bodies was the empty shell that used to hold her father's soul. Lost as she was in her own grief, she had no idea who else had fallen during the battle.

Jona addressed the crowd: "Yesterday, we suffered an unimaginable loss. Though our hearts are broken, we will not forget the sacrifice and bravery of those who died defending our city and our right to freedom and truth. They fought for a better world, and in their memory—in my father's memory—we will fight on. We honor our fallen comrades by rising up to live." Jona paused, taking a moment to compose himself and clearing his throat. "Together, we'll discover and defend the truth. Together, we don't have to fear the darkness, because if there's one thing darkness can't stand, it's hope."

How could Jona speak of hope when there was so much grief?

The pain was a vice around Kenna's heart. All she wanted to do was crawl into her bed and never see the light of day. She wanted to burrow down into her grief, bitter and alone. She let those thoughts drag her under as she sobbed.

Down, down, down, she plummeted to the depths of her raging soul.

But there it was.

A tiny spark of hope beneath all of it. The warmth of possibility wrapped around her. Hope for a different future. A better future.

Kenna wiped her eyes, looking around at the tears in the crowd.

There was so much sadness. Drake clung to her like she was a lifeline, and his face was a mirror of her profound loss.

Maybe this wouldn't crush her. Maybe Jona was right. What if she allowed the tiny remnant of hope to strengthen her? What if she chose to stand with these people who had so much to fight for?

"No," she whispered to the darkness as it threatened to snuff out her inner light. "No," she said again, more firmly this time.

This would not break her. It would forge her. And hope would light a path through this darkness.

Her heart was tattered, but she would find a way to heal. They would all find a way to heal.

Together.

With a breeze at her back, she dragged the single spark of hope up, up, up, to the surface. She stepped forward to stand next to her brother near the bodies. Using her Aqua magic, she dispersed her tears into a fine mist that settled over those they'd lost.

She stood back—an invitation. One by one, the rebels came forward to the white sheets that reflected the bright coral sunrise. One by one, they sprinkled their tears over the fallen. She recognized many of their faces, though she didn't know all their names. The pain was not hers to bear alone. It belonged to all of them.

When everyone had paid tribute, unbidden words welled up from within her. Emerging from the darkness of night into the light of the rising sun, she spoke:

"May the Ancient One bless you and keep you, may truth shine upon you, may hope turn toward you, and offer you eternal peace."

Jona turned towards the lake and raised his hands. He pushed outward, as though forcing back an invisible wall. The stones under the pallets crunched and rolled, tiny, natural wheels carrying the pyres into the glassy water.

As the pallets met the edge of the lake, ripples disturbed the peace. On and on, the ripples spread over the water, just as the ripples of their rebellion would sweep through Mesterra.

Jona twirled his fingers in slow, deliberate pirouettes in the air near his head. The pyres followed the guidance of the gently swirling current into a ring at the center of Lake Audral.

Before Jona could light the pyres, Kenna placed a hand on his arm. "Let me," she whispered.

She reached out for the fire from the torches, gathering it into the spherical cages of her fingers. Like dozens of fishing lines, she cast flaming globes onto the pyres in graceful arcs.

Encouraged by her Flame magic, the pyres ignited quickly. Many glistening eyes reflected the Flame's glowing symphony.

Popping, crackling fire and quiet, muffled sniffles were the only sounds as the gathering watched the flames climb into the sky. The fire grew into mighty spears of light standing with the morning sun. Tiny sparks danced into the sky, and Kenna wondered if each swirling spark was a piece of a departing soul.

"Goodbye," she whispered, tears slipping down her cheeks as she closed her eyes. "I love you. I'll never forget everything you did for me."

Wherever her father's soul was—somewhere *after*—she knew he'd heard her. Within her charred spirit, she knew he'd find peace.

CHAPTER 31

*S*hortly after the funeral, Jona shared the truth with all the people who didn't already know. Even after the battle, there were still a few families who didn't know the Elders were angels or how they'd been using magic to control the memories of the elves in Tormund. How angels had been controlling all the elves throughout Mesterra.

Before the Elders were defeated in the battle, the rebels had taken care to keep their meetings secret. Jona told everyone about the camp in the mountains. Her brother promised to return to Tormund to lead anyone who wanted to the safety of the mountain refuge.

As Jona answered people's questions, Kenna and Drake withdrew to a bench along the shore.

"How are you?" she asked, unsure what else to say.

"I've been better," Drake answered with a humourless laugh. He scrubbed a hand through his messy blond hair. All of his characteristic swagger and confidence had abandoned him in the shadow of his grief.

Silence descended.

"I never would have wished for Ezra to be taken," Kenna said. "Not in a million years. Not even when he gave them Zo and my father's names."

"I know." Drake looked down at his feet. "I know he betrayed us, Kenna, but Ezra was…he is my everything. I don't know how to exist in a world where he doesn't. I have to find him."

Kenna's throat filled with spiky heat. "As much as it hurts, I can understand why he did it. He did it for you. He was afraid he'd lose you in Notos."

"I know he never meant to hurt anyone, but he did." Drake's voice was ragged. "But I can't say I'm sorry. I can't apologize for our love, and what it made him do."

"You never have to apologize for who you love, Drake. Not to me." Kenna reached out and took his hand. "But I need to apologize. I'm sorry. For the way I spoke to you yesterday. I was confused, and afraid. I thought pushing you away was for the best somehow. But I was wrong."

Drake released her hand and hugged her close.

A few minutes passed, and the only sound was the quiet lapping of ripples on the lake's shore. Drake broke the silence. "I need to go with Jona and the others. Into the mountains. Find a way back to Eza. A way to get him out."

"Of course, you do," Kenna said. "I understand, but it doesn't make it any easier to say goodbye."

"Your mother is safe," Ash's voice broke into the space between them, and Kenna turned to face the king. "She's seen the healer, and he's tended her wounds. She will be fine." Kenna sagged in relief. "Is your brother ready to depart?" Ash asked.

"Yes," Kenna said. "Would it be okay if Drake comes, too?"

"I will be happy to give him a ride. Though, this noble steed requires assistance with the straps on his saddle." Ash held out the vest to Kenna.

"Are you alright, Drake?" Ash said, his lips quirking into a smile.

Kenna looked at Drake and very nearly laughed out loud at the way he was gawking at Ash.

"Oh, yes. Sorry. I…Ride. Straps." Drake stammered, his face red. There was nothing odd about the reaction to Ash's magnificence, only that it was coming from Drake, the self-proclaimed master of flirtation.

When Drake shifted his focus to her, she squeezed his hand. "He has that effect on the best of us, my friend." She released Drake's hand and stood. "Let's go get Jona."

"Too late," Jona said. He'd come to them, and he had the harnesses in his hand. Jona set about strapping the makeshift seats to Ash's torso again, and when the apparatus was fixed, he turned to Drake and asked, "Ready?"

Drake looked like he wanted the earth to swallow him whole, but he turned to Kenna with some of his former playful confidence shining through as he winked. "Well, it seems fate has been kind to one of us, at least." As he hugged Kenna, he whispered, "You damn well better take advantage of him and tell me all about it the next time I see you."

It was Kenna's turn to blush. "I love you, Drake. Be careful. I'll wait for news of Ezra and Zo."

Jona placed both hands on her shoulders, looked into her eyes and said, "Stay safe, little sister. I'll see you soon."

"Winter Solstice," she reminded him as he gathered her into a hug. "You be careful, too. I can't lose anyone else."

"I'll do my best."

"I'll meet you at the docks in Notos, Kenna," Ash interrupted. "I've arranged your safe passage with Raziel."

"I thought the crossing was closed when the Elders discovered it?" Kenna asked.

"He made an exception for the king. He will not ask you for any bargains, and I trust him to get you there safely. I would fly you myself, but my energy is still depleted from yesterday."

Kenna felt the faint heat of the affirming thread of truth between them. She gave Drake and her brother final hugs, before setting off once again in the direction of the crossing, headed into the unknown of Notos.

As Ash flew Jona and Drake to the camp in the mountains, he enjoyed getting to know Kenna's brother and her friend. Now that Kenna's mother was out of immediate danger, some of the tension had eased. Jona shared stories of Kenna as a child, and Drake seemed just as enthralled as Ash to learn about these parts of his friend.

"She stole two pixies right from under their noses, and smuggled them out of Dendron and back to Tormund. In twenty-four hours, she'd read three books on pixies, and believed she'd found her life calling in caring for them."

"She never does anything half hearted, does she?" Drake asked. He and Jona shared a laugh that was full of love and admiration for Kenna.

"No," Jona agreed. "She doesn't do anything by halves."

"The pixies didn't complain though," Drake assured Ash. "She nursed them back to health, and they would barely leave her side for a year. By the end, she was so worried they'd get caught she couldn't sleep."

"Yeah. That happens, too. She cares too much and often takes on more than she can handle. It's really important to help her keep balanced and be there to pick up the pieces when the burnout gets the best of her."

Ash had ascertained that Jona knew Kenna was the princess, but no one else did. Not even her closest friends. This story was some sort of cryptic warning to Ash. He brushed against Jona's mind, just enough to read the thoughts just under the surface of the words.

She's going to try to save the humans alone. And it might kill her. Having heard enough, the king pulled back from his intrusion.

"At least the pixies found a new flock eventually," Drake said. "Though, they used to visit her in Iris Meadow sometimes."

When they reached the camp, Hawthorne was waiting for them. They all disentangled themselves from the harnesses, and Jona went to Hawthorne immediately.

"Thank you. For healing my mother," he said, shaking his hand fervently. He turned to Ash, "And thank you for bringing her to him. But I meant what I said. Take care of my sister."

Ash placed a fist over his heart, a sign of sincerity and friendship. "I will do everything in my power to care for her."

Hawthorne pressed a letter into Ash's hand and pulled him off to the side, speaking quietly, "Give this to Pax."

"You won't be able to tell him about the curse," Ash warned.

"I know. When I tried to write the words, they disappeared from the parchment. This letter explains that Pax should allow Kenna to go with you. I've asked him to trust me. At the very least, rest assured Pax and I will try to find a way to stop the ritual."

"Pax is only allowed in Notos because of his position as Kenna's guardian angel. If you enter Notos, your life will be forfeit."

"Let me worry about my life, Ash. You focus on keeping Kenna safe."

Ash's voice was barely a whisper, tinged with warring hope and despair, "Do you think there's a way to stop the curse?"

"I don't know. But even't if I did, I wouldn't tell you in case—"

Nodding, Ash cut him off. "In case Luniva or Samael are able to infiltrate my mental shields. That's wise."

"I know you were already planning to train Kenna, but I can only imagine it was for show. You must train her in earnest and as quickly as possible. Be relentless. If she has any hope of accomplishing the tasks before her, she needs your help. And if anything goes wrong and she ends up in Samael's clutches, she needs to be able to fight him."

"I'll do my best," Ash promised. He gripped his brother's forearm, pulling him close and clapping him on the back. "Thank you for listening. For not judging me too harshly."

"You're my brother, Ash. I would protect you with my life."

Ash blinked against the burning in his eyes and turned away from Hawthorne, wishing he could stay by his brother's side. But there was a princess who needed his help.

When Ash turned to fly away, Drake stopped him. "Ash! I… uh… Your Majesty," he stumbled over his words. "There's a courtesan at the Flaming Arrow in Braktyn. His name is Nik. I spent some time with him a few years ago when I visited Notos. When I brought Kenna across the Veil, we ran into him and I couldn't help feel like I was forgetting something. Probably part of the bargain I made with the ferry master back then."

"Why are you telling me this?"

"I remembered something. Something Nik told me. He said he owed a debt he could never repay to the owner of the brothel. I didn't know whether you might…well, you're the king. Maybe you could help? Maybe give him a job working for you instead or convince the brothel's owner to release him from his debt?"

"I'll see what I can do," Ash said.

"Thanks. And like Jona said, please keep Kenna safe. Don't break her heart."

Ash nodded. It was the only response Ash offered Drake before he took off over the misty mountains. If Hawthorne's plan didn't work, and they couldn't break Ash's curse, a single broken heart was the least of their worries.

CHAPTER 32

On the journey across the Veil, Raziel hardly spoke to Kenna beyond the occasional grunt. Recalling the gleam in his eye as they'd struck their bargain last time, he was likely annoyed at the lack of payment from her. She didn't mind and chose to get some sleep during the crossing.

They arrived at the docks without incident and she thanked Raziel, joining the crowd on the docks. At the end of the pier, she spotted Ash standing beside a midnight blue carriage marked with a sigil matching the one on her wrist, the circle with two shining stars.

She approached the horse at the front, stroking his nose.

"If I knew that you had such an affinity for stroking saddled beasts, I might have kept my saddle on," Ash said. "Would you prefer to fly?"

"Saddled or not," Kenna replied. "I don't plan on riding you anytime soon. A carriage suits me just fine."

Ash's eyes went wide with…confusion? Shock?

The man holding the reins laughed out loud. "Oh, I like you already."

Ash cleared his throat. "Well, I'm afraid you'll have to suffer through my company for roughly seven hours." He climbed into the carriage, seeming a little flustered.

"I'm Wren," the winged man in the driver seat jumped down. "Captain of the Royal Guard at your service milady." He gave Kenna a gallant bow and placed a kiss on the back of her hand like she was some sort of noble. Did he treat all women like royalty?

An adorable dimple appeared in one of his light brown cheeks when he flashed a smile and said, "Don't mind the old man. He's cranky because he missed knitting club yesterday."

"I heard that, asshole!" Ash shouted from inside the carriage.

Kenna decided she liked Wren and she smiled. He was shorter than Ash, probably about six feet tall. He was well-muscled with a navy cape flowing down his back between his yellow-gold wings. He smiled freely, but the number of weapons that Wren had strapped to various parts of his body made Kenna wonder if she should be worried about the journey ahead.

As he took her hand and helped her up into the carriage, she noticed Wren was missing the pinky finger on his left hand. He must have seen her looking because he held up the hand with the missing finger. "Hazards of being fae," he said, before he jumped back up into the driver's seat.

"The captain is nice," Kenna said.

"Yes, well. You should see how cranky the kid gets if he misses his eight o'clock bedtime."

"I heard that, you bastard." Wren shouted through the door from outside where he was busy stowing Kenna's pack.

"How old are you, anyway?" Kenna hadn't thought much about that until now.

"Three-hundred and fifty-four," he said, adjusting the cuff of his sleeve.

Kenna's eyes widened, but she quickly hid her shock. He only looked to be about thirty. That would make him five years her senior, but instead he was centuries old. Of course, he was. Angels were immortal, and he was the king. Stifling her surprise, she opted for a joke. "You'd think after all that time, you'd have learned how to speak to women. Or does comparing yourself to a horse usually work?"

Ash sat back, a half-smile on his lips. "Forgive me for my poor attempts to win your affection. Clearly, this *old man* is out of practice."

Kenna made a noise of agreement as she sank into the embrace of the padded velvet seat. She tried to summon displeasure toward Ash for such an ostentatious display when Mesterra was entering a time of war, but she couldn't be annoyed with him while she was so comfortable.

Normally, she would have enjoyed flirting with someone like him, but there was too much at stake. Even though he'd saved her mother, she'd already lost her father and two of her friends were missing. Mesterra was at war, and she would have stayed if not for the unbreakable oath she'd sworn to the angel king.

She was eager to begin her training, to feel like she was doing *something* that might help the rebels when she returned after Winter Solstice.

"All set," Wren said, rapping on the side of the carriage.

As Ash leaned across to shut the carriage door, his enticing scent wrapped around Kenna. She fought the urge to close her eyes and inhale the alluring aroma of wood smoke in a snowy forest. When had he had time to bathe?

She discreetly sniffed her own armpit, and wrinkled her nose.

"I suppose I should say thank you for your help," she said.

"That might be an appropriate response, but I won't be the one to force you to say or do anything you don't want to do," Ash said. He smiled at her, and the warm truth on her wrist and the genuine softness in his eyes made Kenna's breath catch.

"Well, thank you. For everything," she said.

"You're most welcome."

The carriage jolted into motion and Ash shifted on his seat across from her, completely at ease as he crossed one ankle over the opposite knee. His movement sent another wave of his intoxicating scent over her. In the confines of the carriage, their knees were almost touching.

Why did this suddenly feel so intimate? He'd carried her in his arms to Tormund, but the whole time she'd been afraid to look down or sobbing over her father's death. She hadn't thought much about the feel of Ash's arms around her. The feel of her body pressed against his muscled chest. That beguiling, smoky, evergreen smell.

She was behaving like a schoolgirl, but Ancients, he smelled *so* good. She tried to hold her breath, and clear her mind, but she couldn't hold her breath for the duration of their journey to...to wherever his castle was.

"Can we open a window?" she blurted.

"We can do whatever you want."

Ash's lips quirked as he uncrossed his legs and shifted forward on his seat. Of course, the latch was on her side. Why hadn't she just opened it herself? Their knees brushed again as Ash reached out, and the laces of his shirt shifted revealing the hint of a tattoo on his chest. It looked like the star on her wrist with dozens of thin circles around it. She looked up at his strong, stubbled jaw and closed her eyes, willing her heart and breathing to slow down to normal.

With one hand still on the window, and still very much in Kenna's personal space, he looked down at her. His lips were far too close to hers.

Forget flirting with him. She had the sudden urge to bury her fingers in his unkempt hair and feel her lips on his. She suddenly understood why Sera used sex to cope with trauma. Kenna wondered if feeling Ash moving between her thighs would dull the aching loss and overwhelming helplessness she felt in her chest.

"Better?" he asked, neither of them moving. She nodded once, and then Ash sat back on his side of the carriage with a self-satisfied smirk. "I'd say that's a point to me, wouldn't you agree? Score is one to one."

Bastard. She took a deep breath. As the fresh air cleansed her mind, she glared at him. "I wasn't aware we were playing games, Your Majesty."

"Of course, we're playing." His eyes twinkled. "You scored the first point when you implied I didn't know how to flirt."

"Then you'll find me a worthy opponent. I'm very competitive. If you think you'll win this game, you're mistaken."

His voice took on a sultry quality which made her quiver. "Trust me, love. I could make you beg for me."

"Is that so?" She slowly untied her cloak, arching her back as she removed it. The king's eyes dipped to the swell of her ample breasts just visible over the scooped neck of her top. His pupils dilated, and he swallowed once. "Perhaps *you'll* be the one to beg for me, Your Grace."

He dragged his gaze back to hers, and she gave herself another point for the hungry look in his eyes. "Two to one," she declared.

He cleared his throat and looked away. "Fair enough."

Unsure she liked where this game was leading, she forced a chipper tone into her voice. "Where are we going, anyway?"

"We'll stop in Braktyn. I thought you might like to pay a visit to Pax at the Red Lantern to update him before we go to the castle. Perhaps you'd like to bathe and rest for a few hours as well."

"Oh, that is…surprisingly considerate," she said, genuinely taken aback.

"Surprisingly considerate? Did I not just fly your friends and your ailing mother to safety and healing. Honestly, Kenna, you'd think you had a reason not to trust angels."

She rolled her eyes, and he chuckled.

"After Braktyn, I'll take you to Brumalis Castle. I'm sure you're eager to begin training."

"I…yes. Thank you." He was right.

"I feel I must warn you, though. Many of my brothers and sisters will not take kindly to your presence."

"How many siblings do you have?"

Kenna knew very little about the angels other than the stories she'd heard from the High Council in Mesterra and their altered version of history. Most elvish couples usually only had one child unless they were fated mates. It was odd to think of multiple siblings as a normal occurrence.

"All angels are brothers and sisters. Though, we were not born and bred in the traditional sense."

"But what about children? How do you breed if you're all brothers and sisters?"

"Angels can't procreate with other angels. We were created as children by the Ancients. Luniva and Soldivus are our mother and father. We all grew into men and women, but no angels have been created since the end of the war."

"But you can…" her eyes dipped to his trousers, not daring to ask the question on the tip of her tongue.

"Oh yes. We can do *that* just as well as elves and humans. Better, probably. After all, we've had centuries of practice." He gave her a lopsided smile.

Her entire body warmed. Whatever game they were playing, it was dangerous.

"We can breed with elves. That's where the winged fae like Wren came from and why they are so varied in appearance. Though, I suppose humans and elves were all created with a variety of skin tones and hair colors, just like angels."

"Have the angels ever bred with humans?"

"It was impossible before the war."

"And now?" Kenna asked, a weighty question given the tension coiled around the two of them.

"I think…if you were to bed an angel, it would be wise to make sure you trust him and that he is taking the contraceptive tonic. Unless you're willing to risk becoming pregnant."

"Angel *males* take the tonic?"

Ash nodded. "Most of them would not risk having a winged fae child. Some of them, like Wren's father, refuse to take the tonic. They insist contraception is the woman's responsibility. That's why his father murdered his mother. He blamed her for Wren's existence, and he all but killed his own son."

"That's barbaric." Kenna hardly knew Wren, but she wanted to climb out of the carriage and hug the friendly fae driver.

"It was awful," Ash agreed. "But I couldn't have asked for a better friend."

"So, what would the offspring be of a human and an angel?"

"Honestly? I don't know."

Warm truth flooded the scar on Kenna's wrist. He was being honest with her, not trying to hold back the truth like all the other men and angels in her life. Did he believe she was an ignorant fool for her questions? And why was he bothering to help her or tell her the truth? He was an angel, and Kenna couldn't allow his opinion of her to carry any weight.

"I'm feeling rather tired. I think I'll rest a while," she said.

"Sleep, love." A command. An invitation.

"I HAVE some business to attend to at the Flaming Arrow, so I will meet you back at the Red Lantern in an hour," Ash informed her. "You may want to have some lunch. We will not stop again until we arrive at the castle."

When they stopped outside of the Red Lantern, Kenna practically bounded in to see Pax. She needed his reassurance that she wasn't making a horrible mistake. Not that she had much of a choice. She'd already made an oath with Ash, and there was no going back.

Pax eased her worries over lunch, and then pulled something out of his pocket. "Ye left a leaf from the sacred tree in yer room. I made it a bit easier for ye te keep up with. He held out a long gold chain adorned with a pendant and a charm. The charm was the delicate gold lantern inscribed with the word home. Pax must have kept it from Kenna's employment bracelet. The pendant was a large glass bead, and the leaf inside looked like a tiny replica of the red leaf which she'd kept in her room.

Pax must have seen her confusion. "I shrank the leaf down a bit."

"Thank you." Kenna slipped the necklace over her head and the pendant settled between her breasts. "I'll cherish it."

Pax beamed at her. After they finished lunch, Pax insisted on drawing a hot bath for Kenna in one of the guest rooms. She scrubbed her hair and body and soaked for half an hour in the lavender-scented water. She didn't lie down on the bed, knowing how torturous it would be to have to wake up for her travels.

When she descended the stairs, Pax was outside speaking to Ash. She paused for a moment, watching through the window. Pax had his arms folded across his chest in that protective way of his.

She was still smiling as she exited the Tavern.

"...because I trust Thorne. Ye'll protect her?" Pax was asking.

"With everything I have." Ash bowed slightly.

She cocked her head. Why would Ash have any need to protect her in his own castle? Then again, who could say what threats were carried upon the winds of war and change in the Three Realms?

After the funeral in Tormund, Kenna promised herself never to take a goodbye for granted, so she relished the comfort of Pax's hug. He held her by the shoulders, looking into her eyes. "I'll be seein' ye before ye know it, lass. I reckon ye'll be alright." He gave her a playful flick on the nose.

"I don't know, Pax. I was really looking forward to working with you. Who else would keep me entertained by laughing at their own ridiculous jokes and boring stories?"

"Ye get out of here lass before I put ye te work. I think all the chamber pots need srubbin." Pax smiled, giving her one last squeeze before she climbed back into the carriage with Ash.

CHAPTER 33

Kenna had been asleep again in minutes after they'd left the Red Lantern, and Ash had drifted off for a while too. It had been a long couple of days even for him, so he couldn't imagine how Kenna was coping with the loss and anxiety. She'd had so many painful farewells in the last days. Yet she still found the energy to play with him.

He smiled to himself, watching her dark lashes flutter against her cheeks as she dreamed. Sometime in the last couple of days, his flirtation with her had turned into something genuine and fun, but he'd promised himself he wouldn't touch her. He wouldn't allow himself to cross that line. They could flirt and play games—a little tension would fuel her training—but becoming anything more than friends would be reckless.

She shifted a little and he caught a whiff of lavender. Then, she let out a little snore, waking herself up. His eyes followed her hand as it lifted to her mouth. He was jealous of the thumb she dragged along the soft skin of her bottom lip, wiping away a single droplet of drool at the corner. Everything about this woman beckoned him to her.

Shit.

He looked away quickly.

Every moment he spent with her felt like digging himself deeper and deeper into a hole. He needed to pull himself together and focus on the end goal. He needed to shut this down.

~

KENNA AWOKE with a start to find the carriage window was still cracked. She discreetly used a thumb to wipe a remnant of drool from the corner of her mouth, but when she looked at Ash, he turned away swiftly.

Was he watching me sleep?

Frigid air and the smell of brittle, frozen earth crept into the carriage, scraping at her senses. She shivered and shut the window, snuggling more securely into her cloak.

Ash cleared his throat. When he spoke, his tone was colder and more matter of fact. The warm flirtation from earlier seemed to have vanished. "Apologies. I would have shut it, but I did not want to disturb you. You looked like you needed the rest."

She nodded and looked out the window, but all she could see in the darkness beyond the glass were the shadows of a thick forest of trees in the moonlight.

"Where are we?" she asked.

"Gela Forest. Would you like to begin your training?"

"There's not exactly room to sling weapons and magic within a carriage."

Some of his warmth seeped back in as he laughed. "No, there's not. But there is theory involved in your training as well."

"I had loads of theoretical training in Tormund."

"Did you? Tell me, how would you go about forming a Flame shield?"

"Well, I would reach for my Flame, and then—"

"Wrong," he said abruptly. "Your magic is not something you should have to reach for. It is an extension of *you*. You should be able to use your magic as easily as you move your eyes or your limbs."

"How is that even possible? There are still limitations to magic. It's not like I can just shift the water from an entire lake. Aqua magic can't control the sea at all. And my Terrane magic isn't limitless. I can't move mountains."

"No, but every Vessel has a different capacity for magic. We need time to discover the confines of your power. If you are to fight, you need to know how to push yourself to the threshold without using too much."

"Like Sera did during the battle before you healed her?"

Ash nodded.

It seemed so long ago. Time seemed to move differently in Kenna's tunnel of grief.

Once again, Kenna was confronted with just how little she knew about her own magic. Apparently, it was the same magic the angels possessed, and she wondered what that would mean. How had she settled with learning so little in her four years at the Academy? Then again, maybe she hadn't settled at all. She'd never really been content.

"You don't need to worry. I will help you. The main thing is that—" Ash suddenly stopped, snapping his head toward the dark window.

"What's the matter? Did you hear—"

He held a finger to his lips, demanding silence. Kenna looked out the window but couldn't see anything. She shuddered at the eerie stillness emanating from the forest beyond.

Staring into the blinding darkness, she suddenly saw a silhouette glide past the window in the faint moonlight. The tiny hairs on her arms stood on end. The carriage lurched to a sudden stop, and the immediate stillness was suffocating. Kenna held her breath in the deafening silence, afraid the slightest sound would provoke whatever stalked them.

The silence stretched through the unnaturally slow seconds. What was out there? Why had the carriage stopped?

Then, it began.

Knock. Knock. Knock.

Slow, deliberate, sinister.

Some unknown monster lurked on the other side of the carriage door. She squeezed her eyes shut and opened them again, hoping to wake from the nightmare.

She was not dreaming.

Ash still held his finger to his lips, telling her to stay quiet. In his eyes, she beheld a tempest of the darkest sea, waiting to be unleashed on its foe. There was not a single ounce of fear.

She trembled, terrified not only of the mysterious threat outside their vehicle, but also of the vast power contained in the body across from her. What, exactly, was he capable of?

As silent as the deadliest predator, Ash moved into a crouch by the door, ready to spring forth the moment the carriage door was opened. He extended a firm arm across Kenna's chest, pressing her back into the seat.

"Stay here," he mouthed. His silent command was unnecessary, for when he removed his arm, she was trapped. Invisible manacles held her hands and feet to the bench on which she sat. She wouldn't dare set foot out of the carriage to face whatever waited beyond. Why would he contain her?

As she struggled against her bonds, Kenna was suddenly transported back to that alley in Braktyn, held in place by a brutish angel with foul intentions. Ash had rescued her then, but now he was the one who kept her bound. She felt the panic welling up—panic which had become all to familiar over the last few days.

Just breathe, she reminded herself. *This is not the alley. Ash is not a monster. He's protecting me. Just breathe.*

Still, the feeling of being helpless and trapped was too much. She fixed pleading eyes on Ash, but his mind was already elsewhere as he threw open the door and landed in a defensive position in front of the beast.

The monster outside was poised to attack. It had the upper body of a heavily muscled male, but atop the broad shoulders sat a bull's head with giant, curved horns and gleaming red eyes. It fixed those sinister eyes on Kenna and bellowed a roar so loud she thought her ears might bleed. The biting air and sulfuric smell of rotten eggs washed over her. She shuddered, and her insides churned—still, she could not move.

Ash threw out a hand and a gust of frigid air slammed the carriage door shut. Behind the closed door, her invisible bonds released. She lurched forward, taking a deep gulp of air.

When she drew back the curtain of the window, all Kenna saw was a flurry of glowing eyes and shadowy wings in the darkness. There was vicious growling, bones crunching, flesh tearing, a sickening gurgling sound, and then—silence, followed by the steady approach of footsteps crunching in the snow.

Crunch. Crunch. Crunch.

Slow. Deliberate. Sinister.

There was a silhouette outside the door of the carriage.

Tears of sheer terror stung her eyes as she backed into the corner, away from the approaching monster. Frantically, she looked around for something—anything—she could use to defend herself. There was nothing.

Waiting to be ambushed, she trembled like a coward. Just as she had during the battle in Tormund.

No. No more hiding.

She flung open the door on the opposite side of the carriage and ran.

ASH SWORE VICIOUSLY. At least the monster was dead. For now. They'd need to burn it for it to stay that way. Ash was crunching across the icy earth toward the carriage, when he heard Kenna jump out the other side and run.

Ash would deal with her in a moment. He climbed into the driver seat where Wren was slumped to the side, unconscious but breathing. The monster must have incapacitated him. He shook his friend by the shoulders and Wren awoke, disoriented.

"What the..."

"Are you injured?" Ash asked.

Wren shook his head. He couldn't leave the monster's body; he looked over to where the headless creature laid. Already, it's massive body was crawling toward it's severed head, leaving a slimy trail of bluish black blood. He looked back to Wren, who looked like he might drift back off to sleep.

"Wren!" he snarled. "Wake up. You have to burn it. Now. I'm going after Kenna."

There was only one way to truly destroy an Achetaur, and there was only one reason the Achetaur would have been lurking in these woods.

Wren nodded, eyes still a bit bleary, but he sat up and threw flames toward the monster's body. The body seemed to resist the light of the fire, so Wren sat up a bit straighter, funneling more fire over the creature. When Ash was sure Wren had things under control, he jumped down and jogged after Kenna.

She was a rutting fool for running into the forest alone. If the Achetaur was here, there may be other foul and deadly creatures lurking amongst the trees.

The sound of her labored breathing and twigs cracking under her lumbering gait led him right to her. He could see her running blindly through the trees. She hadn't even thought to use her Flame magic to light her way. He shook his head. The woman knew *nothing* of this realm, and he needed to teach her before it got her killed.

It was mere moments before Ash caught up to Kenna and he wrapped his arms around her, pressing her back against his chest as she thrashed and kicked. "No! No!"

"Kenna. Kenna, stop! It's me! You're okay."

She stilled and he put her down, turning her to face him. Her chest heaved and her brown eyes were wide in the dark. She wasn't able to see Ash in the dim trickle of moonlight in the forest, but he could see her.

Terror and then relief tore through her features as she threw her arms around him, trembling. " I thought it got you and Wren. I thought I was out here alone."

"I'm here. I won't leave you. Not if I can help it."

Ash hugged her for a moment, his jaw resting atop her soft lavender-scented hair, and a flicker of warmth glowed within his shriveled heart. He created a fiery dome around them, shielding them from any other dark creatures lurking in the forest.

Then, Kenna stepped back, illuminated by the orange glow of the flames. There was a look in her eyes like she was having a silent debate with herself. She took a deep breath and Ash thought she was about to kiss him in gratitude. Instead, she slapped him square in the jaw.

Ash's mouth hung open and he held a hand to his cheek. The relief in her eyes a moment earlier had been replaced by vehemence. She poked him hard in the chest, her words pouring out without any regard for his power.

"Don't you ever, *ever*, contain me like that again. Ever. I don't care that you're the king. I don't care if I'm in danger. My free will does not belong to you or any other angel. If you think for one second that you can control or manipulate me, then you're going to find out just how wrong you are."

She squared her shoulders against him, hands on her hips, hair wild.

Damn. It was the second time that night he'd been at a loss in her presence. The second time he'd been taken aback by her tenacity. This woman was utterly perplexing, a tempest destined to rattle the future of the Three Realms. Who was he to try to control her?

"I won't. I promise. I'm sorry." He could feel the warm truth of his words connecting them, and he knew she felt it too when she nodded and stepped back.

Then, she seemed to notice the monsters oily blue-black blood staining his clothes. "Are you...are you okay? Is Wren okay?"

"We're both okay. The blood belongs to the monster. Wren is taking care of the body. Angels bleed red, just like you." Ash gestured to a scratch on her cheek. "May I?"

She nodded once and he brushed a thumb over the bone under her eye, looking at the cut more closely. It was shallow, but he wished he hadn't exhausted his healing magic back in Tormund.

"Just a scratch," he said.

Then he looked into her eyes, and found her staring back at him.

FOR A MOMENT, Kenna was transfixed, his hand still on her cheek. Those eyes had been dark and deadly a few minutes earlier, but the predatory intent had disappeared. He'd had the audacity to bind her, but his apology and the concern evident on his features seemed genuine. In the firelight, something serene and calming in his gaze beckoned her to fall into the deep blue.

He'd come to her rescue, but that did not make him any less deadly. Because he *was* deadly. He must be. How else could he have defeated that monster?

And he was still an angel. She didn't know what to think of this man before her, but if history proved anything, it was that angels and humans were enemies. She took a step backward, extracting her gaze.

"You should have stayed in the carriage," he said.

She shrugged. "Part of learning to fight is taking action instead of letting my fear paralyze me."

Ash nodded slowly and looked at her as though she was a puzzle he couldn't quite piece together.

"Come," he said, walking back to the carriage. The glowing orb of fire still surrounded them but didn't burn any of the trees as they walked. It must require immense power for Ash to control not only the size and shape of his flame, but whether or not it burned the things it came into contact with.

They reached the carriage in a matter of minutes. She hadn't gotten very far in her attempt to flee. Ash opened his shield, wrapping it around the carriage, the horses, and Wren as well.

"Wren, saddle the horses," Ash ordered. "You'll need to ride to the outposts."

Wren nodded, and began following orders like a good soldier. "What was that thing?"

"An Achetaur," Ash answered.

Wren stopped what he was doing and his gaze snapped to Ash like a whip. He must not have realized what the monster was, even as he'd destroyed it. Then, he looked at Kenna, his eyes wide, as though suddenly understanding something.

"Why are you looking at me like that?" she asked.

Wren was no longer playing the good soldier. He looked at his king —his friend—like he might throttle him. "There hasn't been an Achetaur in the Three Realms for over three hundred years. Achetaurs feed on *human* souls." Wren scrubbed a hand down his face. "Fuck, Ash. *Fuck*. She's the human princess? What about—"

"We'll come up with a plan," Ash interrupted. "No one else can find out who she is. If Prince Samael or Lailah find out...that can't happen. Do you understand?" The authority in his tone belonged to a king addressing his Captain of the Guard.

Wren nodded but Kenna could almost feel the anger pulsing off of him. Why was Wren so angry about finding out who she was?

"Whatever the reason for its arrival, the Achetaur shouldn't have been able to pass the wards," Ash stated. "Wren, you need to speak to the Surgati wardens. Tell them it's a routine inspection. Don't mention the attack, but be sure the wards and defenses are strong. If the Achetaur was roaming the forest, there may be a breech. There could be other creatures on the loose."

Wren mounted one of the horses.

"Can't you just fly?" Kenna asked.

He spread his golden wings wide, bumping into a tree on one side and flinching. "My father did me the honor of clipping my flight feathers when I was seventeen. These are just for decoration." He fluttered his feathers closed.

"Oh...I'm sorry," Kenna said. Instinct told her his swagger was hiding the shame and sadness of having such beautiful wings without being able to soar through the skies.

Wren waved a dismissive hand. "I'll meet you back at the castle." With that, he kicked his horse into a gallop.

CHAPTER 34

"We should get out of the forest," Ash said, holding the horse's reins.

"I've never ridden a horse before," Kenna admitted as she tugged her tangled hair into a loose braid. Even though she wanted to prove her bravery and independence, she was desperate to get out of the forest. The darkness between the trees made her feel like she was being watched.

"Then it's a good thing I'll be riding with you. If you don't object, that is." Ash smirked, knowing she didn't have another option.

"Fine. Just get me out of here."

Ash helped her mount the beast, her movements as awkward as a freshly caught fish flopping around on dry land. Then he swung up behind her with infuriating ease, urging the horse into a walk.

If being in a carriage with him had been intoxicating, this was…

No. This was fine. This was just transportation. It didn't matter that his thighs were pressed against hers or that his arms were around her waist. His wood-smoke scent didn't make her want to inhale deeply and lean back into his chest. She didn't wish he'd place a kiss in the exact spot where his warm breath tickled her neck.

She sat up as straight as she could, keeping a couple inches of distance between them as she settled into the steady, swaying rhythm of the horse's gait.

Ash cleared his throat. "Do you mind if we trot?"

"Sure," she said, eager to focus her attention on something other than him. Trying not to fall off the horse sounded like a perfect way to occupy her mind.

He clicked his tongue and the horse obeyed, picking up the pace. Trotting was a little trickier. With every jolt of her ass in the saddle, she resisted the urge to yelp. How did people ride these infernal beasts? This was torture. At least she wasn't thinking about Ash's hand on her hip anymore.

Ash let out a low laugh. "Relax. You're going to bruise your ass if you carry on like that."

"I told you. I've never ridden a horse."

"Can I guide you?" he asked.

She nodded. Ash shifted, making more room for Kenna in the saddle.

"Put your feet in the stirrups," he directed, though he still held the reins with one hand. With his other hand he gently held onto her hip. She couldn't help the warmth that rushed through her as the pad of his fingers brushed over her hipbone.

"When you're in the saddle, you're in control. Relax your upper body." Just as the horse bounced up, Ash said, "Every other time his front legs hit the ground like that, raise your hips up out of the saddle, just a little. Like this."

He gripped her hip and raised her up before the next jarring bump of the horse could bash into her tailbone. Then, he gently lowered her.

"You can count if it helps. One. Two. One. Two." Ash said, but his words fell away as he continued gripping her hip, guiding her up and down. Up and down.

She focused on her movements. It felt more comfortable than before, and the rhythm was soothing. Her concentration shifted to her learning this new skill, but she was aware of his hand on her hip. He seemed to grip her tighter with every passing moment.

"Like that?" she asked.

His voice was gruff. "Just like that." He cleared his throat again. "Want to try galloping?"

"Why not?" she said.

He wrapped his arm around her waist, lifting her so that he was holding her flush against him. None of her weight was in the saddle or stirrups. She yelped but held on to his forearm with all her might.

"What are you—"

There was a smile in his voice as his whisper tickled her ear: "Hold on tight, love."

He kicked the horse, and then they were galloping. No. Not galloping. They were flying through the trees, but this was nothing like being high in the sky, full of terror of falling. This was pure, undiluted joy.

For a few minutes, she forgot all of her worries. She forgot about the angel behind her. She forgot about her friends and family. She forgot her grief. All that was left was speed and wind and glorious freedom. The cold air whipped through her hair, making her eyes water. Then, she tipped her head back and laughed.

It had been torture watching her ass sway with every step the horse took. He shouldn't think of her that way. *Couldn't* think of her that way. She was betrothed to someone else, and she didn't even know it. He couldn't think of her as anything other than a friend—a clever, brave, stunning friend.

He'd thought trotting might be better, but with every rise and fall of her hips, he gripped her hip tighter. Imagining gripping her bare flesh. Imagining…

"Like that?" she asked.

Her breathless question did absolutely nothing to purify the trajectory of his thoughts.

"Just like that," he whispered, the low, rough sound of his voice giving away exactly where his mind had wandered. Had she noticed? He tried to clear the lust from his addled brain by clearing his throat. Ash needed to get out of the woods and get off the horse as soon as fucking possible.

"Want to gallop?"

"Why not?" she answered.

He gathered her in close, inhaling her lavender scent.

"What are you—"

Not trusting himself to hold her close without his mind wandering again, he interrupted, "Hold on tight, love."

He squeezed tight to the sides of the horse, and they were off. A few locks of her hair flew out of her braid, whipping his face. He was glad for the pain washing away the images he'd been playing out in his mind moments ago. Her laughter was a melody and a balm for his aching, tormented soul.

Even if he could find a way to break his curse and free Kenna from the unbreakable oath, Kenna would still have to marry Hawthorne to fulfill the treaty and save the humans. The thought of her in another man's arms stirred something primal and possessive, and he resisted the urge to hold her even tighter.

It didn't matter. This wasn't about what he wanted. It was the only way to save the humans. The only way he might redeem his shredded soul, too. How long could Ash keep her unknown betrothal a secret without destroying the tenuous thread of trust between them?

He told himself she'd been through enough, convincing himself that he was protecting her by hiding her true destiny. The truth was, he was just as selfish as he'd always been. He wanted to be able to pretend his stirring feelings for her weren't cursed to end in heartbreak.

But it would break both of them in the end.

He shook off the thought and lost himself to the feel of her in his arms, the rushing wind, and the horse's pounding hooves.

CHAPTER 35

*A*fter only a few minutes, the edge of the forest came into view and Kenna could breathe again. She relaxed as Ash slowed the horse and climbed off, giving the animal a surprisingly gentle pat on the snout.

If the perpetual autumn of Braktyn was stunning, the glittering winter surrounding her was utterly mesmerizing. The untouched peace of the night swallowed all sound other than the gentle trickle of a nearby stream, settling her frayed nerves.

A wide road stretched endlessly before them, slicing a black path through the ocean of sparkling snow. Barren trees lined either side of the shimmering road, and their dormant branches glittered with frost like they were dusted with crushed diamonds.

"It's like the window," Kenna said, breaking the silence. "In the temple in Braktyn,"

"It is," Ash agreed.

The road was a perfectly smooth black material dappled with what looked like diamonds and sapphires glittering under the luminous moon.

Ash must have noticed her examining the road. "We call it the Sapphire Road."

"What is it made of?"

"Some of the developers I keep on staff discovered crysphalt deep within the earth. They were able to use their elemental power to liquify it, mix it with crushed glass, and pour it into place. It hardened to create crysphaltos, the surface you see now."

"I thought it was flecked with sapphires and diamonds." She smirked at her own foolishness.

Ash laughed. "Sorry to disappoint. Despite what some believe, I am not so frivolous that I would waste precious gems buried on a road beneath my feet."

"How is the road clear of ice and snow when everything else is covered?"

"It is infused with Flame magic."

"Amazing," she mused. "I wish my brother could see it. Jona loves this kind of thing."

"I gathered. His quick thinking with the harnesses was impressive. And the eriksomb he used during the fight… innovative weapons like that could turn the tide of a war."

Kenna huffed. "Yes, he's a genius. Jona is a household name in Mesterra. He created the Geolifts in Dendron and the Fostones." She held up the gem set in a bracelet on her wrist. "It tells the time and lights and extinguishes candles. He's also developing them as a form of communication. That's how he contacted me in Braktyn."

"Are you and your brother close?" Ash asked.

"I thought we were," Kenna said, fighting down the still-raw sting. "He knew who I was for years, but he didn't tell me. My father told him not to, but…I think if our situations were reversed, I would have told him the truth. I've always felt a little different, and I was never sure why. I guess being a human gifted with angel magic from the Ancients will do that to a person." Her words sounded bitter rather than the joking tone she'd intended. "It just…it would have been nice to know sooner."

Ash didn't say anything, but Kenna couldn't bear any silence which might force her to be alone with her thoughts. So, she told him about her friends and about growing up in Tormund. Occasionally, Ash interjected— "Yes." "I see." "Oh?" "Interesting." —confirming he was listening as she blabbered on.

After half an hour of Kenna's incessant chatter, the smooth road gave way to a more familiar cobbled surface and the horse's hooves clopped along through the city of Saphyr.

The buildings, if they could be called that, were hollowed out triangular peaks of snow faced with blocks of ice and wooden doors. The snow-hewn city was a latticework of sapphire blue with twinkling stars serving as the backdrop.

They passed taverns and homes, their internal light offering a full view of their flawless interiors through icy windows. The laughing inhabitants in beautifully decorated rooms stirred a niggling feeling within Kenna—would her life ever be so perfect and carefree?

A few citizens inclined their heads politely to Ash, and he returned their greetings with familiar smiles. He must be a trusted and beloved ruler to elicit such a response from so many of the city's citizens.

"Why didn't anyone seem to recognize you in Braktyn?"

"I only visit Braktyn once a year. It's…tradition to bring a female elf back to the castle for training each year."

Kenna's brow furrowed, and she looked down at him from her perch atop the horse where he walked beside them. That was a strange tradition, and it didn't sound like anything good. She felt for the thread of the oath that connected them.

"Why?"

"Lailah insists."

The warm truth confirmed his words.

"The priestess? But you're the king. Surely, you dictate your own schedule and activities."

He shrugged. "She's the priestess but her authority is as much, if not more, than my own. She works closely with Luniva. You can trust her."

Kenna hissed as the sharp, icy sting of a lie traveled down the thread between them. But his eyes met hers, as though he wanted to tell her the truth but something was stopping him.

"Why are you lying?" she whispered.

When he answered, his words were labored, as though he had to carefully calculate each thought that passed his lips.

"There are…forces stronger than the one between us." Warmth. "I would never purposely cause you harm." Warmth. "You can trust me, Kenna."

There was an icy blast of cold, and that same pleading look in his eyes. Ash was telling her not to trust him.

But why?

Kenna's stomach rumbled as the smell of roasting meat drifted through the air around them, and Ash seized the opportunity to change the subject. "Are you hungry?"

They arrived outside a tavern with a dark blue sign lettered in silver —The Snowed Inn. She almost laughed aloud at the pun. Pax would think it was hilarious. And her father, he would have laughed, too. Kenna smiled sadly.

"I think I could probably eat a whole cow," she admitted.

"I would advise against it. Shall we see if they have an entire goat, perhaps?"

"I'd be happy with whatever. As long as it's big."

Ash's shoulders shook with silent laughter, and it took her a moment to realize what she'd said.

"No. I didn't mean…oh, stop acting like a teenage boy. You know what I meant."

He was obviously holding back from filling the gap in the conversation with a wildly inappropriate comment. She glanced at his face, which had been so serious moments ago, noticing how the freedom of laughter transformed his features, his smile crinkling his eyes at the corners. He looked so utterly…normal. So likeable.

And she did like him.

She couldn't help but laugh along with him at her own expense. The laughter was a balm after having been through so much in such a short period of time.

For tonight, she chose to accept her situation. She couldn't change her path now that they'd already made the unbreakable oath, and she could see no reason or method to flee from Ash. He knew she could feel his lies, and he was obviously trying to warn her about something. She'd have to try to decipher Ash's coded warnings about not trusting him or the priestess later. Perhaps she'd get more answers from Wren when they reached the castle.

For tonight, she'd allow herself the small luxury of imagining she was safe. She could imagine she was a normal princess being whisked away by a king.

Once she began her training in earnest, there would be no more pretending. She would be constantly reminded of her inadequacies in the face of this war. She'd have to learn to fight. To use her magic. To save the humans.

Tonight, she wanted to forget the jumble of pain and responsibilities clattering around her mind, so she said, "I could also use a really, *really* strong drink."

CHAPTER 36

*K*enna's breath hitched when she caught her first glimpse of the towering ivory castle. Brumalis Castle looked like something out of a dream. It was rectangular with six stone towers topped with turrets pointing into the heart of the stars. The castle stood perched in a sea of clouds against a backdrop of obsidian snowcapped mountains.

"Is it floating?" she asked, hoping it wasn't a stupid question. She still didn't understand the limitations of angel magic.

"No, but it does look like it. We'll go down that way and cross the bridge. Ash gestured to the road which veered left and disappeared into the clouds via multiple steep switchbacks.

"Ah, yes. That makes sense." Ash probably thought Kenna had never seen fog before.

The chill seemed to be seeping into her bones even though she'd indulged in three notelixir cocktails at dinner. Her blood was humming pleasantly, but the warmth from the drink couldn't stop her teeth chattering against the frigid night.

The road was wider outside of the city, so Ash was flying slowly along next to her. Suddenly, she nearly slid out of the saddle, giggling.

"I think...I think you should ride with me." Ash didn't look happy about it. Was he mad at her for getting drunk?

He huffed, and settled onto the horse behind her. "You're cold," he said and she nodded.

Without a word, Ash draped his cloak over the front of her, sharing his body heat. The extra layer of material helped to shield her from the worst of the wind.

"Apologies for dropping the heat shield. Even I need to conserve my powers for alternative tasks sometimes. But I rather enjoy the smell of your lavender perfume." He snuffled against her neck, like a dog sniffing about in a grassy meadow.

She giggled, too buzzed to object to his shameless flirtation or care whether his attention meant anything. She hadn't even noticed the heat shield earlier or wondered why she hadn't been freezing in the wintry night. She'd only noticed its absence when Ash let it fall.

"Pray tell, how will you shock and awe me this glorious evening," she said, poking fun at his haughty accent even as his warmth seemed to ease the tension in her body.

"You'll just have to wait and see, love," he said.

She snorted.

"Something wrong?"

"I'm sorry. It's just…you've called me love multiple times now and we barely know each other. Do you give all your friends pet names? Does Wren have a pet name? Do you call him 'love'?"

"I … I apologize. Does it offend you?"

"I don't really mind it with your cute little accent."

A FEW MINUTES LATER, they emerged below the thick cloud and into a wide valley that led to a stone bridge over a pristine, frozen lake. The road led through the rest of the valley to the bottom of another hill— presumably the base of Brumalis Castle.

"I wish it wasn't so cloudy. I bet it's beautiful when you can see the stars," she said.

"One might almost think I had predicted your wish. What would you give me if I could make it come true?"

Her shiver had nothing to do with the cold.

"I…" Was he really implying that his magic was powerful enough to clear the vast, heavy mist and clouds that covered the *entire* valley? And if so, what was he insinuating the payment would be?

"No matter," he said. "I'm sure we can come up with a suitable arrangement at a later date." Ash's arms circled her shoulders. He brought the backs of his hands together in front of her before pushing them outward, as if opening an invisible pair of curtains. The mist above them obeyed his command and parted before fluttering down in walls of snowflakes on either side of the valley.

The ice beneath the bridge was like a vast mirror of black glass, reflecting the tangled pattern of stars overhead. They were surrounded by moonlight, starlight, and midnight. Kenna's mouth hung open, awestruck at the display of beauty before her and the power behind her.

"I really wish I had something clever to say, but I seem to have lost my sense of humor. I've never seen anything so magnificent."

"Wait until you see your bathing chamber," Ash said, and he urged the horse to pick up his pace across the bridge toward the climbing switchbacks on the other side of the valley.

The closer they got to the castle, the more Kenna felt her exhaustion tugging at her. If she had a magnificent bathing chamber, her bed would surely be luxurious. She hoped it was big and had lots of fluffy pillows and blankets. Her eyelids drooped and she struggled to keep them open. It had been over two weeks since she'd had a solid night's sleep. First, she'd been panicked about the Emergence Trial and Ceremony…and so much had happened after that.

They reached high walls built of ice blocks surrounding the castle. The walls must have been fortified with magic, since ice wasn't a suitable material for a defensive structure. Wren was waiting for them the moment they emerged from the icy tunnel that housed the gates and entered the castle courtyard.

"Ash, I need a word," Wren said, his tone serious. "In private,"

Ash dismounted. "I apologize, Kenna. This should only take a moment." She didn't mind. She was too busy admiring the glittering limestone and immense, silver-plated castle gates.

The air was tepid in the courtyard, though they were still outside. She assumed it was cloaked with the same type of magic Ash had used to created that bubble of warmth during their travels.

Ash stood to one side listening to Wren's hushed yet animated words. Then, without a goodbye or any further explanation, Ash took to the sky, abandoning her to her new surroundings. Now that they were in his royal domain, she could no longer pretend she was his priority. Wren walked over, and helped her dismount the horse, handing the reins over to a stable hand.

"Is everything okay?" She asked him.

"Everything is fine," he replied, his former friendliness had returned. "Just a little hiccup the king needed to deal with."

There were a handful of angels milling about the courtyard. They gave Wren and Kenna a wide berth. Wren led her toward the castle doors, which she saw about a quarter of a mile up ahead.

"You get used to it."

"Get used to what?" she asked.

"Their faces." Wren turned to her with a comical sneer, wrinkling his nose. She laughed and he shrugged. "Eventually, the novelty of having someone new to observe with intense judgement will wear off. Then, they'll stop scowling at you and settle for ignoring you."

Kenna had encountered the angels prejudice the day she arrived in Notos and been chastised her for touching her attacker's wings. She shuddered. She wasn't surprised the noble angels present in the court of Brumalis Castle looked down on Wren, a winged fae. Clearly, she wouldn't fare any better as a human disguised as an elf.

"So, how long have you been Captain of the Guard?" she asked Wren.

"Twelve years," he said. "Ash trained me for five years, before I joined the guard. I was a just a grunt for two years before our captain fell ill and died. Ash held a competition for the position of captain, and I beat angels, winged fae, and elves. I earned my place here."

Kenna arched a brow at him. "Well done. And why did such a high-ranking soldier came all the way to Braktyn just to escort us to the castle?"

"Before you left for Tormund, he sent word that *someone* didn't care for heights and would prefer to ride in the carriage." He nudged her with his elbow. "So, I came. My secondary title is the Moody Old Man's Best Friend."

She lowered her voice, "Is he actually over three hundred years old? I mean, elves can live for two hundred years, and we…they…don't look elderly until the last fifty years of their lives. I knew angels were immortal, but…do they age?"

"They age normally until the age of thirty. After that, their appearance doesn't change. They may lose or gain muscle or change their hair style, but they don't appear any older."

"And what about you?" Kenna asked.

"I'm thirty-five. Fae stop aging by the time we reach fifty or sixty, but we're not truly immortal. The average lifespan is about four hundred years. Though, the more often we fly, the longer we live. That's not really an option for me, so I plan to make the most of all the years I've got."

The fact that Wren's own father had shortened his life by clipping his son's wings made Kenna feel sick. "Ash told me about your parents. I'm sorry."

"I thought he might. It's hard for anyone to understand our friendship if they don't know our history."

Kenna had a feeling Wren's father and Drake's father would get along just fine. Drake's father had disowned him four years ago when his son had been honest about his sexuality. Drake's father had chosen social status over his own son.

They reached the doors, and Wren pushed them open, revealing a long hallway with a line of glittering, ostentatious chandeliers. The hallway was a series of arched windows on one side twinned with identically shaped mirrors on the other side, making the whole room glitter with warm, dancing light.

"A servant will show you to your chambers. I need to help Ash deal with a situation near the border."

"What's the situation?" she asked.

"Let's just say our friend in Gela Forest did not come alone."

Kenna's eyes widened, but Wren held a finger to his lips, telling her not to ask any more questions just as a female servant arrived at his side.

"This is Ori," Wren said, and the female servant dipped into a quick curtsey. "She will show you to your chambers. After breakfast in the morning, she'll take you to begin your training," Wren said and handed Ori Kenna's pack.

Ori's blonde hair was slicked back into a polished bun, and golden freckles dusted the fair skin of her slim nose and high cheekbones. Her pink lips were thin, and everything about her looked both solid and breakable at the same time. Like a beautiful piece of glass.

"This way, m'lady," the servant said.

"Oh. Um, I can carry that. You don't have to—"

"No, I insist, m'lady."

Kenna had nothing to do with her hands. What would she do with herself if servants insisted on doing every little thing for her? At least the High Council in Mesterra had one thing right. Servitude should be outlawed, if only to spare people from the sheer awkwardness of having another person do something that she was perfectly capable of doing herself.

Her soft leather boots shuffled along the stone flags and she was reminded of how her mother used to scold her as a child. *Kenna Duras, pick up your feet or you'll wear through your boots in five minutes.* She'd give anything to hear her mother's voice now. At least she knew her mother had seen the healer. She'd be okay.

But her father...she needed to fight to make his death mean something.

They reached a wide stone staircase, and she followed Ori up to the first landing and down the hallway to the left. Ori opened a set of white double doors twice as tall as Kenna, revealing the most opulent bedchamber she'd ever seen.

The floor was made of glittering marbled tile with silver swirls and shining black specks, and the four-poster bed was covered in a mound of plush white pillows with furs draped across the foot. Black organza curtains were drawn back to the head of the bed and pooled on the floor below.

As soon as she saw the bed, Kenna wanted nothing more than to fall into it and sleep for days. She didn't think that would be polite, so she did her best to follow Ori around as she gave her a tour of the room which would serve as her lodging until Winter Solstice.

Ori led her through arched glass doors onto a balcony overlooking the glassy lake and snowy valley. Kenna was grateful for the night's cool kiss on her cheeks instead of the artificial warmth of the courtyard.

"This wing of the castle has the best view," Ori explained.

"It's lovely, thank you. Ash—His Majesty—mentioned a bathing chamber?"

"Yes m'lady, it's just through here." Ori pushed on a single stone next to a mirror, revealing that it was also a hidden door. The door swung inward, and Kenna followed Ori through as the maid started lighting individual candles.

"Let me," Kenna said, tapping the Fostone on her bracelet. Immediately, tiny flames danced into existence in the chandelier and wall sconces.

"Thank you," Ori said. "I lost my Fostone, and have yet to replace it. They're not readily available in Notos."

"How long have you worked at the castle?"

"Two years."

The bathing chamber was a sprawling, tiled room with a sunken marble pool big enough for two or three to sit comfortably. There were various pipes for filling the tub, and the air in the room was warm and humid, the perfect atmosphere for bathing in comfort.

There was a rectangular, eye level window that offered a source of natural light while maintaining the privacy of the chamber. Below the window, a long box of tiny white flowers paid homage to the night—night blooming jasmine.

Mother would love it here.

She longed for her mother's comfort.

"Would you like me to draw you a bath, m'lady?" Ori asked, indicating an array of labeled amber bottles—peppermint, lavender, chamomile, eucalyptus, lemongrass, and many others.

Kenna felt like she might collapse if she didn't lie down. Even though she'd bathed at the Red Lantern, her clothes now stunk of horses. And the bath did look inviting.

"Yes, please." She tried to smile. Ori looked slightly taken aback by the genuine gratitude before she returned Kenna's smile.

While Kenna took off her boots and undressed, Ori ran the bath. Before leaving, the maid said, "I will take my leave then. Would you like me to wake you for breakfast in the morning?"

"Yes, please."

Ori nodded and left Kenna alone in her chambers. Her life was in utter chaos—a nightmare—but her room was magnificent.

After her bath, Kenna dried and dressed in her night shift before sinking into the decadent embrace of the massive bed. The worries about her family, friends, and the future faded to black as she drifted into a dreamless sleep.

CHAPTER 37

Ori opened the room-darkening curtains the following morning, and it took Kenna a moment to remember where she was. In fact, she could barely remember her name. She was nowhere near ready to leave the most comfortable bed she'd ever slept in.

Once awake, her mind spun with the events of the previous few days. Fleeing from Tormund. The battle. Zo and Ezra's capture. Her father's death. Her mother's injury. Jona and her friends flying off to the rebel camp. Staying in bed seemed like the most logical course of action.

She hadn't been there when Zo was taken. She hadn't been able to help at all when the Elders fought her loved ones. She'd hidden like a coward. Frozen and unable to help even if she'd wanted to.

That could never happen again. She couldn't hide anymore. She needed to do *something*.

So, she got up.

Ori cleared her throat. "His majesty took it upon himself to have some suitable clothing left for you in the wardrobe."

"Oh, thank the Ancients," Kenna said.

"I'll wait outside. When you're ready, I will show you down to breakfast."

Kenna opened the massive, wooden wardrobe and found multiple sets of black leather breeches and long sleeve grey blouses. Obviously, she'd need more than one set for her daily training. If it meant she could learn to protect herself and her family, she relished the chance to sweat and bleed. After all, she'd left all expectations of becoming a submissive female behind when she refused to drink from the Emergence Chalice.

And she had no plans to be a simpering princess either.

In addition to the shirts and trousers, there was a single black leather vest, boots, and multiple belts and straps, presumably for holding weapons. Though, Kenna noticed, there weren't any swords or knives among her personal collection yet. That was probably the safest choice for everyone, considering she had no idea how to even hold a blade.

After dressing in the supple trousers and comfortable blouse, she laced up her vest and boots. The vest was fitted, but she twisted, bent, and stretched, and was pleasantly surprised to find the leather was forgiving.

She eyed her reflection in the mirror. The ensemble accentuated all of her feminine curves, and everything about it made her feel empowered. Her long, disheveled locks only added to her fierce appearance. If not for the absence of the grime of battle and the blood of her enemies, she would have looked like she'd stepped off a windswept war field.

Looking at herself, she was certain she could learn to be the warrior she saw standing in the mirror. She ran her fingers through her dark waves, and secured her hair in a braid with a leather cord.

Finally, she pulled out all the belts and straps. They looked like a ball of string, and she didn't have the faintest idea of how to attach them, which made her feel less like a warrior. Refusing to let the self doubt creep in, she shoved the perplexing straps back into the wardrobe.

Ori led her to the dining room for breakfast, and Kenna was surprised to find the table empty. Morning sunlight streamed through large windows with a view of the snowy mountains beyond. Kenna ran a hand along the polished wood of the long table. Though there were twenty chairs around the table, Ash wasn't there. Neither was anyone else.

"Where is everyone?" she asked. Though she wasn't complaining about the absence of the sneering angel courtiers from last night.

"This is His Majesty's private dining room, reserved for his use and that of close friends and family. The rest of the court takes their meals in the great hall while they are visiting."

"Oh. I see." Kenna wasn't sure how she felt about being counted among those lucky enough to dine with the king in such an intimate capacity.

"Would you like some tea?" Ori asked.

"Is there koffee by any chance?" She responded.

"What's koffee?"

"Oh. Nevermind. I'll just have some tea. Thank you."

"The king has created a custom menu for you, so I'll bring your breakfast out." Kenna really hoped her menu included cinnamon buns.

Minutes later, Ori returned with a trolley containing a tea tray, some vile looking green liquid, and a silver cloche. When Kenna removed the cover, she saw a plate piled full of scrambled eggs with vegetables. There was more food than she could ever eat, but there was a sad absence of any toast or jam to accompany the eggs.

"Scrambled eggs with spinach, onion, and mushrooms; green vegetable juice; and a cup of tea. Eat as much as you'd like." At least Ori had the decency to look slightly apologetic about the absence of baked goods.

"Can I have some sugar for my tea?"

"I'm sorry m'lady. The king has advised against sugar at this time."

"Right. Thank you," Kenna fought back the urge to curse and pout like a dissatisfied toddler. The feeling of a man making decisions for her and the absence of koffee did nothing to improve her mood as she ate her breakfast.

"His Majesty sends his apologies that he will not be joining you today, but—"

"What?" she snapped at Ori again. "Sorry."

Ori lowered her gaze at Kenna's snipe.

It wasn't fair of her to punish Ori for delivering the news, but she was seething. Why had she come all this way if Ash wasn't even going to bother to show up for her training? She didn't imagine he'd always be able to train her himself, but she'd hoped that he would at least get her started.

"As I was saying, His Majesty has requested I show you to the training ring. The Captain of the Guard will take you through some basic magic drills and sword craft. The king will return tomorrow."

"Oh," Kenna said. The thought of training with Wren was tolerable. Plus, she might not make as much of a fool of herself in front of Ash if she started her training with the Wren.

"Shall we?" Ori asked.

Kenna followed Ori out of the dining room, passing through the hall of mirrors, down multiple staircases, and around a maze of corridors. Eventually, they descended a stone staircase. At the bottom of the stairs, a hall extended in either direction. Kenna really should have paid more attention to all of the turns as they'd passed through. She'd never be able to make it out of the labyrinth and back to her room without directions or a map.

There were two sets of identical wooden doors at either end of the hallway. Ori gestured to the left, so of course Kenna had to ask, "What happens if I get turned around and end up going the wrong way?" She pointed a thumb to the doors at the opposite end of the hall.

Ori's eyes flashed in warning. "You must not go through those doors. Even if you were allowed, you would not want to. Trust me."

Though Ori hadn't given her any reason to ignore the sensible advice, Kenna made a mental note to see what was behind the forbidden doors at the first available moment. She was no longer content to leave hidden truths undiscovered, and Ash had been trying to warn her about something. For whatever reason, he wouldn't or couldn't be forthcoming with all of his secrets, so Kenna would have to find the answers on her own.

When they reached the door, Ori said, "He'll be waiting for you there. After training, I will take you to your room to bathe and dress for dinner."

"Thank you, Ori," Kenna said.

A draft escaped as Kenna pushed open the door. She stepped into a cavernous, semicircular chamber that reminded her a little of the trial amphitheater in Tormund only larger and more ornate. The curve of the chamber was lined with rows of polished stone benches, presumably for spectators to watch sparring events or competitions. Thankfully, the seats were empty and there were no onlookers to witness her ineptitude. She looked up, noting the opening that revealed a sunny, winter sky above the chamber.

From the shadows of the far side of the ring, a lazy voice drawled, "How nice of you to finally join me."

Her skin prickled in response. Whoever waited in the shadow, it was not Wren.

CHAPTER 38

"Were you expecting me earlier?" she asked the hidden figure.

"Not necessarily. But I was waiting for you, and I do not like to be kept waiting," the voice pointed out.

Should I apologise? For...for not being late?

"Shall we?" A bulky, winged male with porcelain skin and dark curly hair prowled toward her. He had enormous wings with feathers as black as a raven. Both his body and the essence of his presence were incredibly intimidating. Though she was no slight twig herself, he looked like he could snap her in two with half a thought.

He circled her like a shark preparing for a kill. "I'm not sure what about you appeals to him, but here we are." He threw a sword at her feet. "Pick it up."

"I..." She'd never even seen more than the pommel of a sword in a scabbard. She didn't even know how to hold the weapon properly.

"Pick. It. Up." He snarled.

Hands trembling, she obeyed. The metal was cold in her grip, and the sword was heavier than she'd expected. She held it out in front of her with two hands, but her shoulder muscles protested after seconds. Her arms trembled with the effort of holding the heavy weapon aloft.

"What a waste of time. You are pathetic," he spat, and Kenna felt the truth of his words like a hammer against her bones.

"Perhaps if you'd tell me what I'm supposed to do, then I could do it," she ground out.

Learning a new skill was always a challenge, and she hated to fail. The fact that she had no experience didn't make her incompetence any less frustrating. Plus, the condescending male in front of her hadn't even bothered to introduce himself.

"It's a sword. You're meant to try to stab me with the pointy end." His patronizing explanation was unhelpful.

"But...you don't have a weapon."

"And?"

"Is that fair?"

"I can assure you, nothing about this fight is fair. You seem to have forgotten angels are capable of wielding not only steel but also far more dangerous weapons. Let me remind you."

In response to his proclamation, thick white mist clouded the edge of the room. All the candles flickered in their sconces, and the stones beneath their feet rearranged themselves. The large stone tile Kenna was standing on juddered and shifted position, moving her entire body like a pawn in a game of chess.

The gloating male stood before her, an unmoved tower. His eyes, the same silver gray as the sword in her hand, bored into her and sweat trickled down her spine.

"Shall we?" He asked, not bothering to assume a defensive position.

"Where is Wren? I was told that—"

"I dismissed the king's mutt," the male bit back.

"Will you at least tell me your name?"

"Samael. Now, let's get this over with, *Kenna*." He spat her name with such obvious distaste for the sound of it. The way he spoke to her convinced her she was the lowliest creature to ever exist.

His aura made her feel like the entire world would be better if she'd never been born, like everyone would be better off without her.

Despite her utter worthlessness, she struck out with the sword. Samael flicked it away with one finger. The sword struck a shield of solid ice, and the impact reverberated up her arms to her shoulders, making her cry out with pain and drop the weapon.

"Again. Unless you're ready to yield." He sneered.

I should give up. There's no way I can fight him.

Kenna stood. Instead of picking up the sword, she channeled her

Aqua magic, forming spears of bitter ice from the mist surrounding them and launched them at Samael's head. He simply chuffed a viscous laugh, turning the frigid knives to vapour without lifting a finger.

"Pitiful. Have you had enough?"

Her breath heaved in her chest with effort and rage. Rage at herself and her inadequacy. Rage at the High Council and the Elders for lying. Rage at her father for not allowing the females to learn defensive skills at the Academy.

Her rage threatened to drown her in defeat. A still, small voice inside her whispered, reminding her to keep going, reminding her of those she was learning to fight for.

Jona. Zola. Drake. Sera. Father Aryn. Mother.

Their names were her internal war cry as she balled her hands into fists, crushing two large flagstones to rubble, surprising herself with her own strength. She threw every ounce of her effort into propelling the stones toward Samael's legs, hoping to knock him off balance.

He barely moved a muscle, and the pebbles turned to dust, hurling back in her direction. The dust was in her eyes and airway, blinding and choking her. Just when she thought she was going to lose consciousness, Samael withdrew the assaulting debris. She coughed and fell to her knees, tears streaking through the grime on her face.

"Why does he bother with such a worthless female?"

She was broken. She couldn't change anything in the world. Her father was dead. Zo and Ezra were gone. She was going to lose everything until there was nothing left.

What's the point of fighting? If Samael kills me, it will probably be for the best.

Live, a breeze murmured.

By some miracle, she found the will to stand again.

Kenna attacked over and over with no instruction from Samael. Again and again, he thwarted her efforts, humiliated, and berated her. Those dark, hopeless thoughts pressed down on her.

She had no idea how long had passed, but there came a time when she couldn't stand, despite every ounce of effort. She laid on the cold stone floor, trembling and utterly spent. She couldn't even open her eyes to face her own shame and utter worthlessness.

Only then did Samael come anywhere near her. He knelt beside her, his voice vicious and quiet. She imagined she could hear his voice in her mind. "You are nothing. And this is exactly where you belong. In fact, maybe I will end you right now and save the king the trouble of—"

The wooden doors to the training ring opened with a thundering crash. Kenna opened one eye and propped herself up on her elbows to see what was happening.

If lightning had a sound, it was the sound of Ash's voice as he asked, "What is the meaning of this? Where is Wren?"

"I dismissed him." Samael's smile was an ugly, vicious thing. "I thought it would be much more expedient if I trained her myself."

"Is this what you call training?"

"Well, now we know where her weaknesses lie. In case you are wondering, she is one of the weakest I have ever seen. In all aspects." The way Samael spoke about her, it would not have surprised her if he'd turned and spit in her face. "It's interesting though. In spite of her weakness, I was unable to read her thoughts. Why do you think that might be?"

"That is none of your concern. She is none of your concern," Ash said through clenched teeth. "You will not touch her. You will not go near her. You will not even think of her, or I'll show you exactly why I'm the king of the realm and you are only a prince. And you will not live to tell the tale."

"As you wish, *Your Majesty*."

Samael studied his fingernails as though the threat meant nothing. Then, he gave Ash an exaggerated bow and sent a cruel smirk in Kenna's direction. A smirk that suggested his "training" had achieved his desired outcome. She flopped down onto her back again, unable to support her weight on her elbows any longer.

"Kenna," Ash rushed to her side, kneeling. "Did he hurt you?"

She was physically and emotionally exhausted. The oppressive weight of worthlessness she'd felt during her fight with Samael lingered but was fading in the absence of his presence.

"He…he tried to read my thoughts?"

Ash nodded, curtly.

"Why couldn't he?" Kennna asked. "I don't know how to shield against that. I didn't even know angels could do that."

"Only the most powerful angels have the gift of cerelegry—mind reading and mind to mind communication. The glamor I used for your appearance covers your thoughts as well, shielding them from anyone who might take the truth from your mind. Including me."

"But I think he…there were thoughts in my mind that felt…intrusive. Like they didn't belong to me. Was he sending those thoughts?"

Ash nodded. "I'm sorry. Shielding against the intrusive thoughts would have made my protection over you too obvious. We can only hope the prince heeds my warning and stays away from you."

How could anyone presume to take another person's private thoughts or to press such dark and hopeless thoughts onto another? It was despicable.

"Well, at least we know I have room for improvement. I was worried I'd be such a natural warrior that you wouldn't be able to teach me anything." She attempted a weak smile.

"You'll not learn like this," Ash scowled. "From now on, only Wren or I will train you. You have my word." Kenna vaguely noted the glimmering warmth of their oath before she lost consciousness.

CHAPTER 39

$\mathcal{A}$n open book lay on his lap, but he found himself too distracted to read.

For the second time in three days, Ash was watching Kenna sleep, and she'd been sleeping for nearly an entire day.

Why couldn't he tear his eyes away from her?

Kenna curled on her side with her hands tucked under her cheek, still in her training clothes from yesterday morning. Her round, pretty face was still covered in grime, but her tears had left clean slashes through the dirt on her cheeks which looked like scars. He hoped her dreams were pleasant.

She'd been in the castle for less than a day, and Ash had already failed her. Already, she was hurt because of him. He should have done more. He should have at least made Samael suffer. If the Ancient magic of the treaty didn't prevent it, he would have killed the prince, and not just for this. But he couldn't. He couldn't even lock Samael in the dungeon.

This wasn't some staged attack like the one in Braktyn where he knew she'd be okay. If Wren hadn't come to Ash and told him that Samael was with Kenna… He shuddered.

Usually, Samael seemed to enjoy waiting before he pulled a stunt like yesterday's. Whenever Ash's conquests arrived at the castle, it was a game of cat and mouse between the prince and Ash's cursed lovers. Eventually, Samael always pounced.

This time, Samael hadn't waited, and Ash knew why. This morning, Samael had set off to search for the human princess. He knew as well as Ash what this year meant, and Samael was determined to finally earn their mother's approval by marrying the girl.

Ash's single comfort lay in the fact that Samael hadn't guessed Kenna's identity. If not, he wouldn't have left the castle. Her glamor and mental protection had worked against the prince. Kenna would be safer with Samael away from the castle. For the foreseeable future, his brother would be distracted by the impossible task of seeking the human princess he'd unwittingly left in Ash's care.

Seeing Kenna broken and battered on the floor yesterday had stoked a primal need to protect her. Why did Ash feel so drawn to her? Fate seemed to beg him to open his heart to her, but what was the point? He'd had a great love once before with his mate, Elenya. His heart had never recovered from the betrayal and heartbreak that ended their relationship.

If anything, he should push Kenna away. Perhaps he could protect her by remaining cool and distant. If she didn't fall in love with him, then the ritual wouldn't work.

But in all his centuries of being cursed, the women he'd brought to the castle had always fallen for him. He was not so arrogant to believe his flirtation and good looks were enough to make every woman he pursued give him her heart. He was never cruel, but it didn't seem to matter how little or how much attention he paid the targets of his curse. There was likely some mysterious magic which lured the women into loving him.

He was the most dangerous type of foe—handsome, charming, and seductive.

A beautiful, treacherous beast.

Full of self-loathing, Ash slammed the book on his lap shut. He'd brought it with him today to "accidentally" leave it in Kenna's bedchamber so she might read it. Perhaps, the pages he'd folded down might help her begin to uncover the truth for herself. There were no tomes in the castle library holding the true history of Luniva and Soldivus. His mother's true motivation the Void War, but this book was the closest.

It held enough truth about Luniva for Kenna to begin to understand.

When he explained the treaty, she'd have answers to some of her questions. She'd learn about the Shadows. He could tell her about the Hill, the horrible place where her friends Zo and Ezra were being held. She'd understand more about the Emergence serum, how angels had infiltrated and seized control of Mesterra, and how they were meant to leave the elves in peace.

She'd learn the true, extortionate cost of crossing the Veil.

She'd also discover what the treaty required of her as the human princess—a marriage to either save her people or doom them. And she'd find out her unbreakable oath with Ash had likely ruined it.

Their oath would probably prevent her from marrying the prince of Vorra and free the human race.

There was still so much she needed to know that he'd be unable to tell her.

Was it fair for him to tell her about the treaty so soon after everything she'd been through? She'd lost her father and nearly lost her mother. She'd fled from a realm where she'd spent her whole life; she'd discovered her parents had hidden her humanity from her for twenty-five years.

If he told her everything about the treaty, would it change their relationship?

No, he wouldn't tell her just yet. Less than a week ago, she'd believed all angels were her enemy. But she'd chosen to trust him.

For now, he would continue to be her ally, but he would do his best to keep his distance. He would train her, but he would be professional. He'd been a general in Luniva's army hundreds of years ago and a king ever since. Surely, he could abstain from flirtation with a twenty-five-year-old woman.

Kenna began to stir and he resisted the instinct to brush away a strand of hair that fell across her face.

Instead, he clenched his hands into fists and dragged his eyes away from her, looking out the glass balcony doors towards the snowy mountains and clear blue skies beyond.

He didn't wish for love, not really. He only wished he could scoop her up and soar above the clouds. Away from this place, away from his curse, away from the treaty to somewhere they would both be free.

Unfortunately, Ash didn't think freedom was part of either of their destinies. With that truth in mind... at least he could teach her how to fight like Hel.

CHAPTER 40

When Kenna finally awoke, her head was pounding like she'd consumed an entire bottle of notelixir. Her mouth and throat were as dry as dust. It reminded her of the fight—choking on dust, blinded by dust, suffocated by dust. Her breathing constricted in panic, and she bolted upright in bed.

"Good morning to you, too," Ash's silky voice said. "You've been asleep for almost a full day."

He was sitting in a chair next to her bed with a book on his lap, looking immaculate as ever. Kenna looked down at her own rumpled clothes, still dirty from the fight, as though Ash had simply laid her on the bed and covered her with a blanket. She breathed slowly, allowing his presence to ease her racing heart.

"You know," she said. "It seems like you're making a habit of watching me sleep."

Ash twirled his fingers lazily in the air, and a swirl of water from the jug on her bedside table filled a large glass. He passed the glass to her. "Drink. I'll see you downstairs for breakfast in ten minutes."

He seemed to have regressed to that handsome, arrogant stranger from the night they'd met. But now, his tone and demeanor were cool and condescending. She chugged the water in one long swallow.

"You know, after everything that's happened, I think I deserve to get properly drunk. Is that part of today's plan, by any chance?"

"No, we have work to do." Ash stood, leaving the book on the chair and crossed to the door.

"Fine. I bet Ori can find me some of the good stuff later."

From all the way across the room, Ash said, "She's been instructed to provide you only with meals and beverages which will benefit your strength and training."

"How did you—"

Ash tapped one of his pointed ears as he walked out the door.

Kenna made a note to keep any such future monologues contained within her skull. Thankfully, Ash's glamour would protect her thoughts from prying minds. As the puzzle pieces detailing the scope of Ash's abilities slotted into place, Kenna couldn't decide if she felt more or less safe. He had some healing magic, and she'd witnessed him summon the elements without needing a source. She'd seen his immense strength and speed first hand. If Ash had those powers, then so did other angels —so did Prince Samael and the angel courtiers who seemed so averse to her presence.

Ash's behavior this morning was different. There was none of his fierce protection and gentle concern from the moments after the fight. There was none of the playful flirtation they'd shared during the journey to Brumalis Castle. There was nothing she'd seen of him the last few days that had made her begin to trust him.

Had it been only a few days since she'd met him at the Golden Flagon? Since he'd saved her that night in Braktyn? His power had terrified her then. It still scared her, but the more time she'd spent with him, the more it seemed like he was on her side.

But now…

Had she offended him or was he disappointed in the outcome of her training with Samael? He'd acted eager to be her friend and ally, but now he was acting like her presence was an immense inconvenience.

If anything, *he* was the inconvenience. He was the angel king, and she was a human princess. Their races had been on opposite sides of the Void War, a war that ended with the fate of humanity resting on her shoulders.

Kenna threw off the blanket. She was not a teenager. She would not waste her time brooding over the inner workings of an immortal man-child whose moods swung like a pendulum. She deserved a lover who held control of himself and his emotions. A man who knew what he wanted and didn't play games.

She picked up the book Ash had left behind. As she skimmed the page, she discerned that it was a romance story. It wasn't a simple love story. It was the story of the Ancients. Kenna threw it on her bed and looked forward to reading more tonight.

She made her way to the bathing chamber, catching sight of her reflection. Unlike the pristine visage of the previous morning, she was filthy. Perhaps she looked like a real warrior with the dirt and grime streaking her clothes and face, but Samael had shown her how truly inept she was.

She felt further away from her goal than ever.

Kenna sighed and pushed the stone in the wall to open the door, looking longingly at the bathtub. She changed and took care of her body's morning business, making the unfortunate discovery that her cycle had arrived.

Fantastic.

Thankfully, she found the products she needed in a basket near the toilet before she washed and dressed in a fresh set of training clothes.

She joined Ori outside her door. "Well, it seems fate has cursed me. My second day here, and I've just started my cycle."

Ori didn't even acknowledge the effort of female camaraderie.

A few steps passed in awkward silence, until Kenna started babbling about nothing: "You know, I'm pretty sure I could clear out the castle with my stench. I've always just been such a sweaty person. Being surrounded by pompous, judgemental angels all the time doesn't help. I know they have superior power and all, but do they all have something stuck up their asses?"

Ori just blinked at Kenna as they walked. The maid seemed diligent enough in her service, but she had the personality of a blade of grass. Kenna suspected she'd have to find titillating conversation elsewhere. Kenna longed for the easy banter with Sera and Drake. For late night chats with Zo and Aryn.

Even if Ori wasn't the most exciting person, Kenna was trying her best to be polite and take an interest. "Where are you from?"

"Pardon?" Ori looked at her like she had three heads—like no one had ever bothered to ask her anything about herself before.

"I just wondered how you ended up working at the palace?"

"I don't like to talk about it."

"Come now, Ori. I told you all about my profuse sweating. Surely you can tell me more than that."

Ori darted a glance at her. "I was born in Fylios. Just north of Valak. I came to Notos after my Emergence five years ago. I fell in love, but it didn't end well. The male I loved was my everything; he made me believe we could have a beautiful life together. A child. A future. I moved to Saphyr to be with him, but life in Saphyr was expensive. For a while, my lover took care of me. But, eventually…life with him was not what I thought it would be. I found myself in severe debt and under his control."

Suddenly, Kenna felt guilty for coaxing the story out of the maid. She hoped she didn't feel like she'd ordered her to share the painful history. "I'm sorry things didn't work out as you'd hoped. Surely, employment for the royal family must be a coveted position."

Ori shrugged. "Things could be worse. I'm glad to be in the king's service."

"How long will you work for the royal family until you can pay back your debts?

"I'll never be free," Ori said in a near-silent whisper.

"Oh."

Ori's answering smile was wistful as they reached the dining room. "I'll see you this evening to help you dress for dinner."

"I don't need—" Kenna tried to tell her she didn't need help getting dressed, but Ori had already left.

"Feeling better?" Ash asked from the far end of the table, sipping his green juice and finishing off his eggs.

"Not really. Any chance there is bacon this morning? I could really go for some bacon."

Ash shook his head and a servant appeared with a trolley containing black tea, green juice, and a silver dome. She cursed under her breath. She had a sneaking suspicion what was under the cover. The thought of eggs and vegetables only stoked her hormonal irritability.

Call me a female cliché, but I want cheese and chocolate. And lots of both. Eggs and vegetables can go right into the Void.

The male servant placed the offensive breakfast in front of her, and she scowled at the pile of eggs.

"Aren't you going to drink your vegetable juice?" Ash seemed to be fighting back laughter at the disgusted look on Kenna's face.

"How and why do you drink this swill? Better yet, why do *I* have to drink it?" Kenna pinched her nose and brought the glass to her lips to chug the juice.

"Ash looks after his body without complaint because *he* is not a useless piece of rubbish," Samael said, entering the dining room.

"I thought I made it abundantly clear that you are not to speak to her." Ash glared at his brother.

"Oh, I wouldn't dare defy you, Your Majesty. I was just stating facts to the room at large. If your elvish whore happened to overhear, then it's none of my concern."

Now that she wasn't addled by exhaustion and defeat, Kenna wondered what had caused such animosity between the two angels. The brothers glowered at each other, Samael with his steel gray eyes and Ash with his deep blue stare. Samael was slightly shorter and bulkier than Ash, though he was still over six feet tall. Any similarities between them ended with their dark hair and ivory skin. Kenna didn't want to be in the same room as Samael for another second.

Thankfully, Ash said, "I thought you'd already left."

"What kind of brother would I be if I didn't say goodbye?"

"Goodbye, then," Ash said.

"On second thought, I have not eaten. Perhaps, I'll stay for breakfast."

"I've lost my appetite," Kenna said, pushing her plate away and standing to leave.

"Sit, Kenna," Ash commanded.

She glared at him, hands trembling, but sat back down.

Ash snapped his fingers, and a female servant entered the dining room. "The prince would like to take his breakfast with him on his travels this morning."

"Yes, Your Majesty," the servant said.

"I would have preferred room service," Samael muttered

Then, he plucked an apple out of a fruit bowl on the table. Unsheathing a dagger, he fixed Kenna with a stare and peeled the skin off of the ruby fruit. He looked like he'd much rather be skinning her.

"You need to leave, Sam," Ash commanded.

Samael didn't say a word as he strolled out of the dining room.

Kenna stared at her trembling hands, unable to eat. Whenever Samael was around, all she felt was her own utter worthlessness. Even after he left, taking his intrusive thoughts with him, she couldn't manage to summon any positive energy.

She hadn't anticipated Samael's vitriol or the judgemental courtiers. She hadn't expected to miss her friends and family so much already or to feel the lashing pain of defeat so soon.

"My brother will always solicit your most unpleasant thoughts and emotions. When those feelings arise, it's your decision whether his manipulation crushes your purpose or fuels your strength. Which will you choose, Kenna?"

She looked at Ash, unsure what to say. He hadn't called her love or princess or lass or any other condescending nickname. He'd addressed her by name, and challenged her to step in her power.

That was the moment she knew he was truly on her side. Maybe he'd been cool and indifferent earlier, but this man would teach her to fight from somewhere deep inside. She was determined to prove Samael wrong. She had angel magic, and it was past time she learned to wield it.

She didn't speak as she pulled her plate toward her and choked down as many eggs as she could. She'd need the strength.

Then, she stood, putting her hands on her hips, waiting. "Let's go."

The glint in Ash's eye told her she'd made the right choice.

CHAPTER 41

Two weeks later, she was in the ring with Ash, hating everything about his perfect face with every fiber of her being.

"I need a break," she said.

"You have another half an hour before you get a break."

"Can I have a few minutes to visit the facilities to take care of my feminine needs?"

"Right. If you need—yes. Yes, that is fine." Ash seemed to find a very interesting speck of dirt under his nails. She took great pleasure in seeing Ash's composure crack. It was the only pleasing thing that had happened that morning.

She excused herself, mentally reviewing her training as she walked. Other than his concern after her encounter with Samael, Ash had been cold and distant ever since she arrived in the castle. When they trained, he was merciless and pushed her to her limits.

Though her arms were shaking and felt wobbly after each session, the only thing she'd learned so far was how to grip a sword properly and the positions of the different fighting stances. Kenna had never been naturally athletic, so moving through the stances was difficult. But she felt like she was getting stronger each day, and the stances grew easier every time she practiced them.

Still, Ash hadn't even had the decency to give her an actual sword.

Instead, she used a glorified broom handle like a child's plaything. They hadn't even touched on magic.

Running drills with a wooden toy was cumbersome, and Kenna was impatient to move on to more exciting training. At least it was less humiliating than her training with Samael. Her hands were blistered from hours of physical training, and her patience was thin from the lack of progress. Even so, she headed back to the training ring to face her incompetency head on.

"I think I'm ready for a real sword. See? I'm getting pretty good with this thing." She picked up the broomstick and tossed it up in the air. It spun round and round dramatically before she fumbled with it, failing to catch it and it tumbled to the floor.

"Yes, I can see that," Ash said, with a lopsided smile. "You will be glad to know that throwing a sword and catching it dramatically for the sake of performance is not a particularly useful skill for vanquishing your enemies."

She groaned, "When will I learn something useful then? What about magic?"

"Because of your situation, I think it will be beneficial for you to have a strong foundation in weaponry. Just in case."

"In case of what?" she asked.

"You're the only human who's ever had a magical gifts. There's a chance that once the treaty is fulfilled, you may lose your power."

"That's not exactly reassuring."

"It's unlikely, but that's why it's so important to learn physical combat. Also, you cannot expect to handle a sword like a trained soldier after only two weeks," Ash said. "Don't worry, though. I have no doubt we'll make a fighter of you before Winter Solstice."

"I don't know if you realize this or not, but I'm not the most patient or consistent individual you will ever meet. I'm more inclined to attack things with the full force of my wholehearted efforts. Eventually, I either collapse or succeed. Couldn't you just skip to the end so I know if my efforts are going to be worth it?" She snapped her fingers like Ash often did to summon his servants. "You could just use your magical fingers to help me learn everything I need to know."

Ash arched a brow as he purred, "My magic fingers would happily teach you a thing or two. You need only ask."

She gave him an obscene gesture in return, though it was nice to see him smiling and flirting again.

Focus, Kenna.

"Unfortunately, the only way you will learn is with practice. You will not be able to learn everything you need instantly. Even the fiercest warrior has to master the stances first. It's the foundation for every-thing else. But we're done with sword drills for today. Time to hand you over to Wren."

Kenna groaned. "I take it back. I'll do sword drills with you all day. If Wren makes me run up those rutting stairs one more time, I'll—"

"You'll what?" Wren had snuck up behind her.

"Over to you, mate," Ash said, saluting Wren casually and sauntering away to do whatever else kings did all day.

"So, the princess doesn't like to run up the stairs?" He smiled with a mischievous gleam in his eye. "Shall we jump them instead?"

"What?"

"Like this." Wren walked over to the stairs, standing in front of them with his feet shoulder width apart. He squatted and proceeded to spring up onto the first step. Then the next and the one after that, until he was at the top. He jogged back down to where she stood with her arms crossed over her chest. He was barely out of breath.

"I can't do that," she said.

"Why not?"

"I'm not fit enough! You're…you." She gestured to his chiseled physique. "And I'm me." She indicated the soft curves of her own body.

" Anyone who thinks the shape of your body dictates how strong or fierce of an opponent you can be is wrong. Fitness has little to do with the size of your ass. I've got a few female soldiers under my command who are twice your size, but they're as strong as me. I'd trust them to have my back in a battle more than some of the guys who look like they're cut from marble. None of the training we're doing and none of the food you're eating has anything to do with trying to change your physique. We want your body to become as strong as possible, but that starts here." Wren tapped a finger to his temple. "Let go of your perceived limitations. Now, get your ass over here and jump."

Kenna uncrossed her arms, wiping away her glower and moving to the steps. He was right. She'd decided she couldn't do it without even trying. Two weeks ago, she'd barely been able to jog to the top of the steps once. Yesterday, she'd done twenty sets of sprints up the stairs. She was getting stronger, so maybe she could do this.

She wouldn't be able to help anyone if she wasn't willing to work hard and to push through her own discomfort.

"Race you to the top?" she challenged.

Wren's answering smirk told her she was going to regret it, but she smiled back, ready to embrace the fatigue in her muscles and burning in her lungs. She was a princess, but she wasn't going to sit around in pretty dresses. She was going to be a fucking *warrior*. This was why she was here.

Wren settled into his starting position, and she copied him before he said, "Three, two, one, jump!"

She poured all of her grief, loneliness, anxiety, uncertainty into each jump.

Again and again and again until her lungs burned and tears streamed down her face. The physical exertion released the emotions she'd kept locked inside. Under normal circumstances, she did anything she could to distract herself from her feelings.

With each jump, she had to dig deep to remember everything she was fighting for. She thought about losing her father. Zo and Ezra. Almost losing her mother. She thought about her brother and Sera and all the rebels fighting against the angels in Mesterra. Knowing they were all fighting too made her feel a little less alone. It gave her the will to keep moving.

CHAPTER 42

"Stay with me," Wren said. "Two more rounds."

Lost as she was in her breathing, in the intensity of her effort, Kenna had been able to let her feelings out—the grief, the uncertainty, the anxiety. She sobbed as she pushed herself to jump over and over again. Her emotions roiled and she barely noticed the wind howling through the arena.

After the last round, she jogged down the stairs and collapsed on the floor, lying flat on her back.

After a moment, she sat up and clamped a hand over her mouth feeling the rising nausea. Wren already had a bucket ready, and she promptly lost her entire lunch into the metal container.

Wiping away the remnants of his own sweat, Wren tossed her a rag to wipe her mouth and sweaty face. "If you keep moving a little after you're done, the nausea won't hit as hard. You did well today. Continue that level of effort, I might have to recruit you to join the guard."

He mussed her sweat-soaked hair and then grimaced, playfully wiping her sweat off of his hand on the sleeve of her tunic. She batted away his hand, mustering an exhausted smile as she caught her breath and the nausea faded.

Her body was wrecked and her muscles were screaming, but she was proud of herself. The determination she'd found to keep going when she wanted to give up was surprising.

After giving her a few minutes to recover and drink from the water skin, Wren made her do multiple rounds of push ups and situps until her arms trembled and her core burned. When her arms eventually gave out, he finally declared their session over.

"Thank the Ancients," Kenna said. "You're trying to kill me."

"I think you'll find that's the opposite of what we're trying to achieve here. Has Ash trained you with any wind magic yet?"

"We haven't done any magic training, and I don't have wind magic."

Wren looked at her sideways. "Why would you think that?"

"When I was a child, I used to think I could hear the wind whisper to me. Before my magic even manifested. It wanted to play or help me or warn me of things. My parents told me elves don't have wind magic." Kenna shrugged and looked down, playing with the hem of her blouse. "After that, I learned to ignore the wind's voice most of the time. I figured it was just my imagination."

"But you're not an elf," Wren reminded her. "Your magic comes from angels, right?"

"It does but I don't think I could control the wind even if I wanted to."

"You know the wind in here today was from you, right?"

Kenna snapped her head up, looking at him. "What?"

"Yes. You can definitely wield the wind. In fact, your connection to wind magic seems incredibly strong. Stronger than many angel warriors I've known through the years."

"How is that possible?"

"I don't know, princess. But let's just say that once you learn to harness that power, I'll be glad to be on your side of the war."

Before she had time to wonder what he meant, he extended a hand. "Come on. Let's get you up to your room. I think you've earned a nice bath and some time to relax before dinner."

Kenna groaned, remembering the multiple levels of stairs she'd have to climb to reach her chambers. Wren smiled knowingly.

"We'll take it slowly. Let's go."

She stood and followed Wren through the labyrinth of hallways and up the stairs. Needing a distraction from her aching legs, she finally mustered the courage to ask Wren the question in the front of her mind. She was worried he would think her ignorant, but she needed as much information as she could gather if she'd have any hope of making a difference in the Three Realms.

"Can you tell me what you know about Ash's past?"

"Feeling a bit curious, are you? Jealous, maybe? If you're wondering how many lovers he's had, then I really don't think you want an answer to that question." She felt a spike of jealousy, even though that was not what she'd meant at all.

"I don't want any answers about that. But what role did Ash play in the Void War? How did he end up on the throne?"

They turned down a seemingly endless hallway lined with suits of gleaming black metal and polished steel. There must have been fifteen female servants busy polishing the impressive display.

Wren shrugged. "Not all angels have the same amount of power, and Ash is particularly powerful. He was one of Luniva's favorites, and he was the highest ranking general in her army. When the Ancients made the treaty, they each appointed royals to look after Notos and Vorra. If you want to know any more than that, you'll have to ask the old man. History isn't my area of expertise, princess."

"Should you really call me that? I need to keep a low profile, and I don't think calling me princess will help exactly."

"You're adorable. I happen to believe all beautiful women should feel like a princess." Wren slipped his arm through the crook of her elbow and lowered his voice. "Watch this."

They'd reached the end of the hallway where the female servants were busy cleaning and Wren turned to face the direction they'd come. "Hey there, Princess." He spoke loudly enough that the rumbling purr of his voice echoed down the hallway.

Four of the female servants looked at him, and he blew a kiss in their general direction. Each of the four plump women looked at each other knowingly and returned to their duties with blushing smiles. They didn't seem jealous or like they minded their shared nickname.

"See?" Wren winked.

He turned Kenna around and continued walking to her room. "Nevermind the king," she teased. "How many lovers have *you* had?"

"Let's just say I have quite the reputation around the castle and very few complaints."

"Seems like you might be able to make a living at the Flaming Arrow if you set your mind to it."

"Oh, trust me. I've considered it on more than one occasion, mostly on days when Ash turns into a cold, entitled ass. Usually, he ends up giving me a pay raise to keep me around. Plus, they say you shouldn't turn your favorite hobby into a job. You might not like it so much anymore."

"So, is it normal for him to act that way? Cold and distant?"

"Only when he has something weighing on his mind. He'll be back to himself soon enough. He just needs a little time." Wren turned to her and gave her hand a gentle pat where it rested comfortably in his arm.

They passed a group of angel courtiers going in the opposite direction. The haughty angels bustled past with the swishing of silk gowns and clicking of polished boots.

If not for Wren's fae wings and Kenna's sweaty clothes, he was the picture of a proper gentleman escorting a lady. Still, the courtiers looked down their noses at the pair of them, and one of them gave an audible snort.

When they reached her door, Wren bowed and kissed her hand like he had when they met a few days ago. "Milady."

"What? Aren't you going to call me princess?"

Wren wiggled his eyebrows, grinning. "Do you *want* me to call you princess?"

She rolled her eyes and swatted him away.

"I'll see you at dinner," she said before disappearing into her bedchamber.

Wren had a dimple in one cheek and his smile was dazzling against his brown skin and black stubble. In her first couple of weeks training at the castle, Wren had quickly become someone Kenna considered a friend. Everything about him set her at ease, and she could easily imagine him swapping salacious banter with Sera and Drake over a pint of ale. In fact, she would have bet good money that Sera and Wren would end up tangled in the sheets for hours if they ever had the good fortune to meet. Even if Wren seemed to prefer ladies with more generous curves.

Though Pax was an angel and Wren was a winged fae, she got the same sense of brotherly protection from both of them. There wasn't a drop of evil running through their veins.

Then, there was the king. Ash didn't seem malicious. Moody and somewhat cold, yes. But Kenna didn't feel threatened by him, even if she had a constant tinge of warning in the back of her mind when she was in his presence.

Samael on the other hand…

He'd exerted his power and control over her; he'd seemed to draw such pleasure from her humiliation. Based on her limited experience with the controlling Elders and the merciless High Council in Mesterra, his behavior was exactly what she would have expected from all angels

Ash, Pax, and Wren all perplexed her. Even the high priestess she'd met briefly at Braktyn's temple had seemed benevolent and kind, though Ash had tried to warn her not to trust Lailah. Perhaps angels were just like any other race. Maybe angels and fae weren't inherently good or evil, but some of them ended up hateful and cruel after years of selfish and hurtful choices. Maybe, some of them chipped away at their own kindness until only malice remained.

The Elders had killed her father in battle. They'd captured Ezra and Zo. And what about the ferry master? What role did he play in all of this? After all, Raziel's cruel bargain with Ezra was the only reason her father and Zo were targeted.

When she entered her room, the balcony doors were open and the cool evening breeze gently ruffled the gauzy charcoal curtains. Her bed had been made and a simple, beautiful gown was laid out for her. She ran her hand over the silky violet material. The fine craftsmanship made her think of her mother.

Kenna hadn't been able to ask her mother many questions before she left Tormund. Though her parents had lied to her, it didn't lessen the empty ache of missing them. It just added to the thousands of questions she wished she could ask her father, and the questions she would ask her mother when she saw her again.

Exhausted by her swirling thoughts and the grief weighing her down, Kenna laid on her bed and stared into nothing. She wished she could hide in her room and lose herself in a book instead of having to deal with any of this.

Why me? Why not someone stronger?

Somewhere inside, she heard an whisper of her father's advice. Something he'd told her every time she'd felt overwhelmed.

You're not alone, Kenna. Look around. There are people who love you. People who will help you if you'll only let them. All you have to do is take the next small step. One step at a time.

She clung to the kernel of strength and wisdom, shedding a few silent tears as she wished to hear her father speak the words aloud one more time. And with his words in her heart, she summoned the strength to take the next small step.

Her muscles were stiff from training, so she went to draw a bath. She perused the shelf filled with bottles of scented oils, finding the multitude of choices overwhelming after the taxing day. She'd all but decided to use lavender—as usual—when she discovered a small note on a piece of parchment embossed with the royal sigil.

For aching muscles: Five drops cedarwood, four drops eucalyptus, and four drops lemongrass.

Kenna didn't even know there *was* such a thing as cedarwood oil, but she found it amongst the bottles and added it to the water first. The aroma of a winter forest tickled her nose, wafting into the air on clouds of steam. It would have smelled like Ash if it had any notes of lingering bonfire smoke.

Something stirred within her. Was Ash suggesting that she literally bathe in his scent? As quickly as she could, Kenna muddied the aroma with lemongrass and eucalyptus, trying to tamp down her confusing feelings.

She scrubbed herself clean and then relaxed into the perfect curve of the tub. She closed her eyes, feeling weightless in the deep water and let the soothing scent ease her muscles and carry her away.

FALLING DOWN INTO A SWIRLING, black abyss, she landed in a cage within a Void.

Emerging from the inky darkness, a horned figure with gleaming red eyes circled her.

She smelled rancid breath as the beast sneered in her face, tapping its talons against the metal bars of her prison with malevolent intent.

Clink. Clink. Clink.

Knock. Knock. Knock.

Kenna awoke with a start. Someone was knocking.

"Is everything alright?" Ori's voice came from outside the door of her bathing chamber.

Kenna gasped, startled as freezing water splashed over the side of the tub. She'd fallen asleep. Her skin was pebbled into gooseflesh and she shivered before steadying her breath and reminding herself she was safe. It was only a dream.

She cleared her throat, "Yes, Ori. I'm fine. I just dozed off."

"Okay. Let me know when you are ready," the maid said.

Kenna stepped into the shower where she stood under hot water before dousing herself with lavender, hoping the soothing scent would calm her lingering anxiety. After drying, she pulled on the purple dress and invited Ori into the room to help fasten it at the back. As she stood in front of the mirror, Kenna had to admit the simple gown suited her.

She relished the comfort of Ori's hands running through her hair as the maid arranged it for the evening. If Kenna closed her eyes, she could pretend Ori's hands were her mother's, soothing her in the wake of the ghastly nightmare. But behind closed lids, Kenna was accosted by the memory of the ghoulish forms.

Opening her eyes, she was confronted with her ever-present reality —nightmares were real. Evil was on the rise in the realms, and it was hurting her family.

Kenna had grown up in a world seen through a lens of shelter, privilege, and pretending. She'd gone through daily motions with only two objectives: Safety and Emergence.

Now, she faced the seemingly insurmountable task of finding out how to help her family and friends overthrow the ones who'd subdued the elves under the guise of order and safety for so long. Not to mention freeing the humans.

Ash had to know more about all of this. He knew so much of why she was here and what she was fighting for, yet he'd shared no helpful information with her beyond her physical training.

He couldn't answer questions she'd yet to ask. He couldn't read her mind. He'd told her as much.

But she was a princess, damn it. Physical training was only part of the equation, it was time for her to be a part of the political conversation.

Surely, she should have felt some measure of joy as Ori led her to the dining room. She was living in a stunning castle, dining with the king and his handsome Captain of the Guard. But she couldn't lose sight of why she was here.

CHAPTER 43

*E*ach afternoon, Ash had been visiting the various outposts throughout Notos, checking and reinforcing the wards, making sure that no more creatures like the Achetaur could breach them. He trained with Kenna for two hours every morning, and then left her with Wren.

Most nights, he returned to dine with them, and tonight he and Wren were waiting for Kenna to join them.

"How is she progressing with her fitness?" Ash asked. "Her weapons drills are coming along nicely."

Wren laughed. "The woman is a machine. She pushed herself so hard today that she vomited."

The fire in Kenna's belly and her sheer determination to give her sessions every ounce of effort she had was the most stunning thing about her.

His friend's expression grew serious. "Ash, you've got to tell her about the treaty. If you don't tell her soon, she's going to find out some other way. You'll destroy any sense of trust she feels toward you. She's almost ready to train with her magic, and she needs to be able to trust you for that."

"Don't you think I know that?" Ash snapped, then sighed. "Sorry. I'm just...not looking forward to that conversation."

Ash had played out telling her a hundred different ways. The best he'd landed on was *Oh by the way, you're engaged to the prince of Vorra.*

Sorry I didn't tell you sooner. It doesn't matter if you want to marry him or not, if you don't, you'll have to marry Samael instead and all of humanity is doomed.

His delivery still needed work.

Wren's expression grew serious. "Listen. I know you're my king, but you're my friend first. And so is Kenna. She deserves to know. If you don't tell her by the end of your training with her tomorrow, I'll tell her myself."

Ash ground his teeth, not appreciating the ultimatum. Why did Wren have to be right?

One of the servants opened the doors and Kenna entered the dining room. Wren wolf-whistled in approval just as he did every night. "You clean up well, princess."

Kenna rolled her eyes as usual before twirling slowly and winking at Wren over her shoulder. It earned another whistle from his captain, and Ash resisted the urge to fire his best friend then and there.

"Kenna, you look lovely." Ash gave her a tight smile.

Lovely was an understatement. The purple fabric against the olive undertones of her skin, and the way her dark brown hair spilled over her shoulders was mesmerizing. He was trying. Ancients in the Void, he was fucking trying to keep his distance. He couldn't whistle at her or flirt and play with her the way he wanted to. He couldn't have the same easy friendship she had with Wren. If he did...

Wren was right. Ash had to tell her about the treaty. Tomorrow. He would tell her tomorrow.

He dragged his eyes away from her and clicked his fingers to summon the servants. Then, he caught Wren watching him. Wren blinked three times, a silent invitation for Ash to read his thoughts.

You look like you want to punch me, Wren thought.

I don't want to punch anyone, Ash sent back.

Oh. My mistake. It's probably just been too long since you had a good fu—"

Ash slammed the connection shut.

His best friend's golden eyes held a knowing look as he looked at Ash over his goblet of wine.

Kenna took her seat at the opposite end of the table from Ash. "Is it really necessary for me to sit all the way down here?"

"You're my guest of honor, so that's your seat."

The truth was, the table was ten feet long and he needed every single inch between them. Otherwise, he might give into the urge to reach out to wrap one of her silky brown waves around his finger. He couldn't sit next to her, and he'd tried to have as little interaction as possible with her outside of their training and their evening meals as possible.

He didn't know what she thought of his change in behavior, but he couldn't worry about that. He shouldn't be worrying what she thought of him at all. Ash snapped his fingers again and servants appeared. They brought out plates filled with juicy cuts of red meat and mounds of sweet potatoes.

"What is this?" Kenna glowered at Ash, pushing the orange mashed vegetables around her plate.

"Sweet potatoes."

"What's wrong with normal white potatoes?" He fought the smile threatening to lift the corners of his mouth, as Kenna took a tentative bite of the sweet potatoes. She seemed to decide they weren't poisonous.

"These provide longer lasting energy than white potatoes. Your training is about much more than what we accomplish in the ring each day. It's about fueling your body for strength and energy. You're a warrior now, so you'll eat like one." Ash smiled at her. He had no doubt she'd excel in her training with the progress he'd seen within her first two weeks.

"You get used to it," Wren said around a mouthful of steak. "Plus, we have treats and desserts every once in a while. We just don't make it a habit."

"I've checked in with the wardens on the southern edge of Gela forest today," Ash reported. "The wards there are in good shape."

"Have they discovered any weaknesses anywhere else? I still don't understand how the Achetaur got through." Wren shook his head.

"I have a feeling there's something Echelous isn't telling us, but I can't ask him outright without giving away Kenna's identity."

Echelous was the angel charged with keeping the monsters outside of Notos. He oversaw the monsters because he *was* a monster, albeit wrapped in pretty flesh. He'd be visiting in for Autumn Equinox, and Ash was hoping that Kenna would have improved by then. Just in case.

Suddenly, Kenna interrupted them, dropping her silverware onto her empty plate with a clatter. "Are you going to continue to discuss things as though I'm not here or do you plan to include me in your conversation? Will you ever tell me what exactly it is you have planned for me or what is happening beyond the walls of this castle? Or am I a prisoner?"

Ash stopped eating, and felt a wave of annoyance at her irreverence. He was still a king, after all. "Excuse me?"

A flicker of fear crossed Kenna's features.

Wren must have seen it, because he said, "Don't worry Kenna. He just isn't used to anyone questioning his kingly wisdom."

Ash shot his friend a death glare, but it had no effect on Wren.

Kenna squared her shoulders. "I'd like to know what you are planning for my training, and I want to know what's so important about the Winter Solstice. Just because I made an oath with you and accepted your offer of help doesn't mean I have to follow you like a mindless, bleating sheep. I've spent my entire life having men make decisions for me and having people decide what's best for me without any consideration for my opinions. My father..." her voice broke. "My father, my mother, and my brother did so because they loved me, but I will no longer be kept in the dark and steered by other people's motives."

Ash returned to his dinner. He should tell her. He should tell her everything. But the thought of it suddenly made his throat feel dry. He raised his water goblet to take a sip.

ASH DIDN'T ANSWER, offered no explanation. He wouldn't meet Kenna's eyes as he carried on cutting his steak. He had the audacity to continue eating in silence while Kenna waited for answers. Enough.

She'd had enough of his games. He'd brought her here, all lopsided grins and flirtation and helpful intentions, but ever since they'd arrived he'd been cold toward her. She'd trusted him, but he wasn't holding up his end of the bargain. He might not be lying to her, but it was time he told her exactly what was going on.

Ash began to take a sip of water, and Kenna lashed out with her magic, splashing the water right into his handsome face.

Wren howled with laughter and Kenna's anger faded for a split second as she smirked at her comrade. But when she looked at Ash, his expression instantly wiped the smile off of her face. He didn't move—didn't even blink—as the water vanished.

All it took was a thought.

He gritted his teeth as he spoke. "I may be the king, but there are still powers greater than me in this Realm. Have you forgotten that the Ancients are still alive? There are certain things that I cannot speak of. Even if I wanted to." Kenna felt the warm thread of truth between them, and Wren shifted uncomfortably in his seat. Did he know what Ash was talking about?

Ash stood, and threw his napkin down. He leaned forward bracing his palms on the vast table that stretched between them. His eyes were glacial as he said, "You want to fight me, Kenna? Fine. But know this. If you do not follow my instructions and train every day without fail, you will not be ready."

"Ready for what?" Her chair scraped across the stone tiles as she stood to face him, chest heaving. "I told you I trusted you. I left my friends and family and bound myself to you to come train until Winter Solstice. What's so important about the Solstice? What powers are greater than you? Why don't you just tell me?"

A slow, predatory smile spread over Ash's face.

"You might trust me, Kenna, but I warned you not to. Do you know why you're so important? Want to know why you need to train? War and death are coming for us because of the treaty. When you know everything about me, you'll want to run home. But you won't be able to."

The thread which usually grew warm with the truth was boiling. There was nothing reassuring about the scalding hot pain. She yelped, rubbing at the white star on her wrist. Ash rubbed a hand down his face and the pain disappeared. Still, tears stung her eyes.

"Wh—what do you mean?" Her eyes searched his.

His sapphire gaze held hers for a few more seconds, as though there was more he wanted to say. She could have sworn she saw sadness softening his features before he clenched his fists and strode to her side. He stopped next to her. Without looking at her, he said, "Tomorrow, breakfast is at dawn. Then, you'll train with me all day. Don't be late."

He stalked out of the dining room, slamming the doors open, and Kenna sank into her chair. She put her head in her hands. It hadn't been the diplomatic discussion she'd planned. She'd made a mistake coming here, trusting Ash. The burning truth of his words rang through her mind over and over.

You'll want to run home, but you won't be able to.

What had she done?

Moments later, Wren was at her side, a gentle hand squeezing her shoulder.

"What is he talking about?" She whispered.

"He needs to tell you himself. But I'm going to tell you this now— he's not a monster. He thinks he is, but he's not. As for the treaty, I'm sure we'll figure out a way to—"

"Wren!" Ash barked from the hallway, and Wren gave her an apologetic look before following his king.

CHAPTER 44

*O*ri woke her at dawn, but Kenna had hardly slept, going over and over Ash's words in her mind. She dressed in her training gear, the onslaught of thoughts and fears still plaguing her.

What was the treaty and what did it mean for her?

It sounded like he'd purposely tricked her into coming here. Every ounce of warmth and trust she'd felt toward him felt false and unstable. She'd already been led astray by so many people in her life, and she thought she'd been cautious when she made her oath with Ash. She'd worded it so carefully.

There had been times where she'd felt he was giving her subtle warnings. Why not just tell her the truth?

When she reached the dining room, neither Ash nor Wren were there. A servant brought in her breakfast, and she ate in silence with only her anxiety to keep her company.

What did Ash have planned for her training today? Was he going to hurt her? Would she finally understand his true character? Would she finally have an explanation for his cold demeanor since they'd arrived in the castle?

After breakfast, she made her way to the sparring ring. She didn't see a single soul as she trekked through the castle. She reached the door and raised a trembling hand to push it open. There was no bright morning sunlight from overhead lighting the sparring ring, only the cool gray of dawn.

Ash was sitting against the wall, his forearms resting on his bent knees.

"Sit," he ordered.

She obeyed, keeping a few feet between them as she sat cross-legged beside him.

"I'm sorry for losing my temper last night," he said. "And I'm sorry for the information I've kept from you."

He extended his legs and picked at a thread on his sleeve.

"What is so important about the treaty?" Kenna demanded.

Ash shook his head and a harsh laugh escaped. "I should have told you the moment I knew who you were." He looked down, unable to meet her eyes. "I think I might have fucked it up with our oath. I could tell you, but you will understand more if you allow me to show you."

"Show me how?"

"I can share the memory with you. In your mind."

Kenna recoiled, remembering Samael's invasive presence in her mind. The violation of having hateful thoughts forced upon her. Ash seemed to sense her hesitation.

"I would never force my thoughts upon you without permission. I am not like my brother."

"I...I don't think I'm ready for that yet."

Ash scrubbed a hand through his hair, sighing. "The war ended, and the treaty was negotiated on Winter Solstice three hundred and twenty-nine years ago. This year marks the three hundred and thirtieth anniversary of the treaty. Soldivus and a legion of angels, elves, and humans had won the battle. Soldivus had his teeth clamped over Luniva's throat, ready to spill her life on the battlefield."

Kenna interrupted, "His teeth were at her throat?"

Ash nodded. "The Ancients can shift into dragons. The only way to destroy them is to take their life, destroy the source of their power, and cast their soul out of this world and back into the Void."

Kenna's mind reeled. She'd heard myths of dragons who'd existed before the war, but never knew they were the Ancients. She'd always assumed it was a fictional children's tale.

Ash continued, "Soldivus would have killed her and cast her out, though it pained him to do so. They'd created this world together—created all the angels, elves, and humans—but Luniva had grown bitter and hateful toward the less powerful races, particularly the humans.

She considered them weak and useless. But mostly, she hated them because of the way Soldivus loved them.

"The day before the final battle, Luniva sent Samael and his unit to lay siege to the human stronghold. They had been successful, and Samael's unit held the majority of the human race captive, including the children. Luniva agreed to strike a deal with Soldivus to end the war. And so, the treaty was formed."

"Isn't there a signed document? Something marking the end of the war and everyone who agreed to the terms?" Kenna asked.

Ash shook his head. "There's not an official document. There was no need for signatures. The treaty was sealed with binding magic, but I have written the terms down for you. I've been going over them ever since we returned to the castle. Trying to find a way around it." He pulled a piece of parchment from his pocket.

With each term of the treaty, a puzzle piece clicked into place in Kenna's mind.

1. Soldivus and Luniva may only enter Mesterra in Shadow form once a year. Otherwise they must be confined to their angel form in their respective realms of Vorra and Notos for the duration of the treaty.

KENNA CLARIFIED. "So, they can't shift into dragons now?"

"No. Only Shadows."

"I've seen Shadows in Tormund twice. One of them took one of my brother's friend, Holt. Was it one of the Ancients?"

"Yes, though I can't say which one."

"Holt isn't dead though. I heard him on my Fostone when we were in Braktyn. He was locking my best friend, Zo, in some prison called the Hill. Do you know of it?"

Ash nodded gravely. "If the Shadow took him to the Hill, Holt is likely under the influence of Luniva."

Kenna squeezed her eyes shut. If Holt hurt Zo, she'd fucking kill him. No, Kenna would let Sera kill him. She would be more creative. She would make him suffer for what he'd done.

· · ·

2. Angels who followed Soldivus or Luniva can't cross into Vorra or Notos or their life is forfeit. Other than those who disobey the treaty, no angels may be killed or created during the duration of this treaty.

That seemed straightforward enough, except…

"What about Pax? Did he follow Luniva in the war? He's here in Notos."

"Pax, is your guardian angel, Kenna."

"My…what?"

"When the humans roamed the world, there was an entire host of angels tasked with keeping them safe. They grew up with us, but when they chose to become guardians, angels like Pax spent fifty years completing special training. That's why Pax's accent is different from other angels.

Most of them died defending the humans. Since you're an important part of the treaty, both Soldivus and Luniva agreed it was important to keep you safe until you came of age. They agreed you'd have a guardian angel and neither of them would know who it was. Of course, you and I know it's Pax, but he was forbidden from interfering with your life and your decisions. He couldn't inform Soldivus, Luniva, Prince Hawthorne, or Prince Samael of your whereabouts. He was able to provide some protection, but he would never force you to do anything against your will."

"Wasn't it a little reckless for Pax to open a tavern right across the square from Luniva's High Priestess? Wouldn't other angels who still maintain loyalty to Luniva tell her about him?"

"Pax's tavern is warded. Only those who understand the true nature of Luniva's evil and have no love for her may enter. No one who crossed the threshold of the Red Lantern would speak a word of Pax's presence in this realm. Plus, no one apart from you and I know that he's the guardian who was assigned to protect the human princess. Many elves have guardian angels. It's typical of his ridiculous humor to hide himself in plain sight.

He was likely the merchant who offered your father the glamor potion that kept your identity hidden all those years in Mesterra. Didn't you find it odd that you ended up in the Red Lantern with such a kind angel landlord? Even your limited time here should have showed you how angels look down on elves and winged fae."

"But Holt and Jona both advised Drake to stay at the Red Lantern three years ago. I didn't come to Notos at that time."

"No…but whose advice did you take when you *did* end up in Notos?"

"Drake's… it was all part of the way Pax protected me."

"Exactly."

3. Only one angel from Vorra or Notos can cross the Veil into Mesterra each year, but they must stay no longer than one year.

"THIS ONE DOESN'T MAKE sense. There are definitely over three hundred angels from Notos in Mesterra. If you consider the High Council and all of the Elders ruling the towns and cities across the realm…there must be at least a thousand angels."

"One thousand six hundred and forty-five from Notos alone, maybe a few less now if any have been killed in the rebellion."

Kenna's eyebrows rose. "How do you know the exact number?"

"Lailah found a loophole. She used Luniva's magic to create a serum, the same serum the elves drink at the Emergence Ceremony. The Emergence serum acts as a disguise for the angels, diluting their blood just enough for five of them to cross the Veil each year. Once they're in Mesterra, they must simply drink the serum annually. It continues to disguise their angel blood so that they can stay in Mesterra undetected by the treaty's magic. Almost all the angels in Mesterra are Luniva's puppets. The High Council were the original five."

Kenna told Ash about the events during the emergence trial and how the Elders had erased everyone's memories.

"Was the mist from the trial made from the Emergence serum?" When Ash nodded, she asked, "So, what does the Emergence serum do to the elves? When they drink from the Chalice, elves exhibit the Emergence glow and they feel of their Vessel's capacity increasing."

"Nothing but trickery and a temporary sense of euphoria. The original purpose of the serum was to control the elves' minds completely, but Lailah's plan was not entirely successful."

"Why not?" Kenna asked.

"Ancient magic is…complicated."

Kenna remembered the bottle Zo had passed around at the Emergence Ceremony which seemed to bring the elves back to their senses and restore their memories. It was some sort of antidote, then. Where did it come from?

She'd think about that later.

4. Humans will remain in a magical sleep state until the newborn human princess is released from her sleep after three hundred and five years. She will be the only human to awake, and on the three hundred and thirtieth anniversary of the treaty, Winter Solstice, in her twenty-fifth year, she may choose to form a marriage alliance.

If the humans make an alliance with Prince Hawthorne of Vorra, the humans will wake and keep their free will, and Luniva must stay on the eternal shores of the moon for eternity.

If the human princess allies with Prince Samael of Notos, the humans will wake and be controlled by Luniva, and Soldivus must stay on the eternal shores of the sun for eternity.

"I'M...I'M betrothed. To one of the princes."

Ash gave her a moment to let it sink in. She'd only had a few lovers in her twenty-five years. While Sera used sex to cope with all her trauma and Aryn saved herself for her fiancé, both Kenna and Zo had fallen somewhere in the middle. Kenna had always believed she'd find a single great love. She'd always known she deserved someone who would cherish her.

Her parents were mates, which was rare among elves. She'd seen her parent's relationship, and she refused to settle for anything less than true love.

She'd probably never find love like that if she was destined for an arranged marriage to save the humans.

She wasn't naive enough to think she'd come through this experience without having to make any more sacrifices. She'd already lost her father; she could settle for a marriage alliance if the sacrifice allowed her to save her friends and family. To save the humans.

Maybe her marriage to the prince of Vorra would be nothing but a marriage of convenience. Maybe she could find true love elsewhere.

The thought didn't sit well with her, but she could see no other option. Really, true love should be the least of her concerns right now.

"When was anyone going to tell me any of this?" Kenna asked.

"The treaty didn't stipulate. Perhaps the Ancients knew enough about you to know you'd find the answers on your own."

"Obviously, I can't marry Samael. I can't be in the same room with him. I can't..." Kenna forced herself to take deep breaths. "I'll just have to marry the prince of Vorra. Surely, he can't be that bad if he fought for the humans."

There was nothing cold or arrogant or flirty about Ash's tone when he spoke again, "I wish it were as simple as that. I'm afraid we've likely ruined your chances for marrying the prince of Vorra because of your unbreakable oath."

Kenna played over the words of her oath with Ash in her mind. She couldn't leave Notos until Winter Solstice, and the prince of Vorra couldn't come to Notos without forfeiting his life.

"So I'll be forced into a marriage with Samael?"

"I'm almost certain our oath will prevent you from marrying either of the princes. But if Samael finds out who you are, he will try to find a way to make you his wife."

She set the parchment on her lap and hung her head. In her attempts to help, she'd doomed herself to a marriage with a cruel angel. Worse than that, she'd doomed the humans to an eternity of slavery. Rage, disappointment, and helplessness bubbled in her chest, and she wanted to scream.

Ash's voice was so quiet it was almost a whisper: "Turn the page over. There's more."

CHAPTER 45

5. Elves may not cross the Veil into Notos without forfeiting their lives and souls to Luniva for eternal punishment and damnation.

KENNA'S HANDS SHOOK. This term meant...she ran through a list of everyone she knew who'd crossed the Veil. Her father. Her brother. Drake. Ezra. Any of the other rebels who'd ever made the crossing into Notos looking for freedom and answers would be doomed.

She'd crossed the Veil, too, but she was human. She looked at Ash. "Does this apply to me?"

"I'm not sure," Ash answered. His eyes were troubled. "It says elves, but it seems that your glamor fooled Raziel. He made a bargain with you just as he would with any other elf. So...probably. Again, Ancient magic is a mystery, even to angels."

Her heart constricted and wave of nausea passed through her once more.

"If I am to fulfill the treaty, I have to marry Hawthorne or Samael on the anniversary of the treaty this year."

Ash gave her a curt nod.

"But my unbreakable oath with you likely prevents me from marrying either of them, and Prince Hawthorne of Vorra can't come to Notos or he'll be executed."

Ash's gaze was full of torment as he spoke the words she'd already pieced together in her mind, "Even if we find a way to break our oath, you'll likely be forced to marry Samael, and your people will lose their free will forever."

Every shard of belief that coming here had been the right choice came crashing down around her, the truth of it slicing through her like a thousand knives. It slashed and shredded every ounce of hope, every part of her that had thought she might make a difference.

"What's the point of any of this then?" She held her arms wide, gesturing to the sparring ring around them. "Why bother teaching me how to fight if none of it matters?"

"There might be a way to get you out. The prince of Vorra knows you're here. The healer who tended to your mother at the rebel camp—Thorne—is Prince Hawthorne."

"He's...he's helping my family?"

Ash confirmed with a nod.

"He's been working with the rebels, and both of us are trying to come up with a plan."

What cruel irony. Kenna's eyes welled with tears. Had her father sacrificed his life only for her to end up bound to a monster?

Surely, anyone would be better than Samael. The thought of him putting his hands on her—much less having to share his bed—was like thousands of tiny spiders crawling all over her skin. But marrying a total stranger?

She thought about marrying Ash, but he was a king. The treaty stipulated that she marry a prince.

And what about the rest of her friends and family? There were so many rebels fighting for freedom in Mesterra. If she married Samael, and Luniva seized control of humanity, it was only a matter of time before there would be nothing to stop the angels in Notos from marching on Mesterra.

The humans would be expendable puppets in the hands of some divine power. The thought was sickening. She didn't know any of humans, so she didn't have the same love and care for them as she did for her friends, but she had a responsibility to set them free. The king and queen were her biological parents. If they were still alive, she had to save them.

She wouldn't marry Samael. The rebels wouldn't be destroyed. And the humans would be restored with their free will intact. They would find a way. An icy calmness filled her.

Kenna slowly stood. "You were right. You said I'd want to run away when I learned the truth, and you were right. I do want to run, but that's not an option. Luniva and her priestess found loopholes in the treaty. Her minions crossed the Veil year after year until they had enough power to control Mesterra. They used the serum to control the elves' memories, right?"

Some emotion she didn't understand flashed in Ash's eyes. "The loophole she found was very costly."

"Perhaps. But still, she found a way. There must be some way for me to save the humans, to save everyone I love, but I refuse to marry Samael. I refuse to believe there isn't a way out of this. I refuse to be controlled by decisions made over three hundred years ago when I was nothing but a babe in arms. Decisions about *my* fate which I had no voice in. If I have to marry a prince, it will be the prince of Vorra and it will free my people."

"We might have a chance to get you out, and Winter Solstice will be the only opportunity. I can't see a way yet, but Hawthorne and Pax are plotting, so we must hold onto hope. Whatever the outcome, you need to learn to fight. I couldn't live with myself if you were forced into marrying Samael without a way to defend yourself."

Kenna crossed to the weapons cabinet and grabbed her training sword, swinging it deftly through a few of the stances she'd learned. It felt more natural in her hands now. Rather than letting the thoughts swirl, she would focus all her attention on training to keep her uncertainty at bay.

Walking back over to Ash, she extended a hand to help him up. "Get up, Your Grace. You're wasting my time by sitting on your royal ass."

Ash took her hand and stood; he took a deep breath. The weight of his secrets had made Ash appear so aloof, but as he exhaled, all the coldness he'd exuded the last two weeks seemed to vanish.

A slow smile spread over his face, and his eyes swept over her with pure admiration as he stalked toward her. Ash was inches away, close enough for their breath to mingle when she looked up at him. Here was the king with the twinkle in his blue eyes, the man whose gaze followed her so carefully. Here was the handsome man who flirted and teased and filled her stomach with warm butterflies. He placed one hand on the small of her back, pulling her close, and cupped the back of her neck with his other hand.

On instinct, Kenna closed her eyes as he leaned down, and she lost herself to the feel of his lips as they brushed against her earlobe. Her training sword hung limp at her side as the feel of being so close to him turned her body to molten liquid. She didn't know if it was her adrenaline and determination or his cedar and smoke scent which made her want to kiss him.

Was he going to kiss her now? How much time would she have in which she was free to kiss whomever she wanted? She might never have the opportunity to follow her heart or listen to her body once she was married to the prince of Vorra.

"If you want to get a closer look at my royal ass, all you have to do is ask."

The low rumble of his voice made her stomach flutter, and she felt the flood of warmth through their bond. She could have him if she wanted. Not a moment later, he snatched the training sword out of her hand and backed away, winking.

"Three-two, love."

"Oh, so we're back to keeping score, are we?" she asked.

"Only if you *want* to play. Or maybe you're scared you'll lose."

"I never lose."

He'd kept the truth from her about the treaty, but there was no time to dwell on that. After all, he was still trying to help her.

The residual anger and sexual tension coiled deep within her, and she vowed to pour every ounce of both into every single training session, starting today.

CHAPTER 46

Two months passed, and Autumn Equinox was upon them. Ever since Ash had told her about the treaty, Kenna had used the truth of it to fuel her training sessions with both the king and Wren. Her swordsmanship and fitness had improved immensely, and she was so much stronger than when she'd fled Tormund.

Her alliance with Ash had grown into true friendship with undeniable physical chemistry. Ash's coldness had vanished, and their flirtatious game had continued. They were currently tied nine to nine. Neither of them seemed to have any issue driving the other to distraction.

But any romantic feelings between them were doomed to end in heartache if Kenna was to fulfill her destiny and save the humans.

Despite their burgeoning friendship, Ash was keeping something from her. He'd tried to warn her that she couldn't trust him, but she still hadn't figured out why. She wasn't sure if it was something to do with the rebellion or the treaty. Since she didn't know what question to ask, she couldn't coax the words from him and test the truth with their unbreakable oath.

Some evenings, Ash and Wren would leave after training and were busy dealing with other kingdom duties. They continued monitoring the outposts to ensure the Surgati wardens were doing their jobs and keeping any foul creatures from wandering the realm.

On those nights, Kenna dined in her room alone. She didn't mind the solitude, finding it preferable to making small talk with a room full of strangers. In fact, the angel courtiers who took residence within the castle walls probably wouldn't speak to her at all.

There were no fae or elves among the nobility who might befriend her. The servants were all elves who seemed to resent her for her relationship with Ash. And though many fae and elves were part of the royal guard, they all dined at the garrison which was over a mile away on the other side of the sprawling castle compound.

Ash had told Samael to stay away during Kenna's first days at the castle. Ultimately, the king's warning to his brother was unnecessary. She hadn't seen Samael since he'd left the castle in search of the human princess.

Kenna stifled a smile, knowing just how angry the prince would be when he found out she was the one he'd been searching for. Then, her smile faded. Thinking of the sinister prince's ire never ceased to make her shudder.

Today was her first day off in months, and Ash had invited her for a special Equinox lunch instead of their typical evening meal. When she entered the dining room, it was late afternoon, and she was surprised to find six place settings at the long dining table. Her heart thudded in her chest.

Was Samael back? Who else could it be? Ash had never invited any of the courtiers to dine with them before.

She sank into her customary chair at the opposite end of the table from Ash, but the king snapped his fingers at her, and it made her hackles rise.

"I would prefer it if you sat next to me today," he said.

"And I would prefer if you didn't beckon me like some mindless pet."

"As much as I enjoy our games, I do not have the time or patience for them today. Now, move." Ash's glacial indigo gaze bored into her as he leaned forward in his seat.

Kenna swallowed, but defended her dignity, holding her position with a stalwart stare of her own. It took every ounce of her will to stay seated. Everything about Ash drew her to him like a sandy shore pulling the strings of the tide.

"Good afternoon, Your Majesty." The scent of vanilla swirled through the air as Priestess Lailah and her perfect curves floated into the dining room. "Kenna."

"Your Holiness," Ash said without looking in Lailah's direction.

His stare was still occupied with breaking down Kenna's stubborn glare. Kenna sensed Lailah looking back and forth between her and Ash, as though waiting to see which one of them would emerge victorious.

"They're always like this," Wren informed the priestess. "I've lost count of the score, but I think Kenna's winning."

Kenna nearly jumped out of her chair when Ash suddenly slammed a palm down on the table, the cutlery clattering. "You will sit next to me, Kenna. It is not up for debate. Today is not the day for you to test my good graces." It was the command of a king, and she was in no position to disobey.

In her first days of knowing him, she never would have guessed he had a temper, but whatever stirred his anger gave him no excuse to speak to her that way. Kenna rose, glaring at him with every step she took and poured every ounce of bitter sweetness she possessed into her cordial words and graceful curtsey. "As you wish, Your Grace."

Lailah's brows rose.

~

"WHAT NEWS FROM BRAKTYN?" the king asked his sister. Kenna's ears perked. This would be the first news she'd heard from beyond the castle in weeks. She wondered how Pax was doing, but wouldn't draw attention to him by asking the priestess about him.

"There is not much to report that you do not already know. The rebellion rages on in Mesterra. Nearly six hundred elves arrived on our shores this morning. You must thank your captain for allowing me to borrow some of the royal guard to help them find their way to the temple and suitable lodgings." Lailah turned to Kenna, seeming pleased to offer her benevolent services. "It is my sacred duty to help those who flee into our realm on the Equinox and Solstice crossings."

With her new knowledge of the treaty, Kenna found Lailah's curated demeanor slimy. The priestess was one of the highest-ranking members of Notos' royal court, which meant she knew the treaty stipulated every elf who crossed the Veil paid with their soul. Still, Lailah spoke of hundreds of elves being damned for eternity as casually as speaking of the weather.

Kenna's cocked her head. She couldn't understand why Wren and Ash would allow the royal guard to deliver these elves to the priestess. Why wouldn't Ash and Wren inform her of this plan?

She looked at Ash with the silent question in her eyes, begging for permission to confront Lailah about her hypocrisy. Ash seemed to sense Kenna's intent and gave an almost imperceptible shake of his head, urging her to feign ignorance.

Before Kenna could find out anymore, Samael entered the dining room along with a strikingly handsome male she'd never met. Upon seeing the Prince, Kenna's heart started pounding and her palms grew sweaty, remembering all the hateful thoughts Samael had spewed into her mind that first day. Just thinking about it made her head ache.

The prince of Notos was dripping with disgust. "You're still here then. Pity."

Ash said, "I agreed to this meeting, brother, but do not think that I will not have you removed if you can not behave in a respectful manner."

Below the table, Ash squeezed Kenna's knee gently. She suddenly understood why he'd insisted on her sitting next to him. Her breathing slowed, comforted by his touch. She would have to apologize for her petulant behaviour later.

"Apologies, Your Majesty. Wonderful to see you, Lailah," Samael said, pointedly ignoring Wren's presence.

"How long has it been, cousin?" the other male addressed Ash.

"Not long enough, I assure you, Echelous," Ash responded before he snapped his fingers, summoning the servants to bring the food.

Echelous. Ash had spoken of him. He was the leader of the Surgati wardens he controlled the wards to keep unsavory creatures out of Notos. He was also the most beautiful person Kenna had ever laid eyes on, which was saying a great deal considering present company. Echelous' silver blonde waves contrasted beautifully with his tanned skin, and he observed her with eyes in a shade that could only be described as turquoise. He grinned at her, and she got the distinct sense that his disarming smile made him even more dangerous.

Once the servants had served the meal, Ash returned to the discussion of the influx of elves from Mesterra.

Ash turned to Lailah, "I assume we'll soon need to set up refugee camps outside the city. How many more can Braktyn accommodate if there is another wave of arrivals on Winter Solstice?"

"It is difficult to say. If the numbers remain consistent, we should be able to house approximately one hundred more elves in the city's inns. Some folks might be persuaded to open their homes. If there are more than that, we'll need to erect additional shelters before more elves arrive on Winter Solstice."

Ash's jaw clenched and Kenna stopped chewing. There were that many elves arriving in Notos? So many people paying with their souls and completely unaware. Somehow, she needed to find a way to get a message to her brother and tell him to stop any more rebel elves from coming to Notos.

"You know," Echelous drawled. "I could easily accommodate elves within the borders of my lands."

Ash's smile was tight. "As we have previously discussed, your offer is noted but unnecessary."

Echelous leaned back in his seat, sipping a glass of wine. "It's a shame. I grow weary of the monotony. Things grow tiresome without any new faces to liven things up." He surveyed Kenna like he'd devour her if given the chance.

"We all have our burdens to bear." Ash gave Echelous a dark look.

"I suppose we do." Echelous smile was full of sinister knowledge before he turned to Lailah. "And how are things at the temple, Your Holiness?"

"Very well, thank you. More and more elves are recruited to the cause each day. Many of the fae still have doubts, but they do not concern me."

"And what *does* concern you?" Wren's amber eyes flashed, and his uncharacteristic outburst surprised Kenna.

Lailah still ignored Wren, and Samael spoke next, pretended like he hadn't even heard Wren's question: "I must say, you are making excellent headway, Lailah."

"And what of this years Solstice games?" Echelous asked Ash.

"Everything is in place."

Echelous turned his piercing eyes to Kenna, making her feel like he could see through her glamor. "You must be quite the warrior indeed."

Kenna looked at Ash briefly, keeping her features serene, trying not to give anything away. "I have been training diligently. If the king believes I will be ready, then I'm sure he is correct."

Samael laughed. "Oh, you really are a fool, aren't you?" The prince turned to Echelous. "She is one of the weakest he's ever had. Not that it matters."

"Samael, don't be like that," Lailah chided. She turned to Kenna. "You are learning, my child. You can only succeed through determination and will. You must look deep within to find your own power."

Kenna forced a smile and took a long gulp of her wine, trying to avoid meeting Ash's eyes.

Lailah changed the subject abruptly. "The men bore me. How do you find Brumalis Castle? Are you enjoying your stay?"

"I'm quite enjoying it now that the tyrant king has fed me something other than rabbit food," Kenna said, taking a bite of chocolate cake.

Wren chuckled and Lailah released a tinkling laugh. Ash didn't bother to hide his smirk. For a moment, she forgot who these people were and everything they were capable of, and Kenna grinned as well.

"I know all about Ash's training. If his methods have not changed, then I believe you are perfectly justified in having a hidden desire to murder him." Lailah gave Kenna a conspiratorial smile. "His experience is unparalleled, and your efforts will prove fruitful. You will be so proud of yourself when your training is completed and you fulfil your purpose. Your power resides within. Never forget that, my child."

"Well, I hope you are right," Kenna said, fighting the urge to gag on Lailah's condescension. "Now if you'll all excuse me. Today is the only day this week I've been allowed any rest, and I think I'd like some time to relax."

"Of course, dear," Lailah said. She looked out the window, where the afternoon sunlight was quickly fading and pursed her lips. "It's time I take my leave as well."

"Will you not stay for the Equinox festivities?" Kenna asked.

"No," Lailah said. "I only participate on Winter Solstice. The other seasonal festivities cannot drag me away from my sacred duty."

Kenna nodded. "Good evening then," she said, leaving the dining room.

"Kenna, wait!" Ash shouted, just as Kenna reached her bedroom door. "Can we talk?"

"I'm tired, Ash." And she meant it. She was exhausted.

"Please?"

"Fine."

They crossed through her bedroom to the balcony, stepping out into the fresh air to watch the sunset. She'd given everything for almost three months, and all it took was one meal in the presence of three angels to make her doubt everything she'd accomplished.

Being near Samael seemed to drain her body and mind, but it hadn't been as bad as when they'd been alone in the sparring ring.

"Tell me about Echelous," she said. "You called him cousin, but I assumed he was one of your brothers."

A muscle ticked in Ash's jaw. "Echelous and his kind are the result of Luniva attempting to create angels, though it was forbidden by the treaty. They are just as powerful as angels, but with none of the good intentions of Soldivus poured into their creation. Even Luniva is wary of their kind and doesn't know how to destroy them."

"I thought Echelous and the Surgati were supposed to monitor the wards that keep monsters out of Notos. "

"That is his story. But it has long been my suspicion that Echelous's true goal is to let the monsters in."

"And where are the monsters? Are they in a prison somewhere?"

"Something like that," Ash said, making it clear Kenna would find no more answers from him tonight.

"Did you stop Samael from sending horrible thoughts into my mind today?"

"I did. I'm sorry if I overstepped. I should have asked your permission."

"I wish you would have told me they were coming."

"I thought they would dine in the great hall with the courtiers. All three of them enjoy the attention."

"And you don't?"

Ash placed his hands on the balcony rail, hopping up and swinging his legs over the edge of the railing. Kenna's breath caught before she remembered that he had wings. He sat perched on the railing with his legs dangling into the abyss, looking out over his kingdom.

"No. Being dressed up and put on a pedestal in front of a crowd is not something I particularly enjoy."

"Even if you get to wear a shiny crown?" Kenna teased, leaning against the railing next to him.

Ash rested a hand atop her head. "You can have my shiny crown. I never wanted it. I rarely wear it."

He slid his hand down, tucking a strand of hair behind her ear. He plucked the crown, seemingly from thin air, and placed it on her head. "It suits you," Ash said, turning away from her.

"Is this legal?" Kenna asked.

Ash spun his legs around and hopped down onto the balcony. He stood behind her, his arms on either side of her on the balcony railing. They'd trained together regularly, touched often, but something about this moment felt more intimate.

It didn't feel like a game at all when his lips brushed her ear. "I'm the king. Shouldn't I be able to crown whichever queen I choose?"

She closed her eyes, leaning into the feel of his lips on her skin. Ash was treading a thin line. There was something between them. Neither of them was fool enough to deny it, but they were not children. Both of them had kingdoms and responsibilities, and Notos would never be her kingdom.

Still, she couldn't quite bring herself to remove the crown. Kenna watched the sun slip below the horizon as the moon began its ascent. A few stars twinkled to life in the dusky sky. The barren expanse of snow glittered—a beautiful, blank canvas, just waiting for an artist to tell a story.

She turned, facing Ash, looking up at him. An invitation.

He lifted a finger to her chin, tilting her closer. When he leaned in, Kenna's eyes fluttered closed.

The moment his warm lips met hers, a voice from the Fostone on Kenna's wrist startled her, and Ash stepped away from her.

"Kenna?" A garbled voice emanated from her Fostone. Kenna's eyes snapped open and Ash stepped away quickly.

"Jona?" she said to her wrist.

"Yes, it's me. Listen, I can't talk long. The connection is too weak. We know where the Hill is. We know where they're keeping Zo and Ezra. We're making plans to destroy it and get the prisoners out."

Kenna's eyes stung with tears. "You're getting Zo out?"

"We're trying."

"How?"

"Commander!" Someone shouted.

"Not now!" her brother said.

"Commander?" Kenna questioned.

"Apparently."

"Are Sera and Aryn okay? How's mother?"

"Mother worries about you, and losing father… I can't imagine what it must be like for someone to lose their mate. Sera is raring to burn the entire realm to the ground, and Aryn is as delightful as ever."

Kenna laughed, but Ash's eyes looked haunted by some unknown ghost.

Already, she could feel the drain on her Vessel from maintaining the long distance conversation. What else did she need to ask? What did she need to tell him?

"You need to stop elves from making the crossing," she told him. "The ferry master is capturing their souls."

"I know," Jona said.

"You know?" Kenna shouted. "And yet you've made the crossing? You allowed me to make the crossing? Why?"

"Because we're going to win the war, little sister. And we're going to set every one of those souls free."

"But Jona, I…I'm betrothed. I must marry the prince of Vorra if I'm to save the humans and fulfill the treaty. But my oath with Ash—"

"I know. Prince Hawthorne told me about the treaty, but there's a plan in place. Don't worry. Mother is delighted, by the way. She's already planning your dress. She said it's going to be—"

His voice faded away.

"Jona?" Kenna tapped the Fostone, willing it to reconnect.

The sun had faded beyond the horizon, and the balcony was bathed in moonlight. Ash was still standing in front of her. When their eyes met, Kenna removed the crown from her head, handing it back to him.

He unfurled his wings and slowly flew over her head.

In a moment, Ash was in front of her balcony, gracefully moving his wings like he was treading water in the starlit sky. He looked so perfect among the stars, a beacon of pure light in this dark place. But his light would never belong to her.

He looked directly into her eyes, and gently moved a thumb across her cheek, brushing away a single tear.

Perhaps it made her foolish or impulsive, but she didn't care. She wanted to feel his lips on hers again, but not the brief touch of earlier. She wanted to kiss him and wrap her arms around him. Maybe if she joined her broken pieces to his, they could both pretend to be whole. At least for a while.

"Ash," she whispered. The king backed away, suspended just beyond her reach.

"I need to go," he said. "Goodnight, Kenna."

Ash placed his crown atop his head, and the weight of it looked like it caused him pain. Then, Ash twisted his body, throwing himself backward, falling with his wings relaxed uselessly at his side. Why wasn't he flying?

Just as she was about to scream his name, Ash spread his wings wide, soaring above his kingdom like a dream.

Losing him felt like a nightmare.

CHAPTER 48

*A*sh didn't know what would have happened last night if her brother hadn't interrupted their kiss. He'd skipped breakfast.

She'd stopped making a fuss of her appearance weeks ago, saying there was no point because of her sweaty training sessions.

But Ash loved the way she looked in the mornings. He could picture her now, cheeks tinged with pink and hair slightly disheveled from sleep. Then, he pictured laying her out on the long table and burying his face between her thighs.

He scrubbed both hands down his cheeks and exhaled sharply through his nose. They had to cease this flirtation, these games. If there was any hope of helping her escape his curse, then he couldn't allow things to progress between them. He needed to be professional.

Ash thundered into the sparring ring without any greeting or explanation and launched into training mode. "You have made excellent progress with your shields. Today, I'll attempt to breach your magical defences before attacking with the sword. Start with your Terrane shield. When you're ready, take up the second defensive stance and prepare for my attack."

"Ash. We need to talk about last night."

"There's nothing to talk about, Kenna."

Her face crumpled, and he knew he'd hurt her. His resolve from moments earlier faltered.

Damn it.

He couldn't keep doing this. Couldn't keep wanting her and then pushing her away. Was he just as bad as all the other men in her life? Was he trying to decide what was best for her without allowing her input?

Kenna valued making her own choices. She was strong and capable, and he wanted her to know he saw those things in her. He hated the idea of her feeling belittled or incompetent in his presence. So, today, he'd give her a chance to prove to herself how far she'd come. He'd let her choose what happened next.

"Terrane shield," he reminded her. "Now."

Kenna swirled her hands through the air, forming a solid circular shield of dust and stone in front of her. Then, she drew her sword, entered second position, and braced for attack.

"Are you ready?"

She snorted. "You would never warn me if this were a real fight."

Ash attacked with a flaming spear and a metal dagger, striking through her shield in a single swipe. As she ducked into a low squat the spear singed a hole in the sleeve of her blouse, and she narrowly avoided the dagger going through her forehead. The knife clattered off the wall to the stone floor behind her.

Still crouching, she looked at Ash, incredulous.

"Are you actually trying to kill me?"

"If it's a real fight you want, love. Then a real fight you shall have."

Her hair fell in loose waves around her shoulders. She touched her head where a leather cord had previously held her hair in a high, messy bun. Ash had sliced it in half with his dagger, and the cord laid uselessly at her feet. She pointed to the ruined cord with her blade. "I hope you plan on replacing that. Those ties are a precious commodity when your hair is as long as mine."

"I prefer your hair like this." Ash stepped close to her and picked up one of her dark waves, twirling the silky length of it around his fingers. For a moment, their eyes met. His fingers were still entwined in her hair, and he imagined what it would feel like if he gripped her hair and pulled her lips to his. The air around them seemed to vibrate.

～

ASH'S LIPS quirked up in one corner, a telltale sign that he had her right where he wanted her.

Bastard.

Kenna spun away from him, though she missed the feel of his fingers in her hair. She raised a shield with larger stones as quickly as she could. Ash breezed through her Terrane shield again and again. An icy knife turned her breeches into shorts, and a stony spear cleaved off the long sleeves of her blouse. With his final attack, Ash sliced open the laces at the top of her blouse, exposing an indecent amount of cleavage. Kenna clenched her teeth.

"Shall I just strip it all off, or are you going to do the honors?"

But the way he was looking at her...like a starving man who'd just prepared himself a feast. She liked the feel of his eyes roving over her.

"I wasn't aware that my training sessions were your personal peep show."

"I am done coddling you, Kenna. I know things have been hard for you, but you need to face reality. Winter Solstice will be here in three months. If you're to have any chance of success, I need to push you harder than ever before. If you do not fulfill the treaty, it will be my fault."

A flood of truth washed through their oath, and Kenna cocked her head. The man in front of her was willing to do whatever he could to help her step into her own strength. Yes, he'd kept things from her, but he'd never treated her like a child who couldn't make her own decisions.

She found herself thinking about his hands in her hair again, and she blinked away the thought as he ordered, "Use your Flame."

She formed a circular fire shield, but Ash doused it with ease. He was immediately behind her, holding her firmly to the front of his body with an icy dagger to her throat. Sweat slid down her neck, and she welcomed the kiss of his cool blade as she leaned back into his chest.

Suddenly, remembering she was supposed to fight him, Kenna shouldered away from him, and he did not resist. She paced back and forth, catching her breath.

She was getting nowhere. Samael had defeated her again and again that first day, and Ash was doing the same now. How could she hope to learn to fight or make any kind of difference in such a limited time span? If she failed, her father's death would be meaningless. The rebellion would be meaningless.

"Are you alright?" Ash asked.

"I'm fine."

"Are you sure? We can take a br—"

"I said I'm fine. Go again."

She needed his relentless attack. She needed to lose herself. To unleash herself.

With all her effort, Kenna conjured a wall of fire stretching all the way across the arena. A distinctly unladylike amount of sweat dripped down her face with the magical effort and extreme heat. Surely, this shield would be harder to break through, wouldn't it?

But within seconds, Ash walked through the flaming barricade in a cylinder of water and attacked with his sword. Kenna grunted in frustration and lunged at him. He could have disarmed her in an instant, and she couldn't help feeling like he gave her time to channel her emotions into each blow as she attacked. He seemed to understand her need to feel the clash of weapons, to hear the clang of their swords, to be reminded of what she was fighting for.

But then, he was on the offense. Step by step, he attacked; she parried until she was up against the wall. The cool stones pressed into her back as he placed the blunt, metal sword across her throat. She panted, his cedar and smoke scent enveloping her.

"Just think of how much warmer you'd be if I'd not made the alterations to your ensemble." Ash smirked.

"Get. Off."

Ash leaned into the sword holding her to the wall, his mouth inches from her face. "Make me."

"You know I can't." She squeezed her eyes shut.

"Do you yield?"

Kenna grunted and pushed against him with all her might, but he didn't budge. Like a child throwing a tantrum, she used her magic to hurl dust in his eyes. Ash calmly reached up to clear his vision, and she shoved him off and stalked away.

"Again," Ash said.

"No." She was done embarrassing herself.

"We will go again." She paused. Ash rarely used that tone. It was the command of a king, and left no room for argument.

"Fine," she gritted out.

Changing tactics, Kenna wrapped her entire body in a column of Flame. Through the fire, she saw Ash's silhouette circling her with deliberate calculation. Then, a sudden, torrential rain doused both of them. The rain beat down on them from above, as unrelenting as Ash's attack with his sword.

Over and over, their swords met until she realized...he wasn't letting her win. She was holding her own. A knowing smile lit Ash's blue eyes.

But then, he doubled down on his attack, making her work harder. He wouldn't let her win; he knew how important this was. He wouldn't let her win because he *wanted* her to be strong.

Each time their swords crossed, he forced her to shuffle back toward the edge of the ring again.

Finally, he disarmed her. The sword clanged against the flagstones beneath their feet.

This time when he pinned her to the wall, they were both soaking wet in the unnatural, pouring water which still rained from above. His breathing was ragged.

"Tell me what you want," Ash said.

"To free my people. To protect my family."

"Is that all?" His eyes were ravenous as they dropped to her lips, like he would starve if he didn't taste her.

Would it be so bad if they gave in? In three months, Kenna would have to marry a partner chosen by politics. But right now, she could choose. And she chose not to fight her body anymore.

"I want you."

"It's *very* good to hear you say that, love."

Ash dropped his sword and his lips instantly covered hers. The wind swirled around them as he reached his hands around the back of her thighs and hoisted her up. She wrapped her legs around his waist as he pinned her against the wall and kissed her with unhinged passion. And she allowed him to take control.

Their lips and tongues swirled in a battle of passion, both sides victorious as their needs were satisfied.

More. More. More, she thought, over and over, taking no notice of the frenzied wind whipping around them.

Ash's hips grinding into her, the feel of his hard length straining against his trousers as he rubbed against her, and his smoky winter scent wrapping around her was almost enough to send Kenna over the edge. It had been so long since she'd had any sort of release.

She moaned into his mouth. She needed more of his kiss. More of him. She didn't know how long had passed when Ash set her feet back on the ground. All she knew was that it hadn't been long enough.

The wind settled and Ash ran a hand down his face, seeming to return to his senses. "We should go and get ready for the evening," he said.

Kenna's gaze raked down his body. His cheeks were flushed with desire, and his soaking white shirt revealed every line of the defined muscles beneath. She arched a brow.

"You look fine to me," she said.

She could happily look at him in that soaking white shirt for the rest of her life. Slipping one finger into the waistband of his trousers, Kenna tugged him closer. She stood on her tiptoes, and kissed him gently, beginning to unlace his trousers.

Ash stopped her, bracing one arm on the wall beside her head and leaning down. His breath sent delicious shivers through her body. "Have you forgotten that I am king, love?" He snapped his fingers, and the puddles of water in the arena evaporated.

She had. Lost to her passion, she'd forgotten he was the king. She'd forgotten everything that was at stake. For a few glorious minutes, lost in the feel of his lips on hers, she'd forgotten the treaty and their unbreakable oath. She'd forgotten that she was destined to marry someone else, and she'd forgotten that she and Ash would never have a happy ending.

But if it meant she could kiss him—if she could do *more* than kiss him—she would gladly forget all of it.

Ash kissed her on the nose. Then, he took her by the hand and they began the winding trek to her room. As always, the sight of the king accompanying an elf gained a few stares. Thankfully, none of the courtiers commented, but Kenna could practically feel the disapproval radiating from the self-important angels.

When they reached her door, Kenna was still riding high on passion. She could feel the desire pooling deep in her core and recognized a growing physical need which she hadn't satisfied in the last three months of tragedy, lies, and change. Suddenly, that simmering need was burning hot. She spun Ash around, pushing him into the wall beside her door, standing on her toes and kissing him fiercely.

"Do you want to come in?"

"I think…it will be best if I do not."

"Are you sure? The tub is big enough for two."

Ash looked like he was considering it, but he exhaled loudly and said, "As tempting as that sounds, I have things to take care of before dinner."

With that, he gave her a kiss on the cheek and left her there. Alone.

CHAPTER 49

Kenna ran the bath and decided to bathe in the cedarwood oil mixture. After what had just happened, she couldn't get enough of Ash's scent. Her body was awake in a way it hadn't been in a very long time. She touched her lips, still swollen and tingling from Ash's kiss. She could still feel his hips pressing between her legs, see his soaking wet shirt…

She was going to enjoy this bath *very* much.

She sank into the warm water and breathed in the woodsy aroma. As quickly as she could, Kenna scrubbed the grime off her face and out of her hair. Once she was clean, she closed her eyes and slipped a hand between her legs with the intention of dousing the fire Ash had kindled in her core.

But she found herself suddenly exhausted. She'd used so much magic during training today, and the water was so warm, cradling her in its relaxing embrace.

Forgetting the hand between her legs, Kenna relaxed and gave herself over to the seduction of darkness instead.

When Kenna jolted awake once more, the bathroom was dark. The window was open and wintry air clawed at her as she climbed out of the cold water.

Had she opened the window before her bath? She didn't think so. She didn't remember the crisp air snaking through the room when she'd gotten into the tub.

She wrapped herself in a fluffy towel. Then, she heard the shuffling sound of feet approaching from behind. Kenna whirled around, coming face to face with her father's dead, milky white eyes.

"You've never cared about anyone but yourself. At least our real son tried to help us when we were attacked," her father said. Why were his eyes cold and pearly white? They should have been the color of warm chocolate.

Kenna pinched herself and blinked her eyes rapidly, but she didn't wake up. This wasn't a dream.

"Father?"

"You think you can still call me that? She really is a disappointment, isn't she?" her father said, addressing someone over her shoulder. She spun to look behind her.

Her mother's frail body stood behind her. A bloody torso, ivory eyes, and grey sunken cheeks convicting Kenna of her selfishness.

"Don't worry, Kenna." Her mother tenderly placed an icy hand on Kenna's cheek. "We never expected anything more than disappointment from you. Still, you chose to forsake all of us to run away and be nothing. You are nothing."

No. This wasn't right. Her mother was fine. She'd seen the healer. This had to be a dream.

"I–I'm sorry," Kenna stammered.

"She's sorry. She knows exactly who and what he is, and she's *sorry*," her mother spat. Then, both of her parents laughed, but it was…wrong. It was the grating, unnatural sound of metal scraping against stone, not at all the happy sound it should have been.

Kenna stumbled toward the door of the bathing chamber. As she turned to flee, she tripped and crashed to her knees. When she looked down, she saw dark brown feet and raised her eyes.

Zo was surrounded by a silhouette of flame in the night. Her hair was melted into charred clumps and her skin was blackened and covered in a tangle of glowing red cracks. Her bright hazel eyes gleamed, and she spoke with the unnatural voice she'd used when she had her vision all those years ago. A voice that was all at once male and female. Ancient and new. Light and darkness.

"You were never going to help anyone, were you? You're a disgrace. You might be good for keeping house and bearing someone's child. But not the king's. Never the king. Are you enjoying playing house, princess?"

This couldn't be real, but it was. Kenna was awake.

"I don't understand." Tears left rivulets on her face.

"You should be ashamed of yourself," her father said.

Kenna stood and raced through her bedroom and into the hallway, still wrapped in her towel. Every Shadow had horns. Her hair dripped and she left watery footprints on the stone tiles. She could have sworn she saw a gleaming pair of red eyes viciously smiling at her in the hall of mirrors on her way to the dining room. It couldn't be real.

Not real. Not real. Not real. She told herself with every step.

When she finally made it to the dining room, Ash and Wren were there waiting.

Ash looked up in alarm. "Kenna, what—"

Kenna didn't have time to reply before she collapsed to the floor. Ash was there in an instant with his arms wrapped around her, grounding her in reality. His wood-smoke scent mixed with the lingering cedarwood and eucalyptus of her bath oils.

Ash cupped her face in his hands. "What's wrong? What happened?"

"I saw. I saw my parents. It's so wrong. I'm wrong. I can't..." She shook her head.

"Wren, go check her chamber. Make sure it's secure and light the fire. She's freezing." Ash took a deep breath through his nose and wrath flashed in his eyes.

"What did you bathe in?"

"Cedarwood, eucalyptus, and lemongrass oil—the muscle soothing recipe you gave me. The cedarwood oil smells like you and—"

"I did not leave you any such recipe," Ash said.

"Then who—"

"I seem to have missed some special instructions about this evening's dress code. I would not have bothered with these cumbersome trousers if I had known we were meant to arrive dressed solely in our towels." Samael sauntered into the dining room.

Kenna stared at him. *Am I imagining him too?*

"You should not be here at all," Ash spat at his brother. He stood, leaving Kenna trembling in his absence, and was in Samael's face in an instant. "Tell me, brother. Why is it that I can detect the scent of dreamsbane among Kenna's bath oils?"

"Are you accusing me of tampering with the lady's oils, Your Majesty?"

"Who?" Ash growled.

"Perhaps there is *someone* who does not wish the lady well. Perhaps, she is not as safe within the castle walls as she believes."

"Tell me the truth or get the hell out."

"As you wish, brother. I wouldn't want to interrupt your plans." Samael plucked the goblet of wine from where Ash had been seated, and the full carafe of crimson liquid from the table.

Kenna's whole body shuddered with cold and terror. Ash snapped his fingers, and a fur blanket appeared. He wrapped the blanket around her.

Ash plucked a tiny glass filled with black liquid out of his pocket. "Drink this."

"What is it?" She eyed the glass suspiciously.

"Charcoal and water. It will counteract the hallucinogenic properties of the dreamsbane. The taste is vile, but you can wash it down when we get to your room."

It took her a moment to register what he'd said. Dreamsbane. She'd been drugged.

She gulped down the chalky liquid and cringed. Ash nodded his approval and helped her to her feet. Without warning, his warm hands slid beneath her knees and he cradled her in his arms.

Under any other circumstances, she would have felt self-conscious about her nakedness. Ash was not a bulging brute like Samael, but his lean muscles were powerful. Her weight seemed like nothing to him. She relaxed into his strength and snuggled into the blanket leaning her head against his chest as he carried her from the room.

"Not real. Not real. Not real," she whispered repeatedly to herself.

"No, love. It wasn't real. I am real and I am with you. You're okay."

They reached Kenna's chambers where a roaring fire danced in the hearth. Ash set her feet on the ground but kept his arm around her shoulders. Wren joined them, handing Ash her vial of cedarwood oil.

"Dreamsbane," Wren informed them.

"Yes, I could smell it on her. I've given her an antidote," Ash said. "Is the chamber secure?"

"It is."

"Very well. Leave us."

Wren nodded and left.

Ash pulled her to the floor to sit in front of the warmth of the fire. The king sat behind her and hugged her to his chest, with his legs on either side of her. Kenna thought she could see Zo's charred face surrounded by fire, and she clenched her eyes shut against the image. She pulled her knees to her chest, rocking and wishing the antidote would hurry up and work.

"No one will hurt you," Ash promised. "Not while you're here with me." She felt a trickle of warmth through their oath.

When he snapped his fingers again, a tea tray appeared on the floor next to them, complete with steaming cup and a pot of honey. "Now, drink it. All of it."

Rather than putting a teaspoon of honey into the tea, she spooned the syrupy goo directly into her mouth.

Her lungs were raw, and her heart still beat too fast. She felt like she was dying; like the nightmarish images of her loved ones might return at any moment. All she could do was settle back into Ash's chest as he wrapped his arms tightly around her. She focused on the rise and fall of his chest and the tickle of each exhale in her ear, reaching up to feel the sharp line of his stubbled jaw.

He's real. This is real.

Eventually, her heart slowed to its normal rhythm and the black spots on the edges of her vision cleared. The effects of the dreamsbane had finally worn off.

Kenna slowly sat up, reached for her tea. She added a spoonful of honey before sipping the soothing liquid. They must have been sitting there longer than she'd realized because the tea was barely warm. Kenna warmed it with her magic and sipped quietly as Ash idly stroked up and down her back.

"Feeling better?"

"Yes. Thank you." Her cheeks flushed with embarrassment. She must have seemed insane to him. "I'm sorry."

"No, *I'm* sorry," Ash replied, his expression severe. "Someone in this castle drugged you. They will not go unpunished."

Kenna leaned back into him, and he circled his arms around her shoulders. She stared into the fire, allowing their mesmerizing display of color to captivate her.

"Who do you think would poison me? And why?" she asked.

"I have many enemies, Kenna. There are things which will become clear in time, but there are those who would seek to hurt you, and to distract me from accomplishing what needs to be done."

She sat up suddenly. "Why do you always give me only half truths?"

"I fear that you would think badly of me. This kingdom was born out of violence and selfishness, and there are those who thrive on feeding their own murky desires. You've met my brother. Though I try to give him space to take care of his…urges in an appropriate manner, he is difficult to control."

Having been on the receiving end of Samael's darkness, Kenna couldn't imagine there was any appropriate way for Samael to find a release for his evil.

"Has he hurt someone before? Someone you loved?"

"Samael is not happy to simply hurt someone. His craving is not satisfied until his target is decimated and damned for all eternity. He's hurt many people I care about."

"Couldn't you just banish him from the realm?"

"He's protected by the treaty."

Kenna felt the warm truth stretched between them and added dryly, "Right. The treaty that says I might have to marry him."

Ash nodded and Kenna leaned back into Ash's chest once more. For a few minutes, they sat in silence. The only sound was the popping of the fire, and the shifting of logs in the hearth.

KENNA WASN'T sure when they'd fallen asleep. They were laid on the rug in front of the fire, her head resting on his chest. Ash had one arm wrapped around her, and the horrible images from earlier were nothing but a nightmare.

Yes, her father was gone, but she was doing everything she could to make it right. Her mother was okay. Her brother, Sera, and Drake were looking for Zo and Ezra. She had nothing to be ashamed of. She was doing her best.

With the effects of the dreamsbane nullified and her body pressed against Ash, Kenna was suddenly very aware of her nakedness beneath the heavy blanket. It sent a thrilling tingle from her belly down between her legs.

The horrible images weren't real, but the memories from yesterday were real. How he'd kissed her, his hips pinning her to the wall of the sparring ring. Her breathing grew shallow as she felt her desire returning. She imagined their kiss from yesterday but without any clothes hindering her access to him. Imagining feeling him inside her.

Ash interrupted her thoughts, inhaling sharply. She looked at him, her eyes smoldering.

"What are you thinking about?" he asked.

Ash's finger traced a lazy line down her arm, slipping the blanket down to expose her shoulder. The dying embers in the hearth cast a warm glow around them. She wrapped the blanket around herself once more and sat up. Ash mirrored her.

"I was thinking about kissing you," she answered.

"You're lying." So gently, he lifted her hand, and placed a kiss to the scar on her wrist. "Sensing the truth through our oath works both ways. You were thinking about doing more than kissing me."

"And what if I was?" She looked at him, brazen as she shrugged the blanket down farther, exposing her breasts.

His eyes traveled to her peaked nipples and Ash moved behind her, pulling her to his chest the way he had the night before.

He trailed his hand down the top of her leg and then back up the inside of her thigh, barely brushing the coarse hair at the apex of her thighs and skirting around the place where she was desperate for his fingers to land. He inhaled as though breathing in her scent.

"Tell me the truth, Kenna. I know exactly what your body is begging for, but I need to hear you say it."

"I don't know what I want."

"Another lie," he countered. His voice rolled through her like thunder.

"Touch me," she exhaled.

With deft movements, Ash obeyed her whispered plea. The moment his fingers contacted her wet, sensitive flesh, he found further evidence of just how fully she wanted him. The fur blanket pooled around her hips as she leaned her head onto his shoulder behind her. Her legs opened for him as Ash's fingers stroked perfectly.

She was on the edge of release when he stopped.

"No," she whimpered.

Ash moved around to face her, laying her down and kissing her.

There was nothing of the unhinged passion from their kiss in the ring. This was slow and tormenting. He slid his tongue along the seam of her lips, and she opened for him. She could drown in the feel of him and she would die happy.

When their lips parted, he moved down her body with multiple kisses. His tongue flicked across her pert nipple and she gasped. He gave her a wicked grin before he moved further down her body.

He dragged his teeth over her hipbone lightly, before he nipped the flesh there and Kenna drew in a sharp breath.

"You have no idea how long I've wanted to do that." Ash smiled as his eyes met hers and his head hovered between her legs.

"Please," she begged, and he lowered his face, giving her exactly what she wanted. He slipped two fingers inside her and licked up her center. Over and over her tasted her as though he couldn't get enough.

It wasn't long before her back arched and her world shattered. Her breathing was ragged and her heart pounded when Ash moved back up her body and situated the blanket around her. He lay next to her and hugged her to his chest, back in the position they'd been in when she had woken.

It could have all been a dream, if not for the remnants of pleasure she felt.

"That was…"

"*That*, love, was only a sample of everything I can offer you," Ash promised, placing a gentle kiss on her forehead.

"And who is to say there aren't things I can offer you?"

Her naked body had been on full display while Ash was still fully clothed. She reached for the laces of his breeches. She was tired from the ordeal with the dreamsbane, but she wanted him more than ever. Wanted to share the pleasure she felt with him.

He took her hand, raising it to his lips, and placing a kiss to her palm. His eyes twinkled.

"I think you should get some rest. Though, believe me, I will take you up on your offer another time."

"Will you stay with me tonight?" she asked, hoping his presence might keep the nightmarish images out of her head.

"Of course."

Kenna went to change in the bathing chamber. When she returned,

Ash was stretched out on her bed. He patted the bed next to him, and she nestled into him. It wasn't long before she slipped into a dreamless sleep.

281

CHAPTER 50

$\mathcal{A}$s Kenna dressed the next morning, she puzzled over who might have drugged her bath oils. The most likely suspect was Samael, despite his denial.

She shuddered, recalling the horrific images of her ghastly loved ones and their accusing words. Then, her mind drifted to Ash's intimate touch. Their relationship was changing; she could no longer deny her feelings for him.

When they'd met, she'd believed all angels were her immortal enemies, but he had proven himself to be her ally. When she'd accepted his help, he'd been so friendly, warm, and flirtatious. She'd enjoyed his company. Then he'd turned cold, ashamed of keeping the treaty from her.

Two nights ago on her balcony, he'd placed his crown on her head and started to kiss her so gently. He'd stayed with her last night. He'd even refused her when she'd offered to reciprocate the pleasure he'd given her, making it abundantly clear that his feelings went beyond lust.

But was she willing to risk falling in love with him when she knew she'd have to wrench herself away from him in the end? She was destined to marry someone else. Unless she married Samael, she would have to find a way to leave Notos and wed the prince of Vorra.

Whatever she and Ash felt for each other, there could be no happy ending for them.

When Kenna emerged, Ori was not in her usual position outside

Kenna's door, so she walked to breakfast on her own. Ash and Wren were not in the dining room either.

Shoving down her disappointment, Kenna braced herself for a breakfast of eggs and green juice, but when the servant removed the cover over her breakfast dish, she smiled. There were four rashers of bacon and two massive cinnamon swirls on her plate. The familiar scent of cinnamon, sugar, and yeast made tears prick her eyes.

Almost every time she'd visited Zo in the bakery, Kenna had left with a cinnamon bun. The thought of her imprisoned friend sent a jolt of guilt through her. Here Kenna was, basking in the romantic attention of a king, while Zo languished away in some distant Hel.

How did they extract her blood? And what did they need it for? Kenna hoped her best friend wasn't in too much pain.

Kenna knew she needed to eat in order to have strength for her training, but suddenly she didn't have much of an appetite. Sighing, she unrolled her napkin and found a small note tucked in with her silverware.

I apologize for my absence this morning. Samael left to continue his search for the princess this morning. Take time to rest and explore while Wren and I are away today. We'll resume training and additional activities tomorrow. Enjoy the cinnamon buns. After all, I promised that I would bring you pleasure, and I always keep my word. -Ash

A delicious shiver of anticipation shuddered through her body when she read the words, followed by a sense of unease. Someone within the castle had drugged her yesterday, and if Ash was gone, she wasn't under his protection. Even if Samael was not in the castle, why would Ash leave her alone today?

After eating as much as she could, Kenna shoved her hesitation away in favor of Ash's advice to explore the castle.

She didn't bother changing out of her training gear but left the dining room and wandered down toward the sparring chamber. Though she passed many doors that she'd never tried to open, she was fixated on one particular door. Her rigorous training schedule had rendered her too busy and too tired to do much other than eat, train, and sleep during her months of residence, but she had never stopped wondering about the doors Ori had warned her not to open.

At the end of the hallway opposite the sparring chamber, Kenna stood before the identical wooden doors. If the size of the room where

Kenna usually spent her days was any indication, the mysterious room behind the doors would be another large space.

If she was truly going to trust Ash and accept whatever feelings there were between them, she needed to find out if he had anything to hide. He'd invited her to explore the palace, he'd helped her out of danger on multiple occasions, and he'd comforted her the night before. Surely, he couldn't have anything else to hide.

And yet…

Kenna reached out and pushed down on the handles. The doors were locked.

"Can I help you?" Lailah's voice startled her.

"I have the day off training and Ash said I could explore, but…it's locked, so I'll just go."

"Nonsense. One locked door will not block the path of a strong, empowered woman. You wish to enter, and so you shall." Lailah waved her hand and the door unlocked with a click.

How long would Lailah be staying at the castle? The priestess' constant need to turn every situation into a life lesson was exhausting, but at least she'd unlocked the door.

"Thank you," Kenna said. They stood staring at each other awkwardly for a minute. Finally, Kenna added, "Do you want to come with me?"

"Oh no, child. *I* would not be so foolish as to enter those doors. But it is your goal to see what is beyond. What is the meaning of life if we do not accomplish our goals?" With her ominous warning turned motivational statement, Lailah sauntered away down the hallway, trailed by her shimmering wings and flowing skirt.

Kenna rolled her eyes.

Lailah had said crossing the threshold of these doors would be foolish. But she'd opened it for Kenna and encouraged her to see what lay beyond. Apparently, everyone in Brumalis Castle spoke a secret language founded in riddles.

She eyed the door, hesitating. Then, an idea struck. She jogged to the other end of the hallway and entered the sparring chamber where she selected a dagger from the weapons cabinet.

Sheathing the dagger to the strap on her thigh, Kenna returned to the mystery doors. With one hand on the hilt of her dagger, she pressed down on the handle. She pushed against the solid door, and it resisted with a loud creak. It wasn't a large space like she'd expected, but a tiny room no bigger than a broom cupboard. In the dim light of a single sconce with a tiny blue flame, Kenna saw stone steps in front of her. A narrow staircase spiraled down into the unknown.

At once, Kenna detected the stench of waste. If the stairs led to some sort of sewer, it would certainly explain why Lailah didn't want to come with her.

There was no light at all coming from the stairs, so Kenna used the candle in the wall sconce to form a small sphere of flame over her palm. The air seemed hungry for the sound of her steps, swallowing up each slight noise before it could disturb the eerie stillness.

As her foot hit the top step, a frigid wind blew up the stairs and the door behind her slammed shut. Kenna jumped. But in spite of the strong gust, Kenna heard no words of warning on the wind.

"Just a draft from the sewers," she whispered to herself.

Down she descended into the depths of the mysterious chasm, counting her steps as she went. She stopped counting sometime after six hundred and sixty-seven, her knees creaking in protest like they belonged to an elderly woman and not a woman in her mid-twenties. The limestone walls and steps eventually gave way to blocks of ice, and Kenna tread carefully, hoping not to slip.

Eventually, the corkscrew stairs flattened into a long tunnel. She tiptoed to the end of the tunnel, which opened into an enormous, snowy cavern bathed in the same unnatural blue light coming from the upstairs candle.

A narrow, gleaming black bridge cut through the middle of the cavern. Along either side of the length of the bridge, there were multiple icy platforms large enough to hold one or two people. The platforms floated in the air, held aloft by some force Kenna didn't understand.

The snowy walls of the cavern were peppered with hollowed out circles like white honeycomb. Whatever was inside the frozen recesses was set too deep within to see from Kenna's vantage point, so she carefully traversed the frozen earth toward the icy bridge, her breath forming wispy clouds in the air.

The moment her foot hit the glassy surface of the bridge, the silence was broken. Agonized groans, hacking coughs, and hopeless keening filled the air, along with the unmistakable putrid stench of festering waste and unwashed bodies.

And the rotten smell of death.

This was no sewer. It was a prison. If the noises were any indication, being enslaved in the belly of this frigid beast was a fate worse than death.

Is this how Ash treats his prisoners?

He seemed so gentle and kind, but he'd touched her with the same hands that locked people away in here. He kissed her with the same lips that sentenced these prisoners to their gruesome fate.

She needed to leave.

She turned on her heel and ran toward the tunnel leading back to the stairs, but she skidded to a halt when she heard two familiar voices approaching—Samael and Ori.

Drawing her dagger, she shimmied herself into a gap between the tunnel and the cavern wall, listening as the voices descended the winding stairs.

"Did you really think that was good enough? Did you think you would be good enough? After all this time?" Samael accused.

"Please. I can try again. Drugging her oils almost worked. If she hadn't left her chamber…"

"Oh, but she did, didn't she? Thankfully the king thinks quickly on his feet, or rather with his hands and his tongue. But I grow weary of your failure. And so, you can stay here."

Kenna was going to be sick. Ori was the one who had poisoned her bath oils? How did Samael know what had happened with Ash?

Kenna had run right to him for comfort and safety, and he had… what? Given her pleasure as a means of distraction from some darker purpose? What was Ash hiding from her?

"Please, Samael. I'll do anything. You can chain me up. Whip me. I know how you like to punish me, and I want you to. I do. I will submit. Just don't leave me alone here. All I've ever wanted is you. I swear it." Ori was crying.

"We both know that isn't true. You're worthless. And I will take great pleasure in punishing you. But only after you have suffered the consequences of your failure in solitude."

Kenna held her breath as Samael and Ori emerged from the tunnel.

If not for the fact that Ori had just admitted to drugging her, she may have employed her training and attempted to help Ori get away from the prince. Maybe it made her a monster to leave her maid in Samael's hands, but considering Ori's traitorous revelation, Kenna stayed hidden.

The evil angel was merciless.

He dragged a stumbling Ori to the bridge by her hair. Ori's words gave way to unintelligible sobs, begging for a different fate, but the sound of her anguish faded into nothing the moment they reached the bridge. Kenna watched Samael pull Ori to one of the small platforms and push her down onto her knees.

He snapped his fingers the same way Kenna had seen Ash do so many times. But instead of servants, blankets, or hot tea appearing, Samael's fingertips sent the icy disc soaring through the air into one of the holes in the snowy walls. Each snowy recess must house a tormented prisoner.

As soon as Samael and Ori disappeared into the hole, Kenna shimmied out of her hiding place and ran like she'd never run before. She hurtled down the tunnel and up the stairs, not knowing if she'd reach the exit before Samael reappeared. After all, he could move much faster than Kenna if he wanted to. She pumped her legs round and round and round.

"Damn it," she said, as her foot slipped. She slid down a few of the icy steps before she righted herself and began to climb again, moving a bit more carefully.

On and on, she climbed. Her lungs were on fire and her legs felt like they were made of bricks. She willed herself to just keep moving forward. She had to be more than halfway. Finally, she reached the level where the icy steps turned to stone.

But then, she heard footsteps.

CHAPTER 51

The footsteps weren't coming from behind her. They were coming down the stairs toward her. Who was it? Lailah? Ash?

There was nowhere to hide. Kenna moved back down the stairs, pressed herself against the icy wall, gripping her dagger the way Wren had shown her.

Then, she came face to face with a living nightmare.

"I remember you," his gravelly voice rasped as he grinned menacingly. In the narrow stairwell, he was less than a foot away from her, and she was overwhelmed by a smell she would never forget. It was the same rotten breath that had been in her face in the alley outside of the Golden Flagon in Braktyn the night she'd met Ash.

The night Ash had saved her from the brute standing in front of her now.

"What were you doing in my dungeon?"

"Your dungeon? Surely the dungeon belongs to the king," she managed.

"Of course, it does. But even the most powerful king employs a dungeon master. I think I'll enjoy locking you up." Droplets of his fowl spit splattered her face.

Fueled by vengeance, along with her need to survive, Kenna lashed out with her Aqua magic drawing from the icy blocks. Small fissures appeared in the ice wall and steps as she shackled the dungeon master with frigid chains.

"You will do no such thing," she informed him. "But I will have answers. The king saved me from you that day in the alley. Why?"

The angel struggled against his bonds, clearly surprised by her attack, and she doubled her effort to hold him. She panted with the exertion, sweat trickling down her back. She wasn't sure how long she could hold him.

His laugh was full of hateful glee. "I attacked you on his order. I get to play with someone like you once a year. He could just as easily have ordered me to bring you back here and lock you up. But there was no need. You took care of the imprisonment part yourself. You're here now. And you'll never be able to leave."

The revelation sucked the air from Kenna's chest. Everything she thought she'd learned about Ash was a lie. He'd orchestrated the attack in Braktyn. Had tricked her into coming here. Had he been lying about her being able to leave at the end of their oath?

"I'm not a prisoner. I'm leaving after Winter Solstice," she ground out, though the words tasted like bitter lies on her tongue.

"Are you sure?" The brute's eyes gleamed with malicious delight.

"Do you want to know what I'm sure of? I'm sure I remember exactly how you made me feel in the alley that night—the smell of your dank breath, the feel of your grotesque body. I don't care why you attacked. You made me feel weak and helpless. Well, I'm not weak anymore. And you'll never make anyone feel that way ever again. Your memory will never haunt anyone else's nightmares."

Something within her snapped. She drove her dagger through his ribs and into his heart—deep and true—without a moment's hesitation. She swiped her blade before she pulled it out, the way Wren had taught her. Blood spattered the walls and pooled at their feet, and she stared into his soulless eyes as she listened to the rasping sound of the dungeon master struggling for his last breaths. She watched his life fade away to nothing before she released his icy chains. He slid down the wall to rest at her feet.

She'd lied when she'd said he would never haunt anyone ever again.

His dying face would haunt her as long as she lived. For a moment, she stared at her shaking hands and the pool of blood at her feet.

Samael.

Samael would be coming up the stairs. He would find the dungeon master's body and he would know someone had been there. Kenna needed to run.

Her tired legs trudged onward until she finally reached the top of the winding stairs. She hurtled toward the door she'd been so stupidly desperate to look behind.

The door which had changed everything.

She needed to clean the dagger, put it away, and go to her room to gather some supplies. Damn her unbreakable oath. She had to find a way to escape the castle. Tonight.

Then, she looked at the dagger still in her hand, and the knife clattered to the floor. She trembled from head to toe as the reality of what she'd just done washed over her.

Murderer.

Her legs were like lead, but she had to move. She forced herself forward and up the stairs which led back to her chamber—and ran directly into Ash.

~

"KENNA? WHAT ARE—" Ash's brow furrowed as he registered her bloodied appearance. His gaze followed the bloody footprints and sensed the dead body in the stairwell. The haunted look in her eyes. It was the unmistakable look of a person who'd killed for the first time. "Come with me. Now."

She didn't move. She just looked at him and shook her head. "You lied to me."

Shit

"Kenna, I don't know what you think you've discovered or whose body that is, but we need to go. Now. If anyone sees you here..." He shook his head. "There are forces in this realm not even I can protect you from."

"Forces like your dungeon master? The male who attacked me in Braktyn? The male whose job it is to do *your* bidding? He's dead. I killed him."

If she'd killed Varis, the punishment was execution. Even if her crime was discovered, she wouldn't be executed if Samael and Lailah still believed they needed her blood. She would be safe until the ritual on Winter Solstice.

"I will try to explain what I can, but we have to go. You must pretend nothing has changed. Otherwise, you will face a fate worse than death." Ash grabbed hold of her arm.

She wrenched her arm out of his grasp, looking at him with such fear and pain in her eyes. "Isn't that what you want? Varis told me I will never leave this castle. Was he mistaken? Am I free to leave after Winter Solstice?"

Ash hated that she was frightened of him. Hated what she must think of him right now. But she was right to be afraid. He needed to get her away from here.

With a voice he reserved for making his enemies cower before him, he said, "You are too young to comprehend the meaning of imprisonment. You will come with me this instant."

He held out a hand, and she didn't backed away. He'd promised not to take control of her body by magic again. At least he could keep that promise.

"Last chance, Kenna."

She didn't move.

"Suit yourself."

He rushed at her with his shoulder, wrapped his arm around the back of her legs, and hoisted her over his shoulder.

"Put me down right now!" She shrieked.

"Would you rather I carry you to your bedchamber or Samael carry you to the dungeon, Kenna? It's your choice."

She went silent.

Kenna had killed an angel and violated the terms of the treaty in the process. Ash snapped his fingers, and the blood vanished from her hands and the floor. But the treaty was more powerful than his magic. He couldn't shift Varis's body,

Shrouded in dark mist, Ash hurried to Kenna's bedchamber before shutting the door behind them.

He placed her down gently, and she spun away from him, trying to open the locked door to no avail. He couldn't let her out. Not if he had any chance of keeping her safe. Her shoulders went rigid, and she balled her fists at her side. She thought he was going to hurt her.

And she was right. He would hurt her, whether or not he wanted to.

Ash sat on her bed, leaned his elbows on his knees, and put his head in his hands.

"I didn't intend for this to happen," he said, looking at her.

"I don't care what you intended." Tears streaked her beautiful face. "Please. Just let me go."

"I can't. Do me the honor of believing me. I would let you go if it was within my power." It was Ash's turn to beg.

Her laugh was bitter. "You are the *king*. Who has more power than you, other than the Ancients? And where are they?" She gestured to the room, empty save for her and Ash. "I don't see them stepping in to keep me here. I'm trapped in this castle against my will because of you. You know what my freedom means to me. The ability to make my own choices. In the same breath you reveal I am your prisoner, you have the audacity to claim honor? I don't think so, Ash."

He winced and her shoulders slumped as she crossed the room to her bathing chamber, defeat written in her features. "Stay or go. I don't care. Now that I know I'm your lifelong captive, I assume I'll be locked in here either way. I'm going to try to wash away the nightmares I have endured today. Nightmares I've endured because of you."

She slammed the door behind her and the rushing water filling the tub did nothing to stifle the sound of her sobs.

Ash flopped back onto the bed. Everything she'd said was true. He was a monster without a shred of honor. He couldn't endure another moment of his curse hanging between them. He needed to tell her everything, but he didn't think he could.

Ash had tried to tell Kenna once. He'd looked at her and told her she could trust him. He'd let her feel the cold sting of the lie and tried to force the truth into her mind while there was still a chance that she might flee.

Pushing the truth into her thoughts had been as impossible as trying to bring down a mountain with a wooden hammer. The curse wouldn't allow it.

In over three hundred years, the only one of the elvish women he'd ever been able to tell was Elenya. After he'd told his mate the truth, he'd tried to get her out of the castle, but he'd failed her in every way. He'd tried and failed to warn every woman who came after Elenya.

He hadn't allowed himself to fall in love again. Until…

The thought trailed off, the realization dawning like the sun peaking over the horizon.

Ash assumed he'd been able to tell Hawthorne about the curse because of the brotherly love between them; he'd been able to tell his mate because he truly loved her.

With sudden certainty, Ash knew.

He was in love with Kenna. Utterly, hopelessly, deeply in love with her.

She could never replace Elenya. No one could. But he'd been falling for Kenna since the moment he'd met her. Knowing she was destined for something greater, knowing he might somehow redeem himself had allowed him to open his heart in a way he hadn't for hundreds of years.

Ash sprang up from the bed and ran to the bathing chamber, throwing open the door.

Kenna was still crying silently, but she crossed her arms over her breasts in the bath, shrieking. "Get out!"

"I'm cursed!" The words came easily. Laughter bubbled out of him at the freedom. "I couldn't tell you before. I can only tell you now because…" He stopped himself. "I can tell you now."

He shouldn't tell her he loved her. Though he could be honest with her, any love between them was still cursed.

Ash averted his eyes, suddenly realizing she was naked and he'd barged in without warning. "Sorry," he said. When he turned away from her, the water sloshed in the tub as she climbed out.

Elenya *had* to accept him when he told her of the curse. Their souls were entwined by fate, but there was no mating bond with Kenna. There was nothing to protect him from Kenna's disgust as he laid the truth of his curse bare.

Once Kenna knew the truth, she would shrink away from his love. She'd be right to hide her heart away from him the same way covered her body.

"You can turn around," she said. She was wrapped in a white robe, her hair dripping and cheeks flushed.

She was so damned beautiful, and his heart ached with the loss of something he would never have.

CHAPTER 52

Kenna sat on the floor next to her bed, hugging herself as she leaned against the wooden frame. She looked at Ash like he was a monster.

"Well?" she prompted.

"The serum the High Council has been using to control the elve's memories in Mesterra was the priestess' doing. She is gifted with Luniva's power. But to make the serum, she needs to use me or Samael. We were Luniva's highest ranking officers in the Void War, and our mental gifts are particularly strong." Ash tapped his head, indicating his ability to read and control minds.

"The plan was to trick an elf into making an unbreakable oath and falling in love with me. There would be a ritual on Winter Solstice using Ancient magic and the elf's blood to make the Emergence serum. For her blood to be an effective conduit for the magic, the elvish woman would have to love me mind, body, and soul—without mental coercion."

"When you told me about the treaty, you said the serum didn't work properly. That Lailah wanted full control over the elves."

"It did work, but not the way Lailah expected. I wasn't a willing participant. I hesitated because of the cost of creating the serum. Samael offered to do the ritual. He begged to take my place as king, but the thought of Samael ruling...I couldn't bring that fate upon Notos or Mesterra."

Kenna pursed her lips, the only sign that she might agree with his decision.

"I had been on the throne less than a year, and I already regretted following Luniva in the war. But the priestess had no regrets. She swore it was a simple ritual and would only need to take place once for Luniva to control the minds of all the elves in Mesterra. The humans were gone, and this was the only loophole in the treaty that would allow us to control Mesterra. It would give meaning to the war.

Reluctantly, I agreed. I made an unbreakable oath to Lailah to enact her plan and keep it secret. My only condition was that Samael also had to swear an unbreakable oath that he wouldn't be able to kill me and take my throne. Of course, Samael had conditions, too. He wanted to be the one in charge of the palace staff and the dungeons. I couldn't bear the thought of what he might do as king, and I supposed if he was oversaw punishing criminals, it might keep him content.

Just once. That's what I told myself over and over. Lailah graciously chose the female required for the ritual." Ash sneered. "She said it would make it easier if I didn't have to decide. Once she'd chosen the elf, I staged an attack with Varis. I came to the woman's aid before she came to any real harm, earning her trust. She was twenty-five and I was..." Ash swept a hand down his handsome physique. "I usually have a certain effect on women. It didn't take long to trick her into the unbreakable oath."

Kenna's eyes widened and her face blanched. "That's exactly what you did to me when I arrived in Braktyn."

Ash nodded, his voice dropped to a hoarse whisper, "The moment I made the unbreakable oath with Elenya, I was flooded with guilt. I tried to tell her the truth and send her back to Mesterra, but I couldn't. That's when I realized what Lailah had done. I hadn't made an unbreakable oath at all, but I'd willingly walked into a curse. I was bound by Ancient magic, and I couldn't speak a word of it to anyone."

His eyes burned with shame and a few tears escaped. Kenna sat in silence, listening and waiting for him to continue.

"I didn't mean to fall in love with her. I didn't know Elenya was my mate until we first kissed, but Lailah had known when she targeted her. Our mating bond was stronger than the curse. At least, strong enough for me to tell her the truth. But it wasn't strong enough to break the curse's Ancient magic.

When it came time for the ritual, I tried to resist. The curse took hold of my mind and body at midnight on Winter Solstice. I didn't know what I was doing. I never would have known how it all happened if Samael hadn't flooded my mind afterward; Lailah had lied about what the ritual required. Samael took such joy in tormenting me with the images of everything he'd watched play out that night.

For years, I wondered if the images were real or if Samael had conjured them to torture me, but the ritual continued. Year after year after year. When Wren had been here for five years, I finally had the courage to ask him what he'd seen at the Winter Solstice ritual. He confirmed everything Samael showed me as truth."

"Why didn't you refuse to seduce and target anyone after that first year? Surely, if you didn't bring anyone to the castle to fall in love with you, then the ritual couldn't take place."

"The year after my mate died, I tried to resist. Every moment I rebelled against the curse, I was in extreme physical and mental agony. The curse demanded my compliance. It weakened my power, and when I still refused, Samael and Lailah made me watch as they tortured three of my brothers. I gave in."

"What happens at the ritual?"

"It's...I..." Ash's voice broke, and he took a deep breath. He wasn't sure he could get the words out to tell Kenna without collapsing into tears the way he had with Hawthorne.

Kenna's eyes softened ever so slightly. "Would you be able to show me?" She tapped her temple.

She'd never allowed him into her mind before. Ash had suggested it when he told her about the treaty, but she'd refused. Now, even after learning about the dungeon and his curse, she was willing to let him in so she could understand the truth.

He nodded and cleared his throat. "It will be painful. The memory is from Samael's perspective, and it's...it's so much worse than you can imagine. When you come out of the memory, you will feel disoriented and dizzy. You will likely be sick." His eyes dropped to the floor in shame, and his voice was quiet as he said, "You won't ever look at me the same."

She clenched her jaw and squared her shoulders. "Don't tell me what I will or won't do, Ash. Just show me. I'll decide for myself what to do."

"Very well," he said. "But I'm going to get some supplies."

Ash went to the bathing chamber to find a bucket and prepare some cool cloths. Then, he sat next to Kenna on the floor.

"Are you ready?" he asked.

She lifted her chin and sat up straighter. "Yes."

Ash took a deep breath and plunged himself into the darkest part of his mind, losing himself to Samael's horrific memory as he shared it with Kenna.

CHAPTER 53

The long table in the great hall below the dais held hundreds of carafes of sparkling wine and bottles of amber notelixirs. Candlelight sparkled in the crystal goblets and decanters which remained after the Winter Solstice feast. It had been nearly a year since the war ended and the treaty was agreed, and the loyal angels who'd fought for Luniva waited to hear what the priestess would say.

Lailah hadn't shared all of her plans for the ritual with Samael, but it seemed Ash didn't know what she'd say either.

Samael would never understand why their mother, Luniva, had chosen his spineless brother to rule. The only way to keep loyalty was to rule with fear and pain, but Ash didn't have the stomach for tyranny. Samael was hungry for that kind of power.

At least Samael would be allowed to strike fear into the hearts of Notos when they heard the horrors of the castle dungeon. The icy prison was nearly complete. He was also allowed to choose slaves for the castle, and he relished the idea of turning women into subservient wenches. Lailah was the only woman who deserved a position of power in this world.

Samael looked to his left, where Ash and Lailah were seated. Echelous sat at the table directly in front of the dais, his posture relaxed and his smile lopsided, savoring some delicious secret. Samael felt the sting of jealousy in his chest. Had Lailah shared her plans with Echelous?

Lailah stood, sauntering forward and clapping her hands to gain the attention of the assembled court.

Suddenly, the light of thousands of candles winked out with a *whoosh*, plummeting the room into darkness. Winter Solstice marked the annual new moon, so the only light came from Lailah's hands where she held an orb of soft ivory light, as though she'd plucked the moon from the sky.

"Tonight is a very special night. It has been nearly a year since we were cast out of our home in Vorra and sentenced to the endless cold of this realm. The war may not have had the outcome we'd hoped, but the future is not so bleak. We are immortal. We have centuries—millennia if needed—to claim what we've lost."

The faces in the crowd mirrored Samael's scorn for Soldivus.

"For the time being, the human worms are not our concern. But the elves in Mesterra must understand that angels are the superior race. They must never presume to rule themselves. The treaty will not allow more than one angel to cross the Veil into Mesterra each year, but tonight's ritual will make us stronger than the Treaty.

Using Ancient magic and the blood of an elf fully devoted to our king, we have created a serum which will disguise angels enough to allow five to cross the Veil into Mesterra yearly.

Not only will it allow us to infiltrate their land, but we will also seize control of the elves. We will make them believe the serum unlocks their true potential for power. We will call it an Emergence, but it will be nothing more than a temporary euphoria and a physical glow. It will take their memories and free will. We will not let them remember the true beginning of the Void War, but we will make them think it was the worthless humans who caused the conflict. With our control over them, they will have no choice but to become our willing subjects."

Ash was the king of Notos, but would Samael be the one to rule Mesterra? His mouth almost watered at the thought of all that power.

"Each year, we will complete this ritual and five more angels will cross the Veil into Mesterra. Within ten years, there will be fifty angels in Mesterra. Loyal angels will gain the trust of the elvish leaders, assuming roles as their advisors. Eventually, the leaders of every territory of the realm will willingly drink the serum. Once we have infiltrated the minds of their elvish leaders, all the elves will follow.

As time goes on, we will harvest any elves with special gifts and experiment with ways that their blood might enhance the serum. Within a century, not a single elf in Mesterra will remember the truth. Three hundred and twenty-nine years from now, the treaty will be over, and the elves will provide legions of warriors to back our cause. We will go to war with Soldivus again, but this time, we will emerge victorious."

Yes. Yes. It is my turn.

Samael would be the one to rule in Mesterra. Lailah gestured to the table nearest the altar, and her five closest advisors ascended the stairs, joining her on the dais.

"These are the five I have chosen to be Mesterra's High Council. They will drink the serum this year, and the magic will allow them passage across the Veil. Five will be selected each year from now until the end of the treaty so that we have a strong force of angels in Mesterra."

Samael tried to keep the disappointment and rage from his face. The fucking bitch had chosen these five over him? He was the prince of this realm, destined for greater things than being cast aside while his weak brother sat on the throne of Notos.

Lailah placed her hands together and pushed them apart, a graceful breaststroke through invisible water, and the ground before the dais opened up. A cylindrical stone roughly six feet in diameter rose from the gaping hole. The stone circle stood at waist height, like the stump of a tree.

An altar.

"Now let us begin. Varis! Bring her!"

The doors on the opposite side of the great hall swung open. Varis, the dungeon master, descended the stairs with a firm grip on Ash's mate. Samael had never looked twice at her, but now...

He couldn't drag his gaze away from the sight of Elenya in chains while her pink nipples strained against her thin white shift. Terror and despair were written all over her tear-streaked face, and it sent a rush of blood to his cock.

Why had his mother chosen Ash for this purpose and not him? Samael lived for causing this kind of pain.

Varis shoved Elenya and her knees cracked against the stone floor. She knelt in front of Lailah and Ash.

His brother stepped in front of the priestess and called out for his mate. But before he could profess his love, Lailah plunged a long dagger with a cylindrical handle into Ash's back, between his ribs, and straight into his heart.

Samael's face lit with glee. Ash would finally die for his weak-minded insolence.

But Ash's body didn't slump to the floor as Samael expected. Instead, Lailah pushed on the handle, which grew shorter as a smaller cylinder disappeared into a larger one.

When she withdrew the blade, there was no blood and Ash was still standing. It shouldn't be possible.

Ash went preternaturally still and his skin sparkled like a blanket of fresh snow bathed in moonlight. Then his posture turned predatory. He stalked back and forth in front of his mate as though he would pounce on her and feast on her body.

"Please, Lailah. Don't make him do this," Ash's elvish whore whispered to the priestess. "If he hurts me, it will destroy him."

Ash turned to face the priestess, and Samael saw the king's eyes. Normally a deep blue, Ash's eyes were two discs of pure black, filled with feral hunger and unending malice.

Lailah didn't answer aloud, but Samael listened in on the thoughts. Lailah spoke directly into the girl's mind.

Oh you, dear, stupid girl. You think you can save him? If you don't cooperate, I'll make you watch as I torture him.. Slowly.

The girl wouldn't do it. Couldn't allow Ash to be harmed on her behalf when he was her mate. The whole situation was positively delicious. Samael suppressed a shiver of pleasure. He could use this. Tonight's ritual would give him power over his brother, such as he'd never had before.

Lailah nodded to Ash. He stripped down, standing fully nude in front of the entire court, and his black and navy wings unfurled at the sight of his mate on her knees before him. Wings were for flying and fucking. Samael assumed that whenever Elenya spread her legs, Ash spread his wings. It made sex so much more pleasurable.

Now, Ash's feathers were casually displayed in front of the entire court, and he had such burning lust written on his face. The evidence of his desire stood at attention. Samael thrummed with excitement. This ritual was perfectly grotesque, and the plan was brilliant. But *Lailah* made a dire error in casting him aside for his brother, and one day he would have his revenge.

Ash prowled down the steps toward his mate. She was crying silently, her eyes fixed on the king's fathomless black eyes, hoping Ash would recognize her. The girl was a fool.

The king hefted her to her feet, chains clanking against the stones as he unbound her and dragged her toward the altar. Her eyes darted over his face, panic evident.

"Ash, look at me. Ash. Ash. *Ash.*" she said his name over and over as he pushed her down on her back, and climbed atop of her. He hovered over her, not forcing into her as she spoke softly to him. "It's me. Stop. It's me. I love you. Stop. Ash." Her words gave way to whimpering, strangled sobs. Samael's face twisted in disgust. She was foolish if she believed love would have any power over the Ancient magic.

Lailah smiled sweetly and her voice rang through the hall: "Your heart, mind, and soul are entwined. This is your purpose. You should be happy to fulfill your destiny."

Ash's mate squeezed her eyes closed, and she took a deep breath. The king was trembling and sweat beaded on his brow, like he was fighting the magic in his veins. It shouldn't be possible, and yet, his brother hesitated.

～

THE MEMORY CHANGED THEN, becoming foggy and disjointed. In some distant part of her mind, Kenna knew the vision was shifting from Samael's memories to Ash's, and it felt like a half-remembered nightmare.

～

DON'T DO IT. Don't. Don't hurt her. A voice roared in his mind, but it couldn't escape his mouth.

Pain lanced through him and Ash's arms trembled with the need to obey the force demanding his body conquer her, demanding that he take her whether she wanted him or not.

All the while, his soul writhed. The need to protect her was stronger. He couldn't do this to her. But why?

He wanted to. He wanted to be inside her, and he was so close.

But she was crying.

Mate. A distant whisper somewhere within. The woman was his mate. He couldn't hurt her like this. Couldn't force himself on her. Nothing could make him hurt her.

But the pain. Ash's mind felt like it was fracturing into pieces over and over. His body was on fire, and his heart was so cold it ached in his chest.

The woman looked at him, and somewhere in his mind, he heard her.

She opened herself to him, and he recognized her voice in his mind like a soothing song, easing his pain as he fought against himself. He didn't want to hurt her.

I love you. It's okay. I'm okay. It's not your fault. You're mine, and I give myself to you freely.

Ash couldn't bear the pain for another second and he thrust into her.

It's not your fault. I forgive you. I love you. The thoughts poured into him with every thrust of his hips.

He was getting closer now, his pace increasing.

I'll see you again on the eternal shores. Her beautiful voice sang to his soul.

Why was she crying when it was so right for them to be together? When their need for each other was so strong? He could feel the need in their mating bond connecting them. Their souls. Their hearts. Their bodies. This was where they belonged. Why did she offer him forgiveness?

Ash's thrusts grew frantic as the pleasure built. But the moment he groaned and released himself inside her, a blade of ice cleaved his mate's head from her body. His pleasure lingered as the blood pooled from her headless form.

Without a voice, his soul yelled and sobbed inside him. But he had no voice as his heart split in two. He rolled off her corpse, his movements stiff and controlled by the Ancient magic.

He was a monster.

❧

Kenna tugged and tugged on a warm tether of *something*, grappling to pull herself out of the memory.

No more. No more of this. It's too much.

Her vision blurred around the edges, and she turned and vomited into a bucket someone offered her.

What? Who? What was that? Her mind struggled to sort through the images and feelings. The monstrous thoughts she'd had as though they belonged to her. The excitement and mirth she'd felt in Samael's memory.

But then she'd been in Ash's mind. She could still feel the blinding pain. Could still see the headless woman on the stone altar while the ecstasy of release lingered. Ash's mate was beheaded while he was still inside her, and there was so much blood. Such unending, indescribable pain and heartbreak.

She vomited again.

CHAPTER 54

Kenna was pale and vomiting. Though Ash was nauseous, he'd seen the memories enough times that they no longer affected him as much physically. The agony in his soul was still unbearable.

He reached out a hand and stroked Kenna's back, trying to soothe her; she scooted away, unable to bear being touched by a monster.

He couldn't blame her. He'd never reach those eternal shores his mate had promised him. At least not the shores of light where Elenya's soul undoubtedly lived.

Kenna closed her eyes, and a single tear rolled down each of her cheek as she leaned back against her bed.

They sat in silence as Kenna collected herself. She needed time to remember who and where she was. Seeing the memory from Samael's point of view never became any less disgusting.

Eventually, Kenna croaked, "I don't understand."

"The dagger Lailah stabbed into my heart was filled with a serum made with Ancient magic. The moment my mate died, my curse was sealed. I don't know if it was the mating bond or my unwilling participation, but I assume that's why the serum can only control the elves' memories. Of course, that's been enough to keep the elves subdued for centuries."

Kenna stayed silent.

"Lailah took something sacred and beautiful, and turned it into poison," Ash told her. "I've been forced to repeat the ceremony for three hundred and twenty-nine years. An annual celebration in front of an audience of nobles, and I am their beloved king."

Ash sneered, unable to meet her eyes. Kenna reached out a shaky hand, taking Ash's fingers in hers and squeezing. He pulled his hand away. He didn't deserve the compassionate touch.

"I need...I need some time," Kenna said.

"I understand." Ash stood and crossed to the door. He paused, gripping the handle. He wanted to tell her he loved her. Wanted to tell her over and over again how sorry he was. Instead, he said, "For what it's worth, I never wanted to hurt you."

Then, he slipped out of her room.

He sat with his back to Kenna's door. When a servant passed, he summoned her.

"My guest is indisposed. Please, can you summon the Captain of the Guard." The servant bobbed her head, curtseyed, and hurried off to find Wren.

Ash snapped his fingers, summoning two glasses and a bottle of smoky caramel notelixir. He poured a glass full, drained it and poured himself another.

Wren arrived fifteen minutes later, sweaty from training with his soldiers at the garrison.

"How is your training with the new recruits going?" the king asked.

Wren sat next to him on the floor, plucking up the spare glass of elixir. He took a sip. "It's going well. The elf you brought here from Braktyn, Nik, is very promising. He's strong; he has a lot to fight for."

"That's good. He cost me enough. The madam at the brothel was not happy to see him go."

Wren looked at him curiously. "Why'd you pay?"

Ash shrugged and gulped down another burning swallow of his drink. "Why did I rescue a bloodied teenage winged fae twenty years ago?"

Neither of them spoke the answer aloud, though they both knew it. Because ever since the first ritual, Ash had been trying to find a way to redeem himself. So, he helped those he could whenever he could. In this case, Kenna cared about Drake, and Drake had asked for the favor with Nik.

After a few minutes drinking in silence, Wren said, "I don't think you summoned me here to ask about how the new guards are progressing."

After one more sip of his elixir, Ash told his best friend everything that had happened with Kenna.

"She really killed Varis?" Wren asked.

"That's what you took from all of that?"

"She's powerful, Ash. More than I realized."

"I know."

"What if… what if we could get her out?"

"How? The curse won't allow her to leave the castle," Ash said.

"You told me once that the marriage vows are one of the strongest forms of binding Ancient magic. Are you sure the curse would stop her from marrying Hawthorne if we could get him here?"

"I'm almost positive the curse will prevent it. Even if they could be married, he'd be executed if he was discovered in Notos. Hawthorne sneaking into the castle would be suicide. There's no way he'd agree to it."

"Do you actually believe that?" Wren challenged. "Or is there a part of you that hopes he'll refuse?"

"I… Damn it Wren. I love her."

"I know, old man." Wren placed a hand on Ash's shoulder and fixed him with his amber stare. "But if you truly love her, you know we have to try. And I think this is the best chance of getting Kenna away from Samael and Luniva. It's the best chance of saving her life."

"You're right."

If Ash was being honest with himself, he knew Wren was right. The idea had occurred to Ash a while ago, but he had been too selfish to consider it. But Ash truly loved Kenna, and he knew this was the most likely way to save her.

Despite the lingering pain from his memories and the ache he felt from hurting Kenna, a whisper of a smile spread over Ash's face. If he knew anything about the woman he loved, she would want to fight for her freedom.

And as long as Kenna was willing to fight, there was hope.

spent the night puzzling out the details. They'd worked out potential pitfalls, and a backup plan.

It was dawn the following morning when Ash terialized to the outskirts of Braktyn. Like his healing magic, jumping from place to place was one of his weakest powers, so he used it sparingly. But today he urgently needed to speak to Pax.

He wore civilian clothes and walked swiftly towards the Red Lantern to find his brother.

When he reached the city square, he changed his entire demeanor. He staggered through the square like someone who'd spent the whole night drinking. The last thing he wanted was for the priestess to learn that he'd visited his brother.

She'd demand to know why. He'd managed to keep his mind shielded from her all these months, but he'd not given her reason to examine his thoughts too closely. As far as Lailah was concerned, Kenna was just like all the women before her. Lailah needed to believe that was the case in order for their plan to work.

He stumbled to the door of the Red Lantern, and pushed it open. The bell tinkled overhead announcing his arrival, but there were no patrons in the Red Lantern this early Ash dropped his false persona. Pixies flitted around using their magic to clean the floor, light fires, and polish tables.

Pax was whistling as he entered the tavern from the kitchen.

"Ash? What are ye doin' here?"

"I need your help. Can you get a message to Hawthorne?"

"Aye. What do ye need me te tell him?"

"I need you to ask him if he's willing to risk death to save Kenna."

Pax's eyebrows lifted, and Ash explained everything he and Wren had discussed.

"So ye want me and Thorne to sneak in the night before Winter Solstice. And ye want me to perform the marriage rite for Kenna and Thorne. If he isn't executed first. But Kenna hasn't actually agreed to the plan yet, and ye're not even sure he will be able to marry her. But no one can tell me why."

"You and Lailah are the only ones in all of Notos who know the words of the sacred wedding vows. And I can't exactly ask her to perform the ceremony." Ash rolled up his shirt sleeves. "But Hawthorne knows why the marriage vows might not work. Will you speak with him?"

"Aye. Meet me back here in three days."

"Make it four. I won't be able to terialize to Braktyn again before then."

"Right. I'll see ye in four days."

Ash nodded to Pax, and clasped his forearm.

"I missed you, brother," Ash said.

"And I missed ye, too. We'll get her out. I've nae doubts."

Ash blew out a breath. "I certainly hope so."

It TURNED OUT, Ash didn't need to visit Braktyn again. Two days after he'd visited Pax, the king received a cryptic message.

The note didn't need a signature for Ash to know who it was from or what it was about. It simply read:

HE SAYS *he'll do it.*

CHAPTER 55

Kenna woke up before dawn, her whole body still in agony from the events in the dungeon and everything Ash had revealed afterward.

Three days had passed, and Ash had given her time off from training while her body and mind recovered from the trauma. But with the knowledge of Ash's curse, she'd hardly been able to speak. She'd seen everything that had happened. She'd felt his physical anguish as he tried to fight the magic. Her eyes welled with tears any time she dwelled upon the memories.

Either Ash or Wren stood watch outside her door all day while Kenna alternated between numbing herself in the pages of books, crying as she sorted through everything she'd learned, and raging against the injustice of it all.

With a few days of isolation, she'd finally sorted through her feelings and come to a conclusion: she needed to talk to Ash.

They hadn't spoken a word to each other for the last three days, and she'd only seen him each night as he wordlessly laid on the tiled floor beside her bed. Even now, she heard the king's steady breathing. He'd slept there without complaint every night since the dungeon incident.

Other than at night, Ash left her alone in her room. He sent meals up to her, and each one held some sort of sweet treat. A cinnamon bun with breakfast. Chocolate-covered strawberries after lunch. Warm chocolate cake and cream with dinner.

He was a wise man for knowing he could soothe her frayed nerves with such tactics.

She'd suggested that Wren bring in a couch for Ash to sleep on, but the captain said Ash didn't want one. When she looked at Ash lying on the floor each night, Kenna understood why. He was punishing himself.

Ash shifted on the floor next to her, and her thoughts drifted back to the night, four nights ago, when she'd woken up in his arms. He'd given her the release her body had been so desperate for. Part of her wished she were waking up in his arms this morning.

Kenna was still trying to understand his curse and everything that had passed between them, but she was still drawn to him. He'd tricked her into their oath, but something had changed in him these last months. He'd suffered enough.

Tears stung Kenna's eyes at the still-raw memory he'd shared with her. She'd felt everything he felt. Seen the look on his mate's face as she died. Felt Ash's soul cleave into two the moment she was gone. Even now, she heard the words his mate had whispered into his mind: *It's not your fault.*

It was clear that Ash still didn't believe his mate, and over three hundred years later, he still blamed himself for her death. He still believed he was a monster.

He may have made a mistake agreeing to Lailah's plan, but if Samael had been the one in Ash's place, it would have been so much worse.

She'd forgiven him within hours of learning the truth, though she hadn't told him yet. Instead, she'd been stuck in her own head, sorting through everything she'd learned and trying to find the words to express her feelings. Now it was time to talk to him.

As Kenna sat up in bed to rest her back against the pillows, she let out a small whimper of pain. Ash propped himself up on one elbow, staring at her with an unreadable expression. He rubbed the back of his neck, probably sore from another night on the hard floor.

"What?" she asked.

"That noise. It…" Ash cleared his throat. "It reminded me of something."

Kenna flushed. She knew *exactly* what that noise reminded him of, and she vividly recalled his wicked grin as he'd lowered his head between her legs.

"I'd hoped to resume training today, but I don't know if I can walk.

Let alone train. My legs are killing me. Maybe we should just put me out of my misery. Can your curse kill me now or do we have to wait until the Winter Solstice?" Apparently, her instinct was to diffuse the situation with inappropriate jokes.

"Please." His voice cracked. "Please, don't joke about that."

"Sorry." She took a deep breath. It was time to let him back in. She couldn't look him in the eye, but she said, "I forgive you, Ash."

His voice was small, quiet. He sounded so broken and nothing at all like an immortal king when he said, "Perhaps. But I'll never forgive myself."

She patted the bed next to her. "Come here."

He sat on the bed where she'd invited him, stretching his legs out.

"Do you know why I came here with you? Why I accepted your help and made the oath with you in the first place?"

"My charming personality and handsome face. Obviously."

Apparently, they were both going to dance around the truth with jokes this morning. She gave him a stern look, prompting Ash for a more serious answer.

"You made the oath with me to fulfill your dues to the ferry master. You had to accept my help."

"I thought so, too. But I don't think that was the only reason. I made the oath with you because you were the first man who wanted me to be strong. When I was weak and broken, you didn't tell me you would protect me. You told me you'd help me learn to protect myself."

"Kenna, I was telling you what you wanted to hear. I only—"

"Let me finish. That was why I made the oath with you. But do you want to know when my feelings for you started to change?"

She took his hand in hers, holding it on her lap. They studied their entwined fingers and the scar on Kenna's wrist.

"The morning after I'd trained with Samael, he came into the dining room during breakfast. He'd completely humiliated and overwhelmed me on my first day of training. Do you remember what you said?"

Ash gave her a tight nod, but she needed to remind him to help him understand.

"You said it was up to me how I reacted. Samael is a monster, but you reminded me that I get to decide if the monster wins. That was when I knew you were truly my friend.

When you told me about the treaty, I felt trapped by a destiny that had been decided for me before I'd even had a voice. I felt doomed. I felt like I'd failed my life's purpose. If I was lucky, then I might be able to set the humans free if I married some stranger from another realm. Someone I'd never even met."

Ash shifted, as though the thought made him uncomfortable.

Usually, Kenna found it difficult to make eye contact during a meaningful conversation like this, but she was determined for Ash to see the truth in her eyes. She turned toward him, kneeling as she took his face in her hands and met his gaze.

"You helped me see I had a decision. I could choose whether the helplessness of my situation crushed me or gave me a reason to fight. You helped me realize that I *always* have a choice. I never have to simply accept things as they are. I can choose how to move forward. And that's when I knew our friendship might turn into something more. All these months, you have never let me believe I'm helpless. And I won't let you believe you're helpless either. We're going to figure this out. Together."

Kenna poured every ounce of warmth she could summon into their oath. "I know you tricked me, Ash, but I need you to know I forgive you. It's not your fault."

Her words seemed to release him. Ash sat up and wrapped his arms around her waist, and she allowed him to hold her as her tears soaked his shoulder. Ash cried freely, too. Kenna only hoped his tears helped wash away the guilt and shame which had covered him for so long.

When he finally pulled away, Ash said. "There's something else we need to talk about." Kenna blanched, so Ash plowed on. "It's nothing bad. I went to Braktyn to see Pax the day after I told you about the curse. I proposed a plan to Pax, and I was meant to visit him tomorrow, but he sent word last night. We think there might be a way to get you out of here on Winter Solstice."

"How?"

"You marry Hawthorne, just like the treaty stipulates."

"I thought the treaty stipulated that the wedding had to take place on Winter Solstice. I'll be dead before then if I'm forced into the ritual."

"Technically, Winter Solstice lasts for two days. From the stroke of midnight on Winter Solstice Eve until dawn the day after Winter Solstice. During that time, Luniva is at her most powerful. Winter Solstice Eve is when the feast occurs. The ritual takes place at midnight between Winter Solstice Eve and Solstice Day. The games begin the following day. You could marry Hawthorne on Winter Solstice before the ritual takes place."

"Would he risk execution? He's never even met me."

"He may not have met you, but he's an honorable man and a good brother. He would do his duty to rescue you and save the humans."

Ash explained the details of how and when they'd perform the wedding ceremony and sneak Kenna out of the castle.

"You said you thought our unbreakable oath—your curse—would prevent me from marrying another."

"It still might. But the marriage vows are ancient magic, which may be strong enough to undermine the curse."

"And if the curse prevents me from marrying Hawthorne?" Kenna asked.

"We have a backup plan."

"Oh? And what might that be?

"You marry me instead."

Kenna arched a brow at him and tried to ignore the way her heart fluttered. She might be able to marry Ash?

"How, exactly, would being your wife save me from your curse? The mating bond didn't save Elenya."

"I wondered why our bond didn't save her for years. But I didn't find the answers until after her death. Mating bonds are only at their most powerful when the mated couple is also bound by marriage. Marriage is actually a stronger force than the bond. People *choose* to enter into marriage with Ancient magic, whereas the Ancients create perfect mates for people. When mates find each other and choose to be married as well… there's no love bond than that."

"So if you'd married Elenya, the curse wouldn't have been able to make you hurt her. Do you think she would have lived?" Kenna asked, her eyes welling with tears.

Ash's answering smile didn't reach his eyes. "I'm almost certain of it."

They sat in the quiet for a few minutes. Ash seemed to need some time to compose himself before he explained further.

"If you become my wife, my queen, I believe our marriage would prevent Lailah from using either of us for the ritual this year and give us more time to find a way to break the curse. It would also stop Samael from being able to force you into marriage. I think it might put the treaty on hold for a year. Though, if I'm wrong about the delay in the treaty, it could mean the human race is still doomed."

Kenna thought for a moment, and Ash didn't press for answers. But she couldn't see an alternative.

"One way or another, it sounds like I'm getting married on Winter Solstice."

"So, you'd marry Hawthorne?"

"Isn't that what I'm supposed to do?" Kenna tried to keep the bitterness out of her voice. "I guess it's time we start planning a royal wedding."

CHAPTER 56

$\mathcal{A}$ week had passed, and Ash still couldn't believe Kenna had forgiven him. With the hope of Wren's plan and the knowledge that he might save Kenna, he'd started to forgive himself, too.

They were in the training ring, and Kenna had wrapped herself in a cyclone. Through the swirling wind, he saw tendrils of hair coming loose from her braid and floating around her face. She looked like a goddess.

Ash sent a blast of air at the cyclone, and she stumbled back but held her ground. Her face was set with stubborn concentration and she didn't expect him to rain fire down from above. But her reactions were quicker than they'd been when she'd started training.

Months ago, he would have stopped the Flame before it could hurt her, but he didn't need to today. She covered herself in a dome of water. The fire hissed on contact but didn't scathe her. He smiled.

"Good girl," he said. "Now, imagine you're on a battlefield and your enemies are here." Ash summoned multiple columns of water about the size of angel warriors to surround her. "Where do you go?"

"If I'm surrounded like this on a battlefield, I'm dead."

"You need to think creatively, Kenna. You have Aqua, Terrane, Flame, *and* Wind magic at your disposal."

"I suppose if there is dirt beneath my feet, I could launch myself up and over them," she said.

"Excellent. But say the battle takes place on a ship at sea. There's no dirt, no fresh water. You can't wield water from the sea, and there are no fires to draw Flame magic from. What then?"

"Swirling wind around me like I did a minute ago would protect me, but I'm not powerful enough to use it to force my way through all of them." She gestured to her imaginary, watery foes.

"Yes, but you can climb out."

Kenna huffed. "With what? I don't see any stairs or ropes lying around. And unlike you, I can't just snap my fingers to summon something when I want it."

"You don't *see* any ladders, but does that mean there aren't any available to you?"

Slowly, Ash used several currents of air to form and climb an invisible set of stairs. He dropped in front of Kenna, now in the center of the dummy warriors.

"You try."

"There's no space for stairs here." Kenna groaned.

"In the middle of a battle, you must use your wits. Now find a way out, or I'm going to attack. Five, four, three—"

Kenna stole the water from one of the fake opponents and shielded herself as she tried to form an invisible ladder with the wind.

Ash broke through her shield and soaked her with water.

"I almost had it!"

"You're trying too hard. You always try too hard when we work with wind magic. *Feel* it. Listen to it, and allow it to guide you. That's how you'll truly connect with your wind magic. I don't know if you know this, but the voice on the wind and the power to bend the air are gifts from Soldivus."

"No. I didn't know that. But, let me try again."

Once again, the Aqua warriors surrounded her. This time, when she shielded herself, she closed her eyes. Just for a moment, as though she was listening. Allowing the voice of the wind to her guided her hands and her magic, helping her form the ladder.

She climbed up invisible rungs. Then she ran over the top of the water warriors on a platform of air and jumped down the other side, landing in a crouch.

Her chest was rising and falling rapidly, but Ash smirked and sent the water warriors after her. She lashed out at them with fire, pressing down and around them from all sides until they turned to mist.

"Very good," Ash said. "Now do it again."

They ran the maneuver twelve times before Kenna came close to using up her Vessel's capacity for magic. She was sweaty and pale; she swayed on her feet. Ash hurried to her side, easing her down to the ground.

Learning the truth about his curse had unleashed some part of Kenna's magic she hadn't accessed before. She seemed to channel all her emotions into her power, and it was breathtaking.

She was sleeping, and Ash wasn't surprised after witnessing the amount of magic and physical energy she'd used. He'd let her rest for a few minutes before he woke her.

He still hadn't told her he loved her, and he wouldn't. Not unless the plan with Hawthorne failed, and he married her.

If she became his wife, his queen… Ash scrubbed a hand down his face. He shouldn't let himself hope for that.

Obviously, there was something between them. She'd said as much the morning she'd forgiven him. But could she love him after only three months? Especially knowing all the ways he'd betrayed her. Tricked her.

He almost laughed. After over three hundred years of shunning all thoughts of love, this human woman had claimed his heart in a matter of months.

At first it was the hope of redeeming himself, but even when that felt impossible, he couldn't deny the draw he felt to her. It wasn't a mating bond, but there was something special about her that went beyond their physical chemistry.

After a few minutes, Kenna twitched violently and awoke. She took a deep breath and sat up.

"I was in Dendron," she told him. "In my dream, my brother and friends were there. We were fighting the angels. We were winning before I fell off a Geolift."

Ash snapped his fingers and summoned honeyed tea, along with some bread and cheese. She drank a full water skin and an entire pot of tea. She also ate almost the whole loaf of freshly baked bread. Good. The food would replenish the magical energy in her Vessel.

"Feel better?" he asked.

She nodded. "Much. Though my head still feels like it's full of wet sand."

Laughing, she laid down on the stone floor. "I can't believe I did that."

"I can," Ash said, meeting her eyes.

Before the truth could tumble out of him, he helped her to her feet and walked her to her room.

319

CHAPTER 57

*M*orning sunlight streamed into her bedroom, and Kenna shifted in her bed. She needed the bathing chamber, but her legs were in agony; she could barely move under the covers. She dragged herself out of bed to see to her needs and brush her teeth, and hoped that Ash would let her sleep in.

They had a plan. She would marry prince Hawthorne if the unbreakable oath didn't stop it. But was it wrong of her to hope her Ash's curse prevented her from marrying the prince? Was it wrong to hope she would marry Ash instead?

When she returned from the bathing chamber, Ash was seated on the floor. She didn't understand how, but when his hair was messy in the morning, he was even more handsome. It wasn't fair.

Ash chuckled as she hobbled back to bed and gingerly climbed in.

"It's not funny," Kenna scolded. "I think you broke me in yesterday's session."

"It will take more than that to break you, love."

"Possibly, but right now, I feel broken."

Ash stood up. "I may be able to help."

First, he summoned a special tea to help ease her pain. Then he disappeared into the bathing chamber. He kept a toothbrush and things in Kenna's room now, and she figured she should probably allow him to sleep on the bed at some point. The thought of waking up next to him grew more appealing with each day that passed.

Ash returned with a towel and an assortment of oils. "Dreamsbane free," he confirmed. He sat at the end of her bed and gestured to her legs. "May I?"

She nodded and Ash peeled back the covers, revealing her bare legs.

He sucked in a deep breath and kept his gaze fixed on her ankles as he poured the oil along the top of her shins.

"Peppermint?" she asked.

"Yes. And lavender."

"I love the smell of lavender." Kenna leaned back against the headboard and breathed deeply of the familiar aroma.

"I'm quite partial as well," Ash said.

She felt his weight shift on the bed, and he nudged her feet apart to accommodate his kneeling form between her ankles.

Kenna opened her eyes and arched an eyebrow at him as if to say, *'What exactly are you planning on doing in that position?'* The last time he'd been between her legs like that, he'd...

She took a deep, controlled breath.

"Relax. I only intend to ease the tension in your legs."

Ash's smile was tight and Kenna found herself ignoring a twinge of disappointment as she closed her eyes once more. Ash lifted her ankle and bent her left knee, massaging the length of her calf with long, probing strokes, gentle along the tender muscle. Her muscles warmed under his touch and the pain in her legs eased tremendously, probably thanks to the tea.

As he increased the pressure of his fingers, Kenna couldn't help the groan that escaped. Ash's hands stilled and his body went rigid. She slapped a hand over her mouth and giggled, knowing exactly how her groan sounded.

"Sorry," she said, with her eyes still closed. Ash began moving his expert hands again. "Never apologize for making that sound."

She resisted the urge to clamp her legs shut and push him off the bed. It was either that or pull his lips to hers and give her body exactly what it wanted. Instead, she focused on breathing in the familiar, relaxing scent of lavender.

In. Out.

He worked on knots Kenna didn't know she had before moving to her right leg, repeating the process. She thought she might fall asleep, but then Ash's weight shifted again. His hands slowly worked their way up the front of her thighs, warming the muscles there.

When he started kneading her thighs, the sensation teetered between pain and relief. Ash's hands pressed and swirled away the soreness, and she exhaled in the form of another moan.

He flinched, removing his hands and moving away as though she'd burned him. His voice was rough. "That sound."

"I'll be quiet. Don't stop."

Ash scrubbed his oily hand down his face, leaving it shining in the morning sun. "If I don't stop now, you'll beg me not to stop at all. And if we give into what our bodies want... You're betrothed to my *brother*. I can't do this again."

"Can't do what?"

"I can't lose the woman I love!" He closed his eyes, panting. "I'm sorry. I shouldn't have said that."

She sat up. "You love me?"

"Every day I love you more, but you aren't mine. I will lose you to your duty if you marry Hawthorne and save your people. Even if you become my wife, we can't be sure you will survive the curse. But I can't imagine my life without you."

Their oath warmed the scar, confirming Ash's words.

"I need some air." Ash pushed open the balcony doors and paced over the stone flags.

Kenna hadn't allowed herself to dwell on her own feelings for Ash very often. Their friendship had blossomed, and their physical chemistry was... She wanted him. Holy Void, she *really* wanted him.

He'd helped her grow strong and asked for her input and opinion. He hadn't tried to coddle her or shield her from the harsh reality of the world. Though he'd tricked her, Ash was trying to redeem himself, and she believed with all her heart he deserved redemption.

The Winter Solstice was still three months away, and Ash loved her.

She was betrothed to Hawthorne, but it was nothing more than an alliance. Her heart held no loyalty to him.

But if she and Ash gave into their feelings...

The pain he'd felt when he lost his mate roared through her mind. She loathed the idea of hurting him that way. But at this moment, Kenna knew with sudden clarity how much she loved him, too. And damn the consequences.

She sat up, and called, "Ash!"

He turned and walked back into her room. She sensed his hesitation in his too-slow movements. In his tortured blue eyes.

He sat down on the end of her bed, shoulders slumped as if they bore the weight of his forbidden love for her.

"The end of our story may come too soon, and your curse may still claim my life. But whatever my fate may be, I will gladly face it with you by my side."

He turned to face her, and she didn't take her eyes off of his as she took his hand in hers and placed it on her thigh.

"Don't. Stop."

Wordlessly, Ash knelt between her legs again and continued working her knotted muscles. As his hands worked higher up her leg, she felt anticipation coiling tighter and tighter. She closed her eyes and leaned back against the pillows, arching her back and moving her hips toward his fingers. Just when she thought he would set her free from her torment, he moved his hands to her other leg, beginning the same process near the top of her knee.

As his fingers teased the tightness from her muscles, an entirely different sort of tension grew. She squirmed and whimpered, desperate for his hands to be higher. When he pressed his thumb into a knot, she moaned.

Immediately, Ash's mouth was on hers. The weight of his hips and the hardness straining against his breeches pressed into the very spot where she wanted him, needed him—a need greater than her next breath.

He drew back, looking into her eyes, giving her one more chance to change her mind. In answer, she lifted his shirt over his head. The reality of seeing him shirtless above her was so much more satisfying than she'd imagined. It revealed every dip and curve of his muscled chest, but he also opened his wings.

His wings sheltered their bodies beneath a blanket of feathers the color of the midnight sky fading to white. Along the silver tips, the feathers shimmered like ripples of starlight. Kenna ran a finger along the silky underside of his plumage, and he shivered in response.

"That's—" He groaned and kissed her again.

Kenna's silk nightgown was like sandpaper between them. She needed to feel his skin on hers. She pushed his chest away, and he seemed to sense her unspoken request. He tucked a strand of hair behind her ear, tracing a line down her neck and across her collarbone. It was her turn to shiver as he lowered the strap of her shift on one side and then the other.

His pupils dilated as he took in her bare torso, and he left a trail of gentle kisses on her exposed flesh. With a sly smile, he flicked his tongue over her nipple, taking it into his mouth and nipping gently.

Kenna dragged his jaw back up to her lips, staking her claim on him with her mouth and wrapping her legs around him.

The feel of him against her was everything she wanted, but still not enough. She fumbled with the buttons and laces on his trousers. She trembled—not in fear, but in hunger and need for him. He shrugged off his trousers, revealing his proud manhood, and Kenna adjusted the lower half of her shift. There were no more barriers between them.

Ash slid his hand between them, finding her wet and wanting. He curled two fingers inside her and stroked her sensitive bud of flesh with his thumb. Within minutes, she moaned his name as his deft movements brought her over the edge. Panting in the aftermath of her climax, she still needed more.

"Please," she begged.

He placed the tip of his hard length at the wet apex between her legs, sliding it down and positioning himself at her entrance. With self-control gained from centuries of experience, he waited. He offered her a perfect, lopsided smirk as he said, "Since the moment I brought you into this castle, I've wanted you. But I need to know you're sure. Everything I've done..." His smile wavered.

Kenna touched his face with one hand. "Yes. I want this. I want you."

He slid inside her, just an inch. "Then my heart is yours to command. Forever. You are my fucking queen."

In answer to his words, she gripped his ass, pulling him into her. He filled her perfectly, over and over, giving her everything she hadn't known she wanted. His movements were skilled and nuanced, ebbing and flowing like a river. He slid his hand between them, bringing her to the edge again, taking his time until everything inside of both of them gathered into a lake as still as glass and shattered into icy prisms of light.

Ash groaned as he finished inside her, and she rode the waves of pleasure like nothing she'd ever felt. Both of them were breathless as he collapsed on top of her.

"I love you," he whispered, kissing away the single tear that slipped down her cheek.

Kenna clung to him with all her might. "I love you, too."

325

CHAPTER 58

*A*sh soared through the freezing night, and Pax and Hawthorne followed him. The air was thin here in the clouds above the mountains, but they needed to fly above the castle wards. Thank Soldivus, it was cloudy and snowing. Otherwise, the moon would illuminate Ash's location.

His brothers were invisible, cloaked with Pax's magic. Pax couldn't read minds like Ash and Hawthorne, but guardian angels had the gift of being able to make themselves invisible to onlookers. Sharing his ability with Hawthorne required a tremendous amount of effort from Pax, so they needed to move quickly. The guardian angel would need his magic later.

It was half an hour until midnight on Winter Solstice Eve, when the solstice officially began. For Ash, the months three months since Autumn Equinox had passed like a dream. Kenna had given her utmost effort to training every day. They'd continued the flirtatious games, and her sharp wit and sarcasm had only made Ash love her more. And almost every night, they'd made love.

Every morning he'd woken up next to her, and Ash had been happy. Content. After centuries of shame and heartache, he had hope of redemption. They'd rarely spoken about the reality that their happiness couldn't last.

Tonight, Ash's heart would break.

Unless the curse prevented it, Kenna would wed Hawthorne at midnight and fly away from Notos.

As long as Ash snuck Pax and Thorne into the castle and the prince married Kenna before dawn, Lailah could not interfere. The three brothers flew toward a cylindrical structure hidden among the other towers on top of Brumalis Castle. The conical turret looked like all the other towers, but the roof was an illusion of mist. It served as an access point for Samael or his dungeon assistants to reach the icy cavern below the castle without having to use the thousands of stairs.

The shaft into the dungeon was a closely guarded secret and the only part of the castle which wasn't warded against angels. No one would want to fly into that cesspit unless they were delivering prisoners. The snowy cells were full of elves and winged fae who'd been imprisoned there over the years. Even if elves or winged fae managed to escape their cells, the wards would not allow their kind to pass through the shaft.

As for any angels in the dungeon, there was no way they could escape. Samael and Lailah had thoroughly broken their bodies and minds, leaving them in the icy dungeon, lost to their own torment and madness.

Rage and grief rippled through Ash as he thought of his three brothers in that dungeon. The brother's Lailah had tortured to coerce him into complying with the curse all those years ago. He thought of what he would do if Lailah or Samael tried to torture Wren. Protecting his fae friend had been the one remaining thing that kept him from resisting the curse during the last twenty years.

Because Wren was a fae, nothing in the treaty prevented Lailah or Samael from killing him. But Wren knew the risks of helping free Kenna tonight. If Ash hadn't loved Kenna so deeply and hoped to make amends for his part in harming the human race, he wouldn't have risked bringing Lailah and Samael's wrath on Wren.

Unable to pass through the dungeon wards, the captain had stayed behind tonight to guard Kenna.

Having reached their destination, Ash sent the words into his brother's minds.

Follow me.

He tilted forward, tucked his wings into his sides, and dove through the false roof and into the vertical stone tunnel.

When they reached the snowy cavern below, Ash slowed himself to land and then sprinted around and around up the spiral steps and out of the dungeons. Pax and Hawthorne were still shielded from view.

"Hurry it up, lad," Pax whispered. "I can't keep this goin' much longer if ye want me te be able to perform the ceremony."

Ash opened the dungeon's door with a wave of his hand, and the three of them wound their way through the castle to Kenna's chambers.

It's us. Ash sent his thought through the door to Wren, and the Captain of the Guard opened the door just long enough for them to enter.

"Where is she?" Ash asked, panicking slightly when he didn't see Kenna.

"Calm down, old man." Wren jerked his thumb to the door of the bathing chamber. "She's getting ready."

~

KENNA STOOD in her bathing chamber, staring at her reflection. Talking herself into what she needed to do next.

You can do this. You can marry a stranger to save the humans. To escape from here. It's for the good of the Three Realms. It's the right thing to do. It's your best chance to survive.

Reassuring herself she was doing the right thing didn't stop her tears from falling. Her heart from breaking. Not when she knew she was walking away from the man she loved tonight.

She'd known this day would come. Stupidly, she'd thought she deserved those months of happiness with Ash. But why had she let herself fall so deeply in love with him? How was she supposed to marry the Prince of Vorra when her heart belonged wholly to the King of Notos?

She wiped away her tears and splashed water on her face. She'd not worn anything special to mark the occasion. This was no wedding to celebrate.

Someone knocked on the door.

"Kenna? Can I come in?" Ash asked.

She opened the door for him and he entered the bathing room. He closed the door and leaned against it, neither of them speaking as they felt the weight of the moment. They'd already said their goodbyes before Ash flew off to meet Pax and Hawthorne. Silently, Ash stepped towards her and hugged her to his chest. With a shuddering inhale, Kenna breathed in his scent. As she exhaled, her tears began falling again.

After everything they'd been through, was this really goodbye?

Pulling away from him, she tilted her face up to look into his eyes, which were filled with as much anguish as her own. With a gentle swipe of his thumb, he brushed away her tears.

"I love you, Kenella Duras."

"I love you too, Ashton Moonbriar. I just with love was enough." Before Kenna could change her mind, she released him. "Let's get this over with."

When she entered her bedchamber, Pax was there. But Wren and the Prince of Vorra were nowhere to be seen. Pax hugged Kenna, and she clung to her guardian angel. To the first person in this realm who'd made her feel safe.

"I've missed ye."

"You too, Pax." Kenna stepped away from him. "Where is he?"

"I asked him te step outside with Wren fer a minute so I could te talk te ye first."

She sighed. "What is there to say?"

"Are ye sure ye want te do this?"

"Do I have a choice?"

"No one is going te force ye." Compassion lined Pax's features.

"I just want it to be done."

"Well, if yer sure."

Pax crossed to the door and let Wren into the room. Moments after the door closed, the Prince of Vorra materialized in front of them. As Pax released the cloaking magic, Kenna assessed her future husband.

The prince's long brown hair was streaked with gold and tied back from his face. He looked like he was born in a field beneath the summer sunshine and had absorbed its warmth into his bronzed skin. But none of that warmth was evident in his demeanor.

His heavily muscled shoulders were still, and there was no hint of a smile behind his full beard. His moss green eyes found hers, and there was no laughter in his gaze. He looked as serious and miserable as Kenna felt. For the first time, Kenna wondered what the prince thought about their marriage.

Perhaps she wasn't the only one who was here out of duty and desperation.

"It is an honor to meet you, Princess." Hawthorne's voice was as deep as rolling thunder as he acknowledged her with a slight incline of his head. Kenna said nothing.

"Join hands, if ye will," said Pax.

Kenna steeled herself and stepped away from the man she loved toward the prince.

She reached towards him and his warm, calloused hands wrapped around hers. His hands were large and undoubtedly strong, but held hers so gently, as if he might break her. He inhaled through his nose and wrath flashed in his eyes.

Hawthorne's voice was lethal as he asked Ash, "When were you going to tell me, brother, that you'd taken my betrothed to your bed?"

Pax raised his eyebrows. "Ash, is that true?"

"Don't look at Ash. Look at me," Kenna interjected. She fixed both Pax and her future husband with a scathing stare. "No one *took* me anywhere. I love Ash and I was a *very* willing participant." Kenna gave the prince a wicked smile and dared a glance at Ash. His smirk was full of male pride and satisfaction.

Kenna continued, "I value my freedom to make my own choices more than anything. Does Soldivus not value free will as well?"

"My father values free will, yes. But intimacy is a sacred privilege. Bringing a woman to bed when she is betrothed to another?" Hawthorne's heated stare returned to Ash. "It is one of the greatest insults. A betrayal of trust and honor."

Kenna bristled at the way the prince addressed Ash instead of speaking directly to her. She hurled the words at him like daggers. "Forgive me, prince, for following my heart while I still had the choice. A loveless, forced marriage is no way to preserve the free will of humanity. Or will you refuse to help me now that you consider me soiled goods?"

Hawthorne gritted his teeth. "Unlike my brother, I am an honorable man, and I will keep my word."

Pax, Wren, and Ash had silently witnessed the volley of words, and an awkward quiet descended.

Wren was the one who broke the tension. "So congratulations to the happy couple."

Kenna whipped her head towards Wren with a look that said *Shut the Hel up.* And the fae captain held up his hands in silent surrender.

Pax cleared his throat, looking between Hawthorne and Kenna. "I feel like I should ask ye again. Are ye both sure about this?"

"Fine," said Hawthorne.

"Fine," Kenna echoed.

"Aye. Alright, then. We'll begin with the sacred, ancient vows, and then ye can both add something personal if ye want te, but... I'm guessing ye'll not bother with that. If I can get all the way through the vows, we'll know that yer unbreakable oath with Ash couldn't prevent the marriage."

Kenna nodded even as her stomach clenched. She glanced over her shoulder at Ash, at everything she was about to give up if this worked. Anger over Hawthorne's accusations lingered in the king's deep blue eyes, and she could practically feel the tension radiating from him.

Pax began speaking in the Ancient language. Before tonight, Kenna had wondered how no one knew the ancient vows if people had witnessed marriage ceremonies. But every word Pax spoke seemed to evaporate from Kenna's memory as soon as she heard it.

Until Pax said, "Omcumque erlinquite."

At those words, the scar on her wrist scalded her. All-consuming pain like nothing she'd ever felt lanced through the star sigil of her unbreakable oath. Moment by moment, the pain spread, snaking through her veins, up her arm, and into her shoulder. The searing pain was moving toward her heart. Her world was engulfed until she was sure the pain would kill her. Burn her from the inside out. Her eyes rolled back in her head as tremors shook her body. She couldn't move. Couldn't yank her hand away from Hawthorne.

She barely registered the sound of Ash's frantic shouts. "Make it stop. Now! You're killing her!"

The moment Hawthorne released her hand, the pain vanished as though it had never been there at all. Other than her panting breaths and racing heart, she felt perfectly normal. Healthy and whole.

She looked at the scar on her wrist and whispered to herself, "It didn't work."

Then a grin spread over her face. Not sparing a thought for the prince, she turned her back on him to face the king she loved. Ash's face was pale, and his eyes were panicked as he rushed to her, scanning her for injury.

"I'm fine." A laugh tumbled out of her. "It didn't work. I can't marry Hawthorne."

She launched herself into Ash, throwing her arms around his neck. He wrapped his arms around her waist and lifted her off the floor, spinning her around. When he set her feet back on the ground and kissed her gently, there were tears in both of their eyes.

After a moment, Kenna turned to Pax and asked, "What were those last words? What did they mean?"

"Omcumque erlinquite. In the ancient language, it means 'to forsake all others.'"

Ash took her hand and rubbed his thumb across the scar on her wrist. "It looks like you're stuck with me, love."

Kenna stood on her tiptoes, brushing a kiss to Ash's lips. Then, she gave the Hawthorne a sickly sweet smile. "I guess you won't have to debase yourself with me after all."

Wordlessly, Hawthorne clenched and unclenched his fists at his sides as he stalked out onto the balcony and braced his hands on the railing. Pax followed him.

CHAPTER 59

There was a glint in Kenna's eye. "Aren't you going to get down on one knee and ask me properly?"

"I'll get on my knees before you anytime you'd like," he said, kneeling. Damn, he loved the way her cheeks flushed.

"Oi! I'm still here, you know," Wren reminded them.

"Kenella Duras, will you marry me?"

Knowing she loved him didn't stop the nerves tumbling around in his gut as he waited for her answer. She was making him sweat and she damn well knew it. He supposed it was a fair repayment for the way he'd just made her blush.

A devious grin dimpled her cheeks. "Do I get a pretty crown?"

"Anything for you, my queen."

"Mmm. I like the sound of that. Of course, I'll marry you," she said, pulling Ash to his feet and kissing him again.

He smiled against her lips, "Should I be offended that I am your second choice of husband?"

"You are my only choice. There is only you."

There were tears sparkling in her deep brown eyes. And his own cheeks were wet with tears of relief. Tears of joy.

Then she shooed Ash and Wren from the room. "Get out. I need to get ready. It's bad luck for you to see me before the ceremony."

HE ONLY HOPED their marriage would prevent Samael from taking Kenna by force. The thought of losing her wasn't the only thing that made it hard to breathe.

Ash's bride. The thought made him smile, even though he wasn't sure if the rest of the plan would be successful. At least until midnight tomorrow, Kenna would be his wife.

Ash's hands were shaking. He was about to pledge his love and his life to Kenna. She was going to be his queen, and Holy Void, he wanted her to be his queen.

He paced the tiled floor of her room. Was she having second thoughts? Perhaps she felt trapped. Like she had no choice but to marry him.

At least Kenna was no longer being forced to marry a stranger. This way, Ash and Kenna may have a bit more time together while they tried to find out how to break his curse and free the humans. He just hoped their backup plan would keep Kenna safe even though his curse still bound Kenna to the castle.

As far as Lailah knew, Kenna was the elf who was supposed to fall in love with him and provide the sacrifice for the ritual. Once Lailah realized Kenna was human, the priestess would know Kenna's blood would be useless for the ritual to create the Emergence Serum. But if the ritual didn't go ahead, there would be no reason for Lailah to inject Ash with the cursed serum that overtook his mind and body every Winter Solstice.

Ash knew how Lailah loved a spectacle. He'd long suspected that Lailah and Samael knew about Kenna killing Varis, but Kenna would be Ash's queen. This meant Lailah would be bound by Ancient laws protecting the sovereign rulers of Notos from being executed for their crimes.

If the plan worked, Kenna's humanity would protect her from the ritual, and her title would protect her from execution.

But if they were wrong… Ash couldn't bear to think about it.

"I'm going te check on her," Pax said, but before he could, Kenna opened the door.

There wasn't enough air in Ash's lungs. She was stunning in her long black gown. Her kohl-lined brown eyes sparkled as she beheld him. Two braids twisted away from her shimmering cheeks, but the rest of her rich brown waves tumbled freely over her back and shoulders.

The neckline of her gown formed a heart over her breasts, draping off her shoulders. Long gossamer sleeves cuffed at her wrists, and the fabric looked like it had been crafted from an obsidian sky twinkling with hundreds of stars.

"Ye look lovely," Pax said.

"Thank you." Kenna's answer was breathless, and Ash could hear her heart pounding. Was she nervous, too?

"Are ye sure this is what ye want te do?" Pax asked.

Kenna looked to Ash. "I love Ash. I've never wanted anything more."

"And what about you, Ash?" Pax asked.

"Whether I have one day or one century with her, it would never be enough."

Wren clapped Ash on the back. "Well, let's hope this plan works so that you can have a little longer than a day together."

"Aye," Pax agreed, his tone grave. "Let's hope. Now… shall we get ye married?"

"Yes, please," Ash said. Kenna grinned.

Hawthorne scoffed, and Kenna's smile faltered as she beheld the Prince standing at the threshold of the balcony. He shook his head and folded his arms across his chest. The moon illuminated his sullen features.

Kenna was more thankful than ever that she'd not been able to marry the Prince of Vorra as she turned to Pax and said, "I'm ready."

CHAPTER 60

Kenna rolled off of him and collapsed onto the bed in a sweaty heap. Ash had woken with her hand around him. He'd immediately hardened at her touch, and they'd not yet left her chambers. Ever since the first time they'd made love, they seemed to eat breakfast later and later. This morning, the morning after their wedding, they had a good reason to stay in bed a little longer than usual.

Three reasons if Ash was counting. He was so glad she hadn't been able to marry Hawthorne. Did that make him a terrible person?

This backup plan was more dangerous. But she was his *wife.*

He smiled again.

"I never want to leave this bed, but I'm starving," Kenna said.

"Yes. I feel rather ravenous myself." Ash shimmied his way down her body with a mischievous grin, but she stopped him by giving his hair a playful tug.

"I'm serious." She motioned to her curvaceous figure. "If you enjoy the mountains and valleys of this landscape, then you need to feed me, husband."

"If you insist, *my queen.*" Ash squeezed his wife's plump ass, which he did enjoy very, *very* much. Then he gave her a kiss on the nose and snapped his fingers, summoning breakfast.

After breakfast, dressing seemed to break his pleasure-trance. It was Winter Solstice Eve, and the feast was tonight. He might be forced into his cursed trance at midnight. He looked over at his wife. Would this be the last time he saw her in the afterglow of pleasure, cheeks pink and hair disheveled?

His troubled thoughts were interrupted by a knock on the door.

"My lady?" Ori's voice said. Kenna's eyes grew wide and panicked. Ori had been in the dungeon ever since the day Kenna had killed Varis. It was Samael's way of punishing any servant who displeased him.

Ash held a finger to his lips.

"I… just a moment!" Kenna shouted to the door. Then, to Ash: "Why is she here?"

"After Samael punishes servants, he expects them to return to their duties as normal. Speak to her before she gets suspicious. I'll see you in the sparring ring, my queen. Don't expect me to go easy on you. You have a kingdom to defend now."

Ash brushed a quick kiss to her lips, and she smiled before she moved to the door. Kenna cracked it open slightly, stretching and yawning, doing her best impression of someone who'd just woken up. "Sorry, I seem to have overslept."

"Do not fret, my lady. I apologize for my absence of late. I am afraid I have been indisposed. I hope that it was not too much of an inconvenience."

"No. Not at all. I will dress and be out shortly."

While Kenna spoke to the maid, Ash slipped out the balcony doors and flew off into the light of the rising sun toward his bedchamber. He'd ordered the servants to leave him alone today, as he did every year on the eve of Winter Solstice. Usually, he spent the day sulking in his room with a bottle of notelixir. Today, he landed on the balcony of his own room, where Pax and Hawthorne were waiting.

"Did ye have a good night, lad?" Pax asked.

Dressing in his training gear, he said, "A gentleman never tells."

"And since when are you a gentleman?" Hawthorne muttered.

"Do you have a problem, Thorne? You knew the plan was for me to marry Kenna if the curse prevented her from marrying you. Why are you treating me like the villain here?"

"Perhaps I knew the plan, but I might not have had all the information."

Ash pulled on his boots with more force than necessary. "If you're referring to Kenna and I being in love, then forgive me for not telling you. Forgive me for wanting a shred of happiness after all these years."

"It's not that. It's…" The tendons in Hawthorne's neck went taut. "Nevermind. I'm sorry."

"Are you? Because you don't look sorry. Listen, I know what you risked coming here. But if you're not truly on my side, then you're welcome to leave now."

"I am on your side. I'm on Kenna's side."

"Good. Then don't forget what you promised me last night. I'll see you at the feast."

∼

WHEN HE REACHED the sparring chamber, Lailah was waiting.

"What are you doing here?" he asked.

"Just checking in," she said. "Hoping you haven't lost your nerve. You seem rather fond of the girl."

He scoffed. "My *nerve* has nothing to do with it. Your curse takes care of that."

"Hmm." Lailah tapped a finger to her lips. "You know the ritual requires that she fall in love with you, but there are some strange rumors floating around the castle. Some people insist that *you* might actually love the whore."

Ash bared his teeth. "Call her a whore one more time and see what happens."

Lailah's answering snarl was low and vicious. "She's nothing but a whore. Like all the rest."

Ash lashed out, striking out with every ounce of his magic. With a steely glare, and the tiniest effort, she flicked the air in front of him and he flew across the sparring ring with such force that his back cracked the stone wall on the other side and the air was sucked from his lungs.

The blow would have killed an elf or a human, but he could feel his broken ribs and vertebrae already fusing themselves back together. He stood slowly, leaning against the wall with one hand as he recovered.

Lailah prowled closer, a lioness ready to pounce. For a moment, Ash wondered if she'd somehow found a way to kill him despite the treaty. But she wouldn't. Not while she still believed the ritual would take place tonight.

"If you love her, Ashton, then you are a fool. By the end of the feast tonight, I will have the serum, *and* I will have the humans. I know exactly who Kenna Duras is."

Ash's chest constricted. But with centuries of practice, his voice hid his panic. "I don't know what you're talking about."

"Please. Did you think your little angel glamor could hide the human princess's true identity from *me*?"

"You're mistaken. She's not—"

"You disgrace yourself. You cannot lie to me. I was there when you were created. I know she killed Varis, and the consequences for that are clear." A smile bloomed on Lailah's lips, painted a red so dark it was almost black. "Execution."

She clapped her hands together at her chest, giddy. "It's perfect, really. It's been too long since the Winter Solstice festivities included an execution. But first, she'll marry Samael in the morning.

I would have told the prince sooner, but you know your brother. He would have ravaged and killed her before Winter Solstice. He would have ruined everything. Couldn't have our little princess failing to fulfill the treaty before death takes her to the eternal shores.

But after she's married to Samael, you'll be the one to do the honors of executing her for the brutal murder of our dear Varis. That is, if you'd like it to be quick and painless. Otherwise, I'll let Samael have the joy of taking her life. Slowly. A unique wedding gift from husband to wife if there ever was one. Don't you agree?"

Ash's shoulders slumped, and he hung his head. They hadn't anticipated Lailah finding out about Kenna's identity until the Winter Solstice feast tonight.

She donned the sickly sweet voice of the doting priestess. "Oh, you poor dear. It seems I've disappointed you. Will you tell me what I can do to help?"

Lailah probed at his mind. But he'd been fortifying his mental defenses against her for over three centuries, and he let her into his mind just enough for her to read the thoughts and questions she expected.

How did she find out? I thought my glamor hid Kenna's identity. I can't let Samael marry her. There must be a way to stop this.

He felt Lailah withdraw from his mind, and he hid his flicker of relief. She hadn't discovered the truth. The single shred of hope that their plan would still work relied on Ash and Kenna's marriage. If he could keep that from Lailah, they might make it through the Solstice feast.

Even though Lailah wouldn't be able to force Kenna to marry Samael, Kenna was going to have to fight like Hel if she was going to survive.

Ash had never been more glad that he'd insisted on Pax and Hawthorne keeping the details of their backup plan from him. It was looking more and more like they were going to need it.

CHAPTER 61

*A*fter Kenna had dressed, and armed herself with her sword and dagger, she stepped to meet Ori. She tried to sound pleasant, but her tone was clipped. "I've already had breakfast. Straight to the ring this morning."

"Fine," Ori said. Did Kenna detect a hint of annoyance?

She gave her maid a forced smile, attempting nonchalance. She walked beside the woman who'd betrayed her, and her skin felt too tight. She wanted to punch Ori in the face. Though, some small part of her also felt sorry for the woman.

Ash had explained how Samael trapped elvish women, including Ori, into servitude with false promises of love and tenderness. Then he'd cast them aside and treated them with abuse and disdain.

Longing for a scrap of the prince's affection, the maid probably would have killed Kenna in her sleep if Samael ordered it. Thankfully, Kenna spent every night with the reassurance of Ash sleeping next to her. Anyone would be a fool to attack her with the king by her side.

But Ori was the least of Kenna's concerns. She needed to focus on making it through Winter Solstice. If their plan failed and her marriage vows to Ash didn't protect her, she'd be killed at midnight tonight.

There was still something Ash hadn't been able to tell her—an important truth skirting around the edge of her knowledge. But every time she almost found it, it was like trying to see through a dirty window.

"Good luck, *Princess.*"

Kenna's eyes darted to Ori, and the maid gave her a look of mock innocence filled with obvious malice. "What? Isn't that what Wren calls you?"

Before Kenna could answer, Ori was already walking away, humming a romantic tune to herself.

Apparently, she's done pretending now.

Had Ori known Ash was in Kenna's room earlier? Probably. They hadn't exactly kept their affair secret, and the king's dalliances with his elvish visitors were nothing new.

When Kenna pushed open the sparring room door, Ash was standing across the room talking with Lailah, their voices low. Lailah waved a hand, mending some cracked stone tiles on the wall, and walked toward Kenna.

"Hello, my child," Lailah said. She reached a hand out and cupped Kenna's cheek; Kenna resisted, shuddering away from her touch.

"I do hope you feel ready for the festivities. I know I certainly am." The priestess's smile made her stomach churn. "You've worked so tirelessly. Do you feel prepared?"

"I think so," Kenna said.

"Well, one can only hope. After all, what is life's if not the sum of our achievements?"

Kenna fought the urge to punch her. "Will you be at the Winter Solstice games tomorrow?"

"I will be there." Lailah dropped her voice into a conspiratorial whisper. "Is it wrong for a priestess to enjoy the games? I do hope that you fulfill your purpose, child. Good luck." Lailah swayed out of the chamber. Without looking back, she said, "I'll see you tonight, *brother.*"

Ash seemed as troubled as Kenna, if not more so. What had they been speaking about before she arrived? Kenna's pulse quickened. Did Lailah suspect their plans?

She rushed to her husband. Usually, their physical relationship was confined to Kenna's room, not wanting to draw too much attention with public displays of affection. However, sensing Ash's troubled mood, Kenna reached out to draw him into a hug. He brushed her off.

"Aqua shield," Ash said.

"Ash, what did she say to you?"

"Shield up, Kenna." His gaze was dark and guarded. "It's time to see what you've learned."

"Fine." In fact, it was more than fine. Their best training sessions happened when one or both of them were disgruntled.

The sex afterward was always better, too.

Kenna stalked away and raised a dome of water around herself. Without further warning, Ash attacked. He spun and lashed out with two flaming swords, not even bothering to pick up a physical weapon.

Her shield guttered, but she managed to hold it steady. She'd never felt frightened of him, and she knew Ash wouldn't truly hurt her, but today, something was wrong. Lailah had rattled him.

She concentrated on her shield and drew her sword. Ash surrounded her liquid dome with a globe of fire, turning her shield into inconsequential mist.

"I need a break!" she yelled.

The fiery globe morphed into a prison cell, trapping her behind flaming bars. But Ash was the one who was pacing back and forth like a caged animal. "You will not get a break tomorrow if you make it to the Solstice games. You will not get a break from your enemies if you survive to fight in the imminent war. There will be no mercy. Now, fight!"

With a feral shout, Kenna thrust her hands downward, cracking the stones and forming a small ditch with a shield of air above her. She dropped onto her stomach and rolled under the cage. Standing quickly, she drew her sword and took up a defensive stance.

For nearly an hour, Ash pelted every shield she formed with icy daggers, stony projectiles, and flaming spears. The onslaught was relentless, but she ducked, dodged, and parried with her sword and magic until she was utterly exhausted.

He seemed like a different person, lost to some dark place within himself. Kenna's vision blurred around the edges as she clung to the magic keeping the shield of air around her; she felt like she was going to faint.

"Ash, stop," she said quietly. She was too exhausted to defend herself anymore, but he couldn't hear her. "Ash. Stop. Enough!" Kenna sank to her knees, dripping with sweat and dragging air into her ragged lungs as she clung to consciousness.

Seeing her defeat, Ash immediately ceased his attack. He turned away from her and snarled, slamming his hands down. A shower of cracked earth and stone flew away from them.

"Fuck!" His shoulders were heaving, and he leaned forward, placing his hands on his knees.

"Ash, you're scaring me. What's wrong?"

He turned toward Kenna, expression tormented, broken. "Your glamor didn't fool Lailah. My magic wasn't strong enough. She knows who you are. She's known all this time."

"No. But… she'll tell Luniva."

Ash's fists were clenched. "If the priestess knows who you are, Luniva knows who you are." He looked like speaking the words caused him physical agony. His eyes were desperate, pleading with her to understand.

Like the beginning of an avalanche, the truth started cascading down around her, building speed and ferocity as it tumbled down.

Lailah was never in the castle at night when Luniva was confined to the moon. Ash's magic wasn't as strong as Lailah's. The high priestess had constant communication with Luniva.

Kenna spoke her realization aloud. "Lailah isn't just the Luniva's priestess. She *is* Luniva."

Ash nodded.

~

SEATED IN THE ARENA, Ash and Kenna ate a quick lunch to replenish their energy.

"I'm so sorry for how I behaved during training," Ash said. "I slipped into my fighting mentality. The thought of Samael torturing you. Killing you. I needed to see what you were capable of under the sort of relentless attack he would bring. But still… I should have explained."

"Why? Because you think Samael will give me the same courtesy? I couldn't even defeat you, and you would never harm me. I'm not ready," Kenna stated. "Why couldn't you tell me about Lailah sooner? Why couldn't Wren or Pax tell me?"

"It's part of the Ancient magic of the treaty, binding anyone from sharing the identities of Luniva and Soldivus with those who don't already know them. Most people who spend an extended amount of time around Lailah are able to figure it out, but I've tried to keep you away from her as much as possible. I wasn't trying to protect you without your permission, but I couldn't tell you. I thought it would stop her from learning who you were. Apparently, I was wrong."

Hawthorne was meant to arrive this afternoon before the Solstice feast. But everything they'd planned… it was going to be more challenging now that Lailah and Samael knew Kenna's true identity.

Ash pulled her close and kissed her tenderly. "I love you, my queen. Your training is officially finished. I think I'd like to join my wife for a bath, and then I have a surprise for you."

"How can you just pretend like everything is fine?"

"I am the king. If I want to pretend, then I will. Now, will you come with me to your bathing chamber, or do I have to drag you there myself? We are the king and queen, and we have a feast to prepare for."

His worry seemed to have vanished, leaving behind the mischievous glint of intention as he prowled toward her. She backed away slowly, enjoying their game and fighting back her smile.

Ash simply shrugged and said, "So be it."

Then he ran toward her and slung her like a sack of potatoes over his shoulder, giving her a playful whack on her rear end. Ash bounded through the hallway and up the stairs to her chamber. The complete mirth of the moment erased everything else.

She noticed an angel courtier gaping at them in disapproval, and she held up her pinky finger in his direction with a sweet smile. The courtier scoffed and sputtered at the offensive gesture before continuing on his way.

"Put me down," Kenna demanded, though she was breathless with laughter.

"I don't think I will."

Faster than should have been possible, they arrived in her room and he shut the door behind them. Ash set her down gently but pinned her hands against the wall above her head. Then, he kissed her like she was oxygen and he was dying for his next breath.

"Ash," she whispered against his lips.

He snapped his fingers and their clothes vanished. "I believe I mentioned a bath," he said, leading her by the hand to the bathing chamber, which was already full of steam and the heady scent of lavender and peppermint.

Ash pulled her into the steaming water, and she was so lost in the feel of him that she didn't notice his body trying to tell her what his words could not convey. It was only after he left her that she realized he'd been saying goodbye.

Just in case.

CHAPTER 62

Kenna dusted cheeks with shimmering powder, lined her eyes with kohl, and stained her lips before stepping into the bathing chamber once more to don her dress. She wore the black dress she'd worn for their wedding.

When she looked into the mirror, Kenna could hardly recognize herself. She'd changed so drastically since Summer Solstice, and her worries had evolved immeasurably. The previous months had opened her eyes to an entire world full of purpose and responsibilities beyond the confines of her once mundane life. She was a secret human princess with the weight of saving an entire race on her shoulders. She was the queen of Notos now. And tonight, she might die.

Still, she found herself standing in front of her mirror, wondering whether the king would look at her like he had when he'd seen her in this dress last night.

Kenna brushed her hands over the skirt that flared out from her waist, glimmering gems cascading down the fabric like shooting stars.

Her mother would love this dress. Kenna wished she could talk to her, ask her for advice. If their plan worked, hopefully she would get to see her mother soon.

The next right step, her mother had said.

Kenna took a deep breath. She was as ready as she would ever be, so Kenna quietly left her room and headed down to the Great Hall.

A servant opened the door for her, and Kenna found the Great Hall had been utterly transformed by twinkling lights and the low hum of conversation between countless courtiers.

Wren stood on the dais across the room from her, looking quite dashing in a black and gold ensemble that complimented his eyes and wings. Next to him, Ash leaned casually on the arm of his throne, his smiling face crowned with a circlet of white gold and sapphire.

A courtier, some important Lord no doubt, stood next to Ash, telling him an animated story, and Ash tilted his head back and laughed, the picture of a benevolent king.

"Kenella Duras, Royal Mistress to His Majesty King Ashton Moonbriar." The herald announced her arrival, and Kenna wished the floor would swallow her as the chatter died and hundreds of disapproving stares turned in her direction. She was used to the scrutiny, but not from so many people at once.

Lailah—Luniva, Kenna reminded herself—was seated on a smaller throne next to Ash, and she gave Kenna a slight nod. Prince Samael was on another throne on the other side, looking like he had no appetite for the pleasantries of a feast. He didn't acknowledge Kenna at all.

But when Ash saw her standing there, he stood and crossed the silent expanse between them. Wren also weaved his way through the crowd and up the stairs to the herald.

Kenna started to sink into a low curtsey, but Ash caught her by the arm and tilted her chin up to look into his eyes. "You look exquisite. And you do not bow to anyone in this palace. Are you ready?"

She nodded. In front of the entire court, Ash pressed an achingly gentle kiss to her lips, erasing every one of her concerns over what had passed and what was to come. In that moment, he was everything.

When his lips left hers, the worries came flooding back. Lailah and Samael's reaction to what happened next would answer the question. Would Kenna live or die?

Like they'd planned, the herald announced her again, and Ash removed her glamor.

"Ladies and Gentleman, please bow to Her Majesty Kenella Duras, Queen of Notos and princess of the Human race."

As her glamor faded away, Kenna looked to Luniva and Samael, satisfaction and relief flooding her at the looks of shock and fury on their faces. Ash went rigid next to her, poised to fight as he waited for their reactions.

Luniva glared at Kenna and Ash, snapping her fingers and summoning Samael to her side. Kenna could feel the intensity of her icy glare—a cold so frigid it seemed to burn her skin. The Ancient's eyes didn't leave the king and queen as she leaned over to whisper into Samael's ear. Luniva and Samael were so obviously shocked by her title of Queen and the protection it afforded Kenna. They'd need time to recalibrate their plans.

Immediately, Kenna felt the tension leave Ash's body.

"It worked. She just told Samael he can't take you as his wife because of our marriage vows. And now that you're the Queen, they can't execute you for killing Varis. They won't use you for the ritual. She says you'll live. At least for now, you're safe."

Luniva and Samael couldn't kill Ash because of his magical protection under the law, and they would keep Kenna alive long enough to try to find a way to force her to marry Samael and allow Luniva to take control of the humans.

Ash and Kenna's plan had worked. She wouldn't die tonight.

Knowing she wasn't in danger, all Kenna wanted to do was be alone with her husband and celebrate their love surviving another day. But the king and queen couldn't disappear from the great hall before the feast even started.

They crossed to the dais through a sea of bowed heads, whispers, and finally polite applause. Kenna could see the disparaging sneers of so many angels who would never accept her as their queen. And she didn't care one rutting bit.

When they reached Ash's throne, he held up his hands magnanimously, silencing the room as he said, "Please, take your seats. I thank you all for joining me at Brumalis Castle this Winter Solstice eve. It is my sincere hope to provide a diverting Solstice festival that will be recorded as the greatest in history."

There was another round of applause accompanied by the clinking of knives against glasses.

Ash continued, "Now that you've all been introduced to your queen, please join me in welcoming my esteemed and honored guest, His Royal Highness Hawthorne Lightstone, prince of Vorra."

Confused whispers turned to anticipatory silence as Ash gestured to the doors across from the dais. The prince of Vorra had arrived.

Both light and shadows seemed to cling to Prince Hawthorne as he slowly descended the stairs. The crowd parted before him as he crossed the room to stand in front of the dais where the Moonbriar brothers and Luniva sat on their thrones. The atmosphere in the room was charged with unspoken questions. She could almost hear them thinking —would Prince Hawthorne be executed for entering Notos?

Hawthorne's skin might carry lingering notes of summer, but there was no sunshine in his demeanor. He didn't offer her even a hint of a smile. In fact, he looked as though he would rather be anywhere else as he stared at Ash with unyielding, green eyes.

It was Luniva who broke the quiet, still playing priestess, though her words were pointed and fury radiated off her. "Prince Hawthorne, surely you should not look so morose. Will you not smile and bow to your sovereign hosts? We have a new queen, and our king has invited you to join us! He's been very busy, and I'm sure everyone will enjoy tomorrow's Solstice games all the more because of it."

The prince's smile looked more like a grimace as he dropped to one knee on the stone floor, bowing his head in silence.

"You may rise," Ash told the prince. "As our honored guest, you will join us at the royal table."

Something dark flashed in Luniva's eyes. For the sake of the crowd, she seemed to be attempting to maintain her benevolent countenance despite her own shock.

Ash addressed the crowd again. "Please find your seats. Tonight we feast; tomorrow we fight."

Luniva's voice dropped low as she whispered to Kenna. "There's always next year, princess."

The words were no doubt meant as a threat, but Kenna found comfort in the Ancient's promise. Next year. Luniva would keep her alive until next year.

There was more polite applause as Ash extended his arm to Kenna. She looped her hand through the crook of his elbow. Her meaning was clear as she leaned over to whisper, "Can we sneak away for a few minutes?"

His stubbled jaw tickled her ear as he whispered, "Now that you're safe, I want nothing more to find out what's underneath your dress. Unfortunately, we must both be patient. For now, let's be thankful all is going according to plan, and later…"

A cool, intentional current of air wound its way under her skirt and her blood heated. Kenna attempted to maintain a composed smile as he guided her to their table. Ash's angel hearing would have heard Luniva whispering to Kenna. He knew she was safe, too.

Ash seated her across from Hawthorne and the prince looked at her with such obvious disdain that she couldn't help the vehement look she gave him in return.

He'd made her feel like a broken toy when he'd discovered that she and Ash were together. How was Pax friends with this man? What would her life had been like if their marriage had been successful and she'd been tied to the grumpy brute?

Seeing him here now, Kenna was even more glad she'd not been able to marry him. She almost wished she could tell him to leave. She was queen now, so they didn't need his backup plan. Everything would be fine without him.

Instead, she engaged with him as the Queen of Notos. "Tell me, Your Highness, how is it that you come to be in Notos? Surely, the Winter Solstice is not widely celebrated by those as pure and chaste as the citizens of Vorra."

"Clearly, there is much beyond your understanding. I will not bore you with a futile attempt to explain at this time."

The prince's eyes were hard and sharp as pine needles. Now that he was closer, Kenna could see that his eyes were flecked with gold and brown, matching the golden highlights through his beard and hair. He was so dismissive. So patronizing. He was just as bad as the leaders in Mesterra.

She hadn't realized the water in her goblet was boiling until it burned her fingers. She dropped it and the crystal shattered as steam hissed against the stone tiles near her feet. "Sorry," she said to Ash.

"Don't worry," Ash snapped his fingers, and the glass was instantly repaired. She wasn't sure she'd ever understand the limitations of his magic, or rather, the lack thereof.

"How convenient it must be to be able to so easily clean up her messes," Hawthorne said.

Kenna pursed her lips, and Ash placed a steadying hand on her knee under the table.

The servants chose that moment to arrive with platters piled high with food. There was a delicious looking glazed suckling pig, platters of crab and lobster, and a tenderloin of beef cooked to rare perfection. A rainbow of vegetables accompanied the meat and fish, along with potatoes and loaves of bread.

"Please, help yourself," Luniva said to the prince, stabbing a juicy slab of red meat and placing it on her gilded plate.

"I find that I have little appetite in present company," the prince said, swirling the wine in his glass and eyeing Kenna intently.

"Well, I, for one, find that I can always eat," Kenna said, matching his self-important tone as she piled her plate with food. "It matters little if I have smelled the vilest stench. There is nothing that would keep me from enjoying a such succulent feast. Though, I imagine it would be difficult for a swine to enjoy eating pork for dinner."

"I'm no pig, Princess," Hawthorne said.

"And I am no princess. I'm the queen, and you will do well to remember it."

Ash leaned over, running a hand up her thigh as he whispered, "If you do not contain yourself, I'll be forced to remove you from the hall and teach you a lesson."

She kept her eyes on the prince of Vorra. "If you're no pig, Prince Hawthorne, you should try the pork. It is rutting magnificent."

Hawthorne choked on his wine, looking thoroughly disgusted.

Ash said, "Please excuse us for a moment. It seems I need to have a word with my new queen about proper court decorum."

He held her hand and practically dragged her out of the Great Hall, but she knew he wouldn't chastise her. She smiled as she hurried along behind Ash, resisting the urge to stick out her tongue at the haughty, judgemental prince.

The angels in the castle at least had the decency to hide their disdain for her in front of their king. She'd thought the prince of Vorra was supposed to be sympathetic to the human plight, but he seemed to have a lower opinion of her than almost any angel she'd ever met. He'd agreed to risk his life by coming here. He was working with the rebels and he'd healed her mother, but why hadn't Pax and Ash told her that Hawthorne was such an asshole?

As soon as they were alone in an alcove of a deserted corridor, Ash lifted her and sat her on the small marble table. He smiled against her lips as he placed his hands on her waist, kissing her while his magic slowly dragged her skirt up the front of her thighs, and he moved his hips between her legs. "You, my love, have a very filthy mouth. What shall I do about it?"

"What if someone hears us?"

"Then whisper it. Tell me what you want."

Kenna didn't say a word as she slid down from the table and knelt before him, unbuttoning his breeches. She smiled up at him through her lashes. Then, she used her mouth to make amends for her inappropriate behavior at the feast.

When she finished, Ash pulled her up and kissed her fiercely. Then he spun her away from him quickly, pulling her back to his chest with his hands around her waist.

"I told you never to bow before anyone in this castle. How should I punish my queen for disregarding my wishes?"

With one hand, he lifted the front of her dress and dipped his fingers between her legs, torturing her with the friction of her lace undergarments between his fingers and her skin. Then he spun her around so that her back was against the wall and gave her a brief, gentle kiss.

"I think you've learned your lesson," he said, turning away from her and buckling his trousers.

"You're a bastard," she said with a breathy whisper and a grin.

He turned back to her, teasing. "Still such foul language. You haven't learned a thing."

Kenna turned away from him, bending over and bracing one hand against the table. She looked over her shoulder with a smirk as she slid the back of her dress up in invitation. "Perhaps you're right. I don't think I've learned my lesson at all."

Ash prowled closer, unbuckling his belt and unbuttoning his breeches again as he said, "I guess I have some work to do."

He gave her a playful slap on her rear, and Kenna yelped and giggled. When she looked over her shoulder at him again, the king wasn't grinning anymore. Relief and adoration were written all over his face.

"Ash, I'm safe," she said. "I'll be your queen as long as we both live."

Ash slid her undergarments to one side. With both hands firmly gripping her hips, Ash entered her from behind, gently at first. As he thrust into her again and again, she bit her knuckles to stifle her moans of pleasure. He'd said he would teach her a lesson, but they both knew this was a celebration.

She was safe, and she was his.

~

THEY WERE both breathless and smiling in their dark retreat. Ash nuzzled Kenna's neck, breathing in her lavender scent. He pressed kisses to her nose, her lips, her jaw, her collarbone.

"We should get back," he said.

"Very well." Kenna batted her lashes in mock innocence. "I'll try to behave. Though it's entirely possible I may need another lesson later if I forget."

Ash chuckled, leaning his forehead against hers. "I love you, Kenna."

"And I love you, King Ashton Moonbriar," she replied, brushing a kiss to his lips.

"I regret that our relationship began the way it did. I hate that I tricked you into coming here. I'm sorry. I wish I was a better man." Ash cradled her face in his hands, kissing her gently again.

"Look at me," she said, suddenly tearful. "Everyone makes mistakes, Ash. But I see every part of you. Maybe there are things in your past you need to atone for, but I see you fighting for redemption every day. And the things the curse has forced you to do are not your fault. If there is a better man than you, I have not met him."

Ash wanted to take her back to her room right now, but it was nearly midnight, and he was feeling smug. His mother would be sulking since she'd be unable to perform the ritual at midnight. There was no suitable elf in the castle.

Ash helped Kenna fix her hair and adjust her dress, but her cheeks were still tinged with pink in the aftermath of their fun. Everyone would be able to see that Kenna's supposed lesson in court decorum had actually been an excuse for them to find their pleasure in a dark corridor, but Ash didn't care.

They could think whatever they wanted.

Kenna was his wife, and she was alive and safe for the time being. He didn't know what the next days or months would hold for them, but he knew he wouldn't take a single second with her for granted.

Ash replaced the crown on his head and took her hand as he led her through the corridors back to the banquet. Tomorrow, after the games, he was going to give her the crown he'd had made for her. Ash had saved the crown for her Winter Solstice gift, knowing how much more meaningful it would be once they'd survived all of this. He'd had the crown commissioned by a jeweler in Braktyn the day he'd visited Pax, and Ash had paid the jeweler handsomely for his discretion.

Ash had resolved to give her the crown even if she married Hawthorne. Even then, Ash had secretly hoped he would be the man to marry her. And now she was his queen—at least for a little while longer.

But when they returned to the Great Hall, his world stopped. His dreams of broken curses and happiness with Kenna faded like a misty breath on a dark winter night. Wren knelt on the dais, Samael's blade resting across his throat.

CHAPTER 63

Battered and bloody, bound hand, foot, and neck by chains, Wren was held by multiple guards.

"Release him now," Ash demanded. His voice made Kenna tremble.

A cruel, knowing smile was Samael's only answer.

Luniva laughed, and Kenna wondered how the screeching, metallic sound had ever reminded her of ringing bells. "Our dear king and queen seem to have forgotten the reason we are gathered here tonight. It's Winter Solstice. There is a ritual to perform."

No. No. No.

They'd known this was a risk. That Lailah would somehow find a way to make Ash perform the ritual and kill Kenna even though her human blood would be useless for the Emergence serum. After what Ash heard in Samael's mind, they'd thought she was safe.

Was it fear or anger that made Ash's hand tremble in hers?

Ash's voice was still full of icy authority. "Samael, if you do not unhand the Captain of the Guard, I will make you regret every moment of your miserable existence for the rest of your life."

Luniva rolled her eyes. "Oh, Ashton. You always were sympathetic to the lesser creatures of the realms. No matter. The captain will be fine, so long as you perform the ritual."

Kenna's chest seized. Luniva was going to make him choose between Kenna's life and Wren's.

She turned to Ash, gripping his hands and looking into his eyes. His eyes were tidal waves. Hurricanes of blue, filled with torment. Kenna allowed him time to think.

She'd grown so fond of Wren during her time here. She loved him and he meant so much to Ash. All these years, Wren had stood by Ash's side, his only true comrade in this frozen wasteland. But if Ash chose Wren's life over hers, it would doom an entire race of people.

What would her death mean for Mesterra? What would happen if Kenna died and the treaty wasn't fulfilled at all? The humans would waste away and die, but what about her friends and her family? What about her mother and Jona? Zo and Ezra? Drake and Sera?

The questions rolled over her in relentless waves, but there was no right answer. And there was no time to decide.

Kenna clenched her eyes shut for half a second, trying to think of a way out. Her eyes snapped open again when rough hands seized her from behind, pulling her backward away from Ash. Echelous stood behind Ash with a dagger in his hand. A dagger with a cylindrical handle.

Kenna screamed out in warning just as a beaming Echelous plunged the dagger into Ash's back. Echelous must have used the plunger in the dagger's handle to inject the serum into Ash's heart.

Her husband's eyes filled with realization and defeat. "Kenna, I love—"

"No," Kenna sobbed. "No. Ash! Ash!"

The blue faded from the king's eyes, replaced with inky black. And just like that, Ash was gone, and she stood face to face with a predator. Ash had never looked more like Prince Samael than he did as he smirked down at her. The curve of his lips was not flirtatious or teasing. It was a sinister grin that told her exactly how much he looked forward to inflicting pain.

"Ash. It's me. I'm your wife. Your queen." Tears slid down her cheeks. If they'd been right, the Ancient magic of their marriage vows would be strong enough to break through the dark magic that controlled him.

But her king stalked away from her and sat on his throne, his mind now under the thrall of the curse. And Kenna had her answer. Their marriage wasn't enough.

"You cannot kill me in this ritual." Kenna glared at Luniva through her angry tears as she was chained and dragged onto the dais. "I am your queen, and you need me to fulfill the treaty."

"Oh, relax, *Princess*," Lailah said, her insult clear. The Ancient would never acknowledge Kenna as Queen of Notos. "I won't sacrifice you. Your human blood would be useless in the Emergence serum. As for the treaty?" Luniva examined her fingernails. "The humans can rot for all I care. War is coming one way or another, but I don't need the humans to take back my power."

Luniva kicked the back of Kenna's legs, and she buckled, grimacing as her kneecaps hit the marble floor on the dais. Kenna was next to Wren, so close their shoulders were touching.

"Do you honestly think you're the only woman in this castle who is in love with Ashton Moonbriar? There is an entire staff of female elves, just desperate for a scrap of kindness. Six servants offered themselves when we asked for volunteers to take your place."

Kenna looked at Wren, confused. Wren shook his head, warning her to stay quiet. He spoke up on her behalf.

"Surely, the queen does not need to be here for the ritual."

Samael backhanded Wren across the jaw. "Silence, you fae piece of shit."

Then, the main doors of the Grand Hall burst open, and a familiar woman entered the room in a thin white shift.

Ori.

Ori didn't look distressed. She was not in chains. She wore the same simple, revealing white shift Kenna had seen in the memory of the first ritual. The maid's face was radiant, like a jubilant bride pledging herself to the love of her life as she slowly padded through the crowd toward the dais.

Ori knelt in front of the dais, as Luniva moved her arms through the air, and the stone altar raised out of the ground, elevating Kenna's former maid where she bowed.

"I offer myself to you heart, body, and soul, Your Majesty. I am honored to have been chosen as a vessel for your pleasure."

Kenna's stomach churned, and she closed her eyes and lowered her head, unable to stop the tears that flooded her vision, but Luniva stood behind her taking a fistful of her hair and wrenching her head up, forcing her to look.

With a low, malicious whisper, the Ancient said, "A queen of Notos wouldn't avert her eyes from our most sacred ritual. Keep your eyes open, Kenna, or I'll cut them out." She sharpened her voice and ordered, "Echelous. Hold her."

Slipping back into the voice of the magnanimous priestess, Luniva addressed the maid. "Rise, Ori, and come to claim your king."

Ash's eyes were still cold. Black. Empty.

Both Wren and Kenna's hands were both bound in front of them. They were close enough Echelous and Samael didn't notice when the fae's fingers brushed Kenna's. The small act of comfort nearly broke her.

Kenna's former maid stood and climbed up the steps toward the king. When she reached Ash, her cheeks were wet with tears. "Ash. I've loved you since the moment I came to this castle. I thought I loved Samael, but it's been you I loved all along." Samael made a disgusted sort of noise from where he stood, still holding his sword across Wren's throat. Ori continued babbling, "I've longed for this night. I wished I was the one you'd chosen. When Samael told me Kenna was nothing but a human whore, I couldn't believe it. Please. Don't make me wait any longer."

Kenna felt like she'd been doused with frigid water, yet she couldn't look away.

No. She wouldn't let this paralyze her. Not this time. She had to fight.

She struggled and thrashed against her bonds, but Echelous held fast to her hair and placed the tip of a blade on her temple, as though he might drive it into her brain or carry out Luniva's threat to cut out her eyes.

"Eyes open, Princess," Echelous whispered. Kenna went still.

"Ori, you are speaking out of turn," the Ancient said. "You forget yourself, my dear."

"Yes, Your Holiness. Forgive me."

Ash stayed silent. Kenna couldn't let this happen. She looked at Hawthorne. He was sitting on his ass doing nothing. He was supposed to *help* them if things went wrong tonight. And where was Pax? Why weren't either of them doing anything?

The thought of Ash having to perform the ritual made bile rise in Kenna's throat.

A servant appeared in front of Luniva with a crystal goblet filled with a luminescent, swirling white and blue liquid.

"This is a very special notelixir which will enhance your experience. May the light of the Luniva bless your union and bless the realm. Drink and be satisfied." Ori sipped the liquid, and Ash continued standing in his trance-like state.

As soon as Ori sipped the liquid, her adoring gaze turned to something feral and hungry. Her pupils dilated and her cheeks flushed. She licked her lips. Obviously, the liquid had some sort of aphrodisiac effect.

Next, Lailah offered the chalice to Ash, and he took a sip.

Kenna tried to look away again, but she felt the tip of Echelous's blade press a little harder, nearly breaking the skin.

Ash snapped his fingers, and his clothes vanished. Kenna wanted to run to him and cover his indecency before the crowd. His skin was glowing, almost iridescent, as he pulled Ori into a kiss. Kenna's heart fractured in her chest. With his arms wrapped around the maid, Ash's wings unfurled, and he flew them both down the stairs and laid Ori down on the stone altar.

Everything about the ritual was twisted. Wrong.

Ash's wings covered their bodies, but his hips moved in a way that was so familiar. It was like watching one of her own memories performed by actors on a stage. Actors who hadn't connected with the emotion of the character. But this was not some innocent drama. He was her husband, and Kenna knew what was going to happen next.

She kept her eyes open, but her vision blurred and then went black. She blinked but could see nothing. Kenna started to panic, but then she realized someone had blinded her. Her heart rate increased, but as she took deep breaths, the wind whispered. *Calm down.*

Someone was protecting her from watching. Pax had promised he'd be at the feast, invisible. He'd also said something vague about being able to shield her mind from certain things. Perhaps protecting her eyes from having to witness the ritual. But why didn't he stop this?

Though her vision was gone, nothing blocked out the sickening sounds. She heard Ash's movements grow frantic and punishing as Ori's moans spurred him on. She could not escape the familiar groan that tore from her husband's lips as he finished.

"I thank you, my King," Ori said. "And I thank Ancient Luniva for the gifts of pleasure and moonlight." Then there was the unmistakable sound of a blade striking the stone altar and the sickening thud of Ori's head hitting the floor.

Kenna tried to lean forward, but Echelous held her hair firmly. When she vomited, it dripped down her chin and the front of her black wedding dress.

"Fuck," said Echelous, releasing her hair and stepping away from the vomit.

Kenna sobbed while the gathered angel nobility applauded politely, as though they'd just witnessed a diverting performance and not the perversion of one of life's most intimate acts.

When her vision returned, Ash was already dressed and seated, his wings draped over the arms of his throne. His eyes were still bottomless onyx discs, and his skin continued gleaming with that otherworldly light, reminding Kenna of a newly Emerged elf after the Emergence Ceremony. Whatever Ori and Ash had sipped from the chalice before the ritual must be part of the Emergence serum formula.

Ori's body still lay on the stone table, her blood filling carved stone channels along the edge of the altar and funneling in to a small hole to be collected somewhere beneath.

"You poor dear," Luniva said loud enough for the crowd to hear. "That must have been very distressing to watch. Do you know what the law says you are entitled to do if your husband is unfaithful to you?"

Kenna didn't answer.

"Answer me, girl," Luniva said.

"I don't know," Kenna said, gritting her teeth.

"Normally, a wife would be permitted to execute her adulterous husband. Unfortunately, just as our laws prevent us from executing our Queen for murder, we cannot allow our King to be executed. What, then, shall we do? How can the law be satisfied when you both are exempt from the required punishment?"

Lailah tapped her chin, a dramatic farce of searching for a logical solution, even though it was very clear she already had a plan.

"Of course! The Solstice games begin in the morning! But I think we shall begin early. The games will commence tonight, and our king and queen will be amongst the pairs of opponents. They'll fight each other. To the death."

"No," Kenna whispered.

Luniva arched a brow at her and then turned to the crowd. "Our queen says no, but what say you?"

There was a raucous chorus of angels banging on the tables, clinking glasses, and shouting their encouragement with cries of, "Let them fight! Make the human pay!"

Because everyone in the room knew…

If she was forced to fight Ash to the death while he was still under the trance of his curse, there was no way Kenna would walk away with her life.

CHAPTER 64

"Samael, release the captain. Echelous, take Kenna and Wren to her room. I assume she will choose him as her second."

"My second?" Kenna asked.

"You didn't think I would make you fight the king alone, did you? That would be terribly unfair of me. He'd kill you in less than a minute. I assumed you would like Wren to join you in the ring."

"He'll kill Wren as well," Kenna ground out.

"I'm sorry, would you rather have Samael or Echelous as your second? I'm sure they'd be happy to assist you."

"No!" Wren snarled. "I will fight with her." Wren turned to Kenna, acceptance of his fate shining in his golden eyes. She knew Wren would do his best to protect her, but she hated that he'd been hurt to try to coerce Ash.

"Very well. Get on with it then." Lailah waved a dismissive hand, and Echelous pulled Kenna to her feet with rough hands.

The priestess's voice rang after them as Echelous dragged Kenna and Wren through the Great Hall. "Oh, and Kenna? Clean yourself up and dress in something suitable for a fight. A soiled dress is not befitting attire for someone who calls herself a queen."

When they reached Kenna's chambers, Echelous removed Kenna's bonds. "No need to keep a human in chains in a castle full of angels." Then he removed the manacles on Wren's hands and the collar around his neck. He nodded to the chains on Wren's feet. "Not that you can fly, mutt, but those chains stay on. And don't even think about trying to escape. Samael is guarding the balcony. You have fifteen minutes."

Echelous shoved them into her room and slammed the door behind them; Kenna heard the distinct click of a lock.

Immediately, she launched herself into Wren's arms. "How badly did they hurt you? Are you okay?" she asked her friend.

"I've endured worse pain, but I'm not okay with any of this. I worry that Hawthorne has betrayed us. How else would they have planned all this? How else would they know you and Ash were married? Fuck!" Wren punched her wall, and the stone tile cracked under the force of his blow. "It doesn't make sense. And where in the Void is Pax?"

"It's not very nice te speak about someone as though they're not there, ye know," Pax said, coming into view, arms folded and bearing an expression of indignation. "I don't appreciate ye insinuating that Hawthorne's done anything unsavory. We knew there was a risk Lailah would find out what was happenin' and try te pull something like this, which is why Thorne and I had a backup plan."

"We don't have time for you two to fight," Kenna said, trembling. She knew she was in shock, but she needed to use whatever was coursing through her veins to her advantage. She had to keep moving. Otherwise, she might collapse. Then she'd never move again. "We all want the same thing. Somehow, we need to find a way for Ash, Wren, and I to walk away from the games alive. Can we keep him fighting until he returns to his senses? How long until the curse's magic wears off?"

Wren shook his head. "It won't wear off until sunrise."

"Well, then… I don't know. But I need to change."

Kenna's hands were still shaking as she opened her wardrobe to dress in her training clothes, but her normal gear had all disappeared. Instead, she discovered a skillfully crafted set of leather armor and a box. On top of the box rested a small piece of parchment sealed with Ash's sigil.

The note was addressed to her in his familiar, swirling script: "For my beloved queen. You always have a choice."

She didn't dare read the note right now. She didn't have time to fall apart. But she opened the box. Inside, there was a crown. *Her* crown.

Unlike Ash's white gold and sapphire crown, her crown was a delicate circlet made from strands of gold, platinum, and bronze twisted around each other like a cord. In the center of the circlet, there was a diamond-shaped setting filled with tiny rubies, emeralds, sapphires, amethysts, and diamonds. Precious stones of every color—forming a rainbow.

He must have commissioned it for her months ago. He'd been prepared to marry her and make her his queen. Perhaps he'd even hoped for it, the way she had hoped she might be with him. She closed her eyes and said a silent prayer to Soldivus to let her make it through this. She needed to kiss Ash and tell him thank you for a crown more perfect than she could have imagined for herself.

In the privacy of her bathing chamber, Kenna washed away the vomit and dried her tears. She steeled herself and dressed in her new armor, tunneling into the righteous rage she felt toward Lailah and Samael.

The thick navy bodice fastened with metal buckles, and the supple leather moved easily. To protect her throat, there was a platinum and sapphire encrusted gorget designed like the plumage of a blue jay, and the metallic pauldrons over her shoulders were crafted to look like the feathered arch of navy wings. The leather tassets over her thighs were the same deep navy as the center panel of the bodice. She pulled tall boots over her calves and secured bracers over her forearms before fastening the empty scabbard at her back and sheathing her dagger at her waist.

Finally, she set her new crown upon her head. If Lailah's curse forced Ash to kill her, then Kenna would die as his queen. She exited the bathing room, rejoining Pax and Wren.

Echelous didn't bother knocking as he burst into her chamber. "Let's go then," he said.

Pax was nowhere to be seen, but Kenna felt him squeeze her shoulder before she reached out and took Wren's hand.

Hand in hand, they walked to their imminent death.

Death by Ash's hand.

Each click of her heels and the scuff of Wren's chains on the white stone floor echoed through the winding hallways and reverberated through her chest. The palace halls were deserted, but Kenna knew exactly where all the servants and courtiers were.

She'd trained for months, but this fight was only the beginning. Whatever happened tonight, Samael and Lailah would pay. Ash would never stand idly by and let the curse take hold of him again. Not if it forced him to kill his wife and his best friend.

Pax wouldn't stand for Kenna's death, either. He was her guardian angel, and he would spread the news of her death and the truth of everything that happened here to the rebels in Mesterra.

Her brother and the entire rebel force would fight against this. Tears slipped down her cheeks. Kenna dashed them away. She was a warrior now, a queen.

I'm sorry, she thought, wishing she could send the words to everyone she loved.

Whatever the outcome of tonight, this was the beginning of an even greater war than the revolution in Mesterra.

She forced open the large wooden doors of the sparring arena. The benches had been empty during her training sessions, but they were full of people now. Hundreds of eyes focused on Kenna as she and Wren entered the arena. Her ears buzzed with the tinnitus of the bloodthirsty crowd.

King Ashton Moonbriar, High Priestess Lailah, and Prince Samael Moonbriar were seated in the front row across from the doors. All three of the royal siblings looked as regal as Kenna had ever seen them as they fixed their merciless gazes on Kenna.

Samael and Ash were both dressed in intricate fighting leathers, with midnight blue capes attached at their shoulders with silver and sapphire buckles.

Ash was seated on his throne between High Priestess Lailah and Prince Samael. His eyes were still black and unreadable, his posture showing none of his usual humor or swagger. Next to Ash, Prince Samael's steely eyes gleamed as he beheld Kenna's warrior garb. She was sure he couldn't wait to see her battered and torn to shreds.

As always, Lailah was a vision of beauty in swirls of white gossamer and muslin, her shimmering black and silver wings draped behind her. Even though Kenna had learned about the darkness lurking beneath Lailah's pretty exterior, her visage gave no indication of her true nature.

In contrast to Lailah's magnanimous appearance, Prince Hawthorne's eyes were utterly sullen. In his place of honor, a few feet to the right of the priestess, he seemed to be shrouded in shadows, as though he resented being there.

He'd been willing to marry her, but would he help her and Ash tonight? Or had he betrayed them like Wren suspected?

The prince of Vorra wore a crown of twisted gold hawthorn branches atop his dark brown waves. Emerald encrusted leaves and ruby berries appeared along the branches. The sharp coronet only served to make him look more haughty and miserable than ever.

Guards lined the semi-circular wall of the sparring floor. They were ready for their chance to earn victory and glory in the tournament. Kenna, on the other hand, only hoped she might walk away with her life.

When she searched the king's gaze for a glimmer of thought or feeling, Kenna found nothing of the man she loved. Her husband.

"I know you're eager to fight, but you must wait your turn, dear." Lailah indicated for Kenna to take a place along the wall. She stood next to a royal guard who must have been nearly seven feet tall. She didn't recognize him, but she never really went to the garrison. She only trained with Ash and Wren.

That was when Kenna noticed none of the guards acknowledged their captain, and none of them wore the sapphire capes of Notos. Their capes were dark gray, nearly black.

When he joined her, Wren leaned over and whispered, "None of these men are part of my guard. They are Echelous's Surgati wardens."

Perhaps Lailah worried that the angels, fae, and elves who served on Ash's royal guard might try to stop this madness.

Lailah stood and spread her wings and arms, silencing the crowd. "Happy Solstice, my dear brothers and sisters. I hope you've not drunk too deeply at the feast so that you might remember the events of these special Solstice games."

There was a chorus of laughter from the nobility—ironic since angels healed too quickly to be plagued by extreme drunkenness or hangovers.

There were many ashen-faced servants among the crowd, fae and elves, who weren't laughing at all. They'd not been invited to the feast, and most of them looked as though they'd rather be anywhere else.

"Though I have no taste for violence, I would not dream of missing this year's tournament. Without further ado, let the games commence. Echelous's esteemed captain, Brock, will begin the festivities." Lailah gestured to the hulking male next to Kenna.

"Captain, who will you challenge?" Lailah asked.

"I would be remiss if I challenged anyone other than my most skilled comrade. I challenge Magnus."

Brock and Magnus made their way to the center of the ring.

"You will battle until one of you yields or is rendered unconscious. Do you both understand?" Lailah said. Both of the guardians nodded to the priestess. "Very well, please shake on your honor, and begin at the crash of the symbol."

The two Surgati clasped arms, and Kenna leaned over to Wren. "Will they not fight to the death?"

Wren shook his head. "No. Lailah forcing you and Ash to fight to the death is unheard of."

A symbol clanged, and the wardens nodded to each other before they released forearms and drew their swords. The two males were a flurry of steel, stone, ice, and flame. When they were both slicked with sweat and panting, Brock pinned the other warden down under a cage of fire. Through the flaming bars, he held his sword to his captive's throat.

"I yield," said Magnus.

The flaming prison vanished, and Brock extended his arm to help the other Surgati from the ground.

Multiple sets of Echelous's men faced each other in combat, the crowd cheering and jeering in equal measure. Kenna's anxiety climbed higher and higher.

This was part of Lailah's game. Making her watch the display of skill and strength. None of Echelous's men compared to the king. Each combat match was a reminder that there was no hope of Kenna walking away from the fight with Ash.

Even if she and Wren could defend themselves against the king while he was under the curse's control, could either of them take his life to spare their own? Kenna couldn't. She would never forgive herself.

Kenna almost hoped Ash would kill her quickly so that Wren, at least, might be spared. Maybe Lailah wouldn't make them fight to the death. Perhaps this was all just a ploy to terrify and humiliate Kenna.

"While it has been most diverting to see the skills and talents of Echelous's men, I know you've all been anxiously awaiting our *special* source of entertainment. We will now have a short recess, but afterward our king and queen will fight to the death. Our queen will have the

Captain of the Guard, Wren, as her second. Our king's second will be our guest of honor, Prince Hawthorne Lightstone."

"We won't have a chance against both of them," Wren said, his words filled with wrath.

"You said I got a second to make the fight fair!" Kenna yelled.

Lailah shrugged. She examined her perfectly painted nails and then turned to Kenna and simply said, "I lied."

CHAPTER 65

ash and Hawthorne walked along the curve of the wide front aisle and descended the stairs on one side of the stadium seats. On the floor below, Kenna tracked their progress before she and Wren met them at the bottom of the stairs.

"What game are you playing?" she hissed.

Hawthorne looked at her with unforgiving green eyes and set his bearded jaw. "The long game."

He prowled into the ring, swinging his battle axe through the air in practiced arcs. Kenna turned to Ash, whose eyes were still black and vacant.

"Ash?" She searched his face, to no avail.

She remembered seeing his memories of the first ritual. Ash had been haunted all these years by his participation in the ritual when Lailah killed his mate. How would he feel sifting through the fragmented memories of killing Kenna, too?

With tears streaming, Kenna said, "Ash…if you can hear me…" she choked on her emotion. "If you can hear me, know that I love you. I could never kill you, even like this. But if you kill me, if you hurt me because of your curse, it's not your fault. I forgive you. You're not a monster. If I die. I'm just glad…I'm glad I got to be your wife. I'm glad I got to be your queen, even for a single day."

With a blank stare, her husband turned away and followed

Hawthorne into the ring. Wren and Kenna followed the king and the prince into the ring as well.

That was when Kenna knew for certain: she would not survive this fight.

"As I'm sure you can all guess, we are in for an entertaining and enlightening fight indeed. Ash and Kenna, you may begin when the symbol sounds. Wren and Hawthorne, you may only assist by shielding your partner. If you draw a weapon, then you will be disqualified."

Prince Samael's usual sneering face was transcendent, enthralled by the prospect of extreme violence and devastation. Samael practically glowed with elation. He was the image of deadly, ethereal beauty. Next to him, Echelous looked as nonchalant as ever.

Prince Hawthorne stood next to Ash with a hand on his shoulder, and his lips moved. Kenna heard the words on the wind. "Ergiom velias sun bileripio."

It was a language Kenna's ear couldn't decipher, but her heart understood the weight of its authority. The Ancient language.

Before Kenna could wonder at the word's meaning, the symbols crashed.

Ash and Hawthorne stood facing Kenna and Wren, but none of them moved to draw a weapon. The air in the room was ominously charged with the crushing stillness of an approaching storm.

Then Ash spread his wings wide and the very ground beneath the ring began to quake. The wind howled around them, and hailstones the size of grapes pelted the ground, bouncing off the stone tiles. Wren surrounded himself and Kenna in a fiery cube to repel the icy pellets.

"What do we do?" she asked.

"You do exactly what we've trained you to do. Ash would want you to fight. If he kills you, Kenna, it will break him. You have to defend yourself."

In a lightning-bright flash, Ash appeared behind Kenna with two icy daggers suspended near his fingertips. But she'd trained with him every day for six months. She anticipated Ash's move, and she ducked and spun, knocking his feet out from under him. Her king hit the stony floor with a grunt.

His movements were not as quick or skillful as usual, and she wondered if somewhere within he was fighting against this. If he could just hold on. Could she keep him fighting long enough for him to return to himself?

Wren said the curse would keep hold of his mind until dawn. That was still six hours away.

"I'm growing bored, Princess," Ash told her. "I think we'll speed things along."

Thunder peeled, and the wind howled; the flames of hundreds of candles flickered before guttering out. The chamber was dark other than Kenna's flaming daggers and Ash's icy spear reflecting the glowing light of her flames.

Husband and wife, king and queen, they circled each other. It was a dance choreographed by heartbreak and destruction. There was no way out of this. Why didn't he kill her?

Time seemed to slow. A flash of lightning illuminated Ash's face, his black eyes swallowing the blue light. The stone beneath Kenna's feet lurched, tossing her high into the air, and she landed flat on her back. The impact froze the breath in her lungs. Like an executioner, Ash swept his icy sword in an arc toward Kenna's neck.

But before his blade could fall, Hawthorne's battle axe and flaming sword appeared behind Ash, and the Prince of Vorra severed Ash's wings from his body in a single, lethal stroke. One of the few ways to kill an angel. Feathers fluttered around them as Ash fell to the floor, the two bloody stumps at his back gushing.

For the briefest moment, his eyes returned to their normal deep blue, and he brushed a finger down Kenna's cheek. "I love you, my queen."

But then his blue eyes were empty. King Ashton Moonbriar was dead.

"No," Kenna whispered.

Ash's crown clattered to the floor, and Kenna picked it up, scrambling to her knees. She couldn't feel her face, and it took her several seconds to realize the bone chilling scream echoing through her was emanating from her own mouth. She gripped Ash's crown so tightly that blood trickled through her fingers. The pain grounded her in reality.

She was sobbing, but not with grief. With rage.

Rage against Lailah and her curse. Rage against the High Council and their oppression. Rage against the Elders for killing her father.

Rage against Raziel for his bargain and Zo's capture. Above all else, she felt a searing, all-consuming rage against Prince Hawthorne. He had stolen Ash's life. He'd killed him without a shred of honor. He was supposed to be on Ash's side. He was supposed to be here to help, but it seemed like Hawthorne had betrayed Kenna and Ash.

She looked at Lailah and Samael. Surely, they would not stand for the prince of Vorra killing Ash.

Kenna thought she saw a flash of shock in Lailah's eyes. Then, the slight pout of Lailah's sensuous lips looked...bored. As though Ash hadn't been murdered in front of her. Kenna looked at Wren, whose mouth was hanging open in shock. His best friend, his king, was dead.

The crowd seemed to hold its collective breath as they waited for someone to tell them how to react. Lailah clapped her hands slowly, and some of the confused assembly began to applaud.

"Well, I do apologize if anyone is disappointed," Lailah called out. "I had rather hoped the fight would last longer. It seems that we must pause the events for a coronation. All hail, His Majesty King Samael Moonbriar."

As one, everyone in the crowd and all Echelous's wardens dropped to one knee. Kenna was already on her knees next to Ash, but as everyone else bent their knee to the new king, she struggled to her feet in defiance, remembering Ash's words. *You will never bow to anyone in this castle.*

"Kenna, my child. The crown, if you please."

She gripped the crown tighter, blood still dripping in between her fingers.

She couldn't bear the thought of Ash's crown on his brother's head. Lailah fixed her with a burning stare, and Kenna felt the strange sensation of losing control of her own body. Like a puppet, she took stiff, forced steps and extended the crown to the High Priestess. All the while, Kenna's mind protested.

Lailah set the gleaming crown in the nest of Samael's black curls and he smiled in triumph, even as a drop of Kenna's blood trickled down his pale forehead.

Samael spoke next. "Of course, there will be a price to pay, Prince Hawthorne. Surely, you did not expect to come into our realm, murder our king, and walk away unscathed. No. Another round of combat, I think. This time, you can fight our queen. Kenella Duras, will you fight to avenge your lover?"

Fueled by her need for vengeance, she lifted her chin. "I will fight him."

Hawthorne was supposed to help them, but he'd betrayed them instead. Was this some form of cruel payback for her relationship with Ash? Whatever the prince's motivations, none of this was part of any plan Kenna knew about.

And where the *fuck* was Pax?

Her rage would drive her combat. She may not be skilled enough to kill the prince, but she could certainly make him bleed.

Prince Hawthorne still stood in the center of the ring, his hands hanging at his sides, unarmed. When he looked at Kenna, his eyes seemed softer somehow. Apologetic.

She did not care what she saw in his expression. He may kill her just as he'd killed her husband. Even if he regretted killing Ash, Kenna needed vengeance.

Kenna strode forward and clasped his forearm, waiting for the sound of the symbol to mark the beginning of their match. The intelligent thing to do would be to try to kill him quickly. But she would never be able to inflict enough pain to satisfy the debt he owed. Kenna wanted him to suffer.

When the symbol clanged, Kenna didn't hesitate. She aimed for his ribs with an icy dagger, but he shifted to his left. He sucked in a breath through his teeth, as the frigid knife sliced through the flesh on his shoulder. Holding her gaze, he stood still as a stone.

Why wasn't he fighting? His sudden pacifism after his murderous display against Ash only fueled Kenna's hatred.

"Fight me, you fucking murderer," she snarled.

Hawthorne closed his eyes and remained still. Attacking with magic would not satisfy Kenna's need to feel the prince's flesh tear and break under the weight of her wrath.

She hurled a fist at his nose, and bone crunched as his head jerked back violently. Hawthorne wiped his mouth and spat blood out onto the stone floor. Kenna circled around him and swooped his feet out from under him, making him crash to his back next to her.

She placed one knee on his chest and leaned in close as she put her dagger to his throat. "Was it always your plan to betray us? To murder him? Will you stop with Ash, or do you plan to destroy everyone that I love?"

Still, Hawthorne said nothing.

"Fight. Back."

Kenna clenched her teeth as she stood. She drew her sword from the scabbard on her back.

Hawthorne sat up, kneeling before her.

She slammed the broad side of her blade against the back of the prince's skull, sending him sprawling face first onto the unyielding stone.

He raised himself to his knees again.

The crowd jeered. They wanted violence, but not like this.

"It seems that His Highness does not want to play. Perhaps we can persuade him with the right tools," Samael said. The new king snapped his fingers and two whips tipped with icy black spikes appeared at Kenna's feet.

She picked up the whips and snapped them in the air. The crowd cheered. Prince Hawthorne flinched at the sound, giving Kenna some measure of satisfaction. But then, he looked at her with those mossy eyes, as if giving her permission.

And she hated him for it.

Something in her cracked and she flung the whips at him again and again. Shredding leather, flesh, and sinew, she sobbed with every lash of the whips against Hawthorne's skin. He grunted, panted, and fell forward. He laid prostrate before her, but still, he did not fight back.

She let out an incomprehensible shriek of frustration.

He coughed and raised himself onto his knees again, an act which seemed to require tremendous effort. Only then did it occur to Kenna that he wasn't healing. Why? Angels could heal from all but mortal wounds, and Kenna had not even attempted to strike a killing blow.

No, she was a creature ruled by the need to make the prince suffer. She circled to the front of him and kicked his chest. Hawthorne fell backward onto the cold floor. When his ravaged back contacted the stone, he let out a cry like that of a wounded animal.

Kenna leaned down. "A quick, painless death would have been a mercy." She drove an icy spike through one of his hands, pinning it to the floor, and he let out a hoarse yell. "But you don't deserve mercy." She pinned his other hand to the floor with a stony dagger. "I would have preferred for you to die even more slowly. But this will have to suffice."

Then, drawing her sword, she stabbed straight into his heart. She pulled the blade out and turned away, leaving him in a pool of his own blood. Just like she had with Varis.

The crowd cheered their approval, and the sound echoed through the emptiness in her chest.

As the noise of the crowd faded, she heard those strange Ancient words on the wind again. Or were the words in her soul?

"Ergiom velias sun bileripio."

Then, the prince took a final, rattling breath on the floor behind her. He was dead.

Kenna strode towards the doors of the arena. All she wanted to do now was crawl into bed. She wanted to sleep forever, and she didn't care if she ever woke up.

In that moment, she didn't care about her brother or the humans or her friends. She was done. There was no point to any of it anymore.

CHAPTER 66

"Not so fast, Kenna," Samael said.

She no longer had the energy to care about any possible threats. She didn't even try to fight as a controlling force turned her to face the new king.

Samael wiped her blood from his brow, leaving a red streak. He stood and stalked toward her. "Well done, Your Majesty. I could not have planned a more brutal end for the prince if I had done it myself. But watching you kill him was…well, it was everything I could have hoped for, and more."

"He deserved it."

"So it would seem." Samael laughed, a sound that scraped against Kenna's bones. "You're just as stupid as the first day you faced me in the ring. No matter. A wife does not require a brain to do her duties."

Kenna's head whipped around to Samael. She'd forgotten all about the treaty. "That's right, Kenna. It seems that you and I are to be married."

"No. You aren't the prince anymore. And *the priestess* doesn't care about the humans. You don't need to marry me."

Samael was standing inches away from her now. He touched her cheek gently, a perversion of a lover's caress. Then he gripped her chin hard, forcing her to look into his merciless, stone gray eyes. "Perhaps I don't *need* you, but who says I don't *want* you? My spineless wretch of a brother stole the throne from me. He kept you from me, and made me look like a fool. Now, I think I'll take back what's rightfully mine.

"I don't belong to any man, and I'll never speak the vows. I'll never marry you," Kenna promised.

Samael's chuckle sent a shiver of dread through her body.

"Of course you'll marry me. But even if you don't, you and I are going to be together for a very, *very* long time. Would you like to see your new home?"

He fisted her hair, yanking her head to the side as he leaned in close. "Tell me, who did you enjoy killing more—Varis or Hawthorne? Did you enjoy the thrill of watching the light fade from their eyes? Personally, I always find that final moment rather anticlimactic. I much prefer watching someone squirm in anticipation of their end. I absolutely love the pleading look in their eyes as they beg for the mercy of death." He shuddered in pleasure.

"And how you will beg, Kenna. When I'm through with you, you'll beg to become my wife. Whether I keep you alive or not once I've broken you, well..." He crushed her throat with one hand as his hot tongue slurped a sluggish trail from her jawline to her ear. Her instinct was to gag at the violation, but he was choking her and blackness crowded the edges of her vision. She tried to claw at Samael's hand with her fingernails. She couldn't breathe, couldn't think as she reached for her magic.

Before she could defend herself, consciousness deserted her, leaving her alone with the monster in the dark.

THE COLD AIR left a metallic tang on her tongue. The stinging sensation in her mouth and nose threatened to freeze her from the inside. In the natural world, it was the type of cold that would lure someone into a dreamless, forever sleep. Instinctively, Kenna knew the cold she felt was nothing natural, and her fate would be worse than death.

When she sat up on her knees, Kenna could barely make out the faint outline of the rounded white walls. She remembered these holes in towering walls of packed snow and ice. She was in the dungeon.

This was her new home.

Her teeth clacked together, already sore. She was seated on a large slab of onyx stone. No, not stone; it was a sheet of solid ice. She looked down into a never-ending chasm of darkness below the transparent floor of her cell. All it would take was for the ice to crack and she'd be swallowed up forever. She didn't imagine for a single second the awaiting monstrous darkness offered a quick or painless end. Her shivers grew more violent as she thought about it. The blackness below seemed to reach for her, hoping to drag her down into its gaping maw.

There were no bars on her snowy cell, but there was no need. She wouldn't risk falling into the chasm beneath her.

Kenna shuffled to the icy wall farthest away from the opening, searching for something solid to cling to. She found nothing, and the frozen wall of her cell offered no sense of warmth, comfort, or safety. She was utterly alone and abandoned.

Her stomach lurched. Where was Wren?

She groaned against the roiling in her stomach and looked around. There was nowhere in her cell to take care of such business. She took deep breaths, willing the cramps to pass. Perhaps she could ask a guard for a bucket.

She doubted it.

She couldn't even hear the keening sounds of any other prisoners. Which was worse? Complete silence or the sound of others' torturous lives? Deep down, she knew it was far worse to endure her fate alone without even having the company of another suffering soul.

Then, suddenly, she heard a jolly whistling tune so deeply at odds with her surroundings. Probably some sick bastard excited by the prospect of inflicting pain. Samael or Lailah? Echelous? Someone worse than any of them?

She didn't want to know. Kenna shuddered and silently hoped whoever it was didn't come to her cell. She squeezed her eyes shut, self-ishly wishing the floating platform would go anywhere else.

The happy melody grew closer and closer. Then it stopped.

She opened her eyes, barely able to make out the backlit, burly silhouette of the winged figure on the platform.

"Nice place ye've got here, lass."

"Pax?" Kenna let out a relieved sound halfway between a laugh and a sob, but then she remembered his absence during the fight. He was supposed to be her guardian angel.

She sobbed in earnest then. "Where were you? I thought you and Hawthorne had a plan. How could you let this happen?"

"Aye. I know it's hard te understand, but what do ye say we get out of here and I'll explain?"

Kenna nodded.

"Good."

She crawled across the icy floor, trying not to go sprawling into the chasm below. When she got closer to Pax, the bluish glow of the platform illuminated his red hair and kind smile. He extended an arm, and she gripped his hand before embracing him.

Pax half-lifted her onto the platform with a steadying arm and shielding wing around her. Her body started to thaw with the contact. She trembled even as she tried not to think about the platform floating over the expansive drop below.

There was no one she would have rather seen. Pax was one of the few people who had never asked for anything from her—not really. Even though he'd made a bargain for her employment, she knew he'd have let her stay at the Red Lantern for free as long as she'd needed. Instead, he'd given her a sense of purpose in helping him, even though he didn't need her help. He'd released her the moment she'd asked with no demands other than that she take care of herself.

Even after all of Kenna's training, it seemed she couldn't even do that.

The platform came to a stop, and they dismounted. The moment Kenna stepped onto the bridge, she clamped her hands over her ears against the warbling cries of the other prisoners. If Pax hadn't arrived, Kenna would have ended up like them. The thought made her lungs constrict.

"Not nice, is it? Right. Got te keep moving. I need te make one more stop. Ye can wait here for me."

"No!" She clenched Pax's arm, her eyes wide with terror. "No. You can't leave me. What if…" She couldn't finish the question. Couldn't think about if Samael or Lailah found her here. "You can't leave me."

Pax looked over the side of the bridge. "Where I have te go now is even worse than this place. If I bring ye with me, I need to protect ye from seein' what's down there. Like I did in the ritual. Do ye understand? Is that alright?"

"I understand," she said. So, it had been Pax who'd shielded her then.

Pax seemed to debate it for another moment before he nodded curtly. "Right, lass. Hold on tight."

She wrapped her arms around Pax's neck, and he cradled her with surprising gentleness.

Then, they were falling straight into the mouth of the black beast.

Even though Pax had shielded her vision, Kenna's eyes were shut so tight she could see the dancing dots of light behind her eyelids. She shivered against the biting wind as it snapped her hair around her face.

Down and down they went until Pax slowed them with a few beats of his wings, and set Kenna's feet onto a solid surface.

The air was colder than ice. The reek was worse than a rotting corpse. The sound was…sound had ceased to exist entirely, or perhaps no sound would dare venture this far below the dungeon.

"Where is it?" Pax muttered. She clung to his hand. "Stay with me, lass, whatever ye do." The hungry quiet gobbled up his words.

There was nothing that could make her want to leave his side and run into whatever belonged in this pit.

"Ah. There ye are," Pax said. "Ye're going to want te cover your head and yer ears, lass. I need te let go of yer hand a minute, but I'll be right by yer side."

She was reluctant to let go of Pax's hand, but he gave her fingers a little squeeze and she obeyed, covering her ears.

An explosion rocked the ground beneath her feet. It sounded like the very earth being shattered in two. Was Pax still standing next to her? She wanted to look.

"Stand still," Pax reminded her. For a few minutes, she heard Pax shuffling and grunting as he talked to himself. "How the Void do ye attach that? Ah. Right. That goes in there. That'll do."

He grabbed hold of her hand again. "All done, lass. You just hold on to me. This could be slightly more…challenging than our descent, so just be patient." Then Pax lifted her into the safety of his arms.

He let out a mighty groan as he pushed off, and Kenna felt his neck and shoulder muscles straining as he struggled to lift them from the floor. She felt the pull of something infinitely more powerful than the usual force that kept her feet on the ground.

The force was not willing to let them escape so easily. In fact, whatever force existed in this pit didn't want to let them out at all. Kenna felt it pulling, scratching, holding, clinging to them with every beat of Pax's wings.

Kenna's Vessel felt empty in this place, and she had no wings to aid Pax's efforts. And then the thoughts crept in until they crowded out anything else in her mind.

I should let myself fall. That would be best for everyone. I'm a murderer. I'm darkness. I'm nothing. I deserve to fall.

She loosened her grip on Pax, thinking she might jump. But he said, "Keep fightin'."

Pax's wing beats were slowing, as the force seemed to pull him down. Did he feel the same sense of hopelessness as her?

But there was another still, quiet voice in her mind. A voice from somewhere very, very far away. A voice that rang true. An Ancient voice with a whisper stronger than the intrusive shouts of the force that wanted her to give up and die.

Fight, the voice of the wind urged.

Pax must have heard the voice, too, because suddenly his wings flapped and strained again, like he was battling for the very existence of anything good and sincere in the world. He bellowed a furious and triumphant roar as they shot up and out of that sinking pit of lies and despair.

Some time later, they crashed onto their backs onto the glassy bridge, panting.

Kenna couldn't understand why her lungs felt so ravaged when she hadn't even been the one flying. Even though they'd made it out, she squeezed her eyes shut against the haunting call that beckoned her back into the pit.

"Ye can open yer eyes, lass," Pax said, still laying on the bridge next to her.

When she opened her eyes, they were no longer alone.

Next to Pax, secured by the harnesses her brother had created after the battle in Tormund, there were two dead bodies.

CHAPTER 67

*K*enna looked at Ash and Hawthorne's bodies—like lifeless statues—and quickly looked away. She couldn't bear to see Ash like that. Why had Pax dragged their bodies out of the depths?

She looked at her Fostone, but there was no time displayed on its surface.

"How long have I been in here?"

"Three hours," Pax said. "We couldn't leave 'em behind, could we? I'm getting all three of ye out of here."

While Kenna hated the idea of leaving Ash's body behind without a proper funeral, she firmly believed Pax should have left Hawthorne's body to rot.

Pax's breathing had recovered more quickly than Kenna's, and he sat up next to Hawthorne and Ash. Then he fumbled through his pockets and procured a large vial of black liquid. It looked like…

"Koffee? I really don't think now is the time, Pax."

Pax laughed, a foreign sound amid the cacophonous misery around them.

"No, lass. It's just a tad stronger than koffee. Do ye remember what I told ye about where koffee comes from?" He turned the vial over. Though it was the color of koffee, the liquid shimmered with iridescent swirls of silver and gold. Like moonlight and sunlight meeting in the darkness of a black sky.

Kenna tried to remember what he'd said. "You said it was derived from a special elixir."

"Aye. The Elixir of Life." Pax brought the vial to Hawthorne's mouth. "Well, bottom's up, lad," Pax said, and then he tipped the liquid down the prince's throat.

Kenna tried to understand what was happening. The prince who had been as cold and still as a glacier a moment before coughed, sputtered, and rolled over. His wounds vanished as he spread shimmering white wings, tipped with the faintest hint of gleaming silver and gold. He looked…

The only word for it was radiant. He looked like light itself.

He glowed with ethereal light, and Hawthorne blinked at Kenna with eyes as sharp and green as a rose stem. If anything, his eyes gleamed with a more vibrant emerald than they had when she'd looked into them and stabbed him to death.

She had killed Hawthorne. He was supposed to be dead.

"You're dead," she said, fixing him with a heated glare.

"Am I? I certainly don't feel dead," the prince mocked, examining his perfectly whole, bare torso as he unstrapped the harness.

"You…you murdered Ash, and you were supposed to help us."

But if Hawthorne was back…if he was alive again, then that meant…

She shifted her eyes to Pax.

"Bring Ash back. Like you did with him." She indicated Hawthorne, unwilling to taste his name in her mouth.

The prince and Pax shared a look, but it was Hawthorne who spoke. "It's not as simple as—"

"Don't you dare speak to me. Whatever is going on here, I don't trust a single word that comes out of your murderous fucking mouth."

Pax cleared his throat, slicing through the net of vehement tension. Her guardian angel drew out another vial of the shimmering liquid. "As the prince was saying, it's not that simple. The elixir was specially formulated fer Prince Hawthorne in Vorra. Our hope is that it will work fer Ash as well, but we're not sure, since—"

"Give it to me," Kenna choked back a relieved sob and snatched the vial out of Pax's hand, scrambling to Ash's side. She gently tilted his head back and emptied the elixir into his mouth.

"Come on," she whispered.

With Hawthorne, the effect had been instant, but nothing was happening with Ash.

She shook Ash's shoulders, gently at first. "Come back. Come back." As she grew more desperate, she shook him harder. "Ash! Come back!"

She laid her head on his cold, hard chest, hoping to hear his heartbeat, but there was only silence.

"He's gone, lass."

Kenna knew Pax was right. She wrapped her arms around her king and wept, her cries mingling with the hundreds of other tortured lives wasting away in the icy dungeon.

After a minute, Hawthorne cleared his throat. "I'm sorry to interrupt, but I think we should leave this place before we're discovered."

Kenna hated him, but she was ready to get off the damn bridge. She couldn't listen to the wailing prisoners anymore. She collected herself and stood.

"We can't leave him here," Kenna whispered. Even if Ash's soul was gone, she wouldn't leave his body in this horrible place.

"Of course not," Pax said, softly.

He lifted Ash into his arms and they crossed the bridge, away from the echoes of torment and toward the spiral stairs that led up to the castle.

The silence when she stepped off the bridge was a relief. If she never had to come back to this dungeon, it would still be too soon. Pax gently laid Ash's body on the cold floor, and Kenna did her best not to look at Ash's stony, blank features.

"Let's go," Kenna said, walking toward the stairs.

"No," Hawthorne said. "We won't get out that way. We have to go through the shaft."

Kenna froze and turned to face Hawthorne, who was pointing to a large, vertical cylindrical tunnel overhead. Far, far above, Kenna could see the starry sky.

"Okay, then," Kenna said. She walked towards Pax. "Will you carry me? I don't want to be in here another second." She waited for his strong arms to lift her up, but he didn't.

"Aye, I'll carry ye. Though…there's also the wards. They won't let ye out that way unless…"

Pax and Hawthorne shared a look.

"Ye won't be able to get out unless ye're married to an angel. The marriage vows will disguise your blood and allow you past the wards like the Emergence serum allows angels to cross the Veil."

"I am married to an angel," Kenna said.

"You *were* married to an angel," Hawthorne said, his words lacking sympathy.

"The only way out is if ye marry Thorne," Pax said.

"No. He killed Ash. Do you understand? Sliced off his wings in front of me as easy as slicing a piece of cake. And where the fuck were you, Pax? Why didn't you stop him?"

Pax looked down, as though he couldn't meet her eyes. "Ash told us te end him if there was the slightest chance he was going te hurt ye. This plan was our last resort. We'd hoped we'd be able te bring Ash back, but we can't, and I'm sorry. And if Hawthorne deserves no mercy, what about ye? Ye killed Thorne without knowing about the elixir of life."

"He deserved it, Pax. He murdered my husband. And in the end, he didn't even die. Look, here he stands. Whole and breathing. It is not fair that he should live while Ash…" Her throat closed.

"None of it is fair, lass. I know that. The longer ye live, the more ye will understand just how unfair it all is. But this is yer best option. The wards will not let ye past if ye don't take the marriage vows. Plus, have ye fergotten the treaty? The humans will be freed if ye do this. Do ye understand? But no one will force ye. It is yer choice."

"Can't I marry you instead?" she asked, even though she'd never thought about Pax in that way.

Pax wrinkled his nose. "No, lass. It's forbidden. As yer guardian angel, I might as well be yer brother or yer dad."

That was when she started laughing hysterically. Laughing so hard, tears streamed down her face. If she didn't laugh, she thought she might run and hurl herself off the bridge. If she didn't laugh, she might break apart entirely.

"This isn't a choice at all. Who would choose to stay imprisoned when they have the option to be free? What kind of monster would I be if I threw away the chance to save an entire race of people?"

Pax's soft eyes beseeched her. "Listen, I know this is difficult, but ye can trust the prince."

Pax and Hawthorne's eyes both shifted to the stairs, and Kenna sensed the shift in their demeanors.

"Now, Princess," Hawthorne said.

Kenna heard footsteps a moment later.

"Fine. I'll do it." She marched up to Hawthorne. "Don't think for one second I'm going to be your pretty little submissive wife." She gritted her teeth.

Hawthorne raised a brow. "Did I say I wanted a wife like that?"

"This marriage is just another prison. I'll find a way out."

Hawthorne's mouth quirked with the hint of a sad smile.

Kenna knew how this worked. She knew the ancient marriage vows were binding until death, a bond as sacred as the bond between fated mates. When she'd attempted to marry Hawthorne, it was before Ash had become her husband. Before the prince had made her a widow. She hated to mar the sacred words by sharing them with the surly prince. Refusing to make eye contact with him, she clasped his extended hand.

After Pax had spoken the binding words in the Ancient language, he spoke the rest of the vows. "Do ye, Prince Hawthorne Lightstone, take this woman as yer wife? Will ye cherish her and protect her life as though it is more precious than yer own?"

"I do and I will."

Kenna scoffed. There was no way she could repeat those words.

Pax must have seen it in her eyes because he only asked, "Do ye take Prince Hawthorne Lightstone as yer husband?"

"I do."

Kenna fought the urge to vomit as the zing of their vows stung her skin.

The scar on her forearm changed. The star marking her oath with Ash, of their marriage, still remained. Now, it was overlaid with the sun. Hawthorne now bore a matching tattoo on his chest over his heart. She might have thought the swirling elegance of the sun entwined with the star on her wrist was beautiful if she didn't find the words she'd just spoken so abhorrent.

Immediately, Pax snatched her up in his arms.

"Wait!" she shouted. "What about Wren?"

"I used my cloaking magic te get him out of the castle while Samael and Lailah were distracted. We had a horse ready and waitin'. He'll be nearly in Braktyn now. There are rebels there who'll hide him. I'll tell ye more once we get away from here."

Satisfied that she wasn't leaving Wren behind in the clutches of

Lailah and Samael, Kenna nodded. Then, they flew up through the chimney-like tunnel into a black sky with Ash's body dangling from the harness below them.

The darkness was fading to a grey dawn, and she closed her eyes against the rushing wind and her stinging tears.

"I'm sorry, Ash." She whispered it so quietly that the wind was the only one who heard.

CHAPTER 68

The snow beneath them sparkled, bright white under the fuschia and amber sunrise. After a tense hour of flying at full speed, Kenna guessed they were twenty or thirty miles from the Brumalis Castle with no sign of pursuit. She could see the hard line of the Sapphire Road cutting through the winter landscape below them. The road was empty. Mercifully, it seemed no one cared enough to come after her, or they hadn't discovered her absence yet.

Pax slowed his pace, and she asked, "Where are we going? Will it be safe at the Red Lantern?"

"I don't think so." Pax looked a little sad. "I'll miss the pixies who helped me look after the place."

"Pixies?"

"Aye. They kept themselves hidden, but did a great job keepin' the place clean and tidy. Ye didn't think ye were the only one helpin' me out, did ye?"

"I'm sorry, Pax. I know it was your home."

"When ye've lived as long as I have, ye tend not te get too attached te places or things. It's the relationships that count." He squeezed her gently.

"I can't believe everything you risked getting me out. I'm sorry I didn't thank you before." She snuggled into him.

Pax might have shrugged if his shoulders weren't preoccupied with their flight. "I'd do it all again if it meant I could get ye home."

"I don't think I have a home."

"Sure, ye do. Try te get some rest. Ye're safe now." Pax held her close, and she let the steady beat of his wings rock her to sleep.

~

WHEN KENNA AWOKE, her head was fuzzy and clouded as if she'd slept for days. They were still flying. She rubbed her eyes and blinked against the bright morning light. Below, there was nothing but an azure sea.

"Where are we?" she asked.

"We'll be comin' in te Tormund in a few minutes."

"Have we crossed the Veil?"

"The Veil's torn between Notos and Mesterra. Nothing separates those two realms now."

"But...how?"

"I'm not sure."

Kenna dared a glance at the prince flying silently beside them, but he didn't look in her direction.

"Does that mean the elves who paid with their souls no longer have to pay that debt?"

"Not quite," said Pax. "Luniva still has hold of their souls, but with the Veil gone, we've got a fightin' chance te cast her out and get em' free. Ash and Wren have been sneaking weapons te any rebel elves they can find. The elves aren't gonna stop with takin' down the High Council. They're on a mission te take back everything Luniva stole from them."

Before long, Kenna recognized the familiar landscape of the Lithari Mountains overlooking Lake Audral and Iris Meadow. The sight was welcoming. Comforting.

The ice on Lake Audral reflected their flight path, and Kenna grimaced at the sight of the silent, stoic prince flying alongside them, and the dead king suspended from the harness.

"Could we stop for a drink?" She was desperate to relieve herself and couldn't remember the last time she'd had any water.

"Aye. Good thinking." Pax swooped and dived, bringing them in for a graceful landing on the side of the lake near the snow-covered meadow.

After hiding behind a snowdrift to see to her needs, she returned to the lake. She found a spot a healthy distance away from Prince Hawthorne. She broke the thick ice with her magic and scooped up mouthfuls of water, drinking deeply and relishing the familiar, refreshing taste.

"Where do we go from here?" she asked, her words tinged with so much more than the question of geography.

"I told ye, lass. We're taking ye home."

"And I told *you*, I don't have a home. Not anymore." Nothing had ever felt so true.

"Oh, I know a few folk who would disagree. Including me. Up ye get." Pax extended a hand, leaving no room for argument. She couldn't have protested even if she'd wanted to. She was utterly spent and had no fight left.

Kenna let Pax sweep her up into his arms. Her current emotional devastation weighing her down was so similar to her feelings when she'd left Tormund six months ago. After the battle, she'd gone to Notos with Ash, drowning in sadness over her father's death and hoping to learn to fight. Now she was returning, but she felt like she'd failed. Like she was walking backward.

The grief she'd tried so hard to run away from resurfaced, multiplied exponentially in the aftermath of losing Ash. As she let the pain wash over her, she was rocked to sleep again beneath the heavy blanket of exhaustion and loss.

When she next woke, the sun was high in the sky but already past its peak. Past midday, then.

Kenna was stiff and groggy and couldn't imagine how sore and tired Pax must be after flying for hours on end. If she was a better person, she might have let Hawthorne carry her to give Pax a break. But even thinking about being against Hawthorne's bare tanned chest made her want to claw at her own skin. The thought of him carrying Ash when he'd been the one to murder him was just as abhorrent.

The Lithari Mountains stretched endlessly below them, carpeted with spiky pine trees and dusted with snow. A tendril of smoke puffed through the canopy of trees just ahead of them.

"Where are we?"

"Nearly there," Pax said, beginning their descent into the sweeping forest below.

Kenna closed her eyes as they flew down toward the thick trees. She still hated heights. The smell of evergreens in the snow laced with smoke reminded her so much of Ash, and she could almost feel him holding her.

Pax skillfully navigated them down, and when she opened her eyes, they were in a clearing in the rebel camp. Kenna choked on a sob, scrambling out of Pax's arms and into her mother's awaiting embrace. They squeezed each other tightly in a tangled vise of arms and tears. Kenna couldn't breathe.

Eventually, they released each other, and she examined her mother for signs of injury. Mother looked like she'd aged years in the months they'd been apart. Like losing her mate had splintered something within her. She looked thinner than when Kenna had last seen her.

"It's so good to see you," Kenna said.

Her mother's eyes welled up with tears and she hugged her close once more. "I was so worried about you, my girl."

Over her mother's shoulder, Kenna beheld hundreds of tents surrounded by high wooden walls. Near the center of the rebel camp crackled a huge bonfire with a ring of larger tents and many people she didn't recognize. They were chatting and laughing, totally unphased by whatever threat was looming over Mesterra, completely unaware of Kenna's loss.

Her mother put a hand on Kenna's cheek and then looked behind her. Kenna turned to see Pax wrapping Ash's body in a shroud. Hawthorne was already building a funeral pyre. Her heart ached and her eyes burned, but she he had no tears left. There was nothing but an empty chasm in her chest where Ash's love had been.

"Thank you. For bringing her back to us," her mother said to Hawthorne.

The prince gave her mother a curt nod.

"I thought I might never see you again," Kenna said. Quietly, she added, "He was...he was my husband."

"Your husband? Oh, Kenna." Her mother held her tight, letting her cry.

"Well, hello there." Jona's familiar face emerged from a thicket of trees, buckling his trousers as he approached. "Of all the times you could have chosen for a reunion with your big brother, it seems you caught me with my pants down."

Brothers. She rolled her eyes.

"Come here and give me a hug before I punch you," she threatened, wiping away her tears.

Her brother wrapped his arms around her and gave her an extra firm squeeze. "I missed you, little sister."

"You too, Jona."

Releasing her, Jona held his arms wide and gestured to the camp behind him. "Welcome to the heart of the Rebellion." His smile turned solemn. "A force of rebels have been making their way towards the Hill where Zo and Ezra and many others are being held. We're going to get as many elves out as we can. But it will take time to gather the forces without being detected. We have a source on the inside helping us. One of the guards."

"What? Who?"

"Holt."

"But I thought…he was there when they locked Zo up. I thought he was working with the High Council. For Luniva."

"We thought he was working for them, too. As it turns out, the Shadow who stole him away after his Emergence was Soldivus."

"Why would Soldivus take Holt?"

"We aren't sure. But Holt has infiltrated the Hill as a guard. He's the one who's helped us with our plan. He's been smuggling us messages through the rebel forces anytime he makes a supply run."

"Has he…is Zo alright?"

Jona's mouth formed a thin line. "She's alive."

"What is that supposed to mean, Jona?"

"Holt has been doing what he can to look after her without causing suspicion." Jona placed a gentle hand on Kenna's shoulder. "We're going to get her out, but I imagine she'll have a long road of healing ahead."

Kenna nodded. She wouldn't pray. Couldn't pray. She wouldn't pray to Soldivus, whose loyal prince had killed her husband. Perhaps Hawthorne meant to resurrect Ash, but she couldn't be sure. She didn't trust him.

The only reason she'd agreed to marry him was because of…

"The treaty!" Kenna said, suddenly. "We fulfilled the treaty!"

She whirled to Hawthorne, who'd gone utterly still. "Not quite."

"What do you mean?" Kenna spat, holding up her wrist where his vile mark had burned over the faded scar marking her oath with Ash.

"You're my wife, but the humans aren't yet free."

Jona raised an eyebrow at Kenna. "His wife?"

Pax explained everything that had happened, sparing Kenna from speaking about it all. Her brother ground his teeth, and her mother placed a hand over her mouth. Her mother cried silently as she reached out and took Kenna's hand.

"I can't believe…" Her mother shook her head. "I knew you were brave and resilient, but you are so much stronger than I ever imagined."

Kenna huffed. "Maybe. But what's the point? Ash is dead, and the humans are still locked in their sleep state. Why didn't our marriage work?"

"I'm not sure," said Hawthorne. "But I have my suspicions."

"There's still hope, though?" Pax asked. "Ye got married on Winter Solstice, just like the treaty said, and the Veil between here and Notos is gone." Pax turned to Kenna. "I reckon ye'll find a way te save the humans."

Kenna's voice sounded small. "It's too much. Why would Soldivus place the hope of an entire race on one person's shoulders? I can't carry this burden."

"Then don't try to carry it alone." Pax put a heavy arm around her. "I'll help ye."

"Don't forget about me," her mother said.

"Or me," her brother said. "Sera, Aryn, and Drake, too, when they get back."

Kenna couldn't say why, but she looked at her new husband.

His eyes were still sharp and unreadable. "You're my wife. Of course, I'll stand with you."

CHAPTER 69

It was the second funeral Kenna had been to within the last year. At her father's funeral, she'd found the will to fight and moved to Notos with wide-eyed optimism. After Ash had died and she'd woken in the dungeon, despair and hopelessness had filled every crevice within her, and she couldn't seem to let those feelings go.

Less than twelve hours ago, she'd believed she wouldn't see anyone or anything she loved ever again. She'd felt completely trapped and alone, and she'd believed death would have been a kinder fate than being locked in her icy prison.

Kenna felt a sudden flood of gratitude for her broad auburn-haired guardian angel who had carried her all this way. He'd come for her when she'd thought all was lost. Now, Pax stood next to her, talking to her brother with inexplicable peace and hope evident in his gaze.

With everyone gathered, Hawthorne took up a place in front of the rebels where Ash's body lay shrouded atop the funeral pyre.

Kenna tried to blink away the memory of Ash's eyes going black as Echelous plunged the serum-filled dagger into his heart. How many times had his eyes looked into hers? She was already forgetting exactly what shade of blue they were.

Hawthorne had murdered Ash, and yet he stood poised to deliver words of condolence at his funeral. If she had any fight left in her spirit, she would object to his presumption. She didn't know if she'd ever forgive her new husband. Probably not.

Perhaps Ash had told Hawthorne and Pax to sacrifice his life for hers, yet she still believed there should have been some other way. But it was Ash's sacrifice, Pax's rescue, and her marriage to Hawthorne, which allowed her to escape from Samael and Lailah's clutches.

No, not Lailah. Luniva.

Hawthorne's bearded jaw was set without a hint of a smirk. So stoic. Nothing at all like the man Kenna had loved. The man he'd taken from her.

She brushed away her tears as Hawthorne said, "Good evening. I am not sure what to say about my brother. For over three hundred years, I believed him my enemy. Once I realized how his heart had changed, our time together was too short.

I had hoped to rescue him. To bring him out of Notos and back into the light. Instead, it was his time to grace the eternal shores. There was a time I would have thought his soul was destined for the moon. But now, I know with every fiber in my being that I will see him again one day on the shores of the sun. Kenna, you are his queen. Would you like to do the honors?"

Hawthorne turned his back to the crowd, facing the pyre. Pax took her hand and led her forward. Her red-haired friend held an orb of flame over his palm, but Kenna hesitated to light the pyre as Hawthorne spoke quietly to Ash's body:

"I love you, brother. We will make Luniva pay for the pain you have endured all these years. Every life claimed by the curse will not be in vain. Your death will not be in vain. Lost souls will be restored, and everything will be redeemed. I will cherish and protect her with my life, just as you did."

Kenna gave her new husband a sidelong glance. Perhaps he was not as harsh and unfeeling as their initial encounters suggested. But the prince didn't shed a single tear.

She turned back to the pyre.

"I love you, Ash," Kenna whispered. She wanted to say more. Wanted to speak a prayer over Ash, but she couldn't speak past the lump in her throat.

She lit the pyre, and Hawthorne said:

"May the Ancient One bless you and keep you. May truth shine upon you. May hope turn toward you, and offer you eternal peace."

She looked at Hawthorne again. How did his soul know the words the wind had whispered to her all those months ago at her father's funeral?

Then she looked back to the blazing pyre, rivulets of tears flowing down her cheeks as she watched the sparks flutter into the sky, carrying Ash away.

She hoped he was at peace. She hoped he found his mate on the eternal shores. And even though she felt lost without him, she hoped she could find the will to fight.

Ash and her father were gone, but her mother, Jona, and Pax were still here. Sera, Aryn, Drake, Ezra and Zo were still alive. It didn't matter what happened next, as long as Zo and Ezra were returned to them safely. As long as Wren was safe, too. He was in Braktyn with the rebels, but he'd be here soon.

She wasn't alone, and there was still hope of the rebel elves over-throwing the angels in Mesterra and defeating Luniva. There was still hope of saving the human race. There had to be.

Pax had been right.

Home wasn't a place—home was being with the people she loved. Ash had been her home these last six months. He was gone, but she wasn't homeless.

Perhaps everything was a bit ramshackle right now, but Kenna still had a home. After all, the people here with her and the people who would return from the Hill were her firm foundation. And with that knowledge, Kenna knew she'd be able to rebuild herself little by little.

CHAPTER 70

ashton Moonbriar wasn't a king. He wasn't an angel. He wasn't cursed.

He was a soul made of peace and freedom and hope. Redeemed, he floated away from his worldly body. When he opened his eyes, he was embraced by the warmest light.

Elenya walked barefoot toward him through white sand, which shimmered like finely crushed diamonds. "Hello, my love."

Ash embraced the other half of his soul. His mate.

He remembered Kenna with hope and pride. He thought of her with the pure warmth of true love. There was no room for sadness here on the eternal shores of the sun.

Elenya placed a hand on Ash's cheek. "She is a remarkable woman. I'm glad you had time with her. I'm grateful she reminded you that you're worthy of love."

With one final look across the expanse into the world he'd left behind, Ash saw Kenna, surrounded by people who loved her.

"I'm thankful she's safe," Ash said, pulling Elenya close and breathing in her nearness.

"She is," his mate confirmed. "And you'll help her when she needs you."

Ash knew there were subtle ways departed souls could guide those they'd left behind. When she needed it, he'd be the scent of cedar and smoke on the wind to remind her that their love had been real. He'd be a lone blue flower in a field of white daisies to remind her he was watching over her. He'd be the wind at her back, spurring her on when she wanted to give up.

Ash wasn't sure how long he'd stood there, embracing the woman his soul had lost all those years ago. The sound of footsteps broke their reunion. Ash turned towards the footsteps and came face to face with his father, his arms open wide.

He stepped toward Soldivus, accepting his father's welcoming embrace. "Hello, Ash. Your mate is right. We will not abandon the humans and the elves to fight Luniva alone."

"What do you mean? Are you sending us back?"

"Not just yet." Soldivus smiled. "But we will ponder war and death another day. For now, my son has come home, and I would like to celebrate."

ACKNOWLEDGMENTS

Thanks to my husband, James. You're my best friend. Thank you for putting up with me spending hours in the chair in the corner while I've drafted and edited this novella and the first book in the series. Thank you for supporting me unconditionally and never making me feel silly, even though you don't read spicy books about magic and dragons.

To my kiddos, I hope you always feel like you can talk to me. I hope you feel seen and that you know how much I love you. And to Murphy, the best dog ever. Thanks for the best naptime cuddles.

To my parents, who are always my number one fans any time I create anything, thank you for your love and support, and for instilling a love of creativity and entrepreneurship. I'm only a little sorry there are swear words and spicy scenes in my book.

To my framily and the rat pack, you guys are the best. Sorry I'm so slow at responding to texts.

Mariella and Savanna Roberts at Snowridge Press, thank you for all your help as I begin my self-publishing journey. Mariella, your feedback was so helpful, and Savanna, you've been a star.

Rachel, thanks for the amazing map illustrations, even though you weren't sure which way was west. Haha!

To anyone who reads this, thank you for spending some of your precious time in these pages. I hope this story brings you joy and an escape with characters you can relate to.

Last but not least, I want to thank Jesus for always giving me hope and healing, even when things feel dark and broken.

ABOUT THE AUTHOR

E. J. Wightman is an expat mum of three from Alabama, living in Northern England. She spends her days walking dogs, feeding chickens, parenting feral children, volunteering at church, and pretending to be a minimalist.

In her nonexistent free time, she reads lots of books about faeries, takes too many naps and makes silly TikTok videos.

This is E.J. Wightman's debut novel. If you loved the book, please consider sharing on social media. You can also leave a review on Goodreads, Amazon, or Barnes & Noble.

To keep up to date with future releases,
bookish goodies, and more freebies,
subscribe to the newsletter at
EJWightman.com

ALSO BY E.J. WIGHTMAN

Manifest: A Redemption of Realms Prequel Novella
Read for free by subscribing to the newsletter at EJWightman.com

Crown of Flame and Vengeance: Coming in 2023

www.ingramcontent.com/pod-product-compliance
Lightning Source LLC
Chambersburg PA
CBHW050854210726
48290CB00004B/1225